RAVEN

ALSO BY TRACEY SHEARER

Entwine

RAVEN

To Sue-Lynn:
I can't wait to hear
how you like this one!!

Tracey Shearer

TRACEY SHEARER

TWILIGHT
SPARKS
PRESS LLC

ISBN 978-1-7330030-1-8

Cover art © 2020 by Jessica Petersen
Book Design by Jessica Petersen

Printed in the United States of America

Published by Twilight Sparks Press LLC

To Cleo and Feta,
the best furry friends and editors I could have asked for.

CHAPTER 1

THE DEATH VISION WAS CONSIDERATE, EVEN GENTLE IN ITS overture, just the lightest stroke of icy nails along Kate Banberry's skin. A courtesy greeting before things turned ugly. Before things turned terrifying.

She leaned back against the oven, gripping its handle to stop her hands from shaking. Its warmth banished the chill, even for a moment. Her girls sat across from each other on stools at the kitchen island, icing the brownies they'd been making for the local retirement center.

Emily, her nine-year old, dodged a dollop of icing from her sister. Unsuccessfully. Emily promptly scooped it up off her cheek and ate it. "Your aim is getting better." She grinned at her sister, showing off the gap between her two front teeth.

Patty giggled, her brown braids dancing against her shoulders. "I've been practicing." Kate's seven-year-old had taken her father's death the hardest. But she was finally starting to heal.

Kate had a little time before the vision seized control. She only hoped it was enough time to get the girls out of the kitchen. Her daughters had witnessed Kate having her normal visions—eyes turning white, her losing consciousness—but she had no idea if her death visions were the same. It had been sixteen years since she'd had one, and even if nothing had changed, she had no idea what she looked like. She'd never had witnesses before.

Tiny pinpricks of ice darted up her arms. "I think I'll take over the rest," Kate said, forcing a smile and trying to keep her voice even, "since you're frosting each other more than the brownies. Why don't you two go into the study and play?"

"We don't want to go to the study. We can play here, Mommy," Patty announced.

Kate surveyed the icing battlefield of the kitchen island. It's a wonder anything ended up on the brownies. "Only if you want to clean *all* this up." Both girls looked horrified. Kate kissed the top of Patty's head and took the butter knife from her hand. "Now go on. I promise I'll bring you some brownies in a bit."

Emily slid off the stool and gave her a measured look. "What's going on, Mom?"

"Nothing. I'm just worried we'll run out of icing." Kate grabbed a plastic container to load the brownies up for delivery. It was a good excuse not to meet her daughter's eyes as the cold slid under her skin. She was surprised her breath didn't come out in a frigid puff of air.

Patty paused in licking her icing-covered fingers. "She's going to have a look-see."

That's what they'd always called Kate's visions ever since

Emily and Patty had found out about them. She'd managed to keep them hidden from the girls until their father died two years ago.

"How do you know I'm going to have a look-see?" She scooted Patty off her stool. "Now go wash your hands."

Patty busied herself at the sink, a mountain of suds quickly forming in her small hands. "You've got that frosty ring around your eyes."

Emily squinted at Kate. "Oh yeah, I can see it now. We'd better get you upstairs to your bedroom."

Kate paused in packing the brownies up. The vision dived deeper stealing the life from her fingers, her hands. "I'll be fine. I can make it on my own."

The plastic lid slid from her numb fingers. Emily scooped it up from the floor and put it in the sink. "You need our help, Mom."

Guilt spiraled in Kate's stomach. Her girls deserved a normal mother. One who could do something as simple as package up brownies in the kitchen. One who could drive without worrying about blacking out from a vision.

"I should be the one helping you," Kate said. "That's my job. To take care of you."

It was times like these she dearly missed her husband. Paul hadn't known about her abilities, but she could always count on him to take the girls without needing an explanation. She'd been blessed to find a close knit group of friends in Rosebridge, but it wasn't the same as having a partner.

"Family sticks together," Emily said. "You told us that after

Dad died." She took Kate's hand, but Kate couldn't feel it. "Which means we take care of each other. All of us."

Patty dried her hands and hugged Kate. "We love you, Mommy."

Tears flooded Kate's eyes. Somehow, someway, she needed to get control of her visions. Not only for herself, but for her children.

The chill circled around her legs, and then struck, digging painfully into her bones. She swallowed a gasp. Time was running out. As much as she wanted to shelter them from seeing this happen, Emily was right. Kate needed them.

"I'm not going to make it upstairs girls. I can't . . . I can't feel my feet." She blinked her eyes, and hot tears rolled down her cheeks. "Help me to the pantry."

That was the closest room that had a door. Thankfully, no one was staying in the B&B right now. After their recent poltergeist haunting, business hadn't picked back up yet in their small Scottish town. But she didn't want Aggie or Stu, the B&B's caretakers, to find her passed out on the kitchen floor.

Emily put her arm around Kate's waist. Patty took Kate's elbow. Working as a team, they got her inside the pantry. Kate stumbled down to her knees. She couldn't feel anything below her waist.

"It's okay, Mom." Emily's voice trembled slightly, but her face was determined. She helped Kate to sit, scooting her further from the door. Then with a gentle touch, she eased Kate to lie back as Patty slipped her cardigan under Kate's head as a pillow.

"Are you scared, baby?" Kate couldn't help asking.

Patty shook her head. Her youngest didn't look worried. Not one bit. "The Universe wants you to see something, so you're going to be just fine."

Kate looked up at both of them. Trying to hold on, but it was time. The vision couldn't wait any longer.

The soft ovals of her girls' faces disappeared as if someone erased them.

Kate found herself standing. The pantry was completely gone. She knew she'd lost consciousness because she'd traveled to someplace else. In her mind. As much as she hadn't wanted them to see this, it gave her comfort to know the girls would watch over her.

Kate looked down. Blood slid past her in a slow-moving stream, brilliant red against the white floor. Warmth returned to her legs, her body—the usual sign she was on the right track. Much like the hot/cold game she played with the girls. She'd have to follow the blood trail to see what she was meant to see. Then, and only then, would she be able to wake up.

She stared at the blood. There was so much of it. A shudder gripped her shoulders. Kate struggled to breathe normally.

Why was she having a death vision now after so many years? There'd been no doubt when she'd first felt its touch. It was the only kind of vision which gave her time to prepare. As if the horror of the vision was so great, her body had to have time to absorb it.

The corridor was deserted, the far end fading into blackness. Whatever she needed to see would be beyond that veil.

"Why do I always have to see someone getting hurt or

worse? Especially since I can't always save them, no matter how hard I try." She lifted her hands to the ceiling. "Is it too much to ask for an occasional unicorn? A rainbow?" She listened for a moment. Nothing. "A hazelnut Americano?"

Okay, that last one had been a stretch.

As usual, the Universe was radio silence. She'd heard it speak when Sam had brought Robert to life in the forest, but Sam's abilities were epic, worthy of notice. Kate's weren't. If she were the Universe, she probably wouldn't reply either.

Actually, both her best friends were pretty epic in all ways. Sam was a best-selling romance novelist and spoke to ghosts. Beth could find anything and had her own reality show, plus a mansion in Los Angeles.

Kate was thankful they'd come to Scotland to protect her and battle a serial killer. Well, she wasn't thankful about the serial killer part, but she'd managed to get them on speaking terms again. That was progress.

The darkness in the distance beckoned her. It was time to stop stalling.

"All right. Let's get this over with."

The overhead lights flickered with each slow step she took like they were jostled by her movements. Was she somehow starting to affect her visions? She filed that away for later reflection.

She studied the floor and walls for anything significant or meaningful. The floor was dull concrete, and the walls were gray metal. Nothing.

Then she came to the doors.

Each had a number and to the right of each door handle, a

punch pad on the wall had a blinking blue spot for a thumb-print. A few of the doors also had raised black balls next to their number punch pads. She'd seen enough movies to know what they were—retinal scanners.

The last two doors on either side also had thin plastic tubes. She had no idea what kind of security measure that was, but whatever these doors concealed must be more important than the others. In the center of each of these two doors, a crow was engraved into the metal.

Her first thought was of Caleb and his crows. Was the mys-terious ghost who inhabited the forest around her B&B tied to this place?

She ran her hands through her hair, the curls catching in her fingers. She pulled her hands away and found strands of red twined around her knuckles. Was her hair falling out? This hadn't happened in a vision before. Had her powers changed because she was now part of a triumvirate with Sam and Beth? What if she could be harmed in a vision now? Even killed?

Kate shook her head, trying to dispel the hysterical rise of questions before it took hold. Beth would tell her, "Suck it up, Red." Sam would give her that I-believe-in-you-look and then push her forward.

The vision's chill gripped her temples. She was not doing what it wanted.

"I got it, okay?"

She'd seen all she could in the hallway. It was time to get to the main attraction.

Just a few steps away, the wall of black was absolute, like

every speck of light had been sucked into its depth and extinguished. The blood trail disappeared into the shadows.

Kate wiped her palms on her hips. She didn't usually sweat in visions either.

Gunshots rang out. Kate ducked, flattening to the ground instinctively—into the trail of blood. The liquid burned where it hit her skin, coating her entire chest.

She scrambled to her feet, wiping it off as fast as she could, but it seeped through her shirt and into her skin as if she'd absorbed it. Her blood-soaked clothes were left pristine again.

More gunshots. Screams echoed. She needed to know what was going to happen—no what could happen if she didn't stop it. Kate rushed into the darkness.

That's when she saw bodies. In flashes, like someone kept taking one picture after another.

A man, shot in the neck. Blood seeping into hospital scrubs.

Beth, face down, unmoving.

Sam underneath rubble, hands reaching for Kate, then stilling.

Oh for crap's sake.

Of course it would have to be a vision about her friends dying.

CHAPTER 2

ALMOST IMMEDIATELY, THE VISION BEGAN TO SHATTER. Sections of gray wall at the edges of her vision broke off and spun into the darkness.

"No." She needed to know more. She grasped for any details to hold onto.

The acrid scent of metal melting mixed with the copper tang of blood.

More gunshots so close, all other sounds grew muffled. Like she'd damaged her eardrums.

Shadows seeped through the floor, swallowing the bodies.

Kate tried to run forward, but couldn't move. Heat rose from her feet, all the way through her body. As if she'd stepped into a hot bath.

Someone was pulling her out.

She tried to shake it off, but then she heard her name ricocheting through the muffled sounds.

Kate finally gave up, the last of the vision slipping from her. She opened her eyes to find Logan's worried face.

Logan Dunning. The Detective Chief Constable of their small Scottish town and her closest friend. The one person she had never wanted to find out about her gifts.

"Are you alright?" Logan's gaze roamed over her face, eyes too wide. His fingers gripped her wrist, no doubt checking her pulse.

"I'm fine," Kate's throat was dry, and her words came out in a croak. "Really, I am. Where are the girls?"

"In the study." Logan tilted his head toward the door to the kitchen. "I told them to go and play while I helped you."

"Did we have lunch plans I forgot?" She looked at her watch. Barely eleven. Maybe if she didn't bring up being passed out on the floor, he wouldn't either. Who was she kidding? This was Logan.

"I brought by the toy badge and handcuffs the girls had asked for." His fingers touched her temples, moving to the back of her head. Likely searching for evidence of a concussion. "We should get you to hospital."

"No, really I'm okay. Just low blood sugar. Remember? I felt dizzy and got to the floor just in time."

His expression slid into full police mode. Blue eyes calm and assessing. He wasn't in uniform. Just a button-up shirt and some jeans. But he was still a cop through and through. With a high bullshit detection meter.

"I've seen you dizzy before, Kate. This is something . . . different."

Logan had always bought the low blood sugar excuse in the past, but this was the first time he'd seen her unconscious.

"Now you look angry." His tone was relieved. He gave her a hand and lifted her to her feet. "I'd rather see *that* than how you looked before." A shadow passed over his face, wiping away the scrutiny, leaving behind only worry.

"How did I look before?" Kate dug an energy bar out of a box on one of the shelves. At the rate she, Sam, and Beth were going through them to restore energy after using their abilities, she should buy stock in the company.

Logan rubbed his jaw. "Pale. But your eyes were moving underneath your lids, like you were seeing something in a dream. Are you sure you're alright?"

Kate bit into the bar, using the chew time for stalling. Maybe it *was* time to tell him? Her throat seized up, and she struggled to swallow. He knew about Sam's ability to see ghosts and suspected Beth's gifts already. She didn't doubt he'd believe her.

But it was more than that. Almost every person she'd ever told about her gift had run, which is why she'd kept it a secret from her late husband. If she told Logan now, what was said would forever be said.

She unwrapped more of the bar. The crinkling of the wrapper was loud in the pantry. "I'm taking sleep meds. We're working on the dosage. It's still not right. That's why I passed out."

Partial truth. She'd already failed on lying outright.

Sadness seeped through his face. "It's because of what my brother did to you, isn't it? Why you can't sleep through the night."

Logan's brother Graham had been the serial killer they'd been hunting. An awful realization for everyone.

"The sleep issue is just a short term thing," she said, but Logan had already turned away.

"I'll put on some tea." His voice was gruff.

"Logan."

He ignored her. He walked into the kitchen and grabbed the kettle from the stove. The pipes moaned a bit when he turned on the water. Another fix-it to add to the list. Whenever the B&B actually began to make money again.

"Logan." She let her worry bleed into her tone.

He flicked a glance at her over his shoulder. "I know what you're going to say. You've said it already. But I can't forgive myself. Not yet. Maybe not ever. I should have known Graham was the serial killer." Logan put the kettle on the stove, turning the dial. "I'm a constable."

Kate crossed her arms. "And constables are never wrong, is that it?"

"Graham is my brother. How could I have missed it?" Logan gripped the kitchen island, his knuckles white. "All those women died because I didn't see the truth."

Kate walked over to him. "I knew you couldn't be the killer, but I didn't suspect it was Graham either. I missed it too."

Logan's tortured eyes met hers. "I almost lost you."

She suddenly wanted to put her arms around his waist, lean her head against his heart, breathe in the warmth of him.

She blinked. Where had that come from?

Sure she liked Logan. Maybe a bit too much. But she'd always been able to hold the attraction at bay. Still, she'd just had a death vision, and she remembered now that those played havoc with her emotions.

"Hell. I invited Graham in. Had him sit and take tea." She looked down, shaking her head. "Sam and Beth were the ones who saved me." She played with a piece of chipped paint on the utensil drawer. "I was useless."

He grasped her hands. "You weren't useless. If it wasn't for your gift of giving people second chances, neither of them would have been here in Scotland to save you. It's your superpower you know. Knowing what's underneath the surface. What's in their heart."

She looked up at him, happy to see the anguish gone from his eyes. "Beth thinks I'm too soft. That I'm a pushover."

"And since when do you care what Beth thinks?"

Kate smiled. "Never. That's what pisses her off so much."

"You are infuriating, I'll have to agree there." He was already dodging left and right, as if he anticipated the smack she wanted to give him.

She laughed until he joined in. For just a moment, it was like Graham never happened, the Triumvirate never happened, the stupid death vision never happened. Everything was as it had been.

It felt incredible.

"That's your superpower, DCC."

"What is?" His smile dimmed just a bit.

She squeezed his hand. "You always know how to make me laugh."

Logan lifted her hand and kissed the knuckles, resting his lips against her skin for a long moment. "I'll work on making you laugh as often as possible. I promise." His words vibrated against her skin.

Heat rushed through her fingers, to her wrist, up her arm, and into her heart.

"Getting frisky with the law, I see," a voice said from behind her. Kate knew instantly who it was even without the snarky laughter in the tone.

Logan's grip stiffened and he dropped her hand, and Kate turned around. Beth stood at the kitchen entryway looking like a magazine cover. Sharp cheekbones as ruthless as her gaze. Sam joined her, beaming like sunshine itself in an orange sweater that brought out the green of her eyes.

Usually Kate would have shot back a snappy reply, if only to prevent Sam and Beth from bickering about anything and everything. But seeing them here in the kitchen brought the death vision back. They'd been wounded, dying.

She couldn't lose them.

Beth's eyes narrowed, and she was at Kate's side in an instant. "You okay? You're completely white."

"Nice to see you, Logan," Sam said. "The girls asked if you could join them in the study. They said you were showing them how to be constables."

"Go on, Logan." Kate gave him a soft push toward the hallway. "I'll be there in a bit."

"All right." A smile crinkled the edges of his eyes. "Ladies." He nodded at Beth and Sam, then disappeared through the doorway and down the hall.

Beth cast a look over her shoulder. Her dark bob swayed

with the movement. "Do all Scottish men have such great asses? I mean what's up with that?"

A sudden wave of jealousy swept through Kate. It had to be the death vision again, bringing everything to the surface. Beth—or any woman for that matter—had a right to admire Logan. But it didn't mean she had to like it.

"Patty told us you had a vision?" Sam said.

"I did." The kettle rumbled into a whistle, and Kate took it off the burner. "As usual, I don't know what the hell it means."

KATE LOADED UP THE TEAPOT WITH SEVERAL BAGS. THE rich scent of the PJ Tips breakfast blend she loved saturated the air. She took a deep breath, trying to enjoy the brief moment of normalcy, but Logan's words kept crowding back into her head.

His mistake with Graham had been an honest one. Any normal person wouldn't think to suspect their sibling of something as horrible as being a serial killer.

He didn't know Kate had had a vision about Graham which should have revealed him as the killer. Instead it had been vague and unclear. Graham's last victim died because Kate's gift was faulty.

She'd never been able to count on her ability. Never. The old anger seeped its way through her faster because of the death vision.

Don't lose it Kate. Don't do it. Shove it away like always.

She had roles to play. Peacekeeper and supporter to Sam and Beth. Mother to Emily and Patty. She couldn't afford the luxury of being Kate. Just Kate.

"The tea doesn't need to be watched to brew," Beth drawled.

Kate caught her own reflection in the glass of the cabinet. Haunted wouldn't do. She tried to smile.

"Keep your shirt on," she said. "I'm coming." She looked toward the back door. "Grab mugs and my jacket. Let's go outside. You know how the sound carries in this place."

Sam grabbed Kate's jacket and a plateful of brownies. Beth handled the mugs. Kate led them outside to the table and chairs near the garden.

It was chilly, but the sun peeked in and out from behind the clouds.

Beth cleared the table of fallen leaves and helped Kate get everything in place. As usual, Beth looked put-together with her sleek black leggings and leather jacket. Always camera-ready even though she hadn't filmed her reality show in weeks. Kate eyed her tall suede boots. They cost more than Kate had made last month.

Of course, Sam looked like she didn't have a care in the world. A smile on her face, long honey-colored hair looking like a shampoo commercial. She'd twisted the laws of the Universe to bring Robert back to life.

And then there was little 'ol Kate, hair always a tangled mess, mended clothes, struggling to keep a roof over her family's head. Her abilities amounting to nothing tangible that enriched their lives.

"You look pissed." Beth handed her a spoon slowly. "Was the vision something for TOP to handle?"

"TOP?" Kate looked at Beth and Sam. "What's that?"

"Triumvirate of Pluthar," Sam said. "The acronym was Beth's idea."

Though Sam's tone was neutral, Beth immediately bristled. "I never said I wasn't open to other ideas."

Kate shook her head. "We sound like a circus act."

"Saying our whole damn title isn't keeping things on the down low," Beth said.

Sam crossed her arms. "Can we argue later? Kate had a vision, remember?"

Beth looked like she wanted to argue now. Surprising. Not. Instead she looked at Kate. "Spill it, Red. What did you see?"

Kate told them about the place from her vision—the military feel, the security. "Since Logan interrupted me, it means I'll have another one. Hopefully more revealing." She let out a long breath. "And it wasn't a normal vision. It was a death vision."

Sam sat up straight. "You haven't had one of those since—"

"We were fourteen," Kate said.

Beth looked between them. "So this is worse than your usual visions?"

Kate nodded. "I'm always trying to prevent someone from being hurt, but with a death vision, someone will definitely die if I don't stop it."

"Wow. No pressure," Beth muttered.

Kate grabbed a brownie and stabbed it with her fork.

"Welcome to my life."

"Where's the usual plucky let's-love-our-gifts Kate?" Beth's voice was tentative, unsure.

Kate looked at Beth. "That Kate is on ice right now, replaced by the Kate who has two children. Two girls I'm desperately trying to give a normal life—impossible since I blackout whenever I have a vision, and now Patty has abilities too, which means that nothing I do is going to give them what they had before Paul died."

"You're doing an incredible job under awful circumstances," Sam said.

Now that the words were flowing, they didn't want to be stopped. "Incredible job, right. I'm failing at trying to resuscitate an almost flatlined B&B, wondering if we'll be out on the street any moment." She glared at both of them. "So, yeah, I'm a real success story."

Sam's eyes widened, and Beth looked like someone had goosed her with a cattle prod.

Kate had to admit, she was enjoying their reaction. Maybe even reveling in it. "I'm sorry I'm not acting like you think I should. But I just had a death vision and I don't know how I'm going to stop it. And I *have* to stop it."

Because if she didn't, they'd be dead.

Which made her even angrier. Why couldn't she count on her abilities?

"You'll figure it out, Red. It's going to be okay."

"You don't know that." Kate shook her head. "I'm not like the two of you. You can count on your gifts. No question."

Beth opened her mouth and then closed it. Sam stayed silent.

Kate looked at Beth. "Your gift is so certain, you use it every week on your reality show and it works. Every. Single. Time. And don't get me started on your L.A. mansion."

Beth looked ill.

Her gaze shifted to Sam. "And then there's Samantha Hamilton The only time your gift didn't work was when you chose not to use it. Since you've turned it back on, you brought a ghost back to life. Back to *life*. But wait, there's more. You get extra juice each time you help a ghost, so much so, I think you could light the village theater in case they lose power."

Sam tried to hide her hands, but not before Kate saw them sparking at the tips.

Sam got up and walked over to Kate. She put her hands on Kate's shoulders. "Get it out. What else is eating you inside? Tell us. We can take it."

"We can?" Beth asked.

Sam flashed her a hard look. "This friendship only works if we trust each other. If we're honest with each other—about the good and the bad, even if it's painful."

"Which is why I didn't want to do all this in the first place." Beth waved her hand back and forth between them. "I have enough liabilities in my life."

"Friends are not liabilities," Sam said.

Beth crossed her arms. "To me, they are."

"Stop with the excuses, Marshall." Sam's voice was firm. "If you didn't want to be a part of this, you would have left as soon as we saved Robert. Get over here, now."

"Shove it, Princess," Beth almost yelled, stalking over to Sam. "So typical, thinking you're in charge. You never change. I never said the Triumvirate was permanent—or this friendship."

Tears bubbled up in Kate's eyes. Her anger drained away. She would tear them apart, this sisterhood they'd been working to repair, all because she had no control over how this had come out. And that it had all come out at once.

"Stop it you two."

Their bickering just got louder.

"It's my fault. The death vision messing with me," Kate shouted, but they both ignored her.

"Beth, Sam. Stop," she tried again, but they were locked into their usual antagonistic loop.

But there was one thing sure to zap them out of it.

Literally.

Sam's hand was still on Kate's shoulder. Kate grabbed Beth's hands, holding onto one and putting the other on Sam's arm.

The rush of energy jolted through Kate, stealing her breath for a moment. It was much more powerful than before. Like a switch inside, Kate felt control return. Her emotions were still raw, but now she could decide what to reveal. The after effects of the death vision broke apart and dissipated.

Sam's eyes held a mini-thunderstorm with flashes of lightning, dark and light warring with each other for dominance. Beth's eyes were pools of ink, swallowing every ounce of light. Kate had a feeling hers were white and frosty. The way she'd been told she'd always looked when she had her visions.

Closing her eyes, she saw Sam and Beth before her, blazing like twin flames.

Though their light was bright, it held flashes of darkness. She knew what that meant. They were healing, but not yet whole. None of them were. Especially Kate.

"I'm sorry for being such a dick," Kate mumbled. "Death visions really mess with me."

Sam let out a shuddering breath and the energy banked down to a low hum. No one let go of each other.

"It's okay," Sam said. "I did the same thing about the ghosts' emotions, remember? I nearly attacked you in your bedroom while I was channelling Ellie. If that wasn't being a dick, I don't know what is."

Kate laughed and opened her eyes. "I thought I'd have to bean you with my silver hairbrush."

"I missed out on a chance to bean Sammy? I'm crushed."

Sam gave Beth a stink-eye, but it didn't phase her.

"I don't want to lose you." Kate stood and hugged both of them together. Almost the same height, they towered over Kate.

Beth mumbled into her hair. "You'll never lose me, Red. No matter how much I fuss. You're the only thing anchoring me to the human race." She pulled back and looked at Sam. "Sam on the other hand—"

"We can always agree on our love for Kate. That's good enough for now."

A small quirk at the corner of Beth's mouth looked suspiciously like a smile.

Kate didn't want to move out of their embrace, but she had

to sneeze. The loss of that buzz between them suddenly made Kate even colder. She sat back down and hugged her arms to herself.

Beth dug a tissue out of her pocket and handed it to Kate. "She can never handle her tears. She'll be hiccuping next."

"Hot mess, for sure," Sam agreed.

Kate would have argued, but they were both right.

Beth put a hand on her hip. "Do you really think Sam and I have it made? You know, mansions, money, hunky ghosts brought back to life?"

"Having money can make things easier, Beth." Sam shot her a look.

Beth held up her hands. "Agreed."

It felt good to hear them both acknowledge it.

Kate admitted, "Usually I don't think about it too closely, but the death vision shattered my usual defense mechanisms."

"Defense mechanisms like stress baking, deflecting," Sam mused.

Beth added, "Compartmentalizing. I just didn't realize you had some serious messed up shit in that cute little Pip Squeak package."

"I told you I don't answer to that." But her words held no real heat. Right now she'd take anything Beth called her. "I know you two haven't had easy lives. I *know* that intellectually. But emotionally I sometimes get pissed off."

Beth nodded. "I get being pissed off. I'm still working on that every time I look at Sammy."

Sam raised an eyebrow. "Thanks for making the effort."

Beth sat and scooted her chair closer to Kate. "You just always seemed to handle everything like a pro so I thought you were fine. I know things have changed with Paul being gone." She paused. "And Graham was an unexpected nut-job, but even through those challenges, you always seem on top of things. More than I would ever be."

"I'm great at hiding." Kate blew her nose one last time and wiped her eyes.

Sam sat too. "And I never realized you felt you didn't measure up when it comes to our gifts. You were always so supportive of me getting mine back."

"Because it's part of who you are, Sam." Kate took a sip of tea. "When you tried to stop seeing ghosts, you hurt yourself. I knew it."

Beth nodded. "You see the truth. Even when we don't."

"Logan says it's my superpower."

Beth winked. "Fine ass and a smart mind. Quite the combination."

Kate couldn't help smiling. She felt lighter having let some of that crap out of her system. Holding it in had poisoned her more than she'd realized.

Sam reached across the table and touched her arm. "You're one of the strongest people I know, Kate. Everything you've gone through with trying to find your real parents, losing Paul, dealing with the B&B troubles. And then there's us." She stared at Beth.

"What about us?" Beth snapped.

Sam just frowned at her. "Getting us to come to Scotland. And to work together. Hell had truly frozen over courtesy of you." She paused and looked down for a moment. When she glanced back up, her eyes were filled with tears. "I couldn't have saved Robert without the two of you."

"Oh Lord." Beth looked away, suddenly interested in the roof. "I don't do Hallmark moments." Kate laughed, and Sam joined in amidst Beth's grumbling.

Soon they'd be on their way back to their homes in the States. She didn't know what she'd do without them. Kate breathed in and out quickly, trying to ease the tightness in her chest.

"Sorry for the pity party." Kate leaned back in her chair. "It was easier when I didn't have to see your gifts in person. Just being honest."

Sam nodded. "Go on."

"But seeing both of you in action really brought it home. My abilities are faulty at best. Sometimes on, sometimes off, and mostly unpredictable."

Beth grabbed her phone from her jacket. "Since you know you're going to have "Death Vision Part Deux, "I'm going to text Michael. You could use some help on your visions, and he already offered up his brother as mentor/guru extraordinaire."

"I don't know if he can even help." Kate looked down at her hands. "Everyone's gifts are a bit different when it comes to visions."

"Well, I just texted Michael, so you'll get to find out in person." Beth looked extremely proud of herself, like she'd already solved the problem of Kate.

The trees rustled at the forest's edge, and several crows took flight, their wings dark against the gathering clouds.

In all the emotional meltdown, Kate had forgotten to tell them about the crows she'd seen on two of the doors. She filled them in.

"A crow?" Sam raised an eyebrow, then she lowered her voice, glancing at the forest beyond the garden. "I know what we're all thinking, but a shadowy military base is not exactly Caleb's style."

"There's more to him than we know." Beth stared at the forest as well. "I still think he's connected to the Wardens somehow. You don't exist for as long as he has without making a deal of some sort with the powers-that-be in Entwine."

The Wardens ran the ghostly realm of Entwine, which existed between the living world and whatever came after. The realm Robert had been relegated to until Sam had made a Bargain with the Universe. She'd promised never to abandon her gifts again.

Sam nodded. "Beth's right. I'll talk to Caleb and see what I can find out."

The sun firmly disappeared behind the clouds as it dropped lower on the horizon.

Beth's phone vibrated. "Michael will talk to his brother Duncan about timing and get back to us."

Kate's hands were suddenly sweaty. It's one thing to feel inadequate up against Beth and Sam, but if Duncan had gifts like she did, that would be another self-esteem blow if she couldn't figure out how to control them.

But her friends' lives were at stake if the vision was true. And if nothing else, her visions were always true.

CHAPTER 3

THE SUNBEAMS SHOT PAST THE TREE BRANCHES, FEELING like Heaven against Sam's skin. She'd taken Robert with her to see Caleb, to ask about what that military base might be from Kate's vision. But in this moment, it felt wonderful just to be walking through the peaceful forest with him.

Sam breathed in deeply, holding onto the earthy green scent of the leaves mixing with the dirt. It reminded her a bit of upstate New York. Her family home there seemed so far away now.

She glanced down to avoid a cluster of rocks, and when she looked up, Robert was gone. He winked back into sight a second later, right where he'd stood before.

Sam couldn't stop the small gasp from her lips. "It's still happening?"

"I fear so, and since we have promised honesty . . ." Robert rubbed his jaw. "It is getting worse. If I do not concentrate on this world and what is happening in it, I slip away into Entwine."

The thought of losing Robert sent her stomach into free fall.

She'd sacrificed everything for them to be together. They'd fix this. Somehow.

Sam walked over and grabbed his hands. "The Wardens must know what's going on. They work for the Universe, after all, and the Universe brought you back to life."

She looked up at him. Tall, broad shouldered and drool-worthy, as Kate put it, Robert was so much more than that. Once just a ghost needing her help, but now she couldn't imagine living without him.

"The Universe had a little help from you." Robert kissed her nose, sending a trickle of heat across her cheeks.

"Maybe just a little." She wound her arms around him until his lips met hers. For a moment, she didn't know where one of them ended and the other began. If they didn't have so many eyes upon them, she'd have taken him up against a tree. Right then.

She pulled away, knowing Caleb's crows had already gotten an eyeful to report back to their master. But still took her time, basking in the smile beaming from his face. It still amazed her to have someone who knew exactly who she was and loved her. Good and bad. She'd never had that in a romantic partner before.

She definitely owed the Universe.

Dammit.

"We better get going." She looked at a nearby beech tree. Several crows sat on a thick branch. Their glossy black feathers looked like bruises against the pale limbs of the tree. "You know the crows have probably already reported our progress or lack thereof to Caleb."

Robert nodded. Though he'd cut his hair somewhat, that

same unruly lock he'd always had managed to fall into his eyes. He brushed it back easily. "Nothing escapes his notice in *his* forest."

A shift in air pressure warned Sam a ghost was getting ready to appear. Beatrice stepped from behind a tree. Dressed as usual in her maid's outfit, Beatrice managed to look both welcoming and forbidding. Sam now saw the resemblance to Kate, though they were many generations removed.

"Caleb is waiting on you. Impatient as usual," Beatrice said.

Robert rushed to her side and picked her up in a bear hug. "I grew worried when I did not see you for several days. Where have you been?"

"I had work to do." Beatrice's words were muffled against his chest. "Someone has to keep the manor ghosts in line." She pushed back, a smile softening her round face. As Robert's surrogate mother growing up, Beatrice always relaxed her usually stern nature around him. "I still don't know how you can touch other ghosts, but I'm glad for it." She gave him another squeeze.

"And the Wardens still won't see me," Sam said. "I need to find out what they know about Robert's problem and how to stop it." Sam crossed her arms. "I don't suppose Caleb shared any insights with you on Robert's condition?"

"No." Beatrice huffed and smoothed her apron. "That old coot is keeping mum about the whole thing. Saying it's Warden business." She waved her hand toward Caleb's crows. "And you can tell him I'm not happy about it." The crows cawed and took flight, though Sam wasn't sure if it was to inform Caleb or because they feared Beatrice's wrath.

Sam was anxious for any information about Robert. Not only about how he kept slipping in and out of Entwine, but also how could he be in both worlds easily. See and talk to ghosts just like Sam could. At least he didn't have a Bargain to worry about. She might not know what he was, but he definitely wasn't a necromancer.

Robert touched her shoulder. "Do not fret. For now, I shall be as a babe testing out his first steps." A slip of a smile held his lips. "And I am blessed to have two very capable women to guide me on this new journey."

"He's right, you know," Caleb said, stepping out from the nearest beech tree.

Sam stumbled back, her heart racing into a sprint. She hadn't felt him coming. No shift in energy or pressure. "How? Since when . . ."

Caleb smiled. "I have tricks you've yet to see, Necromancer." He crossed his stick-thin arms and gave them all an assessing look. The green glint in his eyes matched the blood pulsing in the veins underneath his pale skin. Sam assumed it was blood, but he was a forest ghost, so perhaps it was sap?

"Where's your cane?" Beatrice gave him a sniff. "You're looking entirely too spry."

Caleb laughed. At least that was the same. The dry rustle of leaves. "Jealous?"

Beatrice flashed him a deadly look and Caleb sobered in a snap.

Robert took a step closer to him, looking the ghost over. "I will not say you look younger, but there is a difference of some kind. You look more a sapling than a tired old stump."

"Stay out of my business, boy." Caleb pointed a finger at Robert, and tiny green shoots climbed the surface. "The Universe might have seen fit to bring you to life, but I made no such bargain to keep you that way."

Sam walked in between Robert and Caleb. "We didn't come here to fight." She gazed into the forest ghost's eyes. "I never got a chance to thank you for saving me. Without you helping me remember who I was, I wouldn't have woken up in time to fight Graham."

The lines on Caleb's face softened. "I did my part. Gave you a push."

Sam reached out to touch his arm, but stopped. She forgot she couldn't touch ghosts like Robert could. "That's two favors you have done for me. I never forget a debt."

"Be careful at reminding him, lass." Beatrice shot her a concerned look. "You may not like what he asks for."

"I'm not worried." Sam crouched and touched her hand to the ground. She let some of the ghostly essence she still had running through her seep out. "I have changed since that night, since bringing Robert back. I see the connections between everything and everyone." She sent a small bit of the energy surging through the dirt to Caleb's feet.

He stepped back quickly. "You've made your point. Now turn down that blasted glow so we can continue our conversation."

She glanced at Robert and Beatrice. Both of them shielded

their eyes. Caleb just looked uncomfortable. They'd always told her she glowed to those in Entwine, but this felt like something more.

Sam pulled the energy back inside her and tried to concentrate on not glowing. It was difficult since she couldn't see what they did, but both Beatrice and Robert dropped their hands.

Robert gave her a quick smile, and then turned a serious face to Caleb. "Thank you for agreeing to speak with us. We have received some troubling news through a vision. There is a specific detail which could possibly link you to what Kate has seen."

Caleb raised an eyebrow, and several pieces of dark bark fell from his brow. "Go on."

"Do you need to sit down?" Beatrice waved her hand at a nearby stump. "Your back?"

Caleb shook his head. "My back doesn't trouble me any longer."

Sam exchanged a quick look with Robert. Caleb appeared younger, wasn't troubled by back pains any longer. Just what had happened to rejuvenate him?

Beatrice sat down on one of the stumps. "Well, mine still bothers me. I'm not hoarding magic and keeping it from my friends like some others I know." She favored him with a semi-stink-eye.

Caleb harrumphed and gave his attention to Robert. "You were saying?"

"Kate saw a military facility in her vision," Robert said. "There was a symbol of a crow on several of the doors."

"A crow?" Caleb looked confused and then a shiver of fear shook his gaze. "I can assure you I have no part in any military bases. The forest is my home. I don't meddle in the outside world."

Beatrice snorted.

"Much," Caleb added.

Sam's ghostly lie detector stayed green. It was an ability she'd always had. She knew when ghosts lied.

"But you know what Robert is talking about." Sam didn't phrase it as a question.

Caleb stared at her for a long moment before finally nodding. "It does me no good to lie to you."

"What do you know?" Sam waited for the cost.

The fear was gone from Caleb's eyes, replaced with interest. "What are you offering?"

Beatrice stood. "Why do we play this game, Caleb? You already know what you want. Spit it out."

"Were you this prickly when you were alive, woman?"

Beatrice pushed her shoulders back. "Even worse."

Caleb smiled, revealing teeth that looked like pieces of pinecone. "I want the Oracle to refuse the offer she received for these lands."

Whatever Sam had been expecting, it definitely wasn't this. "What offer?"

"She'll know the one. The one that is too good to pass up." Caleb narrowed his eyes. "The one that would save her livelihood."

"Caleb's telling the truth as far as he knows it." Sam looked at Beatrice. "Have your informants shared anything?"

"Nothing." Beatrice looked concerned. "It's not like Kate to hide something that could save her family."

Robert gazed toward the manor through the trees. "Unless it is something she does not wish to do, yet is unable to refuse. At least for the moment."

Caleb turned and began to walk deeper into the forest. "She turns down the offer, and I'll tell you everything I know about what that symbol means."

He paused, his face in the shadow of a low hanging branch. "And it better be soon. Because if the Oracle is having a vision about that place, you're all in danger."

EVEN THOUGH THE KITCHEN WINDOW WAS CLOSED, KATE still heard her girls' happy squeals and Logan's laughter. They brought a smile to Kate's lips. She didn't know what she would do without Logan. He'd been her rock ever since she moved to Scotland.

She let out a breath she hadn't realized she'd been holding. "Logan has been so good about coming around for the girls," she said to Sam. "This is two days in a row now."

Sam raised an eyebrow. "No disagreement there, but stop switching subjects. When I saw Caleb yesterday, he was adamant you'd received an offer for the forest lands. Have you?"

"I don't like that he even knows about it." Kate glanced at

the window again. "Do you think his crows come in and snoop around?"

"So there *is* an offer?" Sam looked like she wanted to shake Kate.

"Fine, there's an offer." Kate picked up the spoon and stirred the chicken noodle soup on the stove. "It's enough to save us, Sam. Save this place. I don't want to sell, but I might not have a choice."

She hated that her voice shook at the end. That the thought of losing the lands warred with the hope of saving the girls' future.

Sam sighed. "I'm sorry for pushing you. I can't imagine what you must be going through."

Kate tasted the soup. Almost ready. "I haven't decided what I'm doing about the offer yet. I need to think on it some more."

Sam nodded. "I understand. Besides, Caleb might not know anything truly helpful about the facility. If you want to sell your lands, you need to do what's right for your family. I'll support you either way."

Bronson glided into the kitchen from the front hall. Kate swore she never heard the sound of his feet. He was trying to teach her burgeoning staff the art of ninja-butlery.

And save her B&B. Sam and Bronson were working on a marketing campaign to get more guests, now that they didn't have a poltergeist problem. Though the current angle was "stay in the most haunted B&B in Scotland."

Kate didn't care what they said as long as they could get this place up and running again.

"I have a message for you, Ms. Banberry."

"It's Kate, Bronson. You don't work for me. You're just trying to save my bacon."

Bronson smiled, bringing out a twinkle in his eyes. His gray hair looked tidy as usual, not a strand out of place. Though he wasn't wearing an official uniform, he still looked entirely too elegant for her haphazard B&B.

"We're doing what we can, Kate, to ensure your bacon doesn't burn." He gave her a quick nod. "I have the new maid learning how to make beds efficiently, and I'm pleased to share the dusting tutorial I provided has made all the difference."

"This place is gleaming alright." Sam smiled at her butler, and it was full of love. Kate didn't know what would have happened to Sam after her parents died if Bronson hadn't been there.

Kate wiped her hands on her apron. "Your message, Bronson?"

"Oh yes." The butler put his hands behind his back. "Michael will be by to pick everyone up at four o'clock for the visit to his house. He asked for confirmation."

"Tell him we'll be ready," Kate said.

Another bright burst of laughter vibrated through the window glass, and Kate couldn't resist any longer. She took off her apron and hung it on the hook by the door.

"Can you watch the soup, Sam?" She asked. "It should be done in about ten more minutes."

"As long as I can have some of your freshly baked bread?" Sam inhaled deeply over the loaf on the counter.

Kate laughed. "Absolutely." She loved seeing everyone so interested in her baking. It made her feel useful even when everything else felt like it was in shambles.

She opened the back door and looked around. She finally spied the top of Emily's head coming around the long line of shrubbery. Her red hair gleamed in the early afternoon light.

Kate walked over to the pathway.

"Out of the way, Mom," Emily announced, a determined glint in her eye. "We've got a prisoner here. She's a squirrely one."

"I'm innocent." Patty trailed behind her, a set of toy plastic hand-cuffs around her tiny wrists. Her light brown hair wafted in the breeze around her heart-shaped face. "Don't believe her, Mommy. I didn't do it."

Bringing up the rear was Logan. He grinned at her, bringing out a set of adorable dimples. Her chest tightened, and she suddenly wished she'd combed her hair.

Emily frowned. "I can make the prisoner talk, Mr. Logan. We have ways." She tickled Patty around the ribs.

"No fair," Patty managed in between giggles, then squealed, "Save me."

Logan scooped Patty up and slipped the cuffs free, tucking them away in his pocket. "You can always count on me to save you, Pats. Though your Mommy can certainly handle herself. Have you seen her right hook?"

Patty laughed and snuggled into Logan's arms just like she used to do with her father. Kate turned away quickly and wiped her eyes, hoping they wouldn't see.

"Mommy is the bravest person I know," Patty declared. "But, you're pretty great too, Mr. Logan. *I* never believed you were guilty."

"The evidence was circumstantial at best," Emily said. "I knew it had to be someone else."

Kate loved seeing both her girls so happy. Tears pricked Kate's eyes. A lot of joy had left their lives two years ago, but her girls were finally healing.

"You are truly a smart cookie," Logan said.

Emily beamed and stood a little straighter. He put Patty down and gazed at both of them, his eyes glistening with tears. "Your belief in me means more than you will ever know."

They hugged him, and Kate almost had to look away again. It was ridiculous really. Logan was just a friend. But to see how much her girls loved him reminded her again of what it felt like to have a partner.

Why was she suddenly thinking about having someone in her life again? Why now?

Her gaze moved to the forest in the distance, where Graham had kidnapped her and Sam. Where he would have killed them both.

That was it.

Almost dying had finally opened her up to the possibility of finding someone.

But even though Paul had wanted her to find love again— they'd talked about it in the days before he died—she wasn't even sure Logan really liked her that way. Sure, he was sweet and a little flirtatious, but nothing had ever happened. And the sixty-five year-old-plumber flirted with her worse, but it didn't mean he was serious.

Sam and Beth thought Logan liked her, but what did they know? Sam hadn't been able to find anyone alive to love and Beth goes through men like toilet paper.

Everyone stared at her and Kate realized she'd been inner monologuing again.

"All right you two," Kate said. "Auntie Sam has soup almost ready in the kitchen, and you can both have some bread too."

"And cookies?" Patty asked.

Kate nodded. "But after the soup. Deal?"

"Deal!" they both shouted, and then raced to the back door.

The slap of their shoes on the slate pathway sounded like horses' hooves. Kate turned away and looked a Logan.His light green polo shirt showed off his broad chest. Kate realized she was staring.

"It's sweet of you to agree to their play date," Kate said, finally tearing her eyes away.

"I know things have been hard on them," Logan said. "On all of you for a while now." He glanced at where they'd disappeared down the path. "To be honest, spending time with them is helping me heal from what happened with Graham. To remember how it was before."

"Well then, I have something I need to show you in the shed." She waved her hand at him. "Oh, stop it with that cop look."

"What cop look?"

She grabbed his hand and tugged him down the path toward the shed. "The frowny face one where you look like everything anyone says will be dissected within an inch of its life."

He didn't reply after that, just let himself be led.

"It's not quite done yet," Kate said, looking back over her shoulder at Logan. "But I know the girls wouldn't mind me giving you a sneak preview now if they knew how much you needed it."

She couldn't wait for him to see it. Anything to take some of the Graham burden from his shoulders.

"They made something for me?" The wonder in his voice was clear.

"Yes, for you." She opened the shed door and they went inside.

The pungent scent of potting soil greeted them. The shed was dark with strands of filtered sunlight making their way though some of the wooden slats. Kate flicked on the light.

She let go of his hand and took a drop cloth off of the sign the girls had been working on. It read, *Parking reserved for Mr. Logan.*

Beth had been helping them paint it. They still needed to finish the flowers and vines around the edges.

The look on Logan's face stole her breath away. He touched the sign with trembling fingers.

"They wanted you to know you're always welcome here."

He moved back a step to stand next to her. She was suddenly very aware of him. Alone. In the shed.

"Thank you," Logan said, still staring at the sign. "I really needed this."

She looked up at him. At 5'10", he wasn't a strain on her

neck. "I'm glad we could help. You know how much you mean to me and the girls."

Logan smiled, bringing out his dimples again. "You mean the world to me. All of you."

She felt the flush creep up to her face and to her lips.

She wanted to kiss him.

And if she was right and he didn't like her that way, it would be forever awkward. This was a small town. She'd see him all the time.

Okay. Operation Quick Exit before she did something stupid.

"Ah, well, uh," Kate said. "We should get back to the kitchen and check on the chicken soup."

She ran her hands through her hair and one of her clips flipped open and dropped to the floor. Kate leaned over to get it and so did Logan. They smacked heads. Hard.

The impact almost made her see stars. Kate wobbled on her feet. Logan caught her, steadying her.

"Are you okay?" His eyes searched her face.

"I'm fine."

She took another step and stumbled into the wheelbarrow.

"That's it. I'm not taking any chances." He lifted her up and off her feet before she knew what was happening.

Now she was in his arms. Exactly where she'd yearned to be yesterday after the vision. His eyebrows pinched together. She reached up a finger to smooth them out.

Logan froze. "Kate?" There was a hint of hope in his voice.

She stared at him, her heart hammering against her ribcage.

What was she doing? Maybe she had a concussion?

"I can walk on my own, really." She squirmed in his arms. "You can put me down."

"Hold on, wait a second—"

She knocked him off balance, and they both went down hard on the floor.

Logan shifted so he took the impact, grasping Kate on top of him, their noses touching. Though the rest of her body was twisted off to the side from where he'd held her.

No graceful fall like what they always show in the movies. They were almost a pretzel.

"I'm a hazard," she said. "Aren't I?"

His eyes warmed bringing out a hint of green. She knew without looking that he was smiling.

"You're the most beautiful hazard I've ever seen."

And before she knew what she was about to do, she kissed him.

His lips were softer than she'd imagined. A rush of heat ran through her. That she'd expected. She'd been imagining kissing Logan for some time now. But then the warmth wrapped its tendrils around her heart, seeking, searching—

Kate scrambled back, breaking the kiss. She got to her feet.

"Logan, I am so sorry."

He sat up, looking dazed. "Sorry for . . . what?" His fingers touched his lips as if he didn't believe what had just happened.

She needed to fix this quickly. "It was out of line. I know we're just friends." Kate tapped her head. "The concussion. I wasn't thinking straight. I didn't tell you that I kiss any guy I fall to the floor with? It's a thing. Started in college actually."

Logan's expression had started to lose its dazed look. Now it was inching toward concerned.

Oh God, she was babbling and obviously lying.

The sound of footsteps outside were a welcome interruption.

"Mom," Emily shouted. "It's time for lunch."

"I'll be right there," Kate yelled back. She gave Logan her hand and helped him to his feet. "You're going to love my chicken noodle soup."

"Sounds delicious." He gave her a strained smile.

She'd take anything at this point. Anything to keep things as they were. Status quo.

CHAPTER 4

KATE LOOKED OUT THE WINDOW OF MICHAEL'S CAR AT THE castle in front of her. Okay, maybe it wasn't a full-blown castle, but it had that fairytale feel to it. And it was huge.

Tall gray spires rose high against the blue sky. The gray stone was worn, pocked with crags like it had been through a battle. It was beautiful and elegant too, much like a grand lady who might bear the scars of the past, but did so with pride.

"Shit, you live there?" Beth said, lifting her chin toward the manor. "No wonder why you've got such a stick up your ass."

Michael switched the ignition off and turned around in the front seat, giving her a look worthy of a dragon. "Don't make me regret letting you come. I only did it as a favor to Sam."

Kate didn't jump into the fray. Her mind was still spinning over what had happened with Logan earlier.

The kiss was definite proof she was ready to venture out again. Not for anything serious, but it would be nice to have someone to do things with, to share things with. So, maybe she simply needed a guy in general? And Logan had just been there when her body had finally realized it.

Her inner voice began to pipe up that proximity hadn't been the only reason for the kiss, but she tamped it down. She needed someone with no complications. Someone who didn't live in her town, in case things went sideways.

And it wouldn't hurt if they were hot. She hadn't been in the field for a few years. Yumminess would help to ease her back into the groove.

Kate squinted up through the roof of the car. *You hear that Universe? How about a little payment for all that I've done for you?*

"Does everyone live there?" Sam said. "Your whole family?"

Michael's blond hair was slicked back today, but it was still a bit long, giving him a rakish air. He wore a deliberately weathered gray leather jacket and jeans. It appeared Beth was rubbing off on his fashion sense.

"Almost everyone," Michael said. "My brother, Duncan—the one who has a similar ability to you, Kate—lives in one of the cottages on the grounds. As does my sister, Glenna. Lennox, our eldest brother, lives there too along with my parents."

"How big is this place?" Kate gazed at the house again, trying to count the windows.

"Nine bedrooms, six baths in the main house. There are three cottages fully equipped, stables, and a garden."

Sam's face held wonder. "What do your parents do again?"

"Well, they're retired now, but they invested wisely."

Beth snorted. "Probably due to the handy visions from Duncan. How convenient."

Michael opened his mouth, and Kate opened her car door. "Let's go in, shall we?" she said brightly, shooting a look at Sam. "I'm dying to meet everyone."

"Yes, let's." Sam got out of the car. She looked extra tall and willowy in her plum-colored duster. "There's plenty of room, but I'm surprised your brothers and sister are living at home. Is there a reason? Something to do with their abilities?"

Michael and Beth got out of the car too.

"My father recently suffered an injury, which is why Duncan and Glenna are staying here temporarily."

"Is he okay?" Beth asked, sounding a skosh contrite.

Michael's mouth finally relaxed from its frown. There was even a glimmer of mischief in his eyes. "Feeling sorry for me, Marshall? Or just trying to practice how to show a softer side for your television audience?"

Beth hit him on the arm. "I only feel sorry for your family having to put up with you."

They walked on ahead, still snapping at each other. Sam and Kate followed them up the long drive to the main house. Bird calls echoed through the air. The breeze danced through her hair and a soft shooshing sound rustled from the trees.

It was warmer than it should be for this time of year. Like the estate was cocooned from the outside elements. The sunshine soaked through her pores.

Kate stopped for a moment. "It's so peaceful here." She closed her eyes and let the wind's breath tickle her cheeks.

"You're much more beautiful in person."

The deep voice with a hint of laughter startled her. Kate's eyes flashed open.

A hottie worthy of Sam's book covers gazed down at her. He was at least a foot taller than Kate. Thick red hair lay in tousled waves on top of his head, the sides cut short. A well groomed beard and mustache made him look devilish. And he had broad shoulders. Her weakness.

"I'm Duncan." He slid his hands into the thin green jacket he wore. Faded jeans, red plaid shirt and scuffed workboots completed his ensemble. His gaze searched Kate's face. "I've seen you for weeks now in my visions. I feel like I know you. I realize now that it might have sounded a bit—"

"Creepy?" Kate crossed her arms. She didn't like the idea of a peeping tom, in visions or in person.

Michael walked back to join them. Though he smiled, it was more like a mask. "Always smooth with the introductions, eh, Duncan?"

Michael and Duncan were about the same height and build, but that's where the similarities ended. Duncan had a rounder face, which seemed accustomed to smiling if the crinkles around his eyes were any indication. Michael was all angles, sharp and assessing.

And tension hummed between the brothers. Though Michael stood stiffly next to Duncan, there was a vulnerability in his eyes. Whatever had happened between them, Kate sensed Michael was ready to mend fences, but judging by Duncan's crossed arms and blank stare, no one would be breaking out the hammer and nails anytime soon unless it was to inflict harm.

"This is my friend from the States." Michael gestured at Sam who grinned extra big. She probably sensed the unspoken strain between the brothers.

"My sister Glenna devours your books," Duncan said. "It's a pleasure to finally meet you."

Sam gave him a wink. "Finally someone who knows who *I* am rather than gushing over Beth." She smiled at Beth sweetly with only a little sauciness in her gaze.

Beth's mouth smiled, but her eyes were serious. "So, *you're* Duncan. Michael told us about your power. Sounds like you can do some serious shit."

Duncan nodded. "I'm pretty skilled in the vision department. But we're all curious about you." His eyes narrowed. "You're . . . different."

His words sat in the air like a pronouncement. Beth looked worried, though she quickly hid it. "I don't have a problem being unique. Never have."

"Let's stop scaring the guests, Duncan." Michael's voice was harsh. He took Beth's arm and she let him. "We should go inside so they can meet everyone."

"Lennox is out checking on the horses, and Da's taking a nap, but everyone else is waiting on you."

Michael gave him a quick nod, and then headed up the drive again with Beth in tow.

"Nice to meet you Duncan," Sam said and then turned, calling out to Michael. "Hold up. Are we going to get a tour?"

She jogged to catch up with them leaving Duncan and Kate to bring up the rear.

"Were you intentionally trying to freak Beth out?" Potential teacher regarding her visions or not, no one messed with her friends.

Duncan glanced at Beth's retreating back. "I didn't mean it to come out that way. But it's true." He lowered his voice. "Ever since she started showing up in my visions, I've been trying to figure out how she does what she does. Finding objects. How she knew what to do to hold Robert's form together when you almost lost him in the woods."

Kate froze. "You know about that?"

Duncan gave her a tired smile. "I've seen a lot."

Kate cast a sideways glance at Duncan. It would be amazing to have someone to talk about her visions with. On the technical side.

"If you've been seeing us regularly, it doesn't sound like your visions are preventative like mine are. I'm always directed to stop something from happening." Kate began to walk again. "Though I'm not one hundred percent successful. Are yours more informative?"

"They are." Duncan kicked at a loose pebble sending it sliding across the other stones. "I don't have a mission to save anyone necessarily, though sometimes that happens because of what I've seen." He looked up at the sky for a moment. "It's more like I'm being shown things so I can prepare, be ready."

"Be ready for what?"

"Sometimes it's seeing a disaster happening so we can minimize the damage. Like the fire we had in town last month." Duncan blew out a breath, suddenly looking like a young boy. "I'm not like you. I don't seem to have a direct purpose."

He gave her a look that made her feel like she should be someone important, but that was stupid. She was the weakest member of TOP, regardless of the pep talks from Beth and Sam.

"You were lucky to have a family who believed in your gift," she said, "even if you didn't understand it yourself."

"Your parents didn't?"

"Nope. You wouldn't believe how many psychiatrists my adoptive parents sent me to."

"And your real parents?"

Kate let out a breath. "I've never been able to find them, and believe me I've searched. I'd love to know where my gifts came from and where *I* came from."

Duncan nodded, his face full of understanding. "My family threw a party the first time I saw something." He shook his head. "It put a lot of pressure on me, being in a family with gifts. It's better now that I'm older, but in the beginning, it felt like a constant competition."

"What do you mean about a competition? Of abilities?"

Duncan nodded. "Not a direct one since we're all different, but more about who was the strongest. Lennox always won." His lips twitched into a smile. "Well, until Glenna was born. Then they tied."

How her life might have been so different if she'd had a family who accepted her gifts. Tears suddenly threatened, and Kate quickly looked down. She cleared her throat. "Well, I don't know about having a purpose, like you say. Sometimes I save people, sometimes I can't. But I try my best. Even when people think I'm crazy."

"And have your abilities changed over the years? Mine did."

"They did. I can touch objects now and get info on who owned it, what happened around it." She pursed he lips. "And there's this weird near-sight thing I did in the forest with Graham. I saw what was going to happen right before it did."

Duncan stopped, interest on his face. "You mean chrono-kenisis?"

"Que?"

"At least it sounds around the area of what you did. It means when you can speed up or slow down your perception of time. So, rather than jumping all the way into the future, you can slow that journey down and see what's going to happen right before."

Kate glanced at Duncan. Regardless of her fear of looking like a fool, it was obvious Duncan knew more than she did about visions. Maybe he *could* help her?

"Chrono whatever is a mouthful."

"You can call it whatever you like."

They were getting closer to the front door. "Michael told you about my blackouts?"

"Yep."

"And you really think you can help me with those?"

Duncan paused a few feet from the door. Michael, Beth and

Sam had already disappeared inside. "I'm definitely going to try."

She shook her head, the breeze sending strands to brush her cheeks. "I still can't believe Michael has a brother who can see the future. A brother who might be my answer to getting a more normal life."

A stronger gust of wind sent a chunky strand of curls across her eyes. She reached to grab it.

And touched Duncan's hand instead.

He looked embarrassed. "Sorry. I was trying to get it for you." His fingers slid through hers, sending electric tingles dancing inside her body.

Duncan dropped his hand. "You have the most unruly hair I've ever seen," he said softly. The look on his face was a mixture of shyness and heat, and the tingles grew to pulses. "And the most magnificent."

Kate just stared at him.

Duncan didn't live in her town. Check.

He was gorgeous. Check.

He seemed interested. Check.

Her body was definitely interested. Check.

Potential complications appeared low. Semi-check.

Damn, Universe. Fast work.

She touched her hair. "You should see it first thing in the morning. It's a crazy mess."

Talking about her messy hair? Epic fail in the flirting department. She was definitely rusty.

But Duncan gave her a slow smile, the shyness gone. He

leaned in close and whispered, "If you insist I see, that can be arranged. Though I should warn you, I hog the covers."

He'd thought she had invited him over so he could see her hair in the morning after a night of . . .

Her face burned hot.

"I, uh, oh, I mean, I didn't exactly mean, I . . ."

Duncan laughed and pulled her into a side hug. "You are entirely too much fun to tease."

The feel of his hip, his body next to hers was intoxicating. Screw the stereotypical butterflies, Kate had full grown birds in her stomach.

She glanced up at him. She'd never kissed a man with a beard or a mustache.

She suddenly wanted to find out what it felt like.

"Duncan," Michael's voice cut through the hormone haze in Kate's mind. "Stop monopolizing Kate."

Duncan's arm dropped from her shoulders, but he took her hand. "Are you ready to meet everyone?"

She squeezed his hand, liking the feel of it in hers. "Lead on."

And she realized she meant much more than just taking her into his house. Something was starting. She didn't know where it would take her, but for the first time in a long time, she was interested to find out.

KATE FOLLOWED MICHAEL INTO THE MANOR WITH DUNCAN trailing behind. Her B&B was pretty spacious, but this felt immense.

The creamy white walls added to the airy feeling. Dark wood railing accented the large spiral staircase leading up to the second floor. Kate tried not to gawk at all the rooms she saw leading off of the entryway.

She suddenly felt like the poor church mouse visiting royalty. But she heard Sam's laughter echoing nearby. The sound eased some of the nervousness in her gut.

With Michael at her side, Kate entered the cozy sitting room. It was lit by candles around the edges and a modest fireplace across from the entrance.

A loveseat and easy chairs were clustered around the fireplace. Across from the loveseat was a chocolate-colored leather sofa which seemed well loved. It was nice to see something less than perfect in this beautiful room.

Sam was bent over, holding her stomach and chuckling with an older woman. It had to be Michael's mother. She was Beth's height, so an inch shorter than Sam, and the way she tilted her head looked just like Michael.

A servant bought over a tray of red wine in elegant cut crystal glasses. Kate grabbed a glass and immediately took a healthy swallow.

Michael led her and Duncan over towards the older woman. "Mother, this is Kate Banberry."

"I'm Jean." She took Kate's hand in her strong grip. "It's so wonderful to finally meet you." Her dark hair had strands of fine silver woven throughout, but Kate couldn't tell her age. Fifties, early sixties, maybe?

"I'm so pleased to meet you too," Kate said. "Your house is amazing."

Jean smiled. "It's been in our family for centuries. A beast to keep up. That's why our children help out."

Michael gazed around the room. "Speaking of children, where are Agnes and Isobel?"

"They're off in Romania," Duncan said. "There were rumors of more dampening stones." The light in his eyes dimmed. "We've only got one left and then we'll be at the mercy of—"

Jean touched his arm, stopping his words. "No need to involve our guests in our family business." Though she smiled, the steel in her words was cold.

Dampening stones? Kate raised an eyebrow at Michael, but he gave her a tiny shake of his head, so she let it drop. She needed Duncan's help. No sense making his mother angry.

She latched onto a topic that every mother usually loves to talk about. Their kids.

"With this many children, I'm sure they ran you ragged." Kate smiled at Duncan and Michael. "I have two girls and they're a handful. A handful I wouldn't trade for the world, but I'm not sure how I would have managed more."

Jean hooked her arm through Michael's and pulled him close. She leaned her head on his shoulder. They had the same angular shape to their faces. "We were blessed when Michael came along. Just his presence brought a calming effect to all the children."

Duncan opened his mouth, but Michael held up his hand.

"Let's not bore Kate with our childhood challenges, Mother. Why don't you introduce her to Glenna while Duncan helps me with the appetizers?"

Michael lead a frowning Duncan out of the study. Something had definitely happened in their childhood. Something bad. Maybe having a family of gifted children wasn't the complete blessing she'd originally thought.

"I see Beth and Sam have already found Glenna." Jean gazed towards the far edge of the room. "She's my baby. My miracle baby. I wasn't supposed to be able to have any more children, and then Glenna came into our lives."

The love in her voice was unmistakable. Kate grabbed her arm. "I almost lost Patty, my youngest. I know what it's like when your prayers are answered."

Jean sniffed and Kate saw the moisture in her eyes. "Come on. I know she'll want to meet you."

Though she looked like a teenager, there was something in the way Glenna held herself that spoke of someone older. Leggings and a long gray sweater amplified her slim frame. Her eyes were large, giving her a doll-like appearance, especially with her cropped blonde hair.

Beth hooked her thumb toward Glenna. "You've got some competition in the Pip Squeak department, Red."

For the first time in forever, Kate was taller than someone who wasn't a child.

"I'm so delighted to meet you." Glenna pulled Kate into a hug. Startled, Kate hugged her back, sloshing a bit of her wine on the plush brown rug and hoping no one noticed. When

Glenna pulled back and stepped away, her smile was so infectious, Kate found herself smiling too.

Sam placed her hand on Glenna's shoulder. "Glenna is a writer too. I'm going to look over her first manuscript and see if there's any tips or suggestions I can give her."

"Saint Sammy to the rescue," Beth said under her breath, but everyone heard it.

Sam frowned, but Glenna's smile grew blinding. "I'm still pinching myself. Best-selling author, Samantha Hamilton, looking at my work." She looked at Duncan who was setting out food with Michael in the sitting room. "Everyone needs a teacher. I know Duncan will be able to help you, Kate."

Kate lifted her glass. "I'll drink to that."

She'd been interrupted in her first vision, which meant another one was coming. If Duncan could help her stop blacking out, she'd owe him big time.

Jean led them back toward the fire and the plates of cheese and crackers, shrimp, small quiches, and bruschetta. Kate took a bite of quiche and had to admit, the food was excellent. She was thankful this place wasn't a B&B she had to compete with.

They all settled in. Sam, Beth and Michael on the sofa. Duncan and Glenna on the loveseat. Jean and Kate in easy chairs by the fire.

Jean raised her glass high. "To our new friends. We are always blessed to find others of our kind."

Our kind. The way she said it filled Kate with longing. Kate had been treated differently by almost everyone who found out about what she could do. Because she was different. But everyone here, *everyone* in this room had an ability. She'd never been among so many before who were like her.

Sam lifted her glass. "And thank you for welcoming us into your home."

"And now," Jean said. "As is tradition for new guests, I'll read your palms." She lifted her hand toward Beth. "I can see connections, relationships, and love."

"I don't believe in that cr . . . stuff," Beth said. She drained her wine glass and handed it to Duncan for a refill.

Michael cocked his head at her. "You have the gift of finding things, and your best friends are also talented. You've seen what I can do. And yet you don't believe my mother has the ability to read palms?"

Beth frowned. "I believe she has a gift."

"Then . . ." Michael's eyebrow lifted.

"Then you need to drop it."

Kate knew why Beth didn't want her palm read. She had never believed in love. Time for some helpful deflection. "I know Sam will do it." Kate winked at Sam.

Sam winked back. "Of course." She held out her hand to Jean. "What do you see?" Beth flashed Kate a grateful look.

Jean looked down at Sam's hand and traced the lines on her palm with a long fingernail. "Ah, very interesting."

"What is it?" Sam asked.

"Looks like you found your love." Jean beamed at her. "After some struggle."

Beth lifted her glass. "I call tussling with the Universe a huge struggle."

"I see the lines criss-crossed here that show of great sacrifice."
Her eyes narrowed. "But there is coming strife that will affect
your relationships with the living world and with Entwine.
The lines aren't definitive, so it could go either way, nothing is
pre-determined. As for children—"

Sam pulled her hand back, but patted Jean's lightly. "No,
don't tell me. I don't want to know either way right now. I'm
just happy to have found Robert."

Jean lifted her hand toward Kate. "I can read yours too, if
you'd like."

Kate shook her head. "No point. I've already got my kids,
and I had the love of my life."

Beth frowned. "Kate believes you only get one soul-mate. If
you believe in soulmates, that is."

It was the lie she'd told everyone. No one could really prove
her wrong, so it was safer. If either Beth or Sam knew the truth,
knew that it was her guilt over not seeing Paul's cancer in time,
they wouldn't give up trying to rationalize her out of it.

"That's not how it works in love," Glenna said. She crossed
her legs, tugging the bottom of her gray sweater over her knees.
"You get several soulmates. Our mother is never wrong."

Jean reached across the coffee table and squeezed Glenna's
hand. "She's right. We each have—"

"We have a situation, Mother." A melodic voice said from
the entryway.

Kate looked back over her shoulder. It was a man who had
the same regal tilt of his head that Michael did. His brown hair
was cropped short, emphasizing the harsh angles to his face.

There wasn't an ounce of fat on his compact frame. He'd be handsome if he smiled. Right now, he looked forbidding.

He made his way over to them, moving lightly on his feet. Kate tensed. Whatever he was about to say, she had a feeling she wasn't going to like it.

"What is it, Lennox?" Jean asked.

Michael stood, as did Duncan. Lennox ignored both of them. "One of the Allens' girls is showing off at the pub in Fairweather. We'll need to grab her quickly. And someone needs to go to her house to stop her father from doing anything foolish."

Jean nodded, her face grim. "If you don't reach her in time, RAVEN will surely capture her."

"Raven?" Sam said.

Duncan's face grew serious. "RAVEN. It stands for Research & Acquisition of Valuable Enhanced Neo-Humans. A black-ops military facility. They take our kind. And experiment on them."

Kate's mind spun, and the image of the crows from her vision fluttered through her thoughts. Their wings felt like they wrapped around her, squeezing the breath from her body. Maybe it hadn't been a crow on the doors at all.

Maybe it had been a raven.

CHAPTER 5

A BLACK OPS MILITARY GROUP? BETH LET THAT ANNOUNCE-MENT sit for a moment in her mind. She'd done a bit of work with a mercenary team in Los Angeles, and they were bad-ass enough. A military group hunting people with abilities would be even worse.

"What do they plan to do to her? The woman you want to grab." Beth looked at Lennox.

He had a boxer's frame. Short but sturdy. Stacked with muscle. "Most likely kidnap her to use her abilities."

Figured. Everyone wanted to use you for something.

Beth's right side ached, under her ribs, where she'd been stabbed in Juvie trying to protect her one and only friend in that place. In the end, she'd been used for her abilities. Against her will.

Lennox lifted his hand toward Glenna. "Do you need to charge?"

"Yes, just give me a sec." Glenna ran upstairs.

Beth didn't know why anyone would be charging their

phones, especially when they needed to rush out and save this Allen chick.

"I'll go to the pub with you." Beth stood. She picked up her small cross-body purse and slung it over her shoulder. The extra magazine for her Walther CCP was a comfortable weight. That plus her two Kershaw knives and she was good to go.

Sam always complained that she didn't need to be armed to the teeth for social calls, but you never know when things could get real. Real sudden.

Jean shook her head. "That's not necessary. We can handle this. You should go home."

"Hold on a second—"

But Beth's retort was cut off by Lennox. "Mother is right. And even if you did come, your ability does us no good. We don't need you to *find* anything." He dismissed Beth with a shake of his head.

Anger flared up Beth's chest, heating her face. "*Finding* things isn't all I can do." She was proud her voice was semi-reasonable. Only a bare hint of a growl. "And if you truly have a black ops military group, you'll need all hands on deck."

Lennox gave her a small smile, gazing at her as if she were a child seeking approval. "I know you're just trying to help, but we don't need any TV flash and dazzle. RAVEN will be armed. You'll be a liability."

Once again with the critics.

"She can handle herself." Michael handed Beth's leather jacket to her. "We're taking her."

Was that a compliment? Her hearing must be shot. Usually

Michael didn't miss a chance to get in a dig about her gifts or anything else.

"*We're*? You're not coming either, brother." Lennox's mouth flattened into a straight line. "Feel-good rainbow shit isn't going to cut it. Glenna and I can handle this."

Glenna, their I'm-barely-bigger-than-a-shadow sister. What kind of mojo did she have?

Michael shrugged on his jacket, looking way too dashing. With the distressed leather and his longish blond hair, he looked ready to get into some trouble.

"I'm going, Lennox." Michael stared down his brother. "If someone gets injured, you're going to need a doctor."

"Bloody hell. Saddled with Miss Ratings and the Love Doctor." Lennox turned on his heel, heading toward the door. "Meet me at the car."

Beth waggled her eyebrows at Michael. "We sound like the title of a made-for-TV movie."

Michael gave her a smoldering look worthy of a leading man, but it collapsed into a grin.

Glenna rushed down the stairs. The kid must have the world's fastest phone charger. "Come on."

They hustled out of the manor. The sun had begun to dip below the line of trees, splashing the sky in shades of red and orange.

A running black box-shaped SUV sat waiting for them with Lennox at the wheel. They filed in, Glenna in the front, Beth and Michael in the back. Lennox took off immediately.

Glenna turned around in her seat. "The pub is two towns

over, but with the way Lennox drives, we'll be there before you know it."

Beth noted the glass on the windows was thicker than usual. "This thing stands up against bullets?"

"It'll withstand fire all the way up to armor piercing bullets," Lennox said. He swerved down a side road, and Beth slid into Michael.

He caught her, an arm around her waist. She turned her head and found his mouth inches away. Heat shot through her skin. His stupid bottom lip begged to be bitten.

"Something fascinating about my mouth?" His words were a low whisper. His breath brushed her cheeks.

She suddenly felt the outline of his hand on her waist. Every finger. Had he just gripped her tighter?

"You better not be using that feely shit on me," she whispered, her gaze moving up his face to meet his eyes. In the shadows of the car, she couldn't read them.

Michael pulled back, letting her go. She suddenly felt cold. "I've never used my powers on a woman like that." His words were low. "And I've vowed never to use them to hurt someone again." A flash of light caught his eyes. They were cool and calm. "I keep my word."

Beth shook her head. She'd been obviously getting the wrong vibe from him. Now she just felt stupid thinking . . . whatever she'd been thinking. She needed something, anything to fill the awkward silence. "Tell me more about the van, Glenna."

"The floor is reinforced to help against grenades."

"And why do you need *that* much protection?"

Michael looked more serious than she'd ever seen him. "My father was injured the last time we faced RAVEN. Since then, Lennox . . . upgraded."

"Why does it feel like I've stumbled into a war?"

Lennox gave Beth a knowing smile in the rearview mirror. "I can let you off here, princess, if you're scared."

Invisible hackles raised on Beth's back. No wonder why Sammy hated it when Beth called her that.

She flicked a glance at Lennox. "It'll take much more than soldiers with grenades to scare me."

Lennox didn't say anything further. A victory.

"This girl at the pub, Fiona, right? What can she do?"

"She can see through things," Michael said. "Clothes, buildings, walls, anything really if she concentrates hard enough. She once helped me save her sister when I had to operate because she knew exactly where the tear was in her spleen."

This town got creepier and creepier. Just how many residents had powers?

They took another turn at high speed. Beth was surprised the wheels didn't lift off the ground, but Lennox seemed completely in control, like he'd done this a million times.

"What's the plan when we get there?" Beth asked.

Lennox met her gaze in the rearview mirror. "Glenna will do reconnaissance to confirm RAVEN is here. If not, we grab Fi and get her out of there. If they're there already, we'll have to convince her to leave."

"But she should leave as soon as you ask, right?" Beth glanced between Michael and Lennox. "Unless she doesn't know about RAVEN?"

"She knows," Glenna said. "All our town does, but many don't believe." She turned around and suddenly looked a lot older. Just what had this kid seen? "We've kept them safe this whole time, so RAVEN is just the boogey man to them. A myth."

"Any tranquilizers on hand, doctor?" Beth said to Michael. That would be the easiest route. Get close, inject her, pretend she's passed out drunk and get her out of there.

Michael shook his head. "I wouldn't do that to someone even if I had the medication on me."

Lennox snorted. "Finally drawing some lines you won't cross. It's about time."

Michael stiffened, but didn't say anything.

Beth didn't understand what Lennox meant, but there was obviously some serious damage between these too. And she wasn't here to play therapist.

"The pub's on the corner." Glenna pointed to the far end of the street. They pulled into a tiny parking lot.

They got out of the car and headed toward the rear entrance. Large floodlights filled the parking area with light. A group of smokers leaned against the back wall, laughing. Beer aroma fought with tobacco and sweat. Lovely.

The warm day had turned into a chilly twilight, but she didn't zip up her jacket. She needed easy access to her gun.

Glenna grabbed the backdoor handle. "I'll give you the signal." She opened the door and headed in.

Beth looked at the men. "Is she going to text us or what?"

Michael shook his head. "Just wait."

"I don't like surprises." Beth shot Michael the glare which always sent the recipient whimpering, but he just smiled at her like she'd said something cute.

Lennox walked over to the smokers. "Clear out." His voice had the bark of a drill sergeant, but his order was met with "Piss off" and "Who do you think you are, my Da?"

Michael walked past Lennox. "Always the hammer. No finesse," he muttered. "When will you learn?"

Beth couldn't hear what Michael said to the smoker crowd, but within moments, they'd disbursed. Some even waving back at Michael and promising to call him. Like he was suddenly their best friend.

Lennox turned around, his cell phone to his ear.

"Why does your brother think your ability is weak, fluffy?" Beth whispered to Michael. "You're crazy powerful. I felt it at the police station even from across the room."

Michael had used his powers of persuasion to get Logan's house key and code from Sheila, the department assistant, when they'd been trying to figure out if Logan was the serial killer after Kate. Michael needed a connection, something to make his suggestions plausible to the person he was trying to influence. But if he had that, Beth was sure she'd just seen the tip of his power iceberg.

Michael glanced past Beth. She could tell his thoughts were far away. "There were some problems when we were growing up. Before I got a handle on things." His voice was equally soft.

"You hurt him, didn't you?" Beth already knew the answer.

Michael met her gaze, his eyes sad. "Yes." The one word hung in the air. He took a deep breath. "And he wants to forget it ever happened. I let him get away with the lie. I owe him that."

Suddenly Beth didn't want to know what someone who could twist emotions had done to his overbearing older brother when they were both just kids. Why he'd vowed never to do it again.

She glanced back at Lennox. He turned around, finishing up his call. Beth recognized the guarded look in his eyes now. She saw it in herself every time she looked in a mirror. When you've been used by someone, the mark remains.

The lights flickered overhead and then went out, dousing them in darkness. Not only the lights from the pub, but the streetlights too.

Lennox nodded toward Michael. "Fiona's still here. And RAVEN too. Let's go." He slipped through the back door.

That was the signal? And how had the kid killed the lights in the back?

Michael looked at Beth. "Keep your gun holstered unless things go bad. Otherwise Lennox might damage it for spite."

"How could he damage—"

But Michael had already gone into the pub. She didn't know what she'd gotten herself into, but no one was going to take someone against their will and use them. Not in front of her.

She pulled open the door and slipped inside.

BETH STOPPED FOR A MOMENT, JUST INSIDE THE DOOR, letting her eyesight adjust to the gloom.

The hallway was tight and cramped. And almost completely dark. But it was short, and the light at the end beckoned. Along with the sounds of Led Zeppelin blasting from the sound system.

She made her way quickly through. Bathroom on the right. Storage room to the left. Flyers decorated the walls advertising the latest local band's show. The greasy smell of something fried squatted on the aroma of stale beer.

She turned the corner, coming into the pub proper, and let out a ragged breath. All along the windows and stretching to her left were tables disappearing around another corner. The place was packed.

Beth looked for any signs of RAVEN. The long bar to her right and the closer cluster of tables had the usual assortment of residents she'd expect. Men trying to recapture their wilder days, a few cougars holding court over some young bucks, and a group of kids looking fresh from college.

Glenna was nowhere to be seen, but Michael and Lennox had a girl cornered by a table, but by the mutinous look on her face, they wouldn't have her trapped for long. It had to be the illustrious Fiona they were supposed to rescue. Great.

Beth let her gaze sweep past, like she was looking for her date.

Against the window, were several stools with tall round

tables in between them. Beth's eyes clocked each one.

Boring.

Perking up like he thought Beth might be interested.

Drunk.

Pay dirt.

At the corner table, leaning back against the glass, was a man who looked comfortably slouchy, deep in his drink from his posture, but his eyes were bright and latched onto Fiona. His companion sat so straight she could have been in choir practice.

A bulge from Ms. Posture's jacket might be a gun. Sloucher had a knife sheath in his boot.

None of it meant they were definitely RAVEN. Either way, they needed to get Fiona out of here before there was trouble.

Beth ordered a Smithwick at the bar, and then pretended to watch the dart match, but studied Fiona. She had shoulder-length blonde hair tinged with orange at the ends, a nose ring, and a low cut tank which advertised her black bra's lacy cups.

"Aw, don't stop now Fiona," one of the boys said at their table. He was rocking the vampire look with enough guy-liner to write a novel with. "Do it again. Tell me what I have in my *left* pocket this time."

"Fiona has to get home," Michael said, flashing an endearing smile.

But Fiona waved him off with her hand. "Don't listen to him, Tavis. I'll do it again, but it'll cost you some fags." Tavis took out a pack of cigarettes and offered her a few.

Lennox took a step forward. His voice dropped, and Beth couldn't hear him over the music. But whatever he said wasn't landing. If anything, Fi's glare grew more heated.

"We'll leave when I'm good and ready, *Lord Forbes.*" Fi's voice was thick with disdain. "Sorry, Tavis. Now where were we?"

Lennox looked up at the ceiling, as if hoping to invoke some mystical help, but nothing happened.

"Left pocket," Tavis piped up. "What do I have in my left pocket?"

Fiona looked down. "Two rubbers. One of them is already ripped inside, you should ditch it." She tucked a strand of hair behind her ear. "A mint lip-balm." She squinted for a moment. "And, it looks like you have the very beginning a kidney infection. I'd have it checked out. Soon."

Tavis blanched and took the contents of his pocket out and put them on the alcohol-stained table. Two condom packs. One more crumpled than the other. And a mint lip balm. He took a large swig of his beer. "Do you think it's a serious infection?" His eyes held a shimmer of fear battling with blatant attraction. "How do you do what you do?"

The goons in the corner shifted in their seats. Ms. Posture stood.

Lennox grabbed Fiona's arm. "I've tried to be patient, but show and tell is over. We're taking you home."

Fiona raised a dark eyebrow. "Get tae. What's the point of having a gift if you can't bloody well use it? I'm tired of the Forbes' controlling everything. Using the Covenant crap as a way to justify bullying everyone to do what you say."

The Covenant? What the hell was that?

Michael moved in between them, laughing about something, like they'd had a good joke.

Beth glanced at the corner table. Ms.Posture sat back down. Sloucher ordered another drink. Michael's deflection tactic had worked. For now.

"It's a trick," one of the girls at the table said. She waved her hand at Fiona, seemingly unaware of the tension around her. Probably because she was going to pass out soon, if the glazed look in her eyes was any indication.

The girl's fake eyelashes were so thick, it looked like spiders had taken up residence on her lids. "Even *I* knew you had rubbers. And you always smell minty. Easy guesses." She lifted her chin towards Fiona. "Tell me the color of my panties. No way you'd know that."

Fiona laughed and it had a nasty edge to it. "It's a trick question, Lia. You're not wearing panties." Her voice dropped, snarling like the crack of a whip. "That's why all the guys like to screw you."

Lia rolled her eyes, unaffected. "Always a bitch. You're just jealous because they don't want you." She leaned, almost falling off her chair. Michael moved closer, steadying her, but she was like a limp noodle. "It's time you faced it, Fi. No one cares about you. We're only here because we're bored and you're a *freak*."

Beth instinctively took a step forward, wanting to hit Lia. She'd been called freak too many times in her life. But Fiona beat her to it. Her blow never landed on Lia though, her wrist caught in Lennox's grip. He was fast. She'd give him that.

Fiona pulled on Lennox, but couldn't break free. "If you don't let go of me," she hissed, "I'll put on a show. Prove to everyone what I can do."

Lennox dropped his hand and gave Michael a look, but Beth knew there'd be no hope in using Michael's power. Fiona wasn't open to any suggestions. She wasn't going anywhere unless they dragged her out kicking and screaming. And if those two were RAVEN, this could get messy.

Michael shook his head at Lennox and propped up Lia again. He locked eyes with Beth and she knew he understood what time it was. Time to call in back-up.

Beth grabbed her beer and sauntered over to join them. The dart crowd gave her an appraising look and Tavis perked up like someone had rammed a rod through his spine.

"Hey Fi," Beth said brightly. "It's so awesome to see you again."

Lennox sighed deeply. "Now's not the time, Beth."

Michael laughed. "Let them talk. They haven't seen each other in a while."

Lennox looked at Michael and Beth like they'd lost their minds.

"Are we moving?" Lia asked. She swayed back and forth next to Michael.

Michael wet a napkin and put it to her head. He leaned down and whispered in her ear and she seemed to calm a bit.

"Who the hell are you?" Fiona crossed her arms. "Did my Da send you?"

Beth laughed and gave everyone the full TV grin. The

sloucher shifted in his seat, but continued to just watch. "Okay, I know it's been a while. I deserve that. Come here you."

She pulled a sputtering Fiona into a hug. Beth whispered in her ear. "Your tricks have attracted RAVEN. I know you might not believe in them, but they're here. We need to get you home."

"I don't know you." Fiona pushed against her. "Why would I listen to a word you say?"

"Because I'm different. Like you." Beth called to her own power. Though she wasn't trying to find anything, her power would come nonetheless. Like grasping fingers, it touched her, sinking through her, joining with her. "And I don't want to get captured either. But I'm willing to risk it to convince you."

She pulled back just a bit, until they were almost nose to nose. To anyone else they probably looked like they were about to kiss. Beth was sure tents were erecting in many pairs of pants.

Fiona stared into her eyes. Beth saw her own reflection in the girl's pupils. Beth's eyes were completely black. Demon eyes, as Sammy had so eloquently put it. Which was ridiculous. Beth was fucked up on her own. No possession required.

She saw Michael out of the corner of her eye, still whispering in Lia's ear. She didn't know why he bothered. Lia wasn't the issue.

Beth blinked, letting the power dissipate. She knew her eyes would be back to normal. She kissed Fi on the cheek, then pulled away, giving the girl some space.

Fiona's skin paled. She took a step back and then another

until she stood next to Lia's seat. "RAVEN is *not* real. They can't be." Her voice was a shaky whisper.

"Who's raven?" Tavis asked.

Michael lifted Lia to her feet, and suddenly she stumbled into Fiona and threw up all over Fiona's tank. She'd had something with tomato sauce recently. The acrid smell made Beth's eyes water.

"Bitch." Fiona shoved Lia and Michael caught her, easing her back into her seat. "You've ruined my favorite tank."

Michael gave Beth a wink. Did he just convince Lia to barf?

"Don't feel so good." Lia leaned over and puked on Tavis' boots.

Beth would use whatever advantage Michael had given them. She looked at Tavis. "You. Help Lia get home, and don't think about trying anything with her because I *will* find you." She held his gaze until he nodded frantically.

Beth smiled at Lennox, using her sweet I'm-just-the-girl-next-door voice. "I'm going to help her get cleaned up. Take care of her bill?"

He nodded without argument.

Beth put her arm around Fiona's shoulders, careful to avoid any vomit. "Michael, can I borrow your jacket?" He took it off and handed to her. Fiona hadn't said a word, but Beth felt the trembling rage in her body.

The bathrooms were by the back door. Beth got Fiona inside before the girl exploded. "I'm going to kill her for this. My favorite tank. I'll never get the smell out of it."

Luckily the bathroom was empty. It was a tiny one-seater

with a door and then a pedestal sink shoved on the other side.

"Take off your top and let me rinse it," Beth said.

Fiona took it off quickly, managing to only get a few tomato chunks in her hair. Beth threw it in the chipped sink and turned on the water.

Fiona grabbed some paper towels and ran them under the water. She wiped her chest with sharp, jerky movements. "Lia did this on purpose." Goosebumps rose on her skin.

Beth handed her Michael's jacket. "Here, put this on."

Lia threw out the red stained paper towels and slipped the jacket on.

Beth glanced at the girl. "Lia was right you know."

"About what?"

"About you being a bitch." Beth rinsed out the top, scrubbing it with the gritty soap from the dispenser.

"Piss off." Fiona zipped up Michael's jacket, her movements tight. She tried to make it past Beth, but Beth shoved her hard against the stall door. It creaked.

Her hand gripped Fiona's shoulder, water dripping onto Michael's jacket. "I know a lot about being a bitch. And it always comes from a place of pain."

The girl froze. "You don't know anything about—"

"I know you've got a screwed up family and loads of haters because you're beautiful." Beth turned back to the sink. "That's enough to make you want to lash out before someone gets close enough to really hurt you."

"Why are you helping me?" Fiona's question was genuine, no sense of snark. "You're not part of the Covenant. Not that

I really believe in any of that crap."

"What exactly is the Covenant?"

Fiona shrugged. "It's something the town founders agreed to a long time ago. The Forbes family protects our town from RAVEN, and in return they keep us under their thumb."

Beth considered her words, scrubbing at a particularly stubborn tomato stain. Lennox or Michael wouldn't have wasted their time here if there wasn't danger and they wouldn't have made up something as horrible as RAVEN.

"Hate to burst your ignorance bubble, but they're real." Beth squeezed out the water from the tank as best she could, wrapped it in paper towels and handed it back to Fiona. "And from what I heard, RAVEN is bad news."

She took out her phone. No texts from Michael. If those two in the bar were RAVEN, were they safe to just walk out the back door?

Fiona's eyes widened. "Wait a second, I know who you are now. You're Beth Marshall. Are you filming a show? Is that what all this RAVEN mystery is?" The anger and fear were gone, replaced by that crazy hope Beth had seen many times before. Everyone wanted to be on TV. "A small town plagued by a hush-hush military group . . . wait a second. What are you supposed to find?"

"My sanity," Beth muttered. Ever since she'd come to Scotland, it had been one crazy thing after another.

Truth was definitely stranger than fiction.

Beth's phone vibrated. Michael had finally texted.

Meet us out back. We have a plan.

"Come on." She hustled Fiona out of the bathroom. "Let's go."

They walked out the back door. And came face to face with RAVEN.

CHAPTER 6

KATE LOOKED AT THE ALLEN HOUSE. OLD, WITH A WORN front porch. And no lights on inside. "Are you sure Mr. Allen is home? Maybe he's with his daughter at the pub?"

Jean knocked on the front door again. "Ken, Ruth? It's Jean Forbes."

Duncan and Sam stood next to Kate. Both looked worried. "What can Mr. Allen do?" Sam asked Duncan.

He rubbed his jaw. "He can cause earthquakes."

"What?" Kate said. "So, that's why we're really here. You're afraid he's going to suddenly flip out and cause an earthquake."

"You should go home, Kate." Sam frowned. "It's not safe."

"My gut tells me I need to be here." Kate wasn't sure why that was true, but it was. When Jean, Duncan and Sam were bustling out the door to go to the Allen house, she felt the need to go too. "And I already checked in with the girls. They're working on their homework with Aggie." The B&B's caretakers had truly become surrogate grandparents to her girls. Kate lifted her chin at Sam. "If it's so dangerous, why don't you leave?"

"I might be able to talk to any of the ghosts here."

"So what you mean is that your gifts are valuable and mine won't do any good."

"No, that's not what I'm saying." She took Kate's hand. A spark of blue from Sam's finger tickled her skin. Sam dropped her hand. "Sorry. I don't know how to control this ghostly essence yet. It keeps slipping out."

Kate eyed the worry tightening her face. "We're all still figuring things out, Sam. Which is why it hurts that you think I shouldn't be here."

Sam's posture immediately softened. "I just hate to see you at risk without a good reason. I wouldn't be a prudent aunt to your girls without thinking of your safety."

Those puppy dog eyes Sam employed so well to get her way were in full force. Yup. She thought Kate was less than. Maybe not as a person, but on the ability level. So much for the "we're all equals" feels they'd given her yesterday.

Duncan nodded. "That might be best, Kate."

It appeared everyone had bought a ticket on the "Kate is worthless" train.

She tamped down her first instinct. Yelling wasn't going to prove her point and would just have her look needy.

Kate pushed her shoulders back, standing up straight. There was no way she was leaving now. They'd be happy she'd come before the night was over if she had anything to say about it.

"I'm just here to help, in any way I can," Kate said, her voice smooth. "Duncan, you know the family well. I know what it's like to be frustrated by my daughters. Perhaps I can talk him down from the ledge?"

Duncan nodded his head. "You might. Plus you're not a Forbes." His expression soured. "We're not always the most popular when it comes to things like this."

Jean knocked again, but no answer. She came down the steps from the porch. "Are we sure he's in there?"

A rumbling shook the ground. Jean stumbled, but Sam grabbed her arm, steadying her.

"He's in there all right." Kate pursed her lips.

Sam said, "There are two ghosts by the hedges, and one on the steps with us. I'm Sam." She paused for a moment. "It's nice to meet you Eileen." She looked at Kate, Jean and Duncan. "Eileen is Ken's mother."

Another tremor shook the ground. A small fissure opened in between Jean and Duncan. They jumped back.

Ghosts couldn't physically open doors, and Kate didn't want to be in a full scale earthquake. "We need to get in there now. Plan A is obviously a bust. Onto Plan B." She looked at Duncan. "Can you break the door down?"

He studied the door. "Mr. Allen reinforced it last year. I wouldn't be able to do it alone."

"Plan C." Kate went over to the garden border and dug out a large rock. "We'll use this to break one of the windows. Duncan, get ready with your coat for the glass so we can put it over the sill to crawl in safely." The rock was heavy, but she'd lifted worse in her own garden.

"Eileen says there's a key to the side door," Sam said. "It's in a loose piece of the door jamb."

Kate dropped the rock. Apparently ghosts *could* get doors open.

The made their way around the side of the house and found the key. Duncan opened the door and took the lead. They slipped into the house quietly.

Inside, it looked like a windstorm had whipped through the living room. Lamps were knocked over and picture frames lay cracked on the floor. Even the large wooden coffee table had been flipped completely over.

Yelling echoed in the distance. They followed the noise, making their way further into the house. All the way through, the same devastation.

They went down a narrow hallway. Kate hadn't realized the house was so deep. They were getting closer to the shouting.

Jean knocked on a closed door at the end of the hallway. "Ken, Ruth, it's Jean," she yelled. "We need to talk."

"Ruth's left me," the man's voice said from behind the door. "And you all need to leave too."

Kate recognized the pain in his voice. His whole world was shifting out of his control. He needed to know he wasn't alone.

"You've got people who care about you, Mr. Allen. I'm Kate. You don't know me, but Jean and Duncan are here and worried sick about you."

The ground rumbled under their feet.

"My family is gone." Ken's voice was slurred. "Said I was a danger to them. They're right. It's about time I stopped fighting."

"You're just having a relapse, Ken," Jean said. "We can help you get control of your abilities again. We've done it before."

"I'm tired of being a burden. I need to finally do something about it."

Jean went white. She walked away from the door and gathered them around her. Keeping her voice pitched low, Jean said, "If he keeps it up, no amount of protection is going to stop RAVEN from finding him. And then our entire town will be in danger."

Duncan rubbed his eyes, looking tired. "I hate to say this, but we're within rights."

"I know," Jean said. "But he's under the influence."

Kate didn't know what they were talking about. "Can you break *that* door down?"

Duncan nodded. "But I have no idea what he'll do if we rush in. We could make things worse."

"Eileen said that the main support beam in the house is damaged," Sam said. "One more good shake and we could be buried. We have to stop him quickly before this gets worse."

Kate looked between Jean and Duncan. If they burst through the door, everyone could die. If they didn't, everyone could die.

The clock on the wall bonged loudly. Seven o'clock.

They needed to know what the right decision was. They needed to know *now.*

Kate's entire body suddenly burned, like she had a high fever. She recognized the feeling. She'd had it before when she'd been in the forest with Sam fighting for their lives. Rather than a full vision, this was going to be a snapshot glimpse of the near future.

Everyone disappeared, and Kate was in a different room. A bedroom. Bed in the corner, side table, lamp. A man who looked like he was in his sixties sat in a chair by the window.

"I failed you." From the voice, Kate knew this was Ken. He held a picture. Kate looked at it. A younger Ken, a woman and two small girls smiled from behind the glass. Tears rolled down his stubbly cheeks.

From the other side of the door, she heard the murmur of Duncan's voice and Jean's.

"I'm ready to stop fighting. To let go." A certainty filled his eyes. A resignation. "It's time." He dropped the picture. Glass broke from the frame.

The floorboards buckled. Chunks of roof fell. The ground heaved, and Kate was suddenly airborne. Ken screamed and the house screamed with him, caving in. The ground swallowed them whole.

Flesh, wood, and bone.

A sharp tug, like being on the end of a rubber band, yanked Kate, pulling her back. She was with Jean and Duncan again.

The clock struck seven.

Kate grabbed Duncan's arm. "Break the door down now and knock Ken out."

He didn't hesitate. Just turned and rammed the door with his shoulder, breaking it open and almost off its hinges.

Kate had a quick glimpse of Ken holding the picture she'd seen. He dropped it, getting to his feet and swinging at Duncan.

But Duncan side-stepped and grabbed the older man around the chest. The ground groaned.

Sam rushed into the room with Kate on her heels, and Ken broke free of Duncan's grip and ran at Sam. He barreled into her, pushing her against the wall. The floorboards buckled.

Screaming, Sam pushed him. Blue light flared from her fingers and disappeared into his body. Ken's eyes rolled up into his head. He collapsed backwards, but Duncan caught him and managed to get him to the floor.

Had Sam just zapped him with that ghostly energy?

Tears streamed down Sam's face, her hands shaking. Kate ran to her, pulling Sam into her arms.

"It was like being in the forest with Graham. All over again." Sam's whisper was ragged.

Kate rubbed her back and stroked her hair, just like she did with her girls when they were upset. "It's okay, Sam. You're safe. I've got you."

Sam pulled back and wiped her eyes. "I'm okay. It's just a little too soon."

Kate dug into her purse. "Tissue, baby wipe, or gummy worms?"

"Tissue."

Kate pressed it into her hand, happy to see it more steady.

Jean removed a section of cracked floorboard and took out a whitish stone. The center was milky, but the top was burned black. "We were lucky this time."

Kate glanced at the stone Jean held. "What is that?"

Duncan took the stone from his mother. "This is a dampening stone. They amplify the local ley lines to keep our abilities off the military's sensing equipment. If Ken had burned through this whole thing, if it were completely black, we'd have RAVEN at our doorstep."

Dampening stones. Duncan had mentioned that his sisters were off looking for more.

Her B&B had no dampening stones. RAVEN must already know about them, yet they hadn't acted. Why? Her heart began to race. The girls. Then she took a deep breath. If RAVEN wanted to, her girls would have already been scooped up with none of them being the wiser. She needed to know more in order to protect her family. Her friends.

"When we get back to the house, we're having a drink," Kate paused. "Several drinks. And someone is going to explain to me how this town works, what your family is doing, and who the hell RAVEN is."

SLOUCHER AND MS. POSTURE STOOD IN FRONT OF BETH. She'd been right. RAVEN.

"Excuse us," Beth said with a smile. "I've got to get my friend home. It's been quite a night."

She grabbed the wet tank from Fiona and held it up toward the RAVEN operatives. A plume of pungent tomato scent filled the night air. Apparently she hadn't gotten it rinsed fully. Or Lia had atomic vomit.

Ms. Posture's eyes darted toward Fiona. "*She's* coming with us."

Beth handed the tank back to Fiona and shook her head. "I don't let my friends go off with strangers."

She didn't see Lennox or Michael anywhere. She couldn't believe they'd be *this* incompetent. The plan Michael mentioned had better be good.

She scanned her opponents. Overpowering one might not be an issue, but she couldn't take on two. There was clearly muscle under their jackets. She could pull her gun, but once that happened, all Scottish hell would break free.

"We're on official business, miss. Please don't interfere." The Sloucher flashed a badge of some sort. Officer Colin Mathews. His black hair was shaggy. They obviously didn't have military standards of grooming at RAVEN.

His buddy flashed her own badge. Jennifer Prentiss, aka Ms. Posture. The top part of the badge had a raven's wings outstretched in front of the sun. The feathers blotted out almost all the sunlight. Like that wasn't ominous.

She gave RAVEN what she hoped was a confused look. "I'm just visiting Fi. But I did promise her parents I'd look after her tonight. Can you tell me what this is about, officers?"

Prentiss smiled. It looked smooth and practiced. "Just some questions and then we'll have her back home."

Movement flickered in her periphery. She sized up the two new RAVEN goons flanking Prentiss. Her fingers itched to grab her Walther. Where were Lennox and Michael?

A loud crash sounded from inside the pub. And screams.

None of the RAVEN crew flinched. They were good.

Mathews nodded at the two on his left. "Check it out. Make sure everyone is okay." The last seemed a hasty add-on, probably to keep up the charade.

The two Matthews had ordered disappeared inside.

"There you are," Lennox said, suddenly coming out from behind the dumpster, like it was the most natural thing in the world. "I looked for you inside." His voice was smooth, caring. He was a better actor than Beth had expected.

"Sorry, babe." Beth softened her stance and took a step toward Lennox, with Fiona in tow. "I got stopped by these cops."

Prentiss' smile looked strained now. "Perhaps you both could come with us? Keep Ms. Allen company. Then you could get her home safely afterwards." Though her voice was pleasant, it had a dark undercurrent.

Matthews nodded. "Our van is across the street."

Beth shot a look at Lennox. If they went with them, it was over. And if anyone did supernatural shit, even if they got away, RAVEN wouldn't stop until they tracked them down. Which meant this wasn't just a rescue mission any longer to save Fi. They needed to take out the operatives. No witnesses, meant no one would be after them.

It was what one of her buddies back in L.A. used to tell her about.

Clean-up.

Adrenaline rushed through her. She'd never killed anyone before, but she wasn't letting them take Fiona. Her vision sharpened. She sensed Fiona's heartbeat behind her. The scent of sweat burned her nose.

Pull her gun, take out the two next to Prentiss. Drop. Shoot Matthews. Roll to avoid Prentiss' shots.

Looked good inside her head, but reality was often different. If only they had Red's near future vision right now. It would come in handy.

"Easy, lass." Lennox's hand on her shoulder felt like iron. "No one is going anywhere." His gaze never moved from Prentiss. "We know who you really are. Who RAVEN is."

Guns were suddenly in everyone's hands, including Beth's. She moved back until they were almost against the wall of the pub.

Prentiss lifted her chin toward Lennox. "We've got you outgunned."

One of the operatives looked up from his smart watch. "No manifestations yet, Commander. Potential non-offensive powers."

Lennox laughed. "Oh, I can assure you. I'm very offensive."

"He is," Beth said. "I can vouch for that."

Lennox frowned at her. She saw the tips of his fingers move in her periphery.

"What the hell?" Matthews gazed down at his weapon. It glowed orange. The smell of burning flesh choked the air. All the operatives dropped their weapons, but didn't make a sound though their hands were burned badly. Their guns were bent in the center, melted.

So that's why Michael warned her about her gun. Lennox could manipulate metal.

"Contact HQ," Matthews said, his voice steady, almost calm. "Two NH, potentially three. Send back-up." He took his billy club out and gripped it in his burned hand. Blood leaked out around the blisters, but he showed no sign of pain. "We're taking you all in."

"I don't think so." Beth shot near Mathews' foot. The kick of concrete dust was a thick puff. "*I* still have a gun, and I don't have any problem using it."

"We can't shoot them or stab them, but we *can* beat the shit out of them," Lennox said quietly.

"I can't reach anyone at HQ," one of the operatives said. "It's just static."

"They know what you look like. We need to kill them." Beth's gun remained trained on Prentiss. She tried to ignore the hollow feeling just saying those words brought.

"We've got it covered." He rushed toward Matthews, landing a hard right hook to his jaw. Blood sprayed from Matthews' mouth, through the air.

She didn't know what the hell he was talking about, but this was the Forbes' rodeo. She trusted they knew what they were doing.

One of the other operatives grabbed Lennox from behind, but Michael's brother shook him off easily.

"Oh crap. Oh crap. Oh crap," Fiona sobbed from behind her. "RAVEN's real. It's all real."

Beth couldn't take her focus off Prentiss and her buddy.

"Don't you run off now, Fi. We don't know how many more of them are out there." She tried to keep her voice steady, but the earlier adrenaline was begging to be utilized.

"Level 2 protocol," Prentiss said and stalked forward, the other operative close behind. Easy, on the balls of their feet, billy clubs out. Prentiss had a set of brass knuckles on her left hand.

But they weren't the traditional knuckles she'd seen. They had sharp points on the edges. Black steel if she wasn't mistaken. Beth could ask Lennox to heat them, but he was busy.

And she didn't need his help.

Beth slid the safety on and holstered her gun. Lennox had also said no knives.

Fists, then.

Prentiss reached Beth first, swinging her club. Beth feinted and landed a left hook to her kidneys. Prentiss grunted, and then she came back with her fist, the steel knuckles slicing open Beth's cheek.

The bright flash of pain quickly died with a thought. Her parents had taught her the hard way how to bury it.

Blood flowed down her face, dripping off her jaw. "That the best you got?"

"Beth, watch out!"

Fi's shout reached her too late. A weight slammed behind Beth's knees. One of the operatives had gotten behind her. Crap.

Hands gripped her shoulders. Beth fell but grabbed one of the hands, wrenching it up and twisting, using her body weight to pull with more force while she fell.

The man screamed quick and short, dropping away. Beth tucked and rolled, coming up onto her feet and punching Prentiss in the stomach, aiming for her diaphragm. She bent over, gasping.

Beth dropped to the ground, almost in a side pushup, and swung her legs around, sweeping Prentiss' feet right out from under her. She went down hard, head cracking against the concrete. Out cold.

Hearing a scuffle of feet to her side, Beth turned to see Fiona hanging onto the back of the operative whose shoulder she'd dislocated. Beth aimed for his jaw with her fist, but he jerked suddenly, flinging Fiona off and sending her tumbling to the ground.

Her split second of attention on the fallen girl got Beth a powerful kick to her side. Her lungs burned to breathe suddenly. She fell onto her back.

She had just enough time to grab the boot coming for her face and pull him off balance. He fell on top of her, slamming her head against the concrete.

Her vision spun. No wonder why Prentiss had lost consciousness. The back door of the pub burst open and two Glennas ran out. Followed by two Michaels.

"You leave her alone." Glenna's sweet voice had dropped into a growl. Beth thought she saw something spark in her pupils.

The weight of the RAVEN goon was suddenly lifted off of her, and Beth's vision cleared. Michael grabbed him like he was a marshmallow.

Michael threw the operative at his sister's feet. Glenna thrust her hands towards him and the last standing RAVEN operative fighting Lennox. A flash of electricity arced out of the power lines from the pub running to the wooden utility pole and shot into both men. They dropped immediately.

Their little sister Glenna packed some serious shit. Crazy ass power in a little package.

Beth let Michael help her up. *There is no pain. There is no pain.* She straightened with just the smallest wince.

Lennox wiped his knuckles against his shirt, leaving red streaks behind.

"You let Beth get hurt, Lennox." Michael's voice was quiet, but hummed with tension. "You could have just heated their zippers and buttons. They'd have been easy to knock out then."

Lennox smiled wide, the first real honest humor Beth had seen on his face. "But then I wouldn't have gotten to beat the crap out of someone."

Michael took a step toward Lennox, but Beth pulled him back. "Let it go. I'm fine."

"Come on, Fi." Lennox helped the girl to her feet. "You did good. No broken bones, yeah?"

Fi nodded her head and flashed Beth a frightened smile. Then she shivered, and Lennox gave her a knit hat from his pocket. Seemed Michael's brother did have a softer side. After letting loose with a lot of violence.

Michael turned to Beth. "He's never been good with the consequences of his actions." The longer he gazed at her cheek and then at her side, the colder his eyes became. "You didn't need to get hurt."

She'd never seen the darkness peek out from behind Dr. Perfect's shell. For a moment, it was like looking at herself. She wondered what demons he tangled with, and how he'd won.

"I've had worse. Really." She didn't know the full extent of their sibling drama, but she didn't want to be the cause of anything further.

"Let me." He reached for her cheek, but stopped just short of touching her.

She should protest again. She didn't need his help. But if Kate's vision was about RAVEN, she'd need to be in tiptop fighting strength. "Do your worst."

Lennox picked up Mathews and headed for the back of the pub. "Hurry up, doctor."

When he opened the door, the sounds of a huge brawl flooded out into the night.

Michael touched her cheek. His fingers were warm against her skin and suddenly she felt everything she'd blocked. Biting heat arced through her skin. She hissed, hating she'd shown any reaction.

You couldn't let others see you were hurt. It gave them power.

He placed his other hand over her side, right on top of what she assumed were several bruised ribs, if her breathing was any indication.

Heat radiated from his hands. Not the heat of pain. The heat of healing.

The cut on her cheek trembled, sending a swift bite of pain through her. She inhaled quickly, but remained still. She couldn't look away from Michael. There was something mesmerizing about the concentration on his face. As if he saw inside her, saw what he was fixing.

But he'd only be able to fix the physical. No matter what he saw, the rest was beyond hope.

An itch worked its way up from her jaw to the top of her cheekbone. She felt the skin stitch back together, the blood cooling on her skin. Something shifted in her side and she could breathe easily.

Michael pulled back. The circles under his eyes were darker than before.

A spark of light caught her attention.

"What the hell is *she* doing?"

Glenna had the tip of her finger to Prentiss' forehead. The RAVEN operative convulsed and then went still. She was breathing, but Glenna had done something.

"I'm wiping their short term memory," Glenna said with a tired smile. "I can hold electrical currents in my body. Just a quick jolt to the right spots in the brain does the trick. It's harmless."

Lennox came out of the pub. Glenna nodded towards Prentiss. He lifted her over his shoulder easily.

Beth looked at Lennox. "That's why you didn't want me to shoot them or use my knives. You want them to forget we'd been here, and a bullet or knife wound is hard to forget."

Lennox just nodded, and then looked at Michael. "The brawl you started in there is pretty impressive. Fruity rainbow crap has its uses I guess."

Michael grabbed one of the other operatives in the same

hold. "Their injuries will be explained by the fight."

Beth stared at both of them. "But RAVEN is smart enough to know that something happened to their team."

"True." Michael looked at the door handle, and Beth opened the door for him. "But it won't be traced back to us. Our town isn't even the next one over."

Michael disappeared inside. She waited a few moments and then shook her head. It was true she'd volunteered to come with them, but they'd deliberately held back information. She was tired and pissed.

"Come on Fi." Beth slipped an arm around the girl. The air felt colder now that the adrenaline had faded. Beth felt the chill through her leather jacket. "Let's go wait at the car."

She led Fiona away toward the SUV. She wasn't going to join their Covenant, whatever that was, but if RAVEN was hunting people with abilities, they needed all the information they could get from the Forbes.

The time for secrets was over.

Chapter 7

Kate poured a glass of wine, trying not to sink back into the plushness of her easy chair. Though she loved the beauty of the Forbes' manor, she realized she preferred the homey coziness of her B&B. All she wanted to do was get home, change into her pj's and watch her girls sleeping. But after the Allen adventure, Jean had finally promised to come clean.

Jean and Michael sat on the couch to her left, Beth and Sam on the love-seat to her right, and Duncan had claimed an easy chair across from her.

"Where are Lennox and Glenna?" Kate asked.

"I asked them to retire for the night," Jean said. "I thought this would be easier without the entire family."

"She really means Lennox." Michael's tone was matter-of-fact.

Duncan shot him a hard look. "He got the job done, didn't he? Fiona's safe, and RAVEN was dealt with."

Sam toyed with her glass. The red wine sloshed gently against the sides. "An entire town filled with people who have abilities. Abilities that can kill, like Ken Allen's. It's a lot to take in." She tucked her long legs underneath her and grabbed a nearby throw.

Kate hadn't had a chance to talk to Sam about what she'd done to Ken. That blast of ghostly energy had knocked him out. Could she have killed him?

"It's been a long day." Kate met Jean's eyes. "You promised to tell us about RAVEN."

"You helped us, and we owe you an explanation." Jean nodded. "We don't know how long RAVEN has been in existence, but long before the Forbeses built this town."

"And they've always been interested in people with gifts?" Sam asked.

Duncan settled back into his chair, looking anything but comfortable. "From what we can tell. They're global. Either recruits work with them willingly, or they use leverage to force their compliance."

Sam shook her head slowly. "Peter Kneller, one of the ghosts from my local bookshop in Kingston, was always talking about military groups capturing people with abilities. I wonder if he was one of those willing recruits or a prisoner."

Michael's jaw tensed. "There's a large RAVEN facility near Kingston. Paired with the local military."

Kate looked at Beth and Sam. Both of their faces mirrored her shock. "We used our abilities for years when we were kids, and they were right in our backyard. Why didn't we get snatched?"

"They don't go after children," Jean said. "They need their

gifts fully developed first." Her hands shook and Michael grabbed one of them. "We've heard stories about the experiments. We think they're searching for a way to duplicate what we can do. Or to enhance it."

Beth looked like she wanted to shoot someone. "That's sick."

"But it makes sense on a tactical level." Duncan looked into the fire. "Not only for their soldiers, but also as leverage against other countries and organizations."

Kate looked at Beth and Sam. "Why haven't they grabbed the three of us? Sam must have given them a large energy wake-up call bringing Robert back to life. And we've formed TOP."

"TOP?" Jean asked.

Sam answered, "Triumvirate of Pluthar. We shortened it to make it easier."

Michael leaned forward, his hands on his knees. "I've been wondering the same thing. What you did there, when Robert was brought back to life, probably blew the monitoring circuits at RAVEN."

Kate crossed her arms. "Didn't Caleb make a reference to other TOPs, that we're not the first?"

Sam nodded.

"Then I think they might be doing reconnaissance first," Kate said. "See if we're worth the trouble, especially given Beth and Sam's celebrity status. They can't just disappear without people noticing."

"Good point, Red." Beth gave her a smile. "So we should

keep our eyes open for surveillance. Install some cameras and better security at the B&B. On me. I have connections."

Kate felt her heartbeat finally slow. The measures might not help, but they couldn't hurt. "The dampening stone at the Allens' was almost burned through. Does the strength of someone's abilities affect how the stone reacts?"

Duncan nodded. "It does. Based on the ability, a certain energy signature is given off. What we do, visions, is a low energy signature. We're not affecting the environment itself when we have them."

"But causing an earthquake," Sam said. "That would be a huge energy signature."

Beth's eyes widened. "Who can cause an earthquake?" She glanced at Sam. "You took Kate there?"

"No one *took* me anywhere, Beth," Kate said, proud her voice was even. "And we'll catch you up later on the earthquake piece. So, none of TOP's abilities affect the environment, which might explain why we wouldn't have sparked RAVEN's interest initially, but what happened in the forest with the Universe definitely changed things."

Kate had felt it with every cell of her body. In that moment, she had been connected to time itself. The past, the future, the present, all flowing through her and around her.

It had been incredible and terrifying at the same time.

"What's the Covenant?" Beth asked.

All the Forbeses stiffened.

Kate glanced at Sam. She looked as surprised as Kate felt.

Jean shifted in her seat. "It's an ancient agreement between the families of this town. We've all pledged to conceal our gifts and to protect each other."

"Then why didn't anyone else help out tonight?" Beth asked.

Jean glanced at Michael, but he put up his hands. "I'm not going to recite our family history, Mother. I'm not part of the Covenant any longer."

"The Forbes family is responsible for the Covenant." Jean looked suddenly older. "We were a founding family, and our town was in chaos. The threat of exposure to the outside world was mounting. Jeremiah Forbes had the gift of sight, like Duncan. He saw the oncoming ruin if we were discovered unless order was established."

"He drafted the Covenant," Duncan said, continuing the tale. "It's also why we keep the archives for all the families who have lived here. Tracking their history and their abilities."

"That explains why Lennox was so rah-rah about getting Fi," Beth said. "It really *is* the job."

Michael's posture grew rigid. "One he takes very seriously, even more so since Father was injured."

Kate's intuition guided her to the next question. "What's the penalty for not upholding the Covenant?"

Duncan's face became grim. "Understand first that no one is forced to live here. You can move at any time and leave the protection of the dampening stones."

Sam frowned. "And potentially be discovered by RAVEN, right?"

"Correct." Duncan leaned forward. "Minor penalties are dealt with by the Council. But if you willingly, not by accident, attempt to reveal our existence to RAVEN." He paused and let out a long breath. "The punishment is death."

"You mean you could have killed Ken Allen?" Kate felt the blood drain from her face. "Killed him before he went any further and potentially alerted RAVEN to your town's existence?" She remembered now the cryptic conversation between Duncan and his mother. Something about being within their rights.

Tortured emotions swam across Duncan's eyes. "You don't understand the whole story, Kate. The rest of the town is counting on us to protect them."

Michael looked as upset as Kate felt. "Now you know why I moved away. I can't condone what *they* might do."

"*They* are your family," Duncan said, his voice rough. "I'm your family." The last words seemed like they slipped out before Duncan realized it. He got up and poured himself a whiskey.

Kate saw the pain etched in his tight shoulders, in the hunch as he gave them his back. Even with their family rift, there was still love there, otherwise it wouldn't be tearing each of them up inside.

Michael looked at his brother, the anger falling away to be replaced by sadness. "Duncan, I—"

"I don't like the Covenant rules any more than you do." Duncan turned around. His eyes glimmered in the firelight. "But with Da laid up, you in the States, and Owen in Egypt, someone has to make sure Lennox doesn't go off the rails." His grip on the whiskey glass tightened. "Someone has to make sure *that sentence* is the last resort."

Jean's face was grim. "The rules are harsh to protect the innocent. There must be a consequence for willingly endangering this town and its people. Otherwise there is no safety."

"I know. I know." Michael ran his hands through his hair. "I'll help where I can until Father is back on his feet. I've got time left on my sabbatical. That's all I can offer."

Duncan drank his whiskey in a quick gulp. "We'll be taking you up on that offer, brother."

"Yes, I'll let them know you're here," Sam said, her attention at a spot past Jean. "Uncle Richard says too many of the stones are failing. They can feel it in Entwine."

Jean gave them a weary smile. "Uncle Richard was the guardian of the stones for many years."

Duncan eyes were pensive. "We've known they wouldn't last forever, but the stones themselves are rare. We've been searching for new ones for years."

"The last ones we have came from the Grennings, and they're long gone. No descendants." Jean looked lost.

"Oh, I don't know about that." Kate smiled at Sam. Jean looked at her, confusion on her face.

"You never mentioned the Grennings before, Mother," Duncan said.

Jean waved her hand at him. "Because it didn't matter."

Sam said, "There is a descendant left. Robert."

"The ghost Sam brought back to life." Beth looked like she wanted to grumble about it, but surprisingly her voice was normal. Kate was impressed.

Jean gasped. "This can't be a coincidence."

"I'm not sure if Robert knows anything about the stones,"

Sam said. "But I will definitely ask him when we get home."

Jean's eyes glistened with tears. "You might have just saved us, Sam."

"And that's our cue to go, before everyone gets all gushy on Sam and embarrasses her." Beth stood. She smiled at Jean. "Thanks for the intel on RAVEN. We'll be on the lookout."

Kate stood too. "And we might need your help. Especially if my vision is really about a RAVEN facility."

"I hope it's not." Sam took her coat from Michael.

Duncan held Kate's coat out to her. "If it is, we'll do what we can to help."

"I agree with my son when it comes to providing information," Jean said. "But unless RAVEN attacks our town, we can't become involved in anything more."

"Mother—"

Jean held up her hand, cutting Michael off. "I'm not being cruel. I'm being practical. The town is our responsibility."

Were they really going to have to go up against RAVEN? Kate hoped not, but she couldn't let someone die if there was a way to prevent it somehow.

She needed another vision.

"Is your offer to help with my gift still open?" Kate asked Duncan.

He nodded.

"Good. Does ten tomorrow morning at my B&B work?"

Duncan nodded, looking entirely too eager. She had to admit, it would be nice to talk to him about their abilities. And him being gorgeous didn't hurt either.

In the car on the way home, Beth turned around and gave Kate a wondering look. "Do you really think your vision is about RAVEN?"

"I do."

There were too many coincidences for them to be coincidences.

Sam pursed her lips. "Which means we might have to break into whatever facility you saw in your vision."

Kate looked between the two of them. "I can't let someone die. No matter how dangerous. But this isn't your problem. It's mine. I had the vision. It's my job to stop it if I can." She tucked her freezing hands under her thighs.

"You can count me in," Michael said from the driver's seat. "You were given the vision for a reason." He met her eyes in the rearview mirror. "Besides, saving lives is kinda my thing."

Unexpected tears filled Kate's eyes. For years, she'd gotten used to doing all this on her own. "Thanks, Michael."

Beth hit him on the arm. "Dude, you ruined my thunder. I was all ready to make the TOP speech, how it's all for one and one for all. You know, the three musketeer shit."

Sam laughed. "I'm here for you too, Kate." She squeezed her arm. "You know, the three musketeer shit."

This time Kate laughed too, but inside her mind spun with worry. After what she'd learned tonight about RAVEN, they'd be up against a formidable foe, and everyone would look to her.

As much as she resented their overprotectiveness, she wasn't a leader like Sam or Beth.

What if she ended up getting everyone killed?

DUNCAN GOT OUT OF HIS CAR AND STARED UP AT KATE'S B&B. The peach-colored brick looked bright in the early morning sun.

Ten minutes to ten o'clock. Early for their first lesson. Though he couldn't deny he was attracted to Kate, he was ultimately here to help. RAVEN was no easy opponent.

It felt surreal to see the B&B in person rather than in a vision, like he usually did. Michael had always accused him of escaping from life by using his gift. Always focused on the future, never the present. Seeing his brother again was like picking at a scab. Best to leave it alone.

He walked up to the front door. It opened before he knocked. Sam smiled at him. "Welcome. Come in."

He looked around the entryway. A long staircase on the left climbed up to the second floor. Blue wallpaper set a striking contrast to the mahogany bannister and dark hardwood floors. A chandelier gleamed and winked above, polished to perfection.

"Did Robert know about more dampening stones?" His mother had specifically reminded him to ask. It was all she could talk about this morning.

A dark-haired man joined Sam. Duncan recognized him immediately from his research last night. Lord Robert Grenning. "Unfortunately, I do not. My father did not share any knowledge of such stones. It is quite possible he was unaware."

"Robert, this is Duncan." Sam's smile became almost

blinding. It was obvious she was hopelessly head over heels.

With his noble carriage, he might have been wearing an embroidered waistcoat rather than a dress shirt and slacks. Robert's thick hair came just to the bottom of his ears.

Robert held out his hand. "It is my honor to meet the man who will help our Kate grow in control."

Duncan shook his hand. "I will do my best," Duncan replied, suddenly feeling like a knight who'd been granted a quest by his monarch.

Sam tugged on Robert's arm. "We're going to the study so you and Kate can concentrate on the lesson."

Duncan watched them walk down the hall farther into the manor. He wondered where Kate was, and then heard the squeals of laughter coming from the kitchen.

"No more cookies," Kate admonished, appearing in the kitchen doorway. "Oh Duncan. I'm glad you're here. I'm almost finished with my baking."

Kate had an apron around her waist and a dusting of flour on her face. Her red hair was up in a bun, held in place by a crayon if he wasn't mistaken.

It felt like someone squeezed Duncan's chest. Hard. She looked even more beautiful than last time.

Two girls rushed out behind her and came to a halt, looking up at Duncan. The younger one had light brown hair and a serious face.

The older one placed her hands on her hips and gave him a studious look. She looked like nine going on twenty. "You must be Mr. Duncan. I'm Emily. This is my sister, Patty."

Patty held his gaze. "You're going to help Mommy, right?"

Duncan wasn't sure if he should crouch to be less imposing. Though they didn't seem scared. But he was a stranger after all. He opted for leaning over, his hands on his knees. "Absolutely, Patty. Your mommy's visions will be under control in no time."

Okay, not exactly the truth, more of a hope. But he didn't want them to worry.

Both girls exchanged a long look, and he had the distinct feeling they didn't believe him. He felt like he'd failed a test he hadn't realized he should have studied for.

"We've got to get going, Mom," Emily finally said. "I need to identify three insects for Mrs. O'Connell's class." Her eyes brightened. "And there's extra credit if they're unusual."

Patty nodded, a smile lifting her lips. "And I'm going to help. I know where there are some really cool looking insects."

Kate gave them both an assessing look. "You know the rules, right?"

Both girls nodded. "Stay on our grounds. Stay together. Text you every half hour. Press the screamer if we're scared. Be back before twilight." They intoned the rules like they'd done it a thousand times.

"Show me," Kate said.

Emily pulled a phone out of her jacket as well as a bright pink clicker that looked like a car fob. Patty pulled out a bright green one.

Kate kissed Patty's cheeks, and then smoothed Emily's hair back in place. "All right. Go on, you two."

With shouts of "Yes" and "Okay", they flew past him and out the door.

"The screamer?" Duncan asked.

Kate nodded. "It's a personal noise alarm. It's super loud, and I can hear it in the house. The girls called it a screamer, and it stuck." She turned around and waved him on. "This way."

Kate led him into the kitchen. The enticing smell of cinnamon and peanuts made his stomach grumble. He'd had a large breakfast, but sweets had always been his downfall.

Duncan saw immediately that Kate's kitchen was a place well used and loved.

A large stove sat to the right along with a refrigerator. A long kitchen island was piled in baking pans and plates of cookies. Two round kitchen tables were directly in front of him. One was covered in coloring books and crayons. The other had dirty plates, a paper towel with bacon sitting on top, and an uncapped bottle of maple syrup.

"Sorry for the mess," Kate said. She handed him a wet rag. "Would you mind wiping down the table?"

She pulled open the stove door and took out a metal sheet of cookies. Snickerdoodles, if he were to guess. They would join the peanut butter cookies already cooling on the racks. "So, did you ever black out from your visions?"

Duncan rinsed the rag off in the sink. "I did."

"Really?"

"I still remember my first vision." He stared out the window over the sink. The trees in the forest almost looked like they lifted their limbs to catch the sun's light. "My Ma was hysterical when I came to." He glanced back over his shoulder at Kate. "She'd thought I'd died."

"So did Millie." Kate's voice was soft.

"Your adoptive mom?"

"Yes."

"You don't call her 'Mom'?"

Kate shook her head. "I stopped after I left home." Her heart-shaped face tightened. "I'd like to think they did the best they could, but I always felt like a stranger in their house. Never a part of their family."

Duncan went over to the table to begin clearing the plates. "At least your girls don't have to deal with that. I know you're an amazing mother."

Some of the darkness fled from her face. "Did your visions tell you that? Or the fact that they've taken over an entire table with their artwork?"

He smiled. "Both. And also the calendar on the wall with their homework assignments and events listed out. You seem so at ease, yet you're keeping track of everything."

"Kids know when you're stressed or upset, so I try to keep things light. Normal. But they know they can't get anything by me." She gathered up the crayons, putting them back in their container. "I'm lucky to have a village of people helping me, including Aggie and Stu, the B&B's caretakers. I trust them with my life. They helped keep the girls secluded away from everything that happened last month."

"When Graham tried to kill you and Sam."

Kate nodded. There was no way I was going to let them be

near anything dangerous. Aggie and Stu took them on a trip to her sister's. They thought it was a big adventure."

"And what did you tell them when you got back." He helped gather up the stickers and glue.

"I told them the basics. There was a bad man who had been caught. Logan's brother." She gave Duncan a wry smile. "Of course, Emily found out somehow that Logan had been accused of his brother's crimes. But they don't know what those crimes are. I'm trying to protect them as best I can."

"I think you're doing a heck of a job." He glanced at the peanut butter cookies on the cooling rack. "Can I?"

Kate laughed. "Of course. A downpayment on our lesson."

Duncan took a quick bite and then put his half-eaten cookie down on the counter and quickly stacked the plates expertly in the crook of his arm. Two years of waiting tables during college had stuck with him.

He went over to the sink and rinsed them off, putting them in the dishwasher.

Kate leaned back against the kitchen cabinets, crossing her arms. "Patty recently told me she can see the future too. As much as I try, I don't think I can keep this world from them." Her voice dropped. "And I can barely keep a roof over their heads." She shook her head, eyes bright. "Sorry. Too much information."

The urge to take her in his arms, to comfort her, flowed through him. Seeing her in his visions for weeks had made him feel like he knew her. Another occupational hazard for a psychic.

"It's easier to confide in a stranger. I get it. My advice is to continue doing what you're doing. Keep the really scary bits under wraps, but be honest with them as much as you can. If they know they can trust you, it'll go a long way when you need them to confide in you. Like Patty finally did."

She shook her head. "Your shirt is soaked. That damned shallow sink. We always said we'd replace it, but we never got around to it."

He looked down at his shirt. It was pretty soaked. "It's fine. It's just water."

"There are a few mens' flannels in the pantry if you want to change. Then we can let your shirt dry out during the lesson."

He walked into the pantry and looked at his options. He'd opted for the brown and olive flannel. The lasses always said green made his red hair more vibrant.

Stripping off his cold t-shirt brought a flash of goosebumps. A scuff of noise made him whirl around. Through the open pantry door, he found Kate watching him.

He recognized the look. Pure attraction. Plain and simple. Finally, he was on familiar, uncomplicated ground.

Duncan tapped his rock-hard abs. "I know, too flabby, right?" He left the shirt unbuttoned and walked back out into the kitchen.

She crossed her arms. "I've seen plenty of hard bodies lately. I'm not fazed."

"Oh really? You're an expert on hard bodies, then?"

"Quite." Her lips twitched. "I took an online course. Got a certificate and everything."

He couldn't help laughing, and she joined in, but this time

with an adorable staccato giggle.

She grabbed his arm. "Does the ab thing really work on the ladies?" she said, trying to catch her breath from laughing.

"Usually." He wiped his eyes from the tears. "You're really not impressed?"

Kate gave him a wink. "Oh, they're impressive all right. And I appreciate the eye candy factor, but that alone never does it for me. Beth had a boy-toy a few years back who was just ridiculous." She hit a pose. "I'm God's gift. Bow down before this hotness." Then she collapsed into giggles again.

"I can't figure you out." He shook his head. "And I'm not used to that."

Kate gave him a quick nod. "Get used to it. And remember, we're here for my lesson, not any funny business, so you can stop the whole Don Juan act."

Duncan buttoned his shirt. "So, should we get started with our lesson?" And away from his thoughts about her freckles and how her eyes sparkled when she smiled.

Kate rubbed her hands together. "Absolutely."

Here was someone he could help. Someone who appreciated him for his abilities. And someone his usual tricks didn't work on.

A strange mixture of hope and fear wrestled around his heart.

He gestured to the kitchen chairs. "Let's begin."

CHAPTER 8

KATE SAT DOWN AT THE KITCHEN TABLE WITH DUNCAN. Even though she'd made light of his display, those were some incredible abs. Lord.

Lesson, lesson. They were here for the lesson. Nothing more right now.

"I'm ready." She gave him a salute. "Lead on."

He laughed. "Okay. Let's start with something that has helped me really connect with my abilities. I don't know if it will stop your blackouts, but it's a good place to begin."

"I'm game."

"Have you ever done grounding?"

Kate felt her eyes narrowing, but couldn't help it. "Are we talking about some woo-woo energy stuff?"

Duncan frowned at her. "Energy work isn't woo-woo. Well, some people think it's mumbo jumbo, but it's worked for me."

Kate leaned back in her chair, crossing her arms. "I thought you were going to teach me some real techniques."

If he started burning sage and bringing out crystals, that was it.

"This is real. And how can you call this woo-woo when you see the future?"

Kate pursed her lips. "That's different."

"Why?"

"Because I've done it."

"Oh, so you need to see it to believe it?"

"Something like that." She'd seen her fair share of hacks, especially when she'd been trying to get help for her poltergeist problem.

"Uncross your arms and your ankles. Feet flat on the floor. Rest your arms to the side or you can lay your palms flat on your thighs."

She did as he asked and felt a little tension ease from her body. "Have you taught anyone else this before?"

"I have." He gave her a knowing look. "Someday, you're going to have to go on faith, Kate. I know it's scary, but you can't always see the possibilities out there."

She lifted her chin slightly. "Have you gone on faith before?"

"I have." He looked down, and she suddenly felt the weight he carried. "I denied it once, and my brother, Thomas died. I don't deny it any longer."

"I'm sorry." She felt awful bringing up those memories. All because she was being stubborn. What did she have to lose by not trying what he suggested?

Her phone buzzed on the table. She looked at it. "It's Emily. Apparently they found the perfect place to study bugs which means they'll be a little later coming back. Hold on a sec."

She typed in her reply. And got another one almost immediately. She laughed.

"What did Emily say?"

Kate put the phone back down on the table. "She wished me luck with my lesson. So we best get back to it. Alright, feet flat on the floor," Kate said. "Arms resting. What's next?"

Duncan gazed at her. "Close your eyes."

She did.

"Picture a cord coming from your body, shooting down into the earth. It can be anything you want. Some people picture the roots of a tree, others a metal cord that clicks into place with the earth's core. Whatever feels right to you."

She immediately saw a huge tree trunk, twice her body size. Roots stretching down. An image flashed into her mind. Her forest. She pictured roots wrapping around a hot lava core, though they didn't burn.

"Bring up the earth energy through your grounding cord. It's warm, rich, flowing."

She felt it when it hit the bottom of her feet, moving up through her calves to her knees. "It's hot."

"Good. Now bring it up your thighs, to the base of your spine. And let's let it sit there for a moment."

Again, flashes of her forest filled her mind. Branches, leaves waving, the wind rustling the bits of grass on the ground.

"If there is any energy inside you that's not yours, send it down the grounding cord."

Beth and Sam immediately came to mind. How they didn't

really believe in her. How they made her doubt herself even more. She tried to shove the energy down the grounding cord, but it stuck. She finally crumpled it up into a ball and the energy sucked it down.

Then her girls' faces appeared in her mind. How she worried about her visions, her gift, putting them in danger.

"Will I lose my connection to Emily and Patty if I let go of their energy?"

"No. The energy you're holding onto is not related to your love for them or wanting to protect them. If it's coming to mind as not being yours, you need to release it."

Kate let the worry about RAVEN slip from her grip and it slid easily down her grounding cord.

She exhaled slowly, feeling lighter.

"Open your eyes."

She did so and saw a faint shimmer of silver blue around Duncan. Her eyes must be wigging out from being closed for a bit.

Duncan touched her shoulder. "How do you feel?"

"Good. Balanced." She laughed. "It's weird." And she liked the warmth from his hand. Seemed the woo-woo stuff hadn't shut down her libido.

"It's not weird. It's exactly what we're shooting for." Duncan dropped his hand and leaned back in his chair. "Now, that we have the earth energy running through you, let's talk about your visions. Everyone has different experiences."

She nodded. "What do you want to know?"

"What are the signs you're about to have a vision?"

"I first get chills," she said. "They move up my arms, numbing them, eventually numbing everything."

How long does it take from the initial chill to the vision itself?"

Kate thought about it. "It varies. Some start in seconds, and others take longer. I don't know why there's a difference. The ones that take the longest are death visions."

Duncan raised an eyebrow. "Tell me how a death vision is different than the others."

"You don't get those?"

"Nope."

Kate sat up straight, finally not feeling like a screw-up. Here was Mr. Experienced, and he'd never had a death vision. "I know this is going to sound weird, but with death visions, I feel like they're alive."

"Alive?" Duncan's voice didn't sound skeptical. It sounded interested.

Kate nodded. "Like it's more than a vision. I don't know how to explain it exactly. It's a feeling I get."

Duncan stared at her for a long moment. She tried not to fidget. "Well, you are the Oracle, so you've always had an extra special connection to your gifts. Maybe your death visions are messengers from the Universe." He rubbed his jaw. "You might try communicating with it the next time."

His easy acceptance relaxed the tension in her body. She leaned back in her chair. Communicating with a death vision? That would be strange right? If it wanted to communicate, wouldn't it have done so years ago?

"Well, I'll have that chance soon enough since I got interrupted before I could see everything. Another round will be headed my way."

"How many death visions have you had?"

"Six before. This was the seventh."

Duncan gave her a long look. "Were you able to save everyone you had visions about?"

Kate shrugged. "I'm fifty/fifty."

"And you black out each time, no matter the type of vision it is?"

"I do. Though visions where I see the past are different." She thought about how to describe it. "I get trapped inside someone's head. And just recently, I touched an object and had the same thing happen too."

Duncan nodded. "Being grounded and within your own space, your aura, should help keep you in control."

Duncan sounded so confident, Kate felt tears rising up through her chest. "I'd love to drive again."

His eyes held understanding. "I'll do everything I can to help, Kate."

A few tears made a break for it, spilling down her cheeks. "I know I might not be able to give my girls a completely normal life, but being able to drive without fear of wrecking my car again? That . . . that would help a lot."

Duncan took her hand. It felt like a lifeline. She gripped it with her other hand and held on. They stared at each other for several moments. She wondered again what it would be like to kiss a man with a mustache and beard.

"It's not easy doing what we do," he said finally. "Only someone who's gone through it can truly understand. Not only the physical piece, but the emotional. Seeing what might be. What will be."

Somehow holding his hand felt more intimate than earlier when he'd been half naked.

"I haven't been able to share what I can do with many people." Kate looked towards the sunny backdoor, wishing they were talking about something bright and happy.

"They don't get it. How could they?" His words were almost a whisper. "Our gifts are wondrous, but also a burden."

She glanced back at him. "Every man I've ever told about my gifts has left me," she whispered. Kate let out a breath, feeling suddenly lighter. She'd never told anyone that before. Not even Sam. Not even Beth.

"That's not right," Duncan said. "I'm sorry you had to go through that." He shook his head. "Every woman I've dated has known what I can do and most took advantage of my gift."

Kate shook her head slowly. "I'm sorry for you too. Mine was just rejection, but yours was way worse. No one should be used. I don't care the reason."

Duncan blinked his eyes quickly. Seems she wasn't the only emotional one when it came to their powers.

A single tear escaped past his lashes. Kate wiped it away automatically, like she did with her girls.

His sharp intake of breath and the look in his eyes sent a spike of desire through her. He wanted to kiss her. She just knew it. Maybe she needed to just tell him it was okay?

"You should probably kiss me—" Kate said.

"We should probably get back to—" Duncan said at the same time.

They stopped and looked at each other.

Then Duncan pulled Kate onto his lap, facing him, and his lips were on hers. This close, she smelled a citrus fragrance on his beard. Lemon, lime, tempered by a dusky orange underneath.

His mustache and beard caught his breath, hot against her skin with each press of his lips. Her mouth opened under his. She tasted him. The salty flavor of her peanut butter cookies and something darker. Something that sent her blood rushing even faster.

His hand wound into her hair, bun coming undone, crayon hitting the floor. His other hand slid around her back, under her top.

The feel of his fingers against her ribs made her suck in her breath. It had been so long since anyone had touched her like this.

Kate unbuttoned his shirt quickly, running her hands down his chest to his abs like she'd imagined earlier. They were tighter than she'd expected.

She felt him, hard and hot underneath her. She slid back and forth, enjoying the pressure of him against her. Waves of desire swirled up through her thighs, her hips.

Duncan moaned.

She pulled back from Duncan. "Pantry," she breathed.

"More privacy." Sam and Robert were in the study. She wasn't up for putting on a free show.

Duncan rose to his feet, lifting her easily. They made it to the pantry quickly. He even managed to close the door without losing his grip on her.

Duncan's hands unclasped her bra, pulling her back into the moment.

Suddenly freed, her breasts sang a loud chorus of Hallelujah.

Tap tap tap of ice against her hands. The death vision had returned.

And the timing sucked even more than usual.

Go away. Come back later.

She tried to focus on the feel of Duncan's hands on her skin but the vision's chilled tapping became an icy grip on her wrists.

Sorry

The word whispered through her mind. She instinctively knew it was the death vision speaking. Why was she hearing it now? Because she'd spoken to it?

The vision wrapped frost around her shoulders, her neck. She looked at Duncan through a thin layer of ice.

He pulled back, eyes concerned.

You must see.

Time was up. The vision swept her away.

S AM LOOKED UP FROM THE BOOK IN FRONT OF HER TO WHERE Robert sat at the small desk by the window. The table near the fireplace was littered with everything she could find in the town library about ghosts.

"So far, there's nothing that relates to what you've been experiencing."

He suddenly disappeared, and then was back in his chair. He turned around to face her. Fatigue pulled at the lines in his face. "And I have been unable to locate anything on your Interweb. It appears Entwine is unknown to most." Robert rubbed the bridge of his nose. "As Beatrice keeps reminding me, no ghost has ever been brought back to life as I was, so we will only find guidance from the Wardens."

Beatrice appeared next to the fireplace as if summoned by Robert's words. Her red hair was in its usual untidy bun.

"This is one time I hate to be right," Beatrice said. "But the Wardens will be the ones who have the answers." She crossed her arms. "I already harangued Caleb within an inch of his wooden existence, but he doesn't know anything, so we're out of other options."

"I've talked to every ghost in this manor, and no one knows how to get me in touch with the Wardens." Sam leaned back in the easy chair, quelling her urge to knock all the books from the table. She felt so helpless. What if Robert disappeared into Entwine for good?

"That's why I'm here." Beatrice placed her hands on her hips. "I'll do anything to protect Robert."

He went to her, taking her hands in his. "If the cost is too great, I would not have you pay it."

Beatrice squeezed his hands, smiling up at him. "There is

no cost too great for you, my dear boy." She glanced at Sam. "I have something that can help. It was given to me as payment for a favor, and I can only use it once, but it will get you an audience with a Warden. You can ask them about Robert and about the dampening stones. Might as well get the most out of the visit."

Sam hadn't thought to ask the Wardens about the dampening stones, but they might indeed know something. Sam had a feeling the Wardens had been around for longer than Caleb, which was a long time.

Beatrice took out a beautiful silver tube from her pocket. It had holes within the metal reminding Sam of a whistle. Beatrice blew into the tube.

No sound.

Sam and Robert looked at each other.

Then the air grew thick. Heavy. A ghost was going to appear.

When the shape formed, Sam let out a relieved sigh. It was a ghost they knew. The Runner who'd helped them get Ray, the poltergeist, to move on.

Darrin.

The Runner had on his usual gray shirt and black pants, but this time his black vest was different. It had symbols embroidered on the bottom. Symbols that matched the ones on the silver cuff at his wrist, and Sam realized they matched the ones on Beatrice's whistle. They'd always looked Celtic to her.

He dropped to one knee before Beatrice.

She flushed and waved her hand at him. "Oh come, come. I know the whistle is very special, but there's no need for the extra pomp and circumstance." She gestured toward Sam and Robert. "I called in my favor because they need to talk to a Warden."

Darrin stood and smiled, though it seemed strained. "Hello Sam, Robert. I can take you to Entwine as Beatrice wishes."

"Is everything all right, Darrin?" Robert asked. "You do not appear to be your usual self."

Darrin looked at Robert, his dark eyes heavy. "I have recently lost a friend."

Sam stepped forward. "I'm so sorry, Darrin. I know what it's like to lose someone you love."

"I have lost many over the centuries, but never like this." His resolve seemed to click into place, the sorrow dissolving into purpose. He held out his hand to Robert. "Come. I will take you."

Robert grasped Sam's hand, and then took Darrin's. The study disappeared around them, like it had been suddenly stripped away. Not the changing of a scene like you'd see at a Broadway show—they were in the study, and now they were not.

Underneath their feet was a platform overlooking a bustle of ghosts below. Sam leaned over the railing and looked down. It reminded her of an old fashioned train station.

Her gaze swept further and she saw the archways Robert had spoken of from the last time he was here. There was one made of metal, looking like something out of a scifi movie. A brilliant blast of light engulfed each ghost who walked through.

A bird flew past Sam and landed on a gorgeous archway

made of vines and leaves. Butterflies danced on the edges. A welcoming glow from inside spilled over those waiting in line. Sam felt the heat of the sun from where she stood.

The archway next to it was one of brick, chipped and cracked. Dark soot stained the edges of the stone. Coldness seeped forth, creeping like shadowy tentacles.

"Darrin, I want to know more about these." Sam gestured to the archways.

Darrin shook his head, gazing down below. "That's for another time." Darrin lift a hand toward a long hallway that led away from the platform. "This way."

They followed the Runner. Sam studied the bland corridors, which looked like all the office buildings she'd ever been in.

Wait, that door was different. It was like her old bedroom door as a kid. The walls shifted to wood. Wood paneling just like her dad had put up in their living room.

The corridor changed as they moved, becoming more like her old house. Before she'd remodeled it after her parents' death. She almost expected to see her parents come through one of the doors.

Quick tears pricked her eyes. Sam took several deep breaths, sucking the emotion back inside. She didn't know if the Wardens were trying to make her feel at ease or make her feel vulnerable.

Either way, she didn't like her emotions being manipulated.

Sam stopped. "Enough." Her words were low, but she was sure they'd be heard. This was Entwine. The Wardens knew everything that happened here.

Darrin looked concerned. Robert looked proud.

The wood paneling shuddered, and then disappeared like it had never been there. In its place stood walls of green. They weren't flat. They were made up of what looked like vines.

And they were in constant motion, twisting and sliding against each other. Here and there, Sam found the Celtic symbols on Darrin's cuff in the shape of the vines. Then they would move, and the symbol would disappear.

Sam looked up and down the hallway. She didn't see a beginning or an end to the vines.

For a moment she was back in Caleb's forest, held in the Universe's embrace. That moment when she was connected to everything, living and dead.

"Entwine is never still," Darrin said. Sam heard the respect in his voice. "Come." He turned and hurried down the hall.

Sam and Robert followed him until he stopped in front of a tall door, going almost to the ceiling. Straight on the sides and rounded on the top. The gold doorknob gleamed against the deep crimson of the door.

Darrin knocked and took a few steps back. Then disappeared.

They stood there for a moment. Nothing happened. Robert glanced at her. "Last time I waited to be summoned."

Sam grasped the door handle. "They've ignored me for weeks. I'm not standing here a moment more." She opened the door and stepped into the room beyond.

It was about half the size of Kate's study at the B&B, but it had a similar feel. Dark leather chairs were clustered two by two around tables, with a long divan in front of the crackling fireplace on the right.

In front of her, two people stood by a window, their backs to Robert and Sam. A man and a woman. Outside the window, storm clouds churned in a gray sky. The patter of rain beat against the glass. Was this place still in Entwine?

"It is Sloane," Robert whispered. "I know not the man with her."

The man who stood beside the Warden was tall, over six feet, and slim. He wore a top hat. It didn't look like a costume. Sloane was a bit taller than Kate, but other than that, Sam couldn't tell much.

Their voices reached Sam.

"You're sure?" Sloane asked.

The man in the top hat nodded. "We lost ten."

"He's becoming bolder. Hungrier."

"The others need to be summoned. A rogue necromancer must be handled swiftly."

Ice shot through Sam's body. A rogue necromancer? What did that mean?

Sloane gave the man a short quick nod. "I will issue the mandate."

The man bowed toward Sloane, and then disappeared. Just like Darrin had. The woman turned around and studied Sam and Robert. Woman wasn't quite right. More a girl. Maybe thirteen, fourteen?

She wore jeans and a motorcycle jacket, but the jacket was unlike any Sam had seen before. The fabric looked like heavy brocade, dark purple cloth shot through with strands of red, the color of blood. Strands which seemed to move, swirl through the purple, echoing the vines in the hallway.

Sloane had dark hair. Longer on the top, but buzzed short on the sides. Her left ear was unadorned, pristine, but her right was pierced all the way up to the top with metal studs in shapes similar to those on Darrin's cuff. They gave off wisps of energy that felt familiar. Ghostly essence.

"You've got some moxie barging in here," Sloane said. "But after what you did bringing Robert back to life, I would expect no less." Her tone and pitch were matter-of-fact with a dash of admiration.

"I've been trying to reach one of you these past two weeks. And no answer," Sam said.

Sloane laughed, and the tattoo creeping up the side of her neck flashed gold. Again, the same symbols as those in her ears, in the cuffs.

"*One of you*," the Warden said. "Sounds so harsh. We're not interchangeable you know. We each have our own districts." Her gaze narrowed, and a buzzing of electricity pricked Sam's skin. It suddenly reminded her of how the poltergeist had felt at Kate's B&B. "If you have questions about Robert, you talk to me. Got it?"

Robert gave Sloane a deep bow. "Thank you for enlightening us as to how things are to be handled. We meant no disrespect with our inquiries, and we are thankful for your time."

Sloane's face immediately lost its hard edges. "I just knew Sam would fall in love with you. So polite, yet strong.

Understanding, yet resolute. Exactly what my wayward Necromancer needed." She gave Robert an almost motherly look. "Let's sit by the fire and see how I can help."

What did she mean by knowing Sam would fall in love with Robert? Robert flashed Sam a perplexed look as he took Sam's arm and led her to the divan in front of the fire. Obviously this was strange to him as well. Ghosts were always peeping in on the living, Sam supposed the Wardens would be the same.

Sloane took the chair to the left, next to a small side table. She opened the drawer and took out a pipe made of dark wood, with grooves all along the bowl, and a tin of tobacco. "You don't mind, do you? Ray's gotten me into the habit. It helps me think."

"Ray, the poltergeist?" Sam said. "He didn't move on?"

Sloane scooped some tobacco into the bowl and tamped it down. "He's able to come and go. As you well know." She filled the bowl with another scoopful and repeated the process one last time.

"I don't know what you mean."

Sloane lit the pipe with a shiny silver lighter, taking a few puffs. Then lit it again, holding the flame over the tobacco more slowly this time. A few long deep puffs.

An earthy aroma filled the air with a hint of berry. Like leather mixed with brandy.

"Ray and Mary came back to help when you were dying," Sloane said. "They worked with the others to save you, but it cost them."

"If you have harmed them, I will—" Robert began, but

the Warden held up her hand. Sam noticed her nails were unpolished and short, with strands of darkness through the nail bed like wisps of shadow.

"Relax, Robert. I have done nothing to Ray, or to Mary." Sloane took a deep pull on the pipe, and then let the smoke escape through her lips. "Ray works for me now. In return, Mary can come and go for visits. No cost." She glanced at them both. "I'm not entirely heartless."

Ray was in servitude to the Wardens because of Sam. Sam vowed she'd free Ray somehow, but right now, she needed to focus on the task at hand. "Robert's slipping in and out of Entwine."

Sloane nodded. "I worried that might happen, so I had this made." She took out a silver ring. A heavy band, thick, and carved with the same Warden symbols. Sloane held it out to Robert.

Sam stopped Robert from reaching for it. "Wait. Will this ring harm him?"

"No." Sloane held her gaze. "It will allow him to balance his energy between the two realms. Keep it on, you stay in the world of the living. Take it off, and you may slip back and forth as needed."

"And the cost?" Sam asked. There was always a price.

Sloane smiled. "Robert has already done me a service by helping you realize your place in the Universe. Consider it a gift. No charge. No future promises required."

Sam wasn't sure how to feel about a gift with no strings attached. But Robert needed the ring. And whatever Sloane was, she was still tied enough to Entwine that Sam could tell if she was lying or not.

"You can take it Robert, she's telling the truth."

Robert grasped the ring from Sloane and slid it onto the ring finger of his right hand. It immediately sized down to fit perfectly. The symbols flashed once, twice, and then settled back to silver.

Sloane's eyes shifted to the door they'd come in. "I'm sorry to cut this short. I have another appointment waiting."

Sam leaned forward. "Just one last thing. We're searching for more dampening stones. They might be known by another name, but they've been used to keep a local town safe from RAVEN. To hide the energy signature of their abilities."

Sam didn't miss the tightness that seized Sloane when she mentioned RAVEN.

"Ask Caleb," the Warden replied. "He might know where such stones can be found. Or so I've heard." Sloane stood and lifted her hand. A second door opened to the left of the fireplace where there had only been a wall before. "You have to excuse me. I really must attend to my next appointment."

Why weren't they going back through the original door? Sam suddenly had the feeling Sloane didn't want them to be seen leaving.

Sloane walked them to the door. Darrin waited outside.

The Warden paused. "If you need to talk with me again, have Robert give you his ring. Hold it in your hand, speak my name, and I will know."

Darrin led them back toward the platform, but Sam's mind

kept swirling. Sloane helped Robert without a cost, gave them information about Caleb freely, and they could now talk to her whenever they wished?

Sloane was playing a long game of sorts. Sam wished she knew what it was.

ONE MOMENT, KATE WAS WITH DUNCAN, THE NEXT SHE was back at the military facility. Back in the corridor of doors from her first vision.

Her body yelled at her in frustration, and she completely agreed. Things had just started to get interesting with Duncan, and she got yanked into the vision.

I'm sorry.

Again the Death Vision's voice.

It sounded so regretful, Kate's frustration died.

"It's okay. I needed to see more." And she did. Her body began to argue, but she ignored it.

And it was the perfect time to try out the grounding that Duncan taught her.

Kate tried to focus. Pictured her grounding cord, like she had in the kitchen. Wind tickled her leaves. Leaves? She wasn't just the grounding cord, she was the entire tree. In the B&B's forest.

Her roots didn't only extend down to the earth's core, they burrowed into the dirt, reaching the other trees' roots. She wasn't alone. She was part of something larger.

Then suddenly she found herself back in the kitchen. Though she still saw the dim outline of the corridor in her mind.

She concentrated on the corridor and the kitchen became faint. Then on the kitchen and the corridor grew fuzzy. Whichever she chose to concentrate on became the stronger visual in her mind.

"Kate, can you see me?" Duncan's face was concerned.

"I can."

The vision touched her hand sending a painful shot of cold through her.

Pain which sent her grounding cord jettisoning free and spiraling away into the depths below her. The kitchen disappeared.

But for a moment, it had worked.

"You need to help me stop blacking out too, you know," she said to the space around her. "So no more sudden icy grabs, got it?"

The Death Vision didn't respond, but warmth rose up Kate's arms. Bolstered by that tiny little step of progress, she turned and looked around. She wouldn't get back to Duncan, to the B&B, until she found out more.

The dark opening at the end of the corridor held onto her gaze, dragging it until she fully faced the blackness in the distance. That's where she'd seen Beth and Sam.

The vibration of footsteps shook through her feet and up her legs. It sounded like a lot of people walking. Together.

A flicker of movement caught her eye at the other end of the corridor. Two soldiers walked past, followed by two more, and then two more. They looked to be in formation. No rush, just a measured march.

A man slipped into the corridor after the soldiers had passed. From the white coat, he looked like a doctor.

He walked toward her, and she read his name badge. Doctor Bob Carmichael. In big bold ominous letters, the word RAVEN blazed on his badge with a level number in blue. It said Level 5.

Kate saluted the Universe for being obvious for once. This was RAVEN. No doubt.

The doctor looked tired, his glasses just barely resting on the edge of his nose. Dark circles bruised the area under his eyes.

The warmth moved through her entire body. Okay. He was the one she had to follow. He'd show her what she needed to see. Message received.

He shuffled past Kate to one of the doors she'd seen the time before. One of the ones with the tubes.

Leaning down, he placed his eye in front of the retinal scanner and waited a moment. Then he put a code into the keypad, too fast for Kate to follow. Last of all, he lifted the end of the tube to his mouth, and saliva disappeared down the plastic and into the door.

Aha. It must be DNA verification of some kind.

A short shuck of noise came from the door, metal releasing and sliding back. Then the door cracked open slowly, expelling a gust of air.

Kate peeped around his shoulder. It was a lab. She followed him in.

Like usual, she wasn't sure what would be important, so

she paid attention to everything. Cataloging, committing to memory. The right wall held refrigerated cabinets with clear doors. Test tubes sat inside. A bunch of monitoring devices of some sort covered the left wall, with soft lights and beeps coming from them. In the back, there was a white privacy curtain like in a hospital room.

The door slid shut behind her.

The lighting was stark from thin overhead fluorescent tubes. There was another doctor in a white lab coat behind a long metal table. The table contained laptops on either end, and in between was littered with crumpled paper, open notebooks, and coffee cups. Burnt coffee, by the smell of it.

The other doctor had light brown hair pulled back into a loose bun. She was a little taller than Kate, but thin, like she wasn't taking care of herself, not eating enough. Underneath her sharp features, Kate saw the glimpse of beauty.

Kate moved closer and read her ID. Her name was Doctor Rachel Withers. She had the same blue Level 5 that the other doctor had on his.

"Did the Major extend the timeline?" she asked the other doctor. She had a soft Scottish lilt.

Bob looked up at the corners of the room and Kate followed his gaze. Cameras were watching their every move. Red lights blinking like eyes.

"No." He took off his glasses and rubbed the bridge of his nose. "But I don't know how he expects us to fix the compound, to stop how fast it breaks down in the host's bloodstream. We're scientists, not magicians."

He was American, with a slight Boston edge to his words. Maybe the facility wasn't in Scotland? Kate wondered if it was one of the others Michael had mentioned. Maybe even the one in Kingston, New York.

A siren began to shriek with a throaty "whoop-whoop" of noise. Kate held her hands over her ears. The sound was deafening.

Rachel looked at one of the cameras and held up her hand. The noise abruptly cut off, leaving a ringing silence.

"No cause for concern, doctor." A voice said through a hidden speaker. "Merely an animal caught on the fence setting off the perimeter alarm. Please get back to your work."

Even with the *please*, there was no mistaking it was an order.

Rachel and Bob exchanged a look that Kate couldn't read.

"Take a look again at the slide, Bob." Rachel gestured to the microscope in front of her.

Bob scratched his head, and Kate saw silver gray mixed in with the short brown strands. "I've already looked at it, Rachel. The results are still the same in Patient 3542."

"We saw the glass move." Rachel glanced toward a table in the corner. It was piled up with various objects. Books, feathers, pencils. "And he threw those books across the room. *That* was something."

"The Major wants him to be able to crush things with his mind. Like Patient 244." Bob walked over to the table and opened up his laptop. "And we haven't been able to synthesize a viable compound from her blood."

"I know." Rachel sighed, and then looked toward the hospital curtain. "I'll check on John."

Bob gave her a sharp glance. "Patient 3542." His words were firm.

Dr. Withers ignored him and walked to the back. She pushed aside the curtain. Kate followed quickly.

A young man lay on a hospital bed. Tubes went in and out of him. Sensors were on his head and over his heart. Dr. Withers checked his pulse and looked at the screens over his bed.

Kate froze. This was the man she saw in her first vision. The one in hospital scrubs, bleeding from his neck.

Okay. He was definitely on the "save" list. Got it.

He looked to be in his early twenties. What were they doing to him? Experiments obviously. But what kind?

Kate thought he was asleep, but then his eyes flashed open. He grabbed the doctor's hand. She didn't pull away.

"Please, Rachel," he whispered. "Can I at least go back to my room?"

Her eyes softened, and she sat on the edge of his bed. "It'll be just a bit longer, John. A few more tests. Once we understand how to strengthen your ability, this will all be over."

"But they promised I'd fight terrorists. That they'd send money to my mother. For my service." His words were weak like he couldn't manage anything louder. "It's been over a month."

A shadow of regret passed over her face. She took his hand in both of hers, squeezing it. John's eyes fluttered, and then closed. "We're almost there. And soon you'll be free."

The last two words were almost a whisper. John had already fallen asleep. Rachel sat there for a moment longer in silence. When she rose and walked back into the main lab, there was a sheen of tears in her eyes.

Kate bent to get a better look at his chart. John Anderson. There were probably a million of those names. He wouldn't be easy to find. She quickly rejoined the doctors.

"Not the marrow again." Bob shook his head. "It was powerful, but not lasting."

"A tap then? From Patient 244?" Rachel looked at a chart in her hands.

Bob seemed to consider this. "The cerebrospinal fluid is the most promising but we've tried that on several subjects already."

"But not with the NRP protocol."

Bob lowered his head and flipped up a page on the chart, effectively covering his mouth from the nearest camera. "That new anti-rejection drug isn't working. Look, I know you want to keep the tests going, keep him alive, but he's dead whether the Major kills him now or later. I've told you not to get attached to the subjects."

His voice was low, barely above a whisper. They must not have microphones in the lab. Only cameras.

Rachel tapped on a line of text on the chart. "They're not just subjects, they're people. We know this. *You* know this." Her whisper was urgent.

Bob nodded and flipped another page on the chart. "I *do* know they're people." His voice remained soft. "Just as I know the Major will hunt us down if we try to free any of them."

Whatever was happening here, they weren't willing participants. The doctors were being forced.

"I don't think I can do this anymore." Rachel's hands shook. Bob took the chart from her and set it on the table.

"You can and you will, unless you want to face the consequences." His voice was firm, but there was kindness to it. "I think of that every day. Of my son. My wife. You can do this, Rach."

Kate's heart skipped a beat. Were their families in jeopardy? If so, no wonder they were doing RAVEN's bidding. She imagined the lengths she'd go to if Patty and Emily were in danger. She'd do anything.

This couldn't continue.

RAVEN needed to be stopped.

Rachel straightened her lab coat. "You're right. I know you're right. But what if that were your son in there? Would *you* forgive us for saving ourselves and condemning *your* family?"

Bob wiped his cheek, and the back of his knuckles were wet with tears. "I'm sorry. If I could think of any way out of this, I would. For both of us."

Rachel took a quick breath and then another. She turned and swept aside several balled-up napkins covering a computer tablet. "We'll find a way, Bob, we have to. But for now, I'll continue to play along." She tapped on the screen. "Who's on our intake today?"

Her fingers scrolled for a few moments.

Kate crept forward to look at the screen. Rachel's finger

hovered over three names. One of them Kate knew. She wobbled, suddenly dizzy.

Rachel clicked on that name, and a picture of a cell appeared through a camera feed. They were looking down from the corner of the cell.

There was one occupant. Hooked up to an IV drip and sedated.

Duncan.

CHAPTER 9

DUNCAN. DUNCAN WAS IN DANGER. THE DEATH VISION had spoken the truth. She had needed to see this.

Kate found herself sitting in a chair in her kitchen. All her clothing was back in place. Including her bra. Duncan sat next to her.

She grabbed his arm. "You're still here."

"I wasn't going to leave you." He smiled at her. "And you came back just for a moment. The grounding worked, didn't it?"

Kate nodded. "For a second or two, but I think I just need to practice." She didn't mention feeling like she was suddenly part of her B&B's forest. That she was a tree. That was a bit too out there.

She looked at Duncan again. He was safe. She shook her head, trying to separate the vision echoes from reality. And remembered again that they'd been getting a bit busy before she'd had the vision. Her breasts wanted to lodge a protest that they'd missed the action, but she ignored them.

Should she say something about what happened? She'd been

out of practice for too long. Was there a protocol?

"I enjoyed the last part of our lesson, especially."

She lifted an eyebrow. "You aren't a mind reader, are you?"

A devilish gleam lit his eyes. "No. Were you just thinking about what happened?"

Heat filled her cheeks. She could never hide it when she blushed, and Duncan grinned like a Cheshire cat.

Kate rescued the crayon from the floor and swept her hair back up into a quick french twist. "You're quite the handful, aren't you?"

"I am. Is that a problem?" His tone was light, but Kate felt a brush of worry underneath.

"No." She felt silly saying something this early, but she liked to have things out in the open. "I haven't dated anyone since my husband died two years ago."

He sat up straight.

"And I'm not really sure what I'm doing or what I want." She took his hand. "But I'm not up for anything serious. And even though the Universe sent you, I don't want to lead you on if you're looking for serious."

The edges of his mouth quirked. Not quite into a smile, but close. "The Universe sent me?"

"Yup. I put together an order and there you were."

He squeezed her hand. "What was the order?"

Maybe she shouldn't have brought that piece up. "Someone who didn't live in my town and was low on complications."

He stared at her for a moment and she was sure he knew that wasn't the whole truth.

"Well, since I'm here by way of the Universe, I'm fine with whatever you're open to."

"Really?"

"Really." He got up and grabbed a plateful of cookies, bringing it to the table. "Now that that's settled, back to the business portion of the day, did your vision confirm it was RAVEN?"

"Yes." How was she going to tell him he was in danger?

Duncan frowned. "I had hoped we were wrong."

"Me too."

Movement from the hallway caught Kate's eye. Sam and Robert walked into the kitchen.

"I heard something about RAVEN?" Sam looked back over her shoulder. "Wait a sec. I think Michael and Beth just pulled up."

As if on cue, the front door opened, and the sound of bickering filled the manor.

"I told you it was a right turn, not a left," Beth said.

Michael snorted. "Oh, were you using your ability to find the correct turn? I didn't see your eyes go black."

"Stop speaking out of your assho—"

"Children," Kate said loudly, mother voice in place. They instantly froze. "Get in here and stop poking each other."

Beth bustled through the doorway almost at the same time as Michael. "Poking, *please*," she said. "We weren't even touching each other."

Michael reached out a finger and tapped her shoulder. Beth's face broke out into a grin before she hid it in a scowl.

Duncan grabbed a cookie. "How did the location scouting go for your show?"

Beth took her jacket off and put it on a hook. Her deep pumpkin turtleneck brought out the amber in her brown eyes.

"Can I get some tea, Red?" She said to Kate, then turned to Duncan. "The network is hammering me for the next installment, and your brother, Mr. Know-it-all, wouldn't let me navigate, so we got lost. Twice."

Kate got up and put the kettle on. She could use some tea herself after that vision.

"We got lost once," Michael said. "And can't your reality show be filmed anywhere? You're Beth Marshall." He put his hand on his hip and did the hair flip pose perfectly.

Again Beth tried to frown, but Kate saw the smile struggling underneath. "Not bad, doctor. But don't quit your job just yet."

Michael sat down at the table. With the mischievous gleam in his eye, he looked twelve. Duncan gave him a wink.

Kate yearned for the day they would all be getting together to catch-up, chat about life, you know, the normal things. Not visions and experiments and kidnapping.

Once she told them what she'd seen, anything normal would be thrown out the window again.

"We had a meeting with Sloane. She gave me this." Robert held up his right hand. A silver band gleamed in the kitchen light. For a moment, Kate swore she saw a flash of gold from the symbols in the metal.

"The Wardens finally popped up?" Beth asked.

Sam shook her head. "Beatrice called in a favor so we could get a meeting."

Duncan's eyes narrowed at Robert's ring. "What does that do?"

"It's supposed to help him stop slipping into Entwine without meaning to." Sam took Robert's hand.

"And here I thought you were just trying to be a ninja like Bronson." Beth's words were light, but she looked concerned.

Kate frowned. "Since when? And why didn't you tell us?"

"I didn't want to worry you," Sam said.

Exactly what Kate was doing by stalling. She opened her mouth to tell them, but Michael leaned forward.

"Can I see the ring again?" he asked. Robert handed it to him and Michael held his phone flashlight over the ring. "Definitely Celtic. I can decipher those symbols for you later, but I recognize the one for strength."

"At least they gave you something," Kate said. "Which means they must be on board with what the Universe did."

"I was surprised actually." Sam looked at Robert. "I have a feeling Sloane is happy about it. I think she likes Robert."

"Like *like*?" Beth drew out the last word, worry on her face.

Robert bristled. "I can assure you there are no flames of love to be fanned when it comes to Sloane." Then he relaxed his posture, mirroring Sam's wondering look. "Yet, I do have the sense she is fond of *both* of us."

Sam straightened in her seat. "We also asked about dampening stones. She told us to check with Caleb."

Duncan touched her hand. "Thank you for doing that, Sam. Any lead means a lot."

Beth looked like she wanted to say something rude, but kept quiet instead.

Kate knew she couldn't hold off any longer. "I had another vision. It's definitely RAVEN."

Beth frowned, but didn't look surprised. Michael just shook his head slowly.

"Here's what I found out," Kate said, and then told them about the lab, the doctors, John Anderson. While the words poured out, she rescued the boiling kettle from the stove and made several cups of PJ Tips, the Extra Strong blend. It helped to have her hands busy with something.

"They were experimenting on people with gifts?" Robert said. "It reminds me of the doctors of my time trying to ascertain the answers of something they could not understand." A shudder ran through him. "With horrifying results."

Beth gripped the edge of the table, her fingers turning white. "Please tell me you're getting this vision because we need to stop them."

Kate brought the cups of tea back over to the table plus cream and sugar. "With death visions, I'm supposed to prevent the death of someone or someones. I don't know about the rest."

"You think it's John Anderson?" Sam asked.

"Definitely him." She hadn't seen Beth and Sam this time. Maybe the first time had been a fluke? She hoped with all her heart it was. "And there's someone else I definitely have to save."

"Who?" Duncan asked.

There was no easy way to deliver the news, so she went with her usual approach to rip of the bandaid. "It's you, Duncan. They'd captured *you* in one of their cells."

Michael brought his fist down hard on the table, jostling the cups, spilling tea. "We're not going to let that happen."

Duncan looked surprised at Michael's reaction. "What's your timeline usually, Kate?"

She knew what he was asking, though she'd never termed it that way. "Max a month ahead of time. At least that's what it's usually been."

"So do you think it is a facility here?" Robert said. "In Scotland?"

Kate nodded. "At first I wasn't sure because one of the doctors had a Boston accent. But since both John and Dr. Withers had Scottish accents and Duncan was in the facility, I think it has to be Scotland. Oh, John also mentioned something about being recruited to fight terrorists. What's that about?"

Duncan's eyes grew unfocused. "We had a family move away. One of their sons was recruited by RAVEN. Told him it was to protect lives."

Michael shook his head. "And after they experimented on him, he was wheelchair bound. Protect lives, my ass."

Beth slid her hand down to her boot. Kate knew she was touching her knife—a nervous gesture she'd seen her do before when threatened. Kate found herself clutching the locket around her neck. The one with pictures of her girls and Paul. Looked like both of them needed some comfort in the face of RAVEN.

Robert glanced at Duncan and Michael. "The names Kate supplied of the victim and the doctors, do they mean anything to you? Dr. Withers appears to be a potential ally against this evil."

"None of the names sound familiar," Duncan said. "And if John was a member of our town, I would know. But we can't count on Dr. Withers. It sounds like they're threatening her family, so she might not help even if she wanted to."

"Let's find her first and then we can figure out a way to convince her," Beth said. She took her phone out. "I'm going to check with my contacts. They'll find something."

"I'm going to ask Bronson too," Sam said. "He's well connected."

Beth frowned. "I'll find her first."

"It's not a competition," Kate said, her tone soft. Knowing now how Bronson had unintentionally had a hand in getting Beth sent to Juvie, she didn't blame Beth for holding a grudge. Both of them had barely said a word to each other since he'd arrived to help with the B&B.

"Duncan, you should stay at home until we know more," Michael said. "We have protections in place that will slow them down if they come for you there."

Duncan stood. "Agreed." For once it seemed, the brothers were on the same page. Michael looked relieved.

"I'll call you about my next lesson," Kate said.

Duncan nodded and then was out the door with Michael in a flash.

Robert lifted Sam's hand and kissed it. "I will consult with

Beatrice to see what additional information she can glean." He took off his ring and disappeared.

All that remained was TOP. Kate's phone buzzed. A message from Emily. They were headed back.

Sam took a sip of tea. "Logan might have intel on RAVEN, especially if their facility is nearby."

"I'll call him," Kate said. "Though I'm not sure how to tell him how I know about RAVEN."

"You could finally spill the beans about your gift," Beth suggested.

Kate just stared at Beth until she shrugged. Then Kate turned to Sam. "I turned down the offer for the lands."

Sam perked up. "Good. I'll tell Caleb. That might get us some info on RAVEN, and I can use that visit as an excuse to ask about the dampening stones. See if Sloane's suggestion pans out."

Kate was happy to have potential leads on more intel, but she couldn't rid herself of the dread inside. She hadn't always succeeded with her death visions.

What if she failed this time?

Duncan would die.

CHAPTER 10

LOGAN TURNED OFF THE CAR. IT TICKED AND CREAKED, cooling down in the chilly night air. He glanced over at Beth in the passenger seat, and then met Kate's eyes in the rearview mirror. "That the place?"

Kate had called him with some crazy story about a military group capturing people with abilities and how they needed his help.

He gazed in the rearview mirror at Kate. She was silent, just staring back at him.

Was she thinking about their kiss in the shed? He had been. Over and over again. Did she really think it was a mistake? He didn't.

"Yup," Beth replied. "That's Dr. Withers' house." She pointed to the one on the corner. A copy of all the other houses on the block. Small, one story, gray paint, tiny stoop.

"The one thing you didn't tell me—among a great many things, I have a feeling," Logan said, "is why you two are mixed up in this." Neither woman made eye contact. "And what you're hoping this Dr. Withers is going to do." He noted Kate's tight posture and Beth's failed attempt at appearing relaxed.

"We're hoping the doctor will help us rescue someone," Kate said. "Or someones."

She wasn't lying, of that he was sure. She had a number of tells when she did. But she wasn't sharing everything.

Beth crossed her arms. "Look, I've got abilities. I've been pretty open about that on my show. And you know Sam does. We heard about some local people being taken. We're trying to help."

He'd suspected the truth about Beth, and she was right about Sam. And if both of them were in danger, Kate would be rushing into battle armed with just a wooden spoon if she had to.

"Neither of you are lying, but I'll expect the full truth sooner or later." He glanced at Beth. "It's not good practice to leave someone in the dark on an op."

Beth opened her mouth, and then closed it. She looked down, but not before he saw something like guilt in her eyes.

Kate cleared her throat. "Thanks for agreeing to come with us, Logan. This way I won't have to worry about Beth doing something illegal."

"Illegal?" Logan lifted an eyebrow.

Beth looked out the window. "Allegedly."

The hairs on his arms rose. She was definitely someone to watch out for. He rubbed his face. But then he'd been wrong about Graham.

He just didn't trust his instincts right now.

"And we can't just *call* Dr. Withers, because . . . ?" Logan didn't bother to keep the frustration from his voice.

"Because we're afraid RAVEN is monitoring her phone." Kate leaned back, her face swallowed up by the darkness of the backseat.

"They're called RAVEN?"

Beth nodded. "It's a snazzy acronym for Research and Acquisition of Valuable Enhanced NeoHumans."

This was sounding more and more like a prank. But they both seemed serious.

Beth's pocket buzzed. She took out her cell. "The doc went in about an hour ago and hasn't come out."

"Bronson's information?" Kate asked.

Beth just nodded, looking like she'd sipped something sour. Logan had met Bronson and liked him. Liked him quite a lot. He was capable in his butler duties, of that there wasn't a doubt given the transformation of the B&B. But underneath the charming veneer, Logan recognized a finely honed edge. Bronson had either been in law enforcement or the military . . . or had been a criminal.

Kate looked worried. "RAVEN has her family as leverage. We can't force her to help us. We'll have to convince her. It won't be easy."

"Tell me how you came by this information on RAVEN and Dr. Withers." Logan gave Beth what he hoped was a serious look. "And please tell me it's by legal means."

"It is. I had a private investigator track her down." Beth looked pleased with herself. "Before Bronson could, I might add." Then she frowned. "What Kate said is true. RAVEN is all over her family. If Dr. Withers sneezes wrong, they'll suffer."

Logan sensed Beth's distress. Interesting that under all that armor beat a soft heart. He felt he'd suddenly gotten a glimpse of the person Kate still believed in.

"What's the plan to get her family to safety if she agrees to help you?"

"We're working on it," Kate said quickly. "First we have to talk to Rachel. I mean, Dr. Withers."

He filed away her slip of tongue. Did she have history with the doctor?

"I see."

Kate cleared her throat. "Thanks for believing us."

"Oh, he doesn't believe everything." Beth smiled, and it was the first genuine smile Logan had ever seen from her. "But he's too much of a white knight not to help us."

"I owe you. All three of you," Logan said. "I can't make up for what Graham did, but I can be here when you need me. On that point, besides keeping Beth from breaking any laws, why am I really here?"

"Beth felt having the DCC with us would make us look legit," Kate replied. "Your credentials will help us get inside where we can talk to Dr. Withers."

Beth nodded. "You're window dressing."

Window dressing? His earlier resolve to be nice, crumbled. "I don't remember you being this obnoxious on your show."

Kate laughed. "That's because they edit it out."

"Hey." Beth looked wounded, but she couldn't keep the grin

from her face. "I lobbied for Logan not to be the killer. That should give me some brownie points I can call in now."

"I appreciate your support," Logan said. "Did you make signs?"

Beth laughed loud, surprise in her eyes. "Why Constable, you've got some fire in you. I like it."

For a moment, he felt like his old self. Sending digs at his friends. The tension in his shoulders eased, dropping them back down and into place.

"So, I'm sure you two have already come up with the excuse I'm giving Dr. Withers?"

"Tell her that there was a break-in at the Lancasters next door," Kate said. "And you think it's the same culprit who committed a series of robberies in Rosebridge."

Kate's love of old movies was showing. "People don't say culprit in real life, Kate." His words were gentle. "But I get the gist. How do you know the Lancasters were broken into?"

Beth cleared her throat.

"Plausible deniability." Logan held up his hand. "I don't want to know. Got it?"

Beth nodded, looking pleased with his reaction. "Once we're inside, keep her busy and I'll search for bugs."

He knew this was most likely a mistake, but there was no point turning back now. Kate and Beth would just figure out another way, a potentially more hazardous way, and come back without him. "Let's get this over with." He glanced back over his shoulder at Kate. "Any hope of convincing you to stay in the car?"

"Nope." Her eyes were already sparking, prepared for an argument.

"Duly noted." He winked at her and watched the brightness in her eyes melt into warmth. It gave him a flicker of hope. Maybe she had really wanted to kiss him and just got scared? "Let's go meet your doctor."

Logan stepped out of the car and took a deep breath. The smell of peat smoke clung to the night air. It reminded him of home. Before things had gotten bad. Before his mother had been killed.

He watched Kate close the car door. Graham had been right about one thing. Kate reminded him of his mother. Not in the way she looked necessarily, but in the unconditional love she gave to everyone around her.

Kate caught his look. "Do I have something on my face? I know I shouldn't have eaten that chocolate lava cake before we left. Is it in my teeth?" She walked over to him, baring her teeth in an endearing grimace. There was absolutely nothing she could do to look ugly. At least in his eyes.

He shook his head. "I'm working on counting all your freckles, that's all. Em and I have a bet you know."

Relief flooded Kate's face, and her eyes brightened. "She'll win. I don't know where she got her attention to detail. Certainly not from me."

"At least she didn't get your clumsiness," Logan said.

"Hey you." She hit his arm, and suddenly the tension that had been between them fell apart. He didn't know what would happen next for them, but at least they were back to where they'd been before the kiss. He'd take that for now.

They made their way up the steps to the porch lit by a single wounded lamp, the bulb almost burned out. Logan knocked on the door. Now he'd find out just what was really going on here. And what Kate had gotten herself mixed up in.

Duncan walked through the forest grounds outside Kate's B&B. Every time the moonlight hit Sam's blonde hair, she almost glowed.

Robert walked beside him, eyes wary. "I still believe this to be an unnecessary risk."

Sam's boots kicked a path through the fallen leaves. "Duncan needs to ask Caleb about more dampening stones, since you didn't know where your family got them."

Robert shook his head. "Duncan, you are part of Kate's vision. You should be someplace safe."

"Sam says the ghosts will give her fair warning of RAVEN showing up," Duncan said. "I'm not worried. Anyway, it could be I get captured because the stones fail." Duncan noticed a line of crows siting on a nearby tree branch. Their shiny eyes followed his steps. "We have to try to attack this on all fronts since we don't yet know the timing of when everything happens."

Sam lifted her hand towards a clearing up ahead. "We're almost to Caleb's tree."

The trunk of the beech tree at the far edge of the clearing

was huge, the size of five men. The weight of its branches had long since pulled them down to the ground, stretched wide like tentacles.

Wind rustled through the few remaining leaves, pulling them from the branches and scattering them in small whirlwinds in the air.

Duncan didn't need Sam's gifts to feel the magic in this place. The barrier between worlds was thin here. The energy of Entwine leaking out into these lands, infusing the trees, the earth, the animals with something extra, something more.

They stopped in front of the large beech. The energy humming off the tree tickled the hairs on his arms and sucked the moisture from his eyes. The wind pawed at his jacket, his pants. The temperature had dropped quickly once night had hit.

Sam touched his arm. "Prepare yourself for a long wait. Caleb usually likes to show off."

Duncan looked up at the moon, flickering in and out with the passing clouds overhead. "Hopefully we won't be here all night. It'll be harder for me to hide from RAVEN in the light of day."

A sharp creaking sound filled the air, like the trees cleared their throats.

"Don't talk ill of your host," a voice said. "And wipe that surprised look off your faces. I don't make all visitors wait. Not when there's a Forbes with them."

A tickling charge of energy went up Duncan's leg, reminding him of a dog sniffing at something new. Maybe something familiar that had been forgotten.

The large beech shivered, shaking its limbs. The trunk swayed forward and back. Then Duncan realized the tree itself didn't move. He was seeing something else. Something attached to the tree. A doorway of some sort, perhaps?

The bark stretched forward, and a figure emerged. Tall and thin, brown echoing the dead leaves on the ground, yet shot through with bits of white like the beech. Arms and legs appeared to be made of condensed pieces of twigs with green shoots popping up here and there. It must be the forest ghost, Caleb. He brimmed with vitality.

"How am I seeing him, Sam?" Duncan asked.

Caleb fixed dark brown eyes upon him. "Because I will it so, boy." His words were raspy, but clear. "I can appear to whomever I wish, whenever I wish." The last was delivered with a heavy dose of pride.

Caleb squinted at the air. "Oh hush now, woman. Let me have my moment. Do you know who he is?"

Robert glanced over at Duncan. "Beatrice is here. She raised me after my mother died." He smiled. "She scolds him for taking on airs."

Caleb snapped his fingers and with a short pop, suddenly another voice filled the clearing. A woman's voice, so sharp that Duncan almost took a step back. "I know full well who he is. And they all know who you are. You don't have to get all hoity-toity about it. RAVEN's after him. They don't have all night."

Duncan's mouth dropped open. "I can hear her—Beatrice."

Sam and Robert both looked surprised, but Sam recovered more quickly.

"We're here for information about RAVEN." Her tone was respectful, deferential. "Kate has turned down the offer for her lands as you wished."

Beatrice harrumphed. "And don't be asking for proof. You know as well as I do that your birds have already seen the letter."

Caleb struggled to frown, but his lips kept twitching. "Nothing gets by you, dear Beatrice. I've seen the letter. Knew you'd come. Did you wonder why Kate received such a tempting offer on these grounds?"

Sam gave him a stern look. "We've had more important matters to deal with. As I'm sure you know."

"Very true, very true." Caleb pursed his lips. "But I think it's important that you understand." He paused and looked at all of them. Duncan swallowed a sigh.

"Spill it." Beatrice demanded.

Caleb smiled and revealed even rows of teeth that looked like wood chips. "It was RAVEN. Oh, of course through a false name. They've been trying to buy this land for years."

"Because of Entwine." Duncan's words weren't a question. He knew it from the moment he felt the power in the ground.

"Smart. Though I shouldn't be surprised for a Forbes." Caleb gave him a quick nod, his face growing cold. "This land is one of many which anchors Entwine. If Kate had sold it . . ." A look of utter hopelessness crept into his eyes. "Let's just say I don't know what would have happened."

"Why didn't you tell us?" Sam looked as upset as Caleb. "Kate almost didn't make the decision. She would have easily thrown away their offer if she'd known."

"You couldn't tell them, could you?" Beatrice's voice held a softness.

Life flooded back into Caleb's face. He rubbed his eyes as if waking. "There are Rules we all must follow. I can tell you now because the decision has been made. Kate doesn't realize how important she—" A sudden rumble of thunder overhead drowned out the rest of his words. Caleb looked up at the sky. "I heard you. We don't need a storm, thank you."

The sky cleared, clouds moving away until the moon shone bright in the clearing.

The forest ghost gestured toward the tree stumps nearby. "Sit, and I'll tell you what I know about RAVEN. A deal is a deal."

Sam sat next to Robert on a stump. Duncan took the one to their right. He stretched out his stiff legs.

Caleb didn't sit. His eyes gazed off into the distance. "I remember the first time I knew of RAVEN. Of course, it wasn't called that back then. It's used various names over the centuries. It was just a small group of men who believed if they could harness what gave people their gifts, they could utilize that power. Give it to those who were deserving."

"So, they were always looking to use people with abilities," Duncan said.

"Yes, but for the greater good," Caleb admitted. "At least in their minds. They formed after the Thirty Year's War. They sought to prevent further bloodshed of that magnitude."

"That was in the 16th century." Robert straightened. "Over eight million souls were lost. The conflict raged through many lands."

Sam nodded. "And that's also the time of the witch hunts. Everyone was eager to blame the famine and the pestilence on something supernatural." Robert looked at her in surprise. "Once I grew old enough to understand my abilities, I did research. Tried to figure out why I was the way I was."

Duncan hadn't heard of the war, but he understood why that might have galvanized a group to make sure something like that could be avoided in the future. It didn't excuse what they did now, though.

"What did they do after they formed?" Duncan looked at Caleb.

"They sought answers," the ghost said. "They used people with abilities for experiments. Even came to my forest after hearing of my legend in the villages, but they weren't able to capture the power of Entwine."

Duncan sensed the hesitation in Caleb. The ghost glanced at the sky and seemed to think better of what he'd been about to say.

"Do they have a base here in Scotland?" Sam hugged her arms to herself. Robert took off his coat and slipped it on her shoulders.

Duncan saw his own breath in the air. The temperature felt like it had suddenly dropped even further.

"They do." Caleb held up his hand, and tiny leaves sprouted from his dark palm. "But before you ask, I don't know where it is. I can only *see* so far beyond my lands."

Robert stood. "Then this has been no help at all."

"I could have told you that from the beginning." Beatrice

piped in. "Always promising information, but never giving you what you need."

Caleb frowned. "I do have one bit of information which might be helpful. And I'm not telling them because of you, Beatrice. I'm telling them because Sam kept her word." He crossed his arms.

Beatrice made a sound like a snort, but otherwise kept silent.

"My contacts tell me Oliver Wilson is stationed somewhere in Scotland. Major Oliver Wilson of RAVEN."

Sam looked at Duncan. He knew she was thinking the same thing he was. This could be the Major that the doctors mentioned in Kate's vision. And if Kate and Beth could get Dr. Withers on board, they could verify it. Verify that Kate's visions were of a local base here in Scotland. That would help narrow their search.

"You know him, don't you?" Duncan had seen the way Caleb said the name. With familiarity.

Caleb grunted in approval. "I did. Back when he was a little older than Kate's daughters."

"You met him here in your forest?" Sam asked.

"Yes." Caleb nodded. "My land is no stranger to blood, as you well know, Necromancer. The last day I saw Oliver Wilson, much was spilled into the ground."

Duncan tried to read Caleb's face, but all he saw was the shadow of a memory, and it definitely wasn't the happy kind. "Did he kill someone?"

"No."

The word was strong, yet flimsy at its core. Something had

happened that day. Something horrible.

Duncan opened his mouth to press for details, but Sam shot him a look so fierce, he shut it. She walked over to Caleb and placed her hand on his tree. Her fingers glowed with a blue light, and the ghost sighed almost as if she'd touched him in comfort.

"Thank you, lass." Caleb gave her a thin smile. "I've seen much in my years. And certain horrors stick with you." He glanced up at the sky. "I can't tell you more. I would if I could."

Sam nodded. "I know. My lie detector is still green."

Caleb gave her a stern frown, but it didn't seem to bother Sam in the least.

The ghost sucked on his cheek, creating a disturbing hollow in his face. "Now, onto the Forbes' business." He stared at Duncan. "What are you seeking?"

Duncan had the feeling Caleb already knew everything, but he played along. "We need more dampening stones to protect our town. They mute the energy we give off so RAVEN can't find us."

He pulled a burned one from his pocket. It had failed yesterday. The blackened crystal lay heavy in his hand. He held it out toward Caleb.

The ghost moved closer, studying it. "Hold it up, boy. Shift it so it catches the moonlight."

Duncan did so, and when the moonlight hit the stone, a symbol shone through. He recognized it. A triskele. Three interlocking spirals. He'd never seen that before.

Caleb nodded. "Just as I thought. These were the stones left upon my lands before I came into knowingness."

"Knowingness?" Duncan asked.

"Came to be. To exist." Caleb's gaze touched on the trees and the ground and the sky and the crows. "I took my first breath many years ago, but these are older."

Robert stood. "That is why my family helped the Forbeses initially. The stones were upon our land?"

Caleb's face crinkled, looking annoyed. "I showed your ancestors where to find them on *my land*. But I've heard only rumors of any remaining."

"Again, nothing to help," Beatrice said. "As expected."

"Unless . . ." Caleb scratched his chin, flaking off brown bark with his nails and revealing fresh white bark underneath.

"Please, if you can tell us anything." Duncan took a breath, realizing how desperate he sounded. He put the stone back into his pocket. "People's lives are at stake."

Caleb's eyes narrowed. "What are you offering?"

Duncan had already discussed their options with his family. Saving their town was worth almost any price, but what would Caleb want? In the end, Glenna had come up with an enticing inducement.

Duncan squared his shoulders. "If we secure at least one new stone, the Forbes family is prepared to give the next acre of land bordering your western boundary over to Kate. It shall become part of the B&B's property, and thus will then fall under your control."

The ghost looked surprised. And by the comical nature of

the movement, Duncan was almost certain the experience was a rare one.

"Your house is several towns over," Sam said. "Michael never mentioned your family owned land next to Kate's."

Duncan shrugged. "We have extensive land holdings throughout Scotland."

Beatrice laughed "And Caleb is still speechless."

Caleb frowned at the air and then turned to Duncan. "That is definitely a worthy offer. What if you secure more than one stone?" Cunning burned in Caleb's eyes. Duncan had indeed provided the ghost with something he wanted.

Duncan was prepared. "For each stone thereafter, another acre will be deeded to the B&B, to the south and west of the forest. We have held this land for centuries, as you well know."

Caleb nodded, rubbing his hands together. Duncan was surprised fire didn't flare from the friction. "I do know. Which is why I didn't expect to see a Forbes on these lands with such an offer. They've always refused my help in the past."

"Because they knew what you'd demand," Beatrice said. Her voice changed to a whisper. "You're never going to get this chance again, Caleb. I hope you have something to help this time."

"We can all hear you, woman. I know what this offer means. And I know something to help." He turned to Duncan. "If you manage to find the stones from my information, I will know. And I will expect payment."

Duncan nodded. "Tell us." Anticipation ran through him. There was a chance they could save the town.

Caleb held out his hand. "For a transaction of this magnitude, we must shake on it first."

Duncan looked at the ghost's hand. It was lighter than before, new bark replacing the old. In between his fingers wound vines. Legends of the Green Man swirled in his head. He knew Caleb was more than a ghost, but was he an ancient deity?

Sam walked over to Duncan and stood by him. "Will he be harmed or changed in any way by touching you?" Duncan flashed her what he hoped was a grateful look. She'd picked up on his worry.

"No, lass. I don't seek to harm or change him. Nothing permanently anyway. Though there will be a touch of pain."

"He's speaking the truth." Sam squeezed Duncan's shoulder. "It's up to you. It's your town."

Lennox would do it. Glenna would have already shook on it. Even Michael, with all his reservations, would have done anything to save lives. There really had never been any choice, and Duncan was certain Caleb knew this.

He held out his hand to the ghost. Caleb gripped it tightly. Sharp edges of bark cut into his flesh, and Duncan winced. Blood pooled in his palm and *something* pushed into his skin.

"What are you doing?" He tried to pull back, but Caleb held on.

"Don't fight it," the ghost urged. "You'll need a piece of me inside you if you have any hope of getting her to listen."

"Her, *who?*" Robert asked, staring at their bloody grip in alarm.

Caleb's face grew serious, and the crows all ducked their

heads under their wings. "My daughter, Vivian. It's she who might hold the last of the stones."

"Daughter?" Sam's voice was loud and full of surprise.

Caleb let go of Duncan's hand so fast, Duncan stumbled backwards, tripped over a root and went down hard. But he never hit the ground.

Suddenly, he was in a vision.

CHAPTER 11

KATE SAW A SHADOW CROSS BEHIND THE DOCTOR'S DOOR, blocking the light from the peephole.

"Who's there?" Though the woman's voice was strong, there was an edge of worry to it.

"Detective Chief Constable Dunning," Logan replied. "I'd like to ask you some questions. It's about the Lancaster's break-in next door."

The door opened an inch, a gold chain visible. Half a face. A tired looking face. "I don't know anything about a break-in. I work odd hours."

Logan nodded and smiled. He was being such a good sport and helping them. "I understand, but it's protocol. I need to get statements from the neighbors."

The doctor opened the door a bit wider, giving them all a look over. "A break-in seems a bit below your pay grade, Detective Chief Constable." Skepticism brought a rush of color to her pallid skin.

Logan shifted his stance, leaning back slightly. He instantly seemed smaller, less intimidating. Kate was impressed. Though he was never intimidating to her. He always made her feel safe.

"Very true." Logan ran a hand through his short brown hair. "But we believe these break-ins are related to a larger ring that includes my town of Rosebridge. I'm handling this case personally."

"Let me see your badge."

He handed it over without protest. "Why don't you call the station. They can confirm I'm who I say I am."

She pointed a finger through the door at Kate and Beth. "Where are *their* badges?"

Beth smiled, all teeth and goodwill. "I'm Beth Marshall." She put her hand on her hip and tilted her head to the side.

The usual. Without the hair flip.

Dr. Withers smiled, looking younger. "Beth Marshall." A sparkle flashed in her eyes bringing them to life. "I *thought* you looked familiar. That eye thing is so spooky. It's all smoke and mirrors, right?"

Logan grew still. Kate believed he'd heard the same thing she had. The real interest under the doctor's casual words.

Beth gave her an embarrassed grin. "It's all fake. But promise not to tell anyone?" She leaned toward the doctor, like they were best friends sharing a secret.

Logan's mouth dropped open, and Kate smothered a giggle behind her hand. She loved seeing people react to Beth's smooth act when they knew how she really was.

"I'm doing some research on the local police procedures," Beth said, "and DCC Dunning was kind enough to let me tag along. This is Lacey, my assistant." She elbowed Kate, and Kate waved.

The doctor nodded. "Happy to meet both, I mean, all of you." She held up Logan's badge. "Just give me a minute to check this out. Can't be too careful these days."

The door closed and they heard Dr. Withers on the phone. Logan had already prepped Sheila, his assistant, to field the call.

Logan leaned in close. "What time was the break-in?" He kept his voice low.

Beth whispered, "Four a.m."

The door opened back up. Chain gone. "Come in," Dr. Withers said and handed Logan his badge. They all filed inside.

The house was tiny and smelled of mildew. It reminded Kate of how her B&B felt before Sam and Beth showed up. Neglected and lonely.

The front room was cluttered. Books stacked everywhere, including the overflowing bookshelf. Kate read the titles. They seemed to be a mixture of textbooks on genetics mixed in with self-help books about how to cope with depression and anxiety. And the entire *Lost Fireflies* trilogy written by Sam.

Kate hoped Beth wouldn't see those and get prickly. They needed to handle this the right way.

Glancing back up, she saw a kitchen to the left with a table up against the side window. A hallway disappeared into the back of the house.

Dr. Withers cleared books off the chairs in the living room. "Please sit down. Tea?"

"That would be lovely," Kate said. "Why don't I help you?" They walked back into the kitchen. She knew Beth would sweep for bugs while she kept the doctor busy.

The kitchen matched the feeling of the front room. Neglect. Dirty dishes stacked in the sink, stove covered in a layer of grease. This wasn't a lived-in home. This was a way station.

Dust clung to every surface, except one. A framed picture sitting on the table by the window.

Logan came into the kitchen and beelined for the table. He reminded her of a bloodhound who suddenly picked up a scent. He picked up the picture. "Is this your sister and brother? I can see a family resemblance."

Dr. Withers turned on the heat under the kettle. "Yes. They live in England."

"And your parents?" Kate helped her get mugs down from a cabinet. They would need to protect all of the doctor's family if they wanted a chance of her helping.

"They passed a few years back. Boating accident."

Kate grasped her arm gently. "I'm so sorry for your loss. My husband passed a few years ago. Cancer."

Dr. Withers nodded, a small smile on her face. "I'm sorry for your loss too."

"Why don't you sit down, and we can handle the tea when the kettle boils," Logan said. "I promise you we'll be brief."

Kate and the doctor walked back over to the table.

"Please, call me Rachel." She sank into one of the small wooden chairs. "Now, about the Lancasters. When did you say their place was broken into?"

"Around four in the morning yesterday," Logan replied. He took out his small notebook.

Rachel rubbed her cheek and yawned. "Long day. I was still asleep at four. I'm sorry I won't be much help."

Beth walked into the kitchen and pulled up a chair. She gave Kate a slight shake of her head. Good. That meant no bugs. They could speak freely.

Logan looked out the window toward the Lancaster's house. "Well, we knew it might be a long shot, but we had to check. Are you on call at the local hospital?"

"No." Rachel looked suddenly more alert. "I do freelance research work. Why are you asking?"

"Many times thieves will scope out the neighborhood." Logan closed his notebook and slipped it back into his pocket. "So, they might have been around at other times. Unusual times so as not to alert anyone." Kate was impressed at how smoothly he improvised.

Rachel's face relaxed. "I see. I really wish I could help, but my life lately has consisted of work and reading. I don't see much of my neighbors. Of anyone." There was a sadness in her tone, one of longing.

Kate smiled. "I know what you mean. I have two daughters, seven and nine. I feel like I'm Mommy twenty-four seven. I don't know most of my neighbors either."

Rachel smiled back. Kate hated that they needed her help,

needed to involve her in something dangerous not only to her, but her family. She was a victim just as much as John Anderson was.

"I saw all your books on genes in the other room," Beth said, her face filled with wonder. She was definitely a better actress than anyone gave her credit for. "I'm fascinated about mutations and how we evolved."

And skilled at getting the conversation in the direction they needed. Kate suppressed the urge to give her friend a thumbs-up.

Rachel nodded and leaned back slightly in her chair. "Me too. I've always been curious about what makes us unique, how we've developed as a species." She glanced at Kate and Logan. "Take your eye color for example. Your blue eyes weren't possible thousands of years ago. Everyone had brown eyes due to thicker melanin in the iris, thereby darkening your eye color. Then there was a mutation that affected the OCA2 gene, and suddenly there were blue eyes."

Logan leaned his arms on the table. "Can your studies explain how siblings can be so different in temperament?"

Rachel laughed. "No. I've struggled with that one myself." Then she sobered. "But the real mystery I'm trying to uncover is why genetics fail." She picked up the framed photo again. "My father had Huntington's Disease, and my brother is just now starting to show symptoms."

Beth perked up. "Huntington's? That affects your neurological functions, doesn't it?"

Rachel nodded. "Dementia eventually. But the early

symptoms are mood changes, difficulty speaking, problems walking."

"That's awful," Kate said. She couldn't imagine how horrible it would be to see someone you loved go through that. She was grateful Paul was still Paul up until the end.

"It is." Rachel shook her head. "It's inherited, so we knew there was always a risk for us." She traced her finger over her brother's face in the picture. "He had a child in High School, my niece Zoe. That's why I took the current research project I'm working on. To help him, to help Zoe."

Kate looked out the darkened window, seeing her murky reflection in the glass. "I understand what it's like to fight for your family. If I could have saved my late husband, I would have done anything. Regardless of the personal cost."

The doctor put the picture down, her hands still resting on the frame. "Personal cost?"

Kate met her gaze. "Sometimes we do bad things for good reasons. But eventually it eats away at us. Changing who we are inside."

"I don't understand." The doctor's voice was soft.

Kate felt the crack. The opening she'd sensed in her vision. Her intuition told her to strike.

"You do understand. So does Bob, but you're stronger than he is. Braver."

Rachel stiffened. "How do you know about Bob?"

"Oh Lord," Beth muttered.

Logan touched her arm. "Kate?"

Beth shook her head. "Don't bother."

Kate frowned at them both, and then turned back to the doctor. "Rachel, it's time to cut the crap and be honest."

The doctor's eyes widened. "Who are you people?"

"We know you work for RAVEN," Kate said. "And we need your help."

"RAVEN? What's that?" Rachel's voice was an octave higher.

Beth leaned her elbows on the table. "The jig is up." Then she stopped and grinned. "I've always wanted to say that." Kate shot her a look and Beth sobered. "Listen, Rachel, we know you got involved with their public persona for good reasons." She pointed at the picture. "But you didn't know about RAVEN, did you? And what they were doing to enhanced Neo Humans."

The doctor stood. "You need to leave. Right now." She took her cell phone out of her pocket, her hands shaking so bad, she couldn't hold it steady. "I'm calling the police. You're all crazy."

"Now just wait, Dr. Withers, please," Logan said.

Beth stood and slide a knife out from her boot. "No one's going anywhere, doc. And no one is calling anyone. Not until we talk it out."

Rachel froze, fingers poised over her phone.

Logan shifted his stance, and the tension ratcheted up in the room. "Put the knife down, Beth."

"She needs to understand we're serious," Beth said. "This is life or death."

Logan unhooked the billy club from his belt holster. "I said, put the knife down." His voice was measured. "I won't have you threatening someone. An *unarmed* someone I might add."

Beth always had to take it to Level 200. Immediately. All this was going to do was scare the doctor more.

Kate took the phone from Rachel's hand. The doctor didn't fight. She looked in shock. "It's okay, Beth. I've got this. You can put your knife away."

Beth's eyes darted from Logan to Kate to the doctor. Assessing. On alert.

"Do you trust me?" Kate asked.

Beth exhaled slowly. "Always, Red." Her words were soft, but filled with sincerity. The knife disappeared back into its sheath.

Kate knew there was only one way to get the doctor to listen. Her stomach twisted. If she did this, there would be no going back. She glanced at Logan. She might lose him once he found out about her abilities.

But Beth was right. This was life or death.

Fear made her skin clammy. She was suddenly short of breath. "Logan, please forgive me for not telling you before."

Beth's eyes grew so wide, her eyelashes touched her eyebrows.

The kettle boiled, a rumbling noise, throttling into a bubbling shriek. No one moved.

Kate said, I can see the future. That's how I know about Bob. About what you're doing to John Anderson."

The kettle whistled and Kate removed it from the heat. Logan looked at Kate with questions pouring from his eyes.

"The future?" Interest, then worry, then fear swarmed across Rachel's face. She gasped, her hand going to her mouth.

"RAVEN has been trying to capture a precog since I've been there."

Kate nodded. "Which is why RAVEN is going to capture a friend of mine unless we stop them."

"And John?" Rachel's voice shook.

Kate walked back over to her. "We're going to save John too."

Rachel leaned back in her chair, a stunned look on her face. Kate had provided the opening. Now she just hoped they could persuade the doctor to help.

Beth looked pleased. Logan looked like he'd been hit in the head.

"Rachel, do you have any booze?" Kate asked. "We've got a lot to discuss."

DUNCAN LOOKED AROUND. STILL NIGHTTIME, STILL IN THE forest. But he was definitely in a vision. At his periphery, he saw the telltale silver hue at the edges of his sight, his warning sign that he was not in his world. He was somewhere in between.

His visions always prepared him for an outcome. And sometimes a way to change it. He wondered what Caleb wanted him to see. It couldn't be a coincidence he suddenly had a vision after touching the forest ghost.

Upon a quick glance, the trees were different. Not the beech trees near Caleb's clearing, but strong tall oaks. The ground was covered in a light mist, but underneath the mist, he saw something else.

A pulsing green. The same color as the shoots springing from Caleb's hand. It was a line, a path of sorts, leading past the oaks and into the shadowed woods.

Duncan followed.

The trees changed to yews. Not unheard of in Scotland, but rare, like the beeches. Yew trees were poisonous. He had a feeling this wasn't going to be a pleasant trip.

He came to a tunnel of intertwined yews, their limbs stretching over his head. Barely any moonlight made it through the wood above. The shadows seemed to move in the tunnel. Duncan looked for another way to go around, but the pulsing green path led through the darkness ahead.

And then he heard voices.

His voice.

His voice? A surge of adrenaline arced through him. He never had visions about himself.

Duncan made his way into the tunnel. Not running. He didn't want to fall over a tree root or stumble into an open hole. Though he'd never been hurt before in the past, he'd never seen himself in a vision before, so the usual rules might not apply.

He had to be careful.

Through the tunnel and out the other side felt like it took forever. The green path beckoned forward. The trees he passed held watching eyes. Owls. Tawny owls. They reminded him of Caleb's crows.

His steps ended in a clearing with a massive yew tree in the center, almost split in the middle. Each side stretched out like wings, branches lifting up, catching the moonlight.

Sam and Robert stood to the left of the tree. Future Duncan stood in front of the tree. Waiting.

Some instinct warned Duncan to stay hidden. Even though it shouldn't matter in a vision, he was so out of his usual element, he wasn't taking any chances.

"Vivian," Sam said to the tree. "We have an urgent need and hope you will hear us." She took a dagger from her purse and cut into her palm. Squeezing her hand, Sam let her blood drip onto the ground.

Where the drops hit, the ground began to hiss as if burned. Then everything became quiet. So quiet, Duncan heard the sigh of the land clearly. A deep rumble of satisfaction.

Then an exhale of wind, the leaves circling and jostling on the ground. Suddenly the moonlight hit the area around the tree, almost brightening it to the point of day.

The branches of the nearby trees swayed, their creaking dance whispered, "Necromancer."

The yew tree shivered, and Duncan expected the same display Caleb had used for his grand entrance—the tree stretching and birthing him. But it appeared Vivian didn't take after her father in that respect.

The center of the tree began to glow like it had captured the moonlight. Then the light morphed into blues and greens. Swirling streams of leaves, earth, and small rocks flew into the light.

Robert clasped Sam's hand. The Duncan of the future

didn't move. Just watched the display.

"Two necromancers in my woods in the space of a year. Remarkable." Unlike Caleb's rasp, this voice was smooth. "Who sent you?"

Future Duncan finally spoke. "Your father."

"The last person my father sent never returned to him. He must wish you to die."

"No," Sam said. "Caleb sent us to you for help."

The ground rumbled. Duncan felt movement underneath his feet, like snakes tunneling through the earth.

Future Duncan kept his footing. "Your father gave me a piece of himself. Would he do that if we were being sent to our deaths?"

The ground quieted.

"Show me," the voice said.

Future Duncan held out his palm, and small green shoots sprang from his skin. They turned their leaves towards the tree as if soaking up the wellspring of energy still swirling in its center.

The light blazed so bright that for a moment, Duncan couldn't see. When it faded, a woman stood in front of the tree.

Where Caleb was thin, Vivian was not. The curve of her body echoed the shape of the branches behind her. Dark hair flowed to her waist, shot through with green fresh leaves. Her skin had the same bark-like appearance as Caleb's, but hers was smooth and unblemished. She wore a dress made of autumn leaves—red, gold, brown and even the black of death.

Vivian stalked forward, each movement rustling the leaves

on her dress. She stared closely at Future Duncan's palm. A look of surprise mixed with sudden vulnerability on her face. Then it was gone.

"Why would my father send you here?"

Future Duncan took out the dampening stone from his pocket. "He said you might know where the remaining stones are. We need them for our town."

She glanced briefly at the stone, and then turned her back on Future Duncan. She walked slowly to the right, fingers tracing the length of a low-hanging branch. Where she touched, the leaves alternately burst into green or shriveled into husks. "I know where the stones were last seen. What do you offer for this knowledge?"

"Five acres to the north of your lands. Much more than we offered your father for his assistance." Future Duncan sounded confident.

Duncan nodded from his hiding place. Smart. He was playing on their obvious animosity.

"A generous offer," Vivian admitted. "But what is more land and more responsibility when you have no one to share it with?" She glanced at Sam. "You know what I speak of, do you not, Necromancer? Your loneliness is the reason you sacrificed your soul to the Universe."

Sam was silent for a moment. "It was one of the reasons, yes. A big reason. And I'd do it again."

"We felt what you did," Vivian said. "All of us." She rubbed her hands together, and fragments of bark fell onto the ground. Where they landed, tiny shoots sprouted up. "You connect the living and the dead, part of the power entwining the threads that bind us all." She paused and gave Sam a look Duncan couldn't read. "And in the process of bringing Robert back to life, you awoke many who slumbered. They know *who* you are."

The way she said those last words sent an icicle up Duncan's spine. Who or what had Sam awoken? Duncan had heard myths and stories growing up, of the creatures inhabiting this land—the forest and beyond. Just how far had Sam's reach extended?

Sam had turned as white as Caleb's beech trees. Robert touched her arm.

Vivian lifted a hand toward Robert. "For as long as I have existed, there has never been a ghost brought back to life before." She closed her eyes. "The energy of Entwine runs through you. Still."

Robert bowed very low and held it for a few seconds. "I am very grateful for the generosity of the Universe." He straightened and held her gaze. "We appreciate and are humbled by the time you grant us, Vivian. We would not disturb your peace if the need was not great."

She smiled, and red and orange blossoms sprung from the ground around the tree. "You have a pretty way about you, Lord Robert Grenning. Perhaps you would consider staying here with me?"

Vines crept from where her feet touched the ground. They circled Robert in a ring of green.

"I am flattered by your attention," Robert said. "Yet, I must continue to find my way in this new existence and would not seek to leave Beatrice nor Samantha in my infancy."

"Ah yes, Beatrice. My owls have told me of her." Vivian took a step forward, and her tree's branches swayed overhead. "She can visit you anywhere, so you would still have her company here." She turned and smiled at Sam. "I would welcome your presence as well, Samantha. You could both remain with me."

Duncan's mouth fell open. With that smile, Vivian had gone from beautiful to breathtaking. As if the sun had suddenly filled her skin with a warm glow.

Future Duncan appeared unfazed, his gaze darting around the clearing. Probably searching for the stones.

"There is much I could teach you, Necromancer," Vivian said. "Would you like to know just what your Triumvirate can do together?"

Sam's eyes held interest.

Future Duncan cleared his throat. "Before terms can be decided, do you know where the stones are?"

Vivian turned away from Sam and Robert and shot a glance toward the base of her tree. The wood groaned, moving, shifting, cracking. In the pale moonlight, Duncan saw three stones. Just like the dampening stones in his town.

Caleb's daughter stared at Sam and Robert. "These two stay with me, and the stones will be yours."

"We can't stay. I'm sorry," Sam said. There was understanding in her tone. "Surely there is something else you desire for the stones?"

Vivian shook her head. "I have stated my terms."

Future Duncan lifted his hands to Vivian. "RAVEN will

destroy our town if we don't have these stones." His voice shook, and then steadied. "Please help us."

Vivian just raised a dark eyebrow. "I care nothing for the outside world." Then she sighed. "However, I will adjust my terms to release the Necromancer. But Robert must stay. Then the stones will be yours."

Caleb's daughter snapped her fingers. Vines sprang from the ground, wrapping around Robert's legs. Robert tried to break free, but the vines grew thicker, holding him fast.

"You must listen to reason," he pleaded. "Holding me here against my will is not the way. I can assure you, the fruit born from what you've sown will not be sweet."

Sam's gaze darkened. Duncan saw flashes of light in her eyes, like a lightning storm. "Release him."

"No." Vivian didn't raise her voice, didn't have to. The vines talked for her, wrapping around Robert's waist now.

Sam squatted and placed her bloodied hand above the ground. "Release him now. This doesn't have to get ugly." Blue energy flowed around Sam's hand, licking at it like a gas flame around a pot on the stove.

Vivian's face grew cold. "You know the penalty." Roots plunged up through the ground next to Sam, several feet high, but she didn't move.

Sam shook her head. "I don't know what penalty you're talking about. But I do know your tree is tied to you. Like Caleb, it feeds you, lets you connect more fully with the land. If I wound it, you're weakened." She plunged her fingers into the earth. "Let us leave. I don't want to hurt you."

The wind picked up. Leaves rustled overhead. Whispers of *Necromancer* filled the clearing.

Vivian stared at the branches and the trees around her, a look of resignation settled into her face. For a moment, Duncan felt almost sorry for her. What must her existence have been like if she didn't even have Caleb for company? No wonder why she bargained for Robert to stay.

"I'm sorry, Samantha," Vivian said.

She stretched her fingers out, and a tree erupted from the ground, next to Sam. Its branches impaled her stomach and chest before she could scramble out of the way. She died instantly, blood pouring from her wounds, soaking the ground.

Robert, still bound by vines, screamed and thrashed against Vivian's power. "Samantha!" His cries filled the air, tears streaming down his face.

Thunder rumbled overhead, clouds skidding against each other. The ground quaked underneath Duncan's feet.

Future Duncan ran toward Robert, but vines burst from the ground, tripping him, encircling him, and finally choking him.

He was dead. Sam was dead. Robert was captured. Duncan fell to his knees, all strength gone. Knowing you'll eventually die and *seeing* it are two different things. His skin grew cold. What if he couldn't prevent this?

Rain poured down in hard sheets, kicking up pieces of earth where it hit. Duncan felt the presence of something vast. He couldn't breathe.

Vivian looked up at the sky. "You know the penalty for threatening my tree."

"The penalty of death is reserved for those who have already proven they will carry out the threat." The voice began low and grew in intensity, ending in a shriek of wind.

Duncan wasn't sure if he heard the voice out loud or in his mind. It felt like it spoke through every cell in his body.

A shadow of fear filled the edges of Vivian's eyes. "She would do anything to protect Robert. There was no doubt she'd carry through on her threat."

A crack of thunder boomed above. "Then you knowingly baited her to break the Rules."

"No . . . I . . ." Vivian shook her head frantically. A flash of lightning split the sky above. "Please!"

A lightning bolt arced out so bright, it blinded Duncan for a moment. He smelled the fire before he saw it, gritty and tasting of blood in his throat. Vivian's tree was burning.

Vivian screamed. She fell to the ground. The edges of her dress caught fire. She looked over to Duncan's hiding place, meeting his gaze.

"See you all do better next time, boy." Her voice wasn't Vivian's. It was Caleb's. Her eyes glowed green. "I would not have the Universe destroy my child. Nor have Entwine lose its only hope in Samantha. There's more at stake than your damned stones."

Vines rushed toward him, moving in a blur.

Duncan scrambled back, falling, falling. Finally hitting hard ground.

Sam and Robert loomed over him.

They were in Caleb's forest. Still nighttime—no time had

passed. And they were both looking at him, concerned.

Sam was alive. He was alive.

He looked up to meet Caleb's eyes and saw the understanding there. The ghost had given him a second chance. Somehow. And he wasn't about to squander it.

OUT OF ALL THE THINGS KATE MIGHT HAVE SAID, BEING able to see the future hadn't been on Logan's list of possibilities. He'd never imagined Kate had abilities over and beyond being the most adorable and exasperating woman he'd ever known. Maybe she believed the doctor would help them if she thought Kate had abilities like the others?

He shook his head trying to clear his thoughts. "You can do what again?"

Dr. Withers put a bottle of whiskey on the table. Beth brought over some glasses.

Kate poured out the whiskey. "I have a gift, Logan, like Sam's. I can see things."

Logan turned away, staring into the living room trying to process.

Kate saw the future.

Suddenly little pieces clicked into place over the years he'd known her.

He'd always chalked it up to her intuition, but it had been something more this whole time.

"I wasn't planning to tell you this way, Logan. But helping

those people at RAVEN is too important. More important than keeping this secret." Kate's voice had risen in pitch like it always did when she was nervous.

Logan turned around. He'd been kept in the dark. Lied to. He prided himself on being a keen observer of details, but he'd missed something so huge. Just like what he'd missed with his brother.

Love had blinded him. In both cases.

Graham's offenses were unforgivable. But Kate, the anguish on her face was enough to kill any lingering hurt.

"Slap him, Kate," Beth said. "I think he's in shock." She stood. "I can slap him if you want."

Logan brandished a stern finger toward Beth. "No one is slapping anyone." He grabbed Kate's hand. "Let's talk in here. Without an audience. It'll give Beth time to fill the doctor in on what you know about RAVEN."

Beth grumbled behind him. "Damn. It was just getting good."

He led Kate into the living room. "Why didn't you tell me before?"

Kate looked down, her red hair falling around her face, hiding it. "I didn't know how to. I was afraid you'd look at me differently. Like you're looking at me now."

"How can you tell what's in my eyes if you can't see me?" Logan took her chin gently, lifting it until she met his gaze.

Kate studied him. She hiccuped, sounding just like Emily when she tried not to cry. "You don't look like you're ready to run out the door screaming. At least not yet."

Logan put his hands on her shoulders. He wanted to take her in his arms, reassure her, but he didn't want to spook her. Especially if he was right that she was scared about her feelings for him. "I'm made of sterner stuff than that, Kate."

She just stared at him, not saying anything.

"I could have helped when you had your visions, helped you stop them from coming true. You know you can trust me, right?"

Kate wrapped her arms around his waist and hugged him. It felt like Heaven. The tightness in his chest eased.

"I know. I was just scared." Her words were muffled against his chest. She pulled back, looking up at him. "You're really okay with this? I don't scare you?"

"Yes, I'm okay with this. No, you don't scare me."

And he meant every word. No hesitation. No doubt.

Kate studied him, her gaze flitting across his face. "I've never met anyone quite like you."

He smiled and loved seeing it echoed in her eyes. "I'd never seek to change you, Kate."

No matter how much he wanted to keep her safe.

Her eyes filled with tears, but she blinked them back. "Come on, we have a doctor to convince." She took his hand, leading him back into the kitchen.

He'd follow her anywhere.

Beth slid glasses of whiskey in front of each of them. Kate took hers without hesitation and knocked it back easily. He tried not to let his mouth drop open.

Rachel gazed at Kate with intensity. "Does John die in your

vision? I'm doing everything I can to keep him from the tests the Major wants to perform, but it's only a matter of time."

Kate shook her head. "Not from what I saw. You were both in your lab. The NRP drug had failed. You were thinking of using spinal fluid from Patient 244 as an option. Bob was counseling you to play ball to protect your family." Kate stared at the doctor. "Who's the Major?"

The doctor blanched, losing what little color she had. "You really can see the future."

Kate took out an energy bar from her purse and gave it to her. "Here, eat this. We're buying stock in the company."

"Major Oliver Wilson." Rachel unwrapped the bar and numbly ate it. "He heads up the Scottish arm of RAVEN. Rachel rubbed her eyes. "We're not planning to try the NRP drug on anyone just yet. It's not ready."

Logan nodded. "So, we have a bit of time before what Kate saw comes to pass."

Rachel gazed out the window, and Logan knew her mind was somewhere else. "I'd like to help free the test subjects. But it's too dangerous."

"We're not asking you to do anything directly," Beth said.

Rachel looked between each of them, her eyes narrowing. "Then what *are* you asking?"

"Be our inside woman," Beth said. "Give us intel so we can figure out a way to take RAVEN down."

Rachel laughed, but it was a shadow of sound. "You can't *take them down.* You'd need an army."

Kate nodded. "Our mission isn't to dismantle RAVEN. Our

mission is to save John and our friend, Duncan. Though I feel there might be others I'm supposed to save too."

Kate seemed extra worried. Logan wondered who else she had seen.

Beth looked like she wanted to argue, but then closed her mouth. Logan was glad both of them were finally showing some sense. Taking down a well-placed, well-funded, and well-armed organization was suicide.

Rachel looked at the picture of her family. "I'm afraid," she whispered.

Logan knew they'd need the doctor's help to save the two people Kate mentioned. And it might be the only way to not get Kate killed.

"Do it for John," Logan said. "For the other families who've lost their sons and daughters to RAVEN. I know what it's like to have regret. Eventually it will eat you up inside if you don't find a way to stop it."

Helping Kate and Beth with their mission allowed him to make amends for what Graham had done.

Rachel took a shuddering breath. "If they find out I'm involved, they'll kill my family."

"I will not let that happen," Beth said. "We'll protect them."

Her words were so sure, Logan found himself believing Beth would somehow find a way. Just in case, he had some old favors he could call in if needed. Get them into hiding.

Kate took the doctor's hand. "Family is everything to me. Mine are at risk already, but I have to follow my visions."

Rachel squeezed Kate's hand and nodded. "All right, I'll do

it. I've been praying for a way to help for months."

"And here we are," Kate said. "We're going to get through this. Together."

"Together." Logan repeated and placed his hand on top of theirs.

Beth put her hand on top of his. "Are we supposed to yell 'Go Team' or some shit like that?"

The doctor laughed, and Kate joined in. Beth gave Logan a wink. There was definitely a method to her snark, and this time, he was in full approval. Anything to bring the light back to Kate's eyes.

He knew Kate would try to keep him out of this, out of whatever they planned with RAVEN. But he wasn't going to let her go through this alone. Not like when she faced Graham. This time he'd be by her side, whether she agreed or not.

CHAPTER 12

KATE TOOK A LONG SIP OF COFFEE IN THE DESERTED DINING room of the Forbes' manor. She hid next to the silver chafing dishes. Everyone else was in the sitting room or hadn't arrived yet.

She'd come this morning with Sam and Beth for a brunch briefing to go over what everyone had learned about RAVEN and the stones. But all she could think about was what happened last night. Telling Logan had gone much better than she'd expected.

He said he was fine with it, but they all say that in the beginning.

Until she sees something *they* wished she hadn't.

Her mind wandered to their kiss in the shed. Even if he was interested in something more, how would it look if he was romancing the woman his brother tried to kill?

Not good. Even potentially creepy. And it could ruin his reputation.

Better to stick with no complications. Someone like Duncan.

The object of her thoughts walked into the dining room with a tray filled with empty coffee cups. "I wondered where you'd wandered off to," Duncan said.

His red hair was unruly today. Wild waves on top of his head, like he'd just woken up.

"I needed a moment," she replied. "Lots to process from last night."

He nodded. "Beth mentioned the meeting with the doctor had gone well."

"It did. And I heard you got some intel from Caleb. Sam told me the basics."

He began to fill the cups from the large silver container on the table. "I'm still wrapping my head around the fact that he gave me a vision."

"Me too. When Sam told me, I almost didn't believe it."

Visions came from the Universe. No one else.

Kate ran her hand along the wood of the table. "So, are you going to tell me what you saw?" The air turned heavy, tense.

"I'm going to figure out a way to fix it, Kate. I promise."

Duncan gave her a look so filled with anguish, her heart seized.

"What did you see?" Her voice was almost a whisper.

"Sam died. So did I." Duncan rubbed his eyes with the heels of his hands. "Robert probably died in the fire."

"Repeat that."

"I died, Kate. I watched it happen." Duncan looked down at the coffee mug in his hand.

People who saw the future didn't see themselves. That was the deal. That was the price.

"How?" Was all she could manage.

"I think it's because the vision came from Caleb, not the Universe. He wanted me to see how we screwed it up. Screwed it up royally."

Laughter from the sitting room reached them, sounding too bright and out of place with what he'd just shared.

Kate grabbed his arm. "I know we have to go inside and talk about RAVEN, but I want to know what happened. Now. Reader's Digest version is fine."

He filled her on Vivian, the vines, the impalement. By the time he'd finished, Kate felt dizzy. She slid into a chair.

Duncan sat down next to her. "I haven't told my family yet. They're already on edge about RAVEN taking me." He shook his head slowly. "I feel like I can't win. I'll either die by Vivian's hand or be used by RAVEN."

This wasn't the man who'd flirted with her, who'd sent shivers down her spine from his kiss. Seeing him like this, vulnerable, tugged at her more deeply than any physical attraction could.

That look in his eyes was the same in her own. Not knowing what to do with what you've seen. Hoping you'll find a way to stop a vision coming to pass. And now he'd witnessed his own death.

"Hey." She cupped his cheek, feeling the softness of his beard on her palm. "We're going to figure this out."

"We?"

"Yes, we. You and me. You're kinda my responsibility because of my vision."

"Oh really?" A little darkness lifted from his face.

Kate nodded. "Yup. My sacred duty is to stop you from being captured, and this whole death thing just won't do."

Now the hint of a smile. "And just how are we going to stop Vivian from killing everyone and also get the dampening stones for my town?"

Kate pursed her lips. "I don't know yet, but first off, we're going to change things up on the approach."

Duncan straightened, looking more like his old self. "I've already started thinking about it. We definitely can't have Robert there."

"Nope. He's too tempting to her, but Sam needs to come."

"Why?"

"I have this feeling in my gut that TOP needs to go with you."

Duncan looked off into space. "I can't figure out what to offer her besides land."

"I'll do some research and see what I can find out about dealing with gods. It might give us some ideas."

"You barely know me, and you're willing to go up against a homicidal forest deity to save a town of people you also don't know." He gazed at her, admiration in his eyes. "Do you realize how incredibly brave you are?"

Kate waved a hand. "I'm just doing what needs to be done to save lives. Isn't that what you're doing? Why you're risking everything to save your town?"

He leaned forward and took her hand. "Thank you for giving me just what I needed."

"What's that?"

"Hope."

The look he gave her was filled with gratitude and also a bit of heat. She suddenly had a flashback of the kitchen. His lips on hers.

"Damn, Duncan. You should have a warning sign." She didn't care she sounded breathy. He pushed all her buttons with just a look.

Duncan lifted her chin with his fingers until their lips were almost touching. "And what would my warning sign say?" The tickle of his words frolicked on her skin.

Instant sex, just add Duncan. She swallowed. "Slippery road ahead. Danger of losing control."

He laughed, a wonderful deep belly laugh. "I'll own that. I'd like to get together again." He gave her a charming half smile. "We *were* rudely interrupted by your vision, if you recall."

"I recall." Her entire body felt tingly. Oh yeah, she recalled all right.

He stood, lifting her to her feet. "Do you know what your warning sign would be?"

"Watch out, she stress-bakes?"

He grinned. "Beware. Too enticing to resist."

"Come on. We don't want Beth coming to find us. She would tease us mercilessly."

"I've seen what she puts my brother through," he said with a shudder.

Kate had stepped in to help with no hesitation. Maybe Sam and Beth's automatic leadership was rubbing off on her? Or maybe, she was finally starting to believe, just a little, that she was just a strong as them.

She brushed past Duncan with a smile, taking the lead. "Let's go."

Duncan watched Kate sit in a chair next to his mother's. She was unlike any woman he'd met before. True, there was the attraction he was used to, but there was something more. She actually seemed to care about him. And they'd known each other less than a week.

She definitely had a big heart. Even though it had been broken painfully when her husband had died.

What was he doing? This wasn't just a fun encounter. Kate was quality. She deserved better than him. But maybe he could become better? For her.

Seeing his own death had definitely put things in perspective.

"Should we get started?" Duncan said. His gaze flickered over everyone. Sam and Robert were on the love-seat with Glenna. Lennox and Michael sat on the couch with Beth between them.

"I hope you have good news about another dampening stone," Lennox said. "I installed the final one at the Allen's last night. Though we might not need it. Ken's left town."

Duncan wasn't surprised. Being abandoned by his family had taken away everything that bound Ken to the town. And he was a liability, a danger to keeping everyone safe.

"Caleb gave us a clue about more stones," Sam said. She raised her eyebrow at Duncan. He knew she was leaving it up to him as to how much he wanted to reveal about last night.

Hope filled Jean's gaze. "Caleb agreed to help? For the lands we promised?"

Duncan put his coffee down. "He gave us some information, as Sam said. I've had a vision. I've seen what we're up against to get the stones, and it won't be easy."

"Which is why you won't be doing it alone." Kate's voice was clear and sure. She believed that together they would succeed, but he'd never forgive himself if Vivian hurt her. However, he knew there'd be no way to convince her to stay out of it.

"Just who did you see in the vision?" Michael glanced between Duncan and Kate.

There was no point lying to his family. They needed to know what they were up against for the stones.

"Robert and Sam." Duncan took a deep breath. "And I was there too."

"Crap." Lennox muttered. "That can't be good. You've never seen yourself before."

Duncan leaned back in his chair. "I think it's because Caleb gave me the vision. It wasn't my own."

Everyone started talking at once.

Worry. Concern. Fear.

What did it mean that the forest ghost had given him a vision?

Duncan rubbed his temples against the headache forming.

He had already gone through all of this in his head over and over again.

"Why don't you tell us the rest, brother." Michael's words cut through the noise, though he didn't raise his voice. In fact, his tone was kind, gentle almost. Everyone else instantly shut up.

Duncan's throat tightened. Once he said this to his family, it would become real. What if they couldn't figure out another way? And if he did survive, RAVEN would almost surely capture him. One of their visions would come to pass. Of that he was certain.

"I saw my death. But Caleb gave me the vision for a reason. He wants me to stop it, so I believe that means there's a way."

"In the spirit of full disclosure, I die too." Sam's words were quiet. Beth's gasp was loud, and she instantly looked embarrassed and angry at the same time. "And Robert is held hostage by Caleb's daughter, though he probably died as well once the Universe set her tree on fire."

"We'd heard rumors of his offspring," Jean said.

"Oh, she's real alright." Duncan shook his head slowly. "Powerful and dangerous too."

Beth pointed at Sam. "You are not dying, you hear me?"

Sam nodded, but Duncan saw a flash of tears in her eyes. "I'll do my best."

Beth blinked quickly. "You're not going to the forest, and that's that."

"She has to go," Kate said. "TOP *has* to be there."

Jean brightened. "Have you had a vision too?"

Kate tucked a strand of red hair behind her ear. "No. But I have this gut feeling we need to be there."

"Gut feeling," Lennox muttered, but Kate shot him a look and he shut up. Surprisingly.

Robert put his arm around Sam. "The tragedies foreseen by Duncan will not come to pass. Caleb is unpredictable, but his gift of this vision shows his intent. He seeks to save us from this fate."

"You can't go, Duncan. I don't care about the dampening stones." His mother held his gaze across the coffee table. "Besides the danger of facing Vivian, the forest might be where RAVEN takes you."

"I have to go because Caleb gave me a piece of himself." Duncan tried to keep his words gentle, seeing the worry in her eyes. "Without it, we don't have a hope of getting Vivian to listen."

Lennox nodded. "Duncan's right. Caleb did this for a reason. And it wasn't to get Duncan killed. He's always had a soft spot for him."

Caleb having a soft spot for him? What did that mean? His mom wouldn't meet Duncan's eyes.

"I'm going too," Glenna announced. "I'll charge up before we leave." She laced her small hands together and cracked her knuckles. "Caleb's daughter won't like what I can do."

The smell of Vivian's tree burning filled Duncan's lungs. "No. We can't attack her. That's what ruined everything the last time. You're sitting this one out, Glenna."

His sister glanced at Lennox. He gave her a small nod.

"Fine," she said, "but I'll be parked at the B&B. In case you need me."

Lennox frowned at Glenna. "And I'll be with you in that car so you don't get it in your head to run off and play hero."

Jean sighed and turned to Kate and Beth. "What's the news on the doctor? Will she help us stop Duncan from being captured?"

"Dr. Withers is on board." Kate sipped her coffee. "She's agreed to give us information on RAVEN through a drop site."

"Drop site?" Michael nudged Beth's knee with his. "Your idea, I take it?"

Beth gave him a hooded look. "As a matter of fact, it is. There's a coffee place she visits regularly, so we won't raise suspicion."

"The staff could be on RAVEN's payroll to keep tabs," Glenna said. "It's what I'd do if I wanted to be discreet."

"Good call." Beth nodded in approval. "But the staff won't be an issue. The drop site is a trashcan around the side. There's a space between the can and the outside holder. She'll drop the envelope of information in between."

There was obviously more to Beth than a reality show. "And how will you know she's dropping something?"

Beth scrolled on her phone and then held it up to show a picture of a side window. "She'll lower her shade halfway if there's something to pick up. I've got someone posted to let us know if that happens."

"Thank you for everything you're doing." Jean touched Kate's hand.

Robert glanced at Kate. "Once Kate's visions included

Duncan, we could not sit by. It is only by working together that we have a hope of saving John Anderson and preventing Duncan's capture."

Lennox stood. "We'll keep Duncan safe, but that's it. We're not going up against RAVEN to rescue a stranger."

Duncan got to his feet. "If they need our help saving John and whoever else Kate sees, I'm in." He had to be. She didn't know what she was going up against. The danger.

"You're being foolish." Lennox's voice wasn't unkind, but it was firm. Duncan recognized the beginning of a lecture. Number 37 if he wasn't mistaken. The why-we-don't-ruffle-the-lion's-fur speech.

Michael joined Duncan. "If TOP needs my help, I'm there. No one is forcing you to take part, Lennox."

Beth shook her head. "I'd rather have you with us, Lennox. You could do some serious damage in a facility with a crap ton of metal. But if you're too chicken-shit to take on RAVEN, there's nothing we can do to help you grow a pair in time."

Lennox's fists clenched and unclenched. Beth's fork bent.

"Back down, brother." Michael's words were a harsh whisper.

Instant fear blossomed in Lennox's eyes. He took a step back.

Duncan didn't blame him. They all knew what Michael was capable of. How painful it was to resist when he screwed with your mind.

His breakfast see-sawed in his stomach.

Lennox held up his hands. "We know what attacking RAVEN means. We'll fail, they'll round everyone up, take them away, experiment on them. I won't let that happen."

Robert steepled his fingers. "I fear you might not have a choice in this matter. If we cannot prevent Duncan's capture, would you leave him in RAVEN's clutches?"

Lennox stared at Duncan. "I'd rescue Duncan, no matter the cost."

Duncan hoped he didn't look as shocked as he felt. There wasn't animosity between them, but there hadn't been deep love either.

Kate smiled like she'd already known his answer. "First things first. Since we know Duncan has to visit Vivian, I'm going to do some research and see what intel I can find out on forest deities. Figure out a better approach."

Beth caught Duncan's eye. His phone buzzed. A text from her.

We need your help with Kate. To keep her safe.

He nodded. Duncan wasn't sure what they had in mind, but if it kept Kate out of the path of Vivian, he would do what needed to be done.

And maybe, just maybe, they'd get a chance to see where this attraction went.

This time, in the tangle of emotions around his heart, hope won out over fear.

CHAPTER 13

KATE SHIFTED FROM FOOT TO FOOT IN FRONT OF DUNCAN'S door. After the meeting yesterday, he'd invited her to a thank-you lunch for giving him hope they'd figure out a way to handle Vivian and get the dampening stones his town desperately needed.

Hope was one thing, but she still needed to figure out a bit more about what might smooth things over with the forest deity. The town library would be her next stop. Dig through some books.

But first, lunch at Duncan's cottage on the Forbeses' grounds.

Alone.

Anticipation fluttered through her. She swallowed, her mouth suddenly dry. The last time they'd been relatively alone, things had heated up.

Her breasts were still complaining about her vision interrupting the due care they deserved. It had been a while. A long while since she'd been intimate with anyone.

She knocked on the door.

It opened quickly, as if Duncan had been waiting for her arrival. There was an uncertain air about him. Not the cool, confident teacher from their first lesson. Kate felt instantly better about being a little nervous herself.

He looked handsome, as usual. A dark blue t-shirt that brought out the red in his hair, faded jeans, and bare feet.

Duncan followed her gaze. "I get hot when I cook, so I like to have my feet free." He moved to the side to let her in.

"What are you cooking?" Kate took off her jacket and dropped it with her purse on the couch.

"Lasagna."

Kate took a deep breath, savoring the enticing scents of cheese and red sauce mixing together. "Yum, yum, yum." She smiled at him and looked around. "How long have you lived in the cottage?"

"Just six months this time. We've all lived at home at one time or another."

Soft classical music played from a blue tooth speaker on an old wooden hutch. It sat in a snug dining room to her right. A small living room opened up to her left. It had a fireplace, a couch and a chair. Straight ahead was a hallway that lead to the kitchen, judging by the direction of the delicious scents. The hallway split off left and right. No doubt to bedrooms.

The two round windows in the living room had glowing lights around them—and not your usual string of lights. These looked like stones sticking to the borders around the glass. She noticed now the front door had some too. "What are those?"

"Lennox reinforced the barriers on the cottage. A local witch helped." Duncan looked concerned, but not worried. He was handling things better than she expected. "If RAVEN tries to get to me here, they'd have a nasty surprise, and it would also be loud enough for my family to hear."

"Smart. You can't be too careful." She touched his shoulder. "I really hope my vision doesn't come to pass."

He nodded, a little worry finally seeping into his gaze. "Me too." Then he took a deep breath. "But we have more important things to worry about right now. Like not overcooking the lasagna. I'd better check on it."

She followed him into the kitchen. It was tiny, barely space for two people, but everything looked well used and cared for. And within reach even to her. Short people must have built it.

Duncan turned on the oven light and peeked inside. "It's ready. It'll just need to cool a bit." He slipped on some silicone gloves and took out a huge glass pan of lasagna.

"That's an awful lot of lasagna for just the two of us."

Duncan smiled. "Well, I figured you could take some home to your girls. And as a poor lonely bachelor, I often eat leftovers." He tried to look downcast at that last bit, but couldn't dowse his smile completely.

"I appreciate the offer. It's not often someone cooks for me." Like never. "Now, what can I help with?"

"I've got a green salad we can whip together if that works." He opened the fridge and started loading up the wooden kitchen island in the center with salad fixings.

Kate grabbed the cucumbers and went to the sink. "Vegetable wash?"

"By the dish drainer."

He joined her by the sink with the carrots. Their bodies almost touching. The heat from his arm warmed hers.

Desire sent tendrils through her. Her legs felt unsteady.

"I'm still thinking about our first lesson."

He reached across her to grab the vegetable wash. "I've been thinking of it too."

Kate turned to face him. "And you're still okay with just seeing where this goes? No expectations?"

He dried off the carrots and turned to her. "I'm good. No expectations necessary."

If this didn't work out, it might get a little awkward seeing him, especially if he was still helping her with her abilities, but that would be the extent of it. They weren't close friends yet, and the girls hardly knew him.

Nobody would get too hurt at this stage.

"Okay, then." She looked up at Duncan. Damn he was handsome. And with the heat in his eyes, they didn't need a stove to cook anything.

Her nails caught on the squeaky clean cucumber.

Duncan took the cucumbers from her hands and put them on the counter with the carrots. "They're as clean as they're going to be."

"I like to be thorough."

The tendrils had turned into rivers. Attraction, heat, desire, you name it, was on the Kate highway.

He grinned. "I have something better than a cucumber."

The laugh exploded from her. "Ah, well I wouldn't really be able to verify that. I've never tried veggies *that* way before." Her words were a little garbled with giggles.

Duncan gave her a quick kiss. Her laughter died instantly. "I think the salad can wait for a bit."

He put his hands on her hips and gently pulled her in front of him, turning her so her back was to the kitchen island.

Her clothes felt suddenly too cloying in the warm kitchen. "I agree." She rested her hands on his chest. He let out a small sigh. She definitely wasn't the only one feeling whatever this was between them.

"I guess that means we'll have to heat up the lasagna later."

She lifted his t-shirt up, and he raised his arms to help. "I never mind a little heat-up."

She let her eyes run over his chest. The red hair formed a v against his fair skin, then trickled down to a trail through those incredible abs.

Kate ran her hands down his chest until she reached his jeans. She unbuttoned them and then eased the zipper down. Tugging them past his hips, they slid down his legs and pooled onto the floor. He stepped out of them and kicked them aside.

Duncan's eyes had turned a hazy blue. He was letting her explore and wasn't trying to rush anything. That alone was a turn-on.

"Green is one of my favorite colors," Kate said, eyeing his plaid boxer briefs. She cupped him through the fabric.

He groaned and gripped the back counter.

She ran her hand down the length of him and back up again. Then she slid her fingers under his waistband. His skin was burning. She gripped him, stroking him.

His hips started to rock back and forth. Stepping closer, she kissed his neck, moving up to his jawline.

He grasped her shoulders, pushing her back up against the kitchen island.

The bottle of olive oil teetered and hit the floor.

Kate tensed, expecting the sound of glass, but it only bounced.

"Plastic," Duncan murmured.

She laughed. "I see you planned ahead."

He gently took her hand and raised both her arms up, then lifted her shirt over her head. He carefully laid it on the counter, out of the way.

Very considerate.

"Poor Mr. Salad." Kate unclasped her bra and flung it through the air. "He has to wait a bit."

Duncan followed its path through the air and then let out a sigh. "It just missed the bowl of extra tomato sauce."

"Darn it. My aim is off."

He turned back to her and his smile moved into one of wonder.

"Oh, Kate." Duncan sounded like Christmas had arrived. And her breasts were ready and willing to be an early present.

He kissed her, the warmth of his beard embracing her. His hands caressed her breasts. Duncan's tongue darted into her mouth. She captured it with her own, deepening the kiss.

His fingers pinched her nipples, bringing sharp moans from her throat. He kissed his way down and replaced the tiny, delicious pain with warm pleasure. He moved back and forth between her nipples, leaving a trail of heat with his beard. Every brush of his hair pulled things tighter within her.

They hadn't even done much yet, and she felt close to exploding.

He moved away from her breasts to untie her sneakers.

"Hey," Kate protested.

Then he rubbed her feet, hitting her inner arch, the top tendons. She closed her eyes, luxuriating in the feel of his hands.

Duncan moved up her legs, massaging her calves, her thighs, then stopping at her hips. He tugged on her yoga pants, inching them down. She scooted up a bit so he could get them off. Then her panties came next.

His lips went back to her breasts and his fingers brushed gently against her. Teasing. Her breathing grew short, faster. Then he slid his fingers inside while his thumb pulsed in a rhythm against her. Faster and faster.

Her orgasm shot through her so fast, she barely made a sound, her entire body clenching in release.

Well, she knew she'd been ready to pop.

Duncan gave her a shy smile and kissed down her belly to her hips.

He hooked his arms underneath her knees and tilted her back slowly.

She leaned back, arms going out to the sides, knocking the croutons to the floor along with the head of lettuce.

"Sorry, Mr. Salad," she whispered, but he just laughed.

He ran his lips along the inside of her thighs. Each movement brushing his beard against her. Then he paused, looking up at her from between her legs. A slow deliberate lick, then another.

Kate writhed underneath him, but she couldn't tear her gaze from his.

He slid his hands under her, lifting her up to his mouth. His lips latched on, sucking—and oh god, was he humming? The vibrations rumbled through her.

Could someone pass out from too much pleasure?

She couldn't hold on, but this time she rode the wave as it built. Her hands tangled in his hair. The desire sent sparks through her vision. The kitchen shimmered in her gaze.

Oh God. Don't let another vision happen. Not now.

She thought she might have screamed. She wasn't sure. Her senses were on overload.

The kitchen was back in focus. Her body still warm. No vision. Whew.

"Kate? How far?" His words were strained. Duncan stood. Completely naked now. She wondered where his green plaid had gone to.

She sat up, feeling like her limbs were jelly. "No home runs just yet. Let's run the bases a bit more. 'Kay?"

He nodded.

Kate eased off the kitchen island and patted the wooden surface. "Up here. I've never gone on my knees in front of a man. For one, it never felt equal to me. And two, I've got bad knees."

He laughed again, and this time it was the full belly laugh

she loved. He lifted himself to sit on the kitchen island. "No sugar coating. I love it."

"No sugar coating here." She gazed down at him. "But I happen to like salty too."

It had been years since she'd done this, but her body remembered. She moved up, grasped the length of him with her right hand, feeling him pulse underneath her. Then she began to stroke. Slowly at first.

Duncan leaned back, hands splayed wide on the kitchen island.

She kissed her way up his length, alternately stroking and licking. Nibbling here and there. Until she took his tip into her mouth and circled her tongue round and round, underneath the ridge and then up to the smooth top. Then back again.

Duncan's breath quickened. He pushed her hair back, away from her face, his fingers shaky. She met his gaze. His eyes were even darker than before. Need pulsing in their depths.

She tightened her grip at his base and took him in and out of her mouth. His breath grew to pants. Tension thrummed in his legs. She upped the rhythm. Quicker and quicker.

With a yell, he filled her mouth. Duncan fell back and the tomatoes flew off the kitchen island, joining the other casualties.

Kate gave him a last slow lick and then went over to the sink, soaking a paper towel with warm water. She gently ran the paper towel over him.

"Am I still alive?" he croaked.

"I hope so. You still owe me lunch." She eyed the produce on the floor. "Though I'm not sure if the tomatoes will be make it."

He hopped off the island and grabbed his boxer briefs from the handle on one of the kitchen drawers. He handed Kate her clothes. They quickly dressed.

"Why don't you take the plates to the table while I whip up the salad?" He gave her a quick kiss and placed the plates into her hands.

Kate walked down the hall to the dining room. Her body felt amazing. Okay, sore, but amazing. What they'd just done had been fabulous. No complaints.

Then why did she feel like something was missing? It wasn't like you needed love to be intimate with someone.

She looked back over her shoulder at Duncan bustling in the kitchen. She liked him. She really did.

And this was nothing serious. No expectations. And no complications.

Not like with Logan.

If she did give something a try with Logan and it didn't work out, the girls would never forgive her if she ruined what they had right now. They adored him.

It couldn't be an accident she was thinking of Logan after just being with Duncan.

Kate placed the plates on the table and sat down, looking at the white round porcelain in front of her.

"Speak, oh King of Salad Plates. I need some guidance," she whispered.

Of course, the plate didn't reply, but her inner voice did.

Maybe she needed expectations?

Maybe she needed complications?

Maybe she really needed Logan.

LOGAN WALKED THROUGH THE BAKERY DOORS, INHALING the delicious aroma of cinnamon rolls and chocolate croissants. He spied Kate's flame of hair by the front windows.

He'd been happily surprised by her call. After what had happened at Dr. Withers' place, he wasn't sure if she'd still worry things had changed between them.

They had, but for the better. He felt closer to her than ever before. It was obvious she'd kept her distance from him because of her secret. But now that he knew, maybe things could move beyond friendship finally?

Logan grabbed his order at the counter and made his way back to her, winding through the crowded tables.

She looked up and waved at him. He stumbled, almost knocking over one of the chairs. With her hair long and loose, and her skin glowing, she looked like a goddess.

He held up the book she'd asked him to bring. "I found it in my mother's boxes."

She stood, took a step forward, then back, as if unsure whether to hug him.

He put the book down and pulled her into his arms. She

froze for a moment and then hugged him back. Squeezed him so tight, he lost his breath.

Logan pulled back slightly. "You okay?"

Kate blinked quickly, but not before he saw the shine of tears in her eyes. "I'm good. Just happy to see you."

She wasn't telling the entire truth, but he didn't press her. They sat down and he looked at the pile of books to her left.

Nature Gods

Legends of the Woods

Forest Deities

"No wonder why you wanted me to bring this." He slid his mother's book over to her.

The History of Rosebridge

Kate brightened "According to their records, they're supposed to have three copies, but they scoured the library yesterday, top to bottom, and couldn't find a copy. It's not in print any longer. It's the only book written about this town."

Duncan took a sip of his coffee. "I'm glad I could help. So, who are we going up against?"

"I've already involved you more than I should have."

"Kate, stop that right now."

She gave him a guarded look.

He pushed on. "I'm honored you confided in me about what you can do, but it doesn't change who you are, who you've always been." He leaned forward and lowered his voice. "There is nothing you can do or say that would change the way I feel about you. Ever. I'm not going anywhere."

The tears were back again and this time, several slid down

her cheeks. She took his hand. "You don't know how much that means right now."

He squeezed her hand. "Your visions are frightening, but we're going to prevent them. Together."

She nodded and pulled her hand away to reach for a napkin to wipe her eyes.

He felt like there might be something more than the visions worrying her, but now was not the time to push. She was the strongest person he knew, but that didn't mean she didn't have her fragile times.

"Tell me what you're looking for in these books."

Kate took a deep breath and seemed more focused. "What do you know of the Green Man?"

"He's the embodiment of nature itself. A legend that's lasted through the centuries." For a moment he was back in time, a boy lying in bed while his mother wove stories about fairies and the enchanted forestlands of Rosebridge.

"What's that smile for?"

"Just fond memories of my mother. Before she died." He shook his head, and the past from his thoughts. "She used to tell me of when she'd sneak into the forests around your B&B and talk with the Green Man. Though she also told me my slippers could fly, so there is that."

Kate laughed. "Well, your mom was right about there being a ghost in my forest."

Logan sat up straight. "There is?"

"There is. It was his crows that attacked Graham before he could hurt Beth."

The familiar guilt flowed through him over his brother's actions. Not as acidic as before, but still there.

"I see what's going on behind those eyes, Logan."

"You do?"

"I do."

He really didn't need another lecture on how to move on from the guilt. He wasn't there yet. He stayed silent.

Kate raised an eyebrow. "Though I want to tattoo 'Graham was not my fault' on your arm, I know we're all struggling with our own damage. Everyone has their own speed of recovery."

Logan glanced down at the Freemasons' tattoo on the inside of his forearm. His brother had one too. It had been one of the reasons they'd thought Logan was the killer at first.

The top of the tattoo was a drawing/drafting compass with the sharp edges facing downward over two rulers joined together. Logan had always thought of it like two hands reaching toward each other, fingers and thumbs touching. In the center was an R for Rosebridge and a small rose.

He lifted his arm slightly. "I could put it over this. *This* has only brought me pain."

He glanced at her and saw understanding.

"There are a lot of things I'd like to change too," she said, "but they remind us of who we are, how far we've come, and how much farther we need to go."

"I see you're branching into counseling along with your culinary skills."

That brought the smile he was hoping for. Chasing away

some of the darkness he hadn't meant to cause. "I am multi-talented."

"I agree. I love your talents."

They stared at each other for a moment. Kate's face reddened. Had he just made her blush? He hadn't even been flirting. Not intentionally anyway. He tamped down the hope that sparked within him.

"So, why do you need to research your forest ghost?"

Kate rustled with her notebook. "Not Caleb. His daughter. We need to figure out a way to safely meet with her."

All gods were dangerous in their own way, at least according to his mother. Though he could never tell if it was fancy or because she'd seen it up close. "You'll need an offering."

Kate stabbed her notebook with her pen. "That's exactly what I was thinking too. But none of these books give me an idea of what that could be."

Logan grabbed back his mother's book and flipped through the well-worn pages. "I remember something in here. Something my mother said. She used to bring treats when she went." He found the page and the underlined words. He showed Kate. "Gifts of the hearth made with clear intention and love."

She took the book and scanned it, nodding. "For me, it would have to be baked goods then."

"Baking comes from your heart and always with good intent."

Kate grinned. "You might have just saved the day, Logan."

She leaned across the table and kissed him on the cheek. She sat back and held his gaze for a moment, a question in her eyes. "I . . ." Kate reached for his hand and knocked his coffee over spilling it onto his chocolate croissant. "Clumsy me again. Sorry." She mopped up the spill, not looking at him.

The warmth of her lips stayed on his skin. Maybe there was hope for them?

He needed to make her see that he could be part of her world if she'd just let him.

CHAPTER 14

KATE LISTENED TO THE NIGHT RAIN PATTERING AGAINST the windows of Duncan's cottage. The fire was crackling nicely in his living room. The cottage was snug and cozy.

Duncan had offered another lesson since their trek to see Vivian had to be delayed due to the rain. No point in delivering soggy offerings.

An open bottle of Cairn O'Mohr Elderberry wine sat between them with a plate of cheese and crackers.

Duncan leaned forward in his chair. The firelight played in his hair, bringing out copper strands. "I'm sorry we couldn't see Vivian tonight."

"As long as we can keep you safe from RAVEN, another day isn't going to matter." Though she had really wanted to get it over with so she could stop worrying about what might happen.

"No more visions about RAVEN?" he asked.

She took a sip of the wine. It was rich and smooth on her tongue. She'd always loved dessert wines.

"Nothing yet," she said, "but I feel like I haven't seen enough.

There are more people to save besides you and John."

"The Universe won't leave you hanging. If there is something you need to see to help you succeed, it'll come."

She stared at him a moment, weighing whether to tell him. But he had her gifts. If anyone would understand about seeing people they love in a vision, he would.

"I saw Sam and Beth in my first vision of RAVEN. Just briefly, and then nothing in the second vision."

Duncan sat up straight. "Have you told them?"

"No. It could be a fluke. Just my worry about them." Her voice didn't sound very convincing. "But what about you? Have you ever had a vision about RAVEN?"

By the ashen look on Duncan's face, she immediately wanted to take her question back.

"I can't see anything related to RAVEN, no matter how hard I try."

"I understand about not being able to see something specific, believe me. But it's not like we can choose the channel we want. We're not TVs."

"I can choose the channel." Duncan held her gaze.

"What?"

"Even pick the time and place I want to see."

"You're playing with me." She couldn't read him. Not like Logan. The way Logan's eyebrows would lift slightly when he was trying to pull one over on her.

"I'm not."

"I've never come across anyone who could direct their visions."

"I'm the only one that I know of." He lifted his wine glass. "Only the people in our town know. And now you. I don't like to advertise that aspect of what I do."

She wasn't surprised. Sam used to get the dial-a-ghost requests when they were kids. If people knew Duncan could pinpoint what he wanted to see . . .

"That's why they want you." It was clear now.

"Excuse me?"

"RAVEN. They already know about me." Kate got up and paced. "Too much has happened around the B&B. But they haven't grabbed me, even though Dr. Withers said they'd been dying to get someone with our abilities. Maybe it's because I'm unreliable on timing. I can't direct what I see. But you can." She stopped and stared at Duncan. "Someone is going to tell them about your ability . . . or someone already has."

He shook his head. "That's ridiculous. Our town is sworn to secrecy about everyone who lives there."

"But they can leverage someone's family, like they did with Dr. Withers."

They stared at each other a moment. Kate decided to switch gears. She needed to know more about what Duncan did.

"Can you choose *who* you want to see?"

Duncan frowned. "Yes, but I don't usually narrow it down like that. There are costs." Duncan's gaze shifted away, towards the fire.

It was mind-boggling enough to think he could choose the time and place, but the person? If she'd been able to control her visions like he could, things would have been so different.

She could have seen Paul's cancer early.

She looked down into her glass, into the purple depths. The old regret flickered and then flamed within her, tightening around her heart. She should have seen it. Should have stopped it.

Compartmentalize Kate. Now is not the time. Back in its box.

The internal controls worked smoothly, gears well-oiled, used to the motions. The past locked away once again. She realized she'd been holding her breath. And Duncan had given her space and his silence almost as if he knew of her internal struggles.

"Okay, tell me how you switch channels to the show you want to see."

Duncan gazed at her a moment longer before he spoke. "I need a calendar, a photo, and a clock, things that help me visualize the time, place and date."

"So you stare at these and you suddenly have your vision?"

He closed his eyes. "I use them to focus, and then I go to a place inside my head. There's always a door that combines all three. The time, the date, and the place. It opens. I walk through. And I see what I need to see."

Kate sensed there was more to it than that. "And what are the costs you mentioned before? When you try to narrow it down to a particular person?"

Duncan smoothed his beard down with his forefinger and thumb. "When we let our gifts speak what they need, there's just the usual drain. Tired, needing a bit more sleep." His eyes grew haunted. "But when you force your gifts to bend to your will, it takes a lot of life force. Both physical and emotional. Essentially you're in the Universe's river of consciousness, but swimming against the flow. Or directing it out of its natural path."

"My blackouts with my visions, I'm not trying to swim against any stream."

"I've been thinking about that. I believe it's just a case of not being fully connected to your abilities," he said. "We know that grounding helped you this last time. Once you get that down as a reflex, happening automatically, you should be able to stay conscious. But the next step is to remove yourself from being inside the vision. That will help you keep control."

"Removing myself? What do you mean?"

"Are you an Apple gal?"

"Fruit or technology?"

A smile quirked his lips. "Technology."

She nodded.

"Okay, so you'll gather the energy and send it into an iPad that you're holding in your hands. Like you just downloaded a video."

"Real or metaphysical?"

"A metaphysical iPad."

Kate tapped her fingers against her wine glass. "My visions used to be like movies when I was a kid. And then things changed after I hit puberty. That's when I started to black out."

Duncan nodded. "Puberty sends our abilities into overdrive. And it tends to break the early easy connection we had with our minds, gifts, and bodies." He put his wine glass down. "All those hormones racing, flooding the body with new needs and desires."

She didn't mistake the heat in his eyes.

He tilted his head toward the hallway. "Speaking of desires, I think the kitchen island is still scandalized from our non-cooking skills, but my bedroom wouldn't be shocked."

"No." The word was out of her mouth before her body could protest. She might just be confused about her feelings for Logan or maybe there was something there between her and Logan she should pursue, but either way, she didn't want to hurt Duncan with continuing anything until she was sure.

Duncan's face fell.

She reached out and took his hand. "I don't mean my body isn't up for it. What we did was pretty mind-blowing. Though I do feel bad we killed the tomatoes." His lips moved into an almost smile. "But I'm not ready up here." She tapped her forehead. No point mentioning her heart. Not until she figured things out. "With the Vivian trip coming up, working out what to do about RAVEN, and getting another vision, I'm too distracted to focus on much else. Let alone pleasure. I wouldn't be fully there, and that's not fair to you."

"You do have a lot on your plate."

"I do."

He sighed. "And here I had a whipped cream and honey extravaganza planned. With chocolate sauce on hold as backup." A grin blossomed on his face, ruining the dejected act.

Kate smiled. "I see. Well, at least none of those will spoil by a delay."

"True." He squeezed her hand, and then let it go.

A weight slid from her back. She was relieved he was okay waiting on moving forward.

"What about when I get visions of the past?" she asked, Getting back on the neutral road. "Glimpses of things that have happened. Can I do the same thing? Channel it into the iPad?"

"Are these visions of the past tied to objects?'

"I don't—" Kate hadn't thought so, but maybe they'd always been attached to objects. She'd thought Ray's pipe was the first, but maybe not. "Let's say, I'm not sure if they're connected to objects."

"If we're talking objects, those are a bit tougher because they can only show you the past," Duncan admitted. "They're not as fluid in energy. It's more of a track or loop that's happened. Unlike the future visions which are still malleable, visions of the past can never be changed."

"Maybe that's why I sometimes get stuck in the memory of who that person was." Kate nodded. "When I held Ray's pipe, the poltergeist, I saw his life and almost came back as him. Not *him* him, but his feelings, his motivations."

Duncan stared at her, and she felt like a piece of white lint on a black suit. "I've never heard of psychometry being that immersive. When did that kind of vision start for you?"

Kate didn't even have to think about it. She knew the first one she'd had. She'd touched the B&B's staircase bannister and saw a young woman. Thnking back on it now, it was most likely Robert's sister. They had the same inquisitive look in their eyes.

"Five years ago," she said. "When we bought the B&B and moved in. But I didn't connect it at the time with something I had touched."

Duncan's gaze flicked to the window. "Interesting."

Kate crossed her ankles. "Is there a way to block visions from objects?"

Duncan brightened. "That I can help with. Phoebe in town has a clear silicone cream that forms a bond around your skin. It prevents the memories from an object from getting through. It's temporary though—only lasts eight hours, so you have to keep applying.

"Sign me up!" she practically yelled. Finally some good news.

Duncan laughed. "Anything to help." His phone buzzed. He grabbed it from the side table and glanced at the screen. "I best drive you home now. It's getting late."

She tried to see who'd texted him, but he slid his phone into his pocket too quickly. Kate grabbed her coat. "Come by around six tomorrow night, and then we'll head into the forest to see Vivian. It's supposed to be a clear night."

They slipped outside. The rain had stopped, but it was still chilly. They could see their breath.

She felt good they had a plan when it came to Vivian, but the bigger problem was RAVEN. She needed another vision to figure out what they needed to do next.

Hey Death Vision, you there?

Duncan stopped when they reached the car and looked at her. "Something wrong?"

"Just trying to see if my new friend was coming back soon. I need another vision. Stat."

Before RAVEN made its move on Duncan.

BETH STARED AT THE TUNNEL, MADE OF ENTWINED YEW branches just like Duncan had described. The moonlight danced back and forth with the clouds overhead, but from what she could see in the light making its way through the branches, the tunnel looked pretty empty except for leaves.

"I feel bad about lying to Kate," Sam said. "Telling her we were going off to do some research on Vivian."

Beth glanced at Sam. She barely made out the oval of her face under her huge ass rain hood. Sam probably didn't want to ruin her makeup.

"It's not a lie," Beth said. "We're doing research. Do you really want her to come up against Vivian without knowing more? And short of tying her up, we're not keeping her from visiting Caleb's daughter."

"I know. And I want to give her as much help as we can. But we could have told her the truth. That we wanted to scout around. Get intel before we come back tomorrow."

"And our sweet little Kate would just sit there and let us tramp out to the forest without her? Even on a reconnaissance mission?"

Sam let out a breath. "You're right. She would have wanted to come."

A gust of wind ran through the forest, creaking the yew tunnel. And sending rain up under Beth's baseball cap. She wiped her face with the back of her hand.

"Thanks for coming with me," Beth said.

Sam nodded. "Of course."

It felt weird not snapping at each other. Beth rolled her shoulders back. "Uh, okay, let's take a look around, see if Vivian shows us anything we can use to make the mission a more successful one, and then we get back home. Easy peasy."

Sam turned around in a circle. "I don't think those would be the words I'd use. All the ghosts just disappeared in one big poof. Like they were snuffed out."

"Great." Beth looked at the tunnel again.

And found it completely dark. Inky black. No light except for the opening at the other end, which now seemed miles away. The moon had been swallowed by clouds.

Bad things happened in the dark.

Something rose up in the distance, black against the light of the far opening.

Was it a snake? A tentacle? Was she losing her mind?

Beth wrapped her arms around herself.

Sam turned on her flashlight, but it flickered and wouldn't hold steady. "Damn batteries." She slid it back into her bag. "I'm cold. Let's get this over with." She'd taken a few steps before she stopped and turned around. "Come on, Beth."

Mildew, dankness, the familiar scents from Beth's childhood

filled her lungs. The root cellar. Barely the size of a coffin. Where they'd lock her away when she'd refused to steal for her parents.

Sometimes they'd put things in there with her. To teach her a lesson.

Scary things.

You know what happens to girls who don't obey their parents.

The words came from the trees. Her mother's voice.

Beth looked frantically around, but didn't see anything.

This hurts us more than it does you.

Her father's voice, saying what he always used to say before he latched the door. Locking her in.

"I'll be good, I'll be good," Beth whispered. "I'll do what you want."

Hands gripped her arms.

She screamed.

"Beth!" Sam's face was inches from hers. Beth's baseball hat was suddenly gone. Rain slid down her face. Sam pulled her over to one of the trees. The leaves above offering a semi-shelter from the rain. "What's going on?" She took Beth's hands in her own.

"It's nothing." Warmth mixed with the rain on her face. She'd been crying and hadn't even realized it. She was more fucked up than usual.

She'd never told another soul what her parents had done. And there was no way she was telling Sam now. She'd just think she was being ridiculous. Letting past childhood trauma stop her from walking through a perfectly fine tunnel in the woods to protect and help their friend.

Okay, a creepy ass tunnel in the woods of a crazy murderous lady of the forest, but that was beside the point.

She tried to remember the coping technique her therapist had taught her. Some crazy breathing exercise? She remembered pinching her nose and almost passing out. She probably should have kept going after the second session.

Sam pushed her hood back, the edges of her blonde hair dark with rain. "It's something, Beth. Just tell me."

Beth moved out from under the tree, letting the rain hit her fully, washing away her tears. "We didn't all have the perfect parents, Princess. Bad shit happened to me. More than the beatings. Let's leave it at that."

She tried to ignore the hurt in Sam's eyes. Using the nickname Sam hated was a dick move, but Beth just needed to get control of herself. Quickly.

Beth grabbed her hat from the ground, wiping off the mud as best she could before putting it back on her head. "Let's just go home. Tomorrow will be clear weather. We'll put new batteries in the flashlights, and everything will be fine."

Sam walked out into the rain. Her hair and face quickly soaked. "One day I hope you'll trust me again, Beth. Otherwise our friendship, our triumvirate, is never going to work." She poked Beth hard in the chest. "I love you, dammit. I never stopped. Which means you can hurt me. And I'm tired of being hurt by you." Disappointment filled Sam's eyes. "Really. Frickin'. Tired."

She walked past Beth and back the way they'd come. This time she didn't turn around. Didn't wait to see if Beth followed.

A flurry of leaves caught in the wind, spiraling around Beth like she was the eye of a hurricane.

Coward

The word raced through the branches, followed by something that sounded suspiciously like laughter.

Beth sprinted to catch up to Sam. It wasn't cowardice. It was self preservation.

She glanced quickly back over her shoulder at the retreating tunnel.

Okay. Self preservation and a bit of fear.

She wouldn't be able to chicken-shit out of it tomorrow night, otherwise Kate would know something was up.

And if Kate asked her . . . Beth knew she'd crack. Like an egg. Secrets spilling out like runny yolk.

Friendship. Love. Kate and Sam.

Liabilities someone would use against her. Sooner or later.

CHAPTER 15

"ARE YOU SURE ABOUT THIS, RED?" BETH ASKED HER. FOR the twelfth time since she'd arrived at the B&B.

Kate turned away from the muffins and faced her. "Why? Do you have a better idea? Maybe head out to the woods again without me?"

"We already apologized for keeping you in the dark."

Beth's face was full of real anguish, but Kate was still mad. Still fuming after they fessed up to their failed venture this morning.

Sam joined them, leaving Robert and Duncan at the table. "We were just trying to protect you."

Kate grabbed the muffin tray and slammed it on the counter. Beth and Sam both flinched.

"I know you think I'm weak no matter what you say. I might not have your powers, but I'm not a coward. I don't back down from a fight, or from visiting a nature deity, no matter how homicidal she might be."

Beth hung her head. "I don't think you're weak. That's not it."

"Oh really." Kate crossed her arms.

Beth's words were soft. "I don't know what I'd do if you were hurt, if you died." She finally looked up, and tears shimmered in her eyes. "I can't lose you."

Sam leaned on the kitchen island. "I can't lose you either, Kate. I won't." She held Kate's gaze. "I've lost so much already with my parents. You're precious to me. Do you understand?"

The boiling anger moved to a simmer.

"I love you both too, but I won't be coddled." Kate uncrossed her arms, letting them fall to her sides. "I don't need to be left behind or locked away. I have visions for a reason. I need to see them through." She sighed. The last of her anger draining away. "And it would make me incredibly sad if my two best friends didn't believe in me."

"I'm sorry," Beth whispered.

Sam handed Beth a tissue for her runny nose. "Me too, Kate."

Kate nodded. "Apologies accepted. We're friends. We forgive. But if you pull that shit one more time . . ."

"We won't," Sam and Beth said in unison. They sounded so much like her girls, Kate couldn't help smiling.

"All right. Get those totes over there so we can start packing up the goods."

Robert walked over to join them, his steps tentative. "Perhaps I should also accompany you to ensure Samantha's protection."

"I'm sorry, Robert, but no." Kate kept her voice gentle. She knew Robert was worried sick over Sam, and she didn't blame him. "Vivian is interested in you, which contributes to all the tragedy Duncan witnessed in his vision. We can't risk it." He frowned at her, but didn't protest further.

Kate glanced at Duncan, who stood by the back door. The sunset behind him lit the sky in beautiful reds and oranges. "I take it your mom is still upset with you going too?"

Duncan nodded, his face serious. "But she understands I need to do this. My family owes you, and I'm not sure how we'll ever repay the debt."

Beth crossed her arms. "It's kinda what we do as TOP." She glanced at Sam and Kate. "Right? Saving people and shit?"

Kate laughed softly. "Maybe it could be an idea for another reality show."

Sam let out a sharp laugh. "I can see it now. The big letters spelling TOP and then us in silhouette."

"In capes," Beth added.

Kate lifted a finger toward her. "No capes. Or spandex." She grabbed her boobs. "But I'd take a super charged push-up bra. Wait. It's television, they can tape me up or something, right?"

Sam, Beth and Duncan collapsed into laughter. Robert looked horrified.

Kate got back to the task at hand. She catalogued all the treats, counting off her fingers. "All right, we have snicker-doodles, oatmeal raisin, and peanut butter cookies. Cranberry scones. Blueberry muffins and lemon poppyseed."

Duncan leaned on the kitchen island. "And you're sure these will work as an offering?"

"No. But based on what I read in the book Logan gave me,

it's the best we got." Kate untied her apron and hung it on a hook by the fridge. "In your vision, you immediately asked for something. There was no show of respect besides words. Actions are important." Kate packaged up the last of the cookies. "Everyone appreciates kindness and consideration. Why not a forest deity too?"

"Just how did Caleb have a kid?" Beth said. "I've been trying to figure that out."

"Me too," Kate said. All the research Kate had done didn't talk about gods/deities/whatever they were procreating except in the old Roman and Greek mythologies. And many times those were with humans.

"I felt something in Caleb's tree the last time I saw him," Sam said. "There's more life, more vitality than he used to have." She glanced at both of them. "And he's looking younger too. When Robert, Duncan, and I went out there, he had newer bark coming to the surface of his skin."

"Samantha speaks the truth," Robert said. "He also appeared to have the energy of a lad rather than an old man. Perhaps when he enters these growth phases, so to speak, he can give birth to another of his kind?"

"I think something we did caused this change." Sam glanced back towards the window and the forest beyond. "Either becoming the triumvirate or when the Universe filled me with energy. Something changed that night."

The words hung in the air. Kate waited for Sam or Beth to say something. Say what they felt when Sam exploded with that energy. But they looked everywhere but at her. Interesting.

Beth tapped her fingers on the kitchen island. "Just thinking ahead . . . given our track record, what are we supposed to do if things go south? Join hands and chant? We still don't know how to work well as TOP."

"What's top?" Emily's voice startled Kate.

She jerked, sending a tote tumbling off the counter, but Duncan caught it.

Her daughter stood in the doorway of the kitchen, her red hair a wild halo around her head. Kate really needed to get a brush through that. Soon.

Patty peeped from around her shoulder. They were both supposed to be at Stu and Aggie's. She'd made sure they'd be out of the way and wouldn't know what was going on tonight.

"Did movie night get cancelled?" Her voice was steadier than she'd expected. She walked over to the girls.

Patty nodded. "Their TV is broken."

Emily eyed the boxes of muffins, cookies, and scones on the counter. "Are we having a party?"

Beth shook her head. "Nope. Just a boring adult thing we have to go to." She faked a yawn. "Your mom is dragging us there so she can offload all this sugar she stress-baked."

Kate shot her a look, but both girls laughed.

"She does that a lot," Emily said, the split between her two front teeth showing when she smiled.

Patty giggled. "I like when she stress-bakes. More for us."

"How did this become a verb in my house?" Kate tried to give them all the sharpest of looks, but they ignored her and kept laughing. She crouched and hugged them both to her, smelling their wonderful mix of shampoo, candy, and dirt. "We're going off to visit someone in the woods. Someone very powerful who can help Mr. Duncan protect the people he loves."

Emily gave her a shrewd look. "Are you scared?"

"A little. I've never met this woman before, so I'm nervous. But that's why I have Auntie Beth, Auntie Sam, and Mr. Duncan going with me. Moral support."

She couldn't tell them the truth about how dangerous Vivian was. It would just scare them, and they'd beg her not to go. But she'd also found that telling them a softened version of the truth helped. They knew when she lied outright. Somehow they could tell.

"I'll go with you." Emily straightened. "We both can."

Kate gripped her shoulder. "Thank you, sweetie. But that word, TOP, you asked about. That's what we are." She pointed to Sam and Beth and herself. "We are a magical trio of—"

"Kick-butt heroes." Sam finished for her. She slashed through the air with some very lame karate moves.

Both girls dissolved into giggles. Sam pretended to be offended.

"All right you two," Kate gently pushed them toward the stairs. "We've got to go. I bet Bronson would host movie night here. He's upstairs. You can call Riley and have him sleep over."

Patty brightened and ran up the stairs. "Bronson!" she yelled. "We're having movie night here. And we have to call Riley."

Emily hung back, waiting until Patty disappeared from

sight. She took her Tardis figure out of her pocket. She loved watching Doctor Who with Robert, who'd become an instant fan.

"Take this, Mom."

"But it's your favorite."

Emily took her hand and put the Tardis in it. "You need it more than I do. Remember, it can take you to any time, any place you want. You'll always find your way back to us."

Kate grasped it, the edges cutting into her skin, and blinked her eyes quickly. She needed to hold it together. If she cried, Emily would definitely know something was wrong.

"Thanks, sweetie. I feel much better now." She hugged Emily, holding on a little longer this time.

Robert walked over and bowed to Emily. "I hope you will allow me to join your movie night."

She gave him a considered look.

"Should I mention, I will also make my special popcorn?"

"Deal." Emily grabbed his hand and pulled him toward the stairs. She waved at everyone through the slats.

Beth laughed softly. "Your kids are something else."

"They are." Kate grabbed her coat, tucking the Tardis into a pocket. "We better get going. We've got a nature deity to visit. And hopefully she likes snickerdoodles."

EVERYONE WAS SILENT WHILE THEY MADE THEIR WAY NORTH deeper into the forest. The only sound was the muted crunch of damp leaves underfoot and the rustle of their bags filled to the brim with the offerings.

"Did you notice the crows?" Kate looked over at the trees. Here and there, shiny dark eyes glimmered in the moonlight. "I read up on them. They're not supposed to be nocturnal."

Sam nodded. "Caleb's will is stronger than nature, it appears."

"His crows give me the willies." Beth shrugged like she'd had a shiver. "Especially the ones doing that hop/walk thing beside us."

Beth was right. Kate wondered what they'd report back to their master.

Duncan stopped in front of a long tunnel of yew trees with their branches entwined overhead. Kate couldn't see the moon through the dense branches. It was complete blackness inside the tunnel. At the very far end, she saw the exit.

"We have to go through there." Duncan pointed into the tunnel.

"I'm just going to climb over the top," Beth said. "I've seen too many horror movies to go through a pitch black tunnel."

The crows cawed out a warning behind them, and the trees making up the yew tunnel suddenly filled with tawny colored owls. Their eyes caught the moonlight, flashing yellow. The crows took off in a flutter of black wings and wind, deserting them.

The hair on Kate's arms rose, and it had nothing to do with the chilly air. "Vivian's got to be controlling the owls. Like Caleb with his crows. Though this feels worse. They're not going to let you climb, Beth." Her voice was a whisper.

No one protested or disputed her words. They must feel the presence in the owls' eyes like she did. Watching.

Sam took a step toward the tunnel. "It's settled then. This is the only way through." Sam handed Beth a flashlight. "New batteries all around." She clasped Beth's shoulder. "You're going to be fine."

Sam was comforting Beth?

Kate looked at both of them. "What am I missing?"

Beth shrugged off Sam's grip. "You're not missing anything major." She turned on the flashlight. It flickered and went out. "Piece of shit equipment." Beth threw it to the ground. Sam picked it up and put it back in her bag without saying a word.

Sam tried her flashlight too. Same thing. The only one that worked was Duncan's.

Kate took in Beth's white face, shaking hands, and the coating of sweat on her forehead. The flashlights. The way the dark tunnel reflected in Beth's eyes. Not to mention the kid gloves Sam was using with Beth.

This is why they failed when they came last night.

"You're afraid of the dark, Beth."

Beth look down, just giving Kate a tight nod. "My parents."

Anger shot through Kate. She'd seen as a child firsthand how Beth's parents had tortured her mentally and physically. She fisted her hands, and then released them. Beth didn't need her rage, she needed her friend.

"What did they do?" Kate asked.

Beth hesitated and Kate sensed her struggle inside.

"They used to lock me away when I was bad."

Beth's voice sounded fragile, like it had when Kate first met her in school. There was more to what Beth's parents had done, but now was not the time to take a deep dive into the damage.

Duncan's face held sympathy. "Look, this isn't your town, Beth. And not your fight. I'll go alone. Maybe without Robert or Sam, things won't get so bad."

"No." Kate's voice rang out in the forest. The owls rustled, looking unsure. "We're all going. Duncan, you lead."

Duncan nodded and turned his flashlight back on.

Kate looked at Beth and Sam. "We're TOP. We've got this. We're all stuck with each other. For better or worse. At least I bring awesome baked goodies to the table." She tried to get a little spark of anything out of Beth. But Beth's eyes were latched onto the tunnel.

Sam sighed. "Your scones are incredible, I'll give you that. Which means, I'm going to definitely gain weight with all your stress-baking. Maybe we need to open our own gym, Beth." She took Beth's hand.

Beth kept staring at the tunnel. "I don't think I can do this."

"You can. You faced down a serial killer. This is small potatoes compared to that," Sam said. Her words didn't banish the fear in Beth's eyes.

Beth's parents hadn't taken care of her, hadn't protected her. Instinct spurred Kate words. "I'm not going to let anything happen to you." She grabbed Beth's free hand. "You trust me, right?"

Beth inhaled, and then nodded. "Always."

"I'm not going to let go of your hand," Kate continued. "And neither is Sam. You're safe in between us."

"I've got you, Beth," Sam said. "I won't ever let go." A fierce light shone in Sam's eyes. She meant every word.

Beth turned and looked at each of them. "Promise?"

"Promise," Kate said, with Sam echoing the word.

Beth squeezed her eyes shut, and then opened them. She took a tiny step forward. And then another.

Kate wasn't a violent person, but she'd have done some serious harm to Beth's parents if they were here. Lucky for them, they were still in prison.

Duncan's flashlight was a bobbing beacon ahead.

Kate blew out a breath and followed, her grip still on Beth. "I like your idea of a gym, Sam. What would you call it?"

"We could call it Princess Moves," Sam said, obviously picking up on Kate's lead. Keep talking, and maybe they'd distract Beth, just a bit.

"Always thinking about yourself. Typical." Beth's voice was one fourth of the usual snark, but it gave Kate hope that they could get through this.

She couldn't see Sam or Beth clearly in the darkness. Just the bobbing light of Duncan's flashlight.

Halfway through the tunnel, something skittered to the right, and Beth jerked, stumbling into Kate.

"I think something brushed by my leg." Sam sounded worried, but still holding it together. "Probably a squirrel."

Duncan's flashlight sputtered. Flickering. He hit it against his hand. It flared one more time, and then went out.

Beth's grip on Kate's hand tightened painfully.

"Oh fuck, oh fuck, oh fuck," Beth repeated over and over.

A low growl sounded from behind them. Beth tried to break from Kate's grip, but she held on.

They needed light. Otherwise Beth would bolt and who knows what the hell was in this tunnel with them.

"Sam, give me your other hand," Kate urged.

Even in total darkness, Sam managed to slip her hand into Kate's. The energy circuit between them hummed immediately into place. Kate hoped it would calm Beth a little.

But they needed light. It didn't make sense, but she felt compelled to call it, to summon it somehow. "I see through time," Kate said loudly. "Let me see now. Bring us light."

"Something touched me." Beth's words were hysterical. She started struggling again.

"Hold her, Sam!" Kate yelled.

"Kate." Duncan's voice held a note of panic. "There's something blocking the exit."

They needed to get through the tunnel. Now.

She knew she wasn't saying it right. She'd been close before. Then the words were out of her mouth before she realized it. "I am the Oracle. I command time. Let me *see.*"

A glowing dot winked and glistened near Kate's hand. Like an ember from a bonfire. She could see movement within. Almost as if it was a small bright TV screen.

"What is that?" Sam asked.

"I'm not sure," Kate replied.

More embers floated down through the yew branches. They

hovered above their heads, illuminating the area around them. Within each, Kate sensed there was more than light.

Eyes shone from the shadows, and then retreated. Kate concentrated on the glow, willing it larger, and it flooded the tunnel with light. Flashes of fur and feather and teeth and claws retreated from the oncoming glow.

"What the hell is that thing?" Beth lifted a shaking hand toward the lumbering mass moving away from the exit.

"No clue," Sam replied. "But Kate just kicked butt without raising a finger."

Kate smiled, feeling the glow of warmth inside her, just like the light outside. "Let's get out of here."

They hustled through the remaining tunnel without incident. When they stepped through the exit, the lights slowly died out. Embers blowing away in the wind.

That had been a warning shot across their bow. Vivian had wanted to scare them off.

She'd underestimated them.

Kate adjusted the bag on her shoulder. "Come on. Let's get this done."

KATE HEADED OFF DOWN THE PATH, FOLLOWING THE LINE of owls in the trees on either side.

"Am I the only one who still thinks this is a bad idea?" Beth said.

Kate turned around. "Bad idea or not, we're going this way.

Through the scary forest, to the scary tree, to meet Caleb's scary daughter. Got it?"

"Geez, she conjures up some fairy lights, and she thinks she's all that. Our little Pip," Beth said behind her.

Sam laughed softly. "Our little Squeak never let anything stop her."

She knew what they were doing. Trying to make things light because they were both scared. She was scared too.

"I told you both I don't answer to Pip or Squeak any more." Kate tried to be stern, but couldn't help the smile on her face.

She'd missed having her friends here. Not across an ocean, not across a phone line. Here. Well, maybe it wasn't the most appropriate friend time to be tromping through a forest towards potential death armed only with snickerdoodles, but they were still together.

Duncan took the lead with her. He hadn't joined in their bantering. His eyes locked on the forest ahead as if waiting for Vivian to suddenly appear. She didn't blame him. He'd already seen what Vivian could do.

They continued on for a bit until Kate felt the forest change. The trees were still the same, but there was a stillness. They were being watched, by more than just the owls.

And it was colder suddenly. She wrapped her scarf tighter, her breath sending plumes of mist. Sudden deep hoots filled the air. Kate jerked and noticed Sam did as well. Duncan and Beth were still, their eyes scanning the trees.

The entire forest felt alive and on alert. "Do you sense anything, Sam?"

"Energy coming up through my boots. Like with Caleb, though this feels different." Sam crouched to the ground and dug a bit through the hard surface. She plunged her fingers into the dark soil underneath. "Caleb's energy always feels like life itself, bright. Vivian's is the whisper of death, pulling rather than giving."

"Pretty accurate," Duncan muttered. "She definitely has an air of destruction around her."

"This is usually the place in the horror movie where everyone is screaming that we should go back now," Beth said.

Kate couldn't argue. The urge to run through that tunnel back into her lands vibrated in Kate's legs.

Her lands. She'd always felt that way. That connection. But not here. These lands were foreign. Hostile.

Kate led on. The path only went one way.

Just a few minutes later, they came into a clearing surrounded by trees resplendent in all the colors of autumn. They were so perfect in placement and color, it felt like someone had painted them.

"That's her tree." Duncan indicated the massive yew tree in the center of the clearing. It was almost split into two, like it had been struck by lightning and reformed after the damage.

"What now?" Kate asked.

Duncan looked at Sam. "You summon her by cutting your hand with one of your daggers and letting the blood soak into the ground. It gets her attention."

Kate looked around. "Let's begin this differently then. She already knows we're here. She might like to make a big show of things like Caleb. Let's let her have her moment."

Kate started unpacking the baked goods. She placed them in front of the tree. Several owls watched her from their branches, but didn't move.

The forest was still quiet. It didn't look like Vivian was going to make an entrance.

Okay, onto Plan B.

Kate held her arms wide. "Vivian, we seek your help. As a show of our good faith, we have brought you gifts from my hearth. Made by hand, with intent, with love, with hope."

Beth gave her a "you crazy" look, Sam nodded encouragingly, and Duncan watched the clearing as if waiting for the inevitable attack.

Sam gasped. "She's coming."

Several leaves wafted to the ground though there was no wind.

"It has been a long time since a Triumvirate of Pluthar has ventured into my woods." The voice was smooth, like liquid moonlight. Delicate, yet unnerving.

Kate was dying to ask how many TOPs there had been, but she didn't think a Q&A with Vivian was the right way to start things. She glanced at Duncan, not sure what to do next.

He jumped in. "We do not seek your counsel lightly. We have a great need."

"There has never been a Triumvirate of Pluthar such as you three. I want to taste the power in your veins. And your truth. The blood never lies." Again the voice sounded pleasant, but underneath there was a clear threat.

At least this was different than what Duncan had seen. Though Kate felt queasy just thinking about cutting her hand.

"Unless you don't truly want my help." The tone was dismissive, as if any moment, it would be gone.

The look in Duncan's eyes was desperate. She couldn't blame him. His town was at stake.

Kate held out her hand to Sam. "You've got your daggers with you, right?"

Beth held up her own. "What's wrong with mine?"

"I don't know where yours has been." Kate gave her a wink.

Beth nodded. "Point taken. Are you sure about this, Red?"

Kate nodded. Sam handed her one of her daggers. The iron felt like ice in her hand.

They stood in front of Vivian's tree in a line, Sam in the center as always, and together they cut into their palms. Kate hissed at the sharp pain, and then it was gone. They curled their hands into fists and let the blood drip down into the grass around Vivian's tree.

A wind whipped up, sending Kate's hair this way and that.

Necromancer

The whisper sounded on the wind.

Seeker

The leaves rustled the name.

Oracle

The tree limbs creaked her title.

Clouds rolled in overhead, sending the moon alternately into shadow and brightness.

This wasn't creepy. Not creepy at all.

Duncan moved in closer, guarding their backs, his attention on the rest of the clearing.

A brightness grew in front of them. In the tree. The center began to glow like it had captured the disappearing moonlight above. Then the light flashed with blues and greens. The wind increased and picked up bits of leaves, rocks, and earth, sending them into the light.

"If an alien comes out through a transdimensional portal," Beth said, "I'm running. Screw this."

Kate and Sam laughed. It was nervous laughter, but it felt good. On instinct, Kate grabbed Sam's hand, and she saw Beth do the same.

"Let's make sure Vivian sees our strength, up close and personal," Kate said, reaching across for Beth's free hand. "Not just through her owls' eyes."

When Beth's hand clenched Kate's, the circuit between them felt stronger this time. The blood from their cuts flowing into each other. Joining them even stronger.

Flashes of lightning arced through Sam's green eyes. Beth's eyes had gone completely black. Kate knew hers had turned white.

It suddenly felt like they stood ten feet tall. Together, they could accomplish anything. And for the first time, she knew they all believed it. Even just for a moment.

Vivian's voice cut through the air. "Impressive." She sounded bored, but Kate didn't miss the undercurrent of respect. "How did you know where to find me?"

Kate quickly dropped her hands, breaking the connection.

They'd shown their worth. There was no reason to look threatening.

Duncan stepped forward. "Your father, Caleb."

"I don't believe you. My father doesn't even remember I exist."

There. A tremor at the edge of her voice. Duncan's vision had been right—she was lonely. She missed Caleb.

"He gave me a piece of himself." Duncan held out his palm, and small green shoots burst from his skin, mixed with blood. His face tightened in pain. Leaves sprang from the shoots, and they turned toward the energy still swirling in the center of the tree as if it were the sun.

The light from the center of the tree blazed so bright, Kate was blinded. Then it faded, and a woman stood in front of them.

Vivian had curves just like Kate's. Long dark hair fell to her waist, but here and there were strands of copper and the green color of moss. She had the same bark-like skin of Caleb, from what Kate had seen that one night, but it was smooth and clear. If she wasn't looking hard, she wouldn't have known it wasn't skin. Her dress looked like the Autumn leaf section of a craft store had exploded, but in a tasteful way.

Vivian stalked forward, the leaves of her dress whispering with each step. She grabbed Duncan's wrist and brought his palm close to her face. Her eyes were rings within rings. Black on the edges, then gold, then green, then ending in a swirl of reddish brown.

Her mouth opened slightly as if in surprise, and Kate caught a glimpse of sharp teeth, almost in the shape of an owl's talons. A sudden look of longing swept across her face, and then it disappeared.

She released his wrist, and Duncan rubbed it. The red imprint of her fingers remained on his skin as if he'd been burned.

"Why would my father send you?"

Duncan took out a dampening stone from his pocket. One that had been burned black. "He told us you might know where we can find more of these. We use them to protect our town."

Vivian walked to the left, and everywhere her feet touched, flowers sprung to life, then withered, then sprung to life again.

"I might know where they were last seen." She stopped for a moment in front of the boxes of cookies, muffins, and scones. Vivian's fingers brushed across the top of one of the cookies. Then she snatched it up in a blur of motion and took a bite.

Kate tensed. This would go one of two ways. She hoped it was the good way.

A look of pleasure filled Vivian's face. "It has been too long since I have enjoyed the food of humans." Her multi-colored eyes fixed upon Kate. "I taste the love you have, the longing for something you have sought for years, and the fear of my reaction." Vivian finished the cookie in one large bite. "No further sacrifice will be required to be in my presence. These offerings will suffice." She started on a scone next.

"Thank you." Kate bowed low. She had a feeling some acknowledgment was required for Vivian's pronouncement.

Vivian resumed her walk, nibbling on the scone. "However, the knowledge of the stones is another matter. What are you prepared to offer for that information?"

Kate knew that the lands wouldn't entice Vivian. Duncan's vision had told her that much. Like Caleb, she craved companionship.

"As long as any member of the Triumvirate of Pluthar remains in Scotland, we will come and visit you."

Vivian arched an eyebrow. "This offer is weak. All members of the Triumvirate must remain in Scotland."

Kate looked at Beth and Sam. She hadn't expected this outcome.

"I've already decided to remain," Sam said. "I can write from anywhere."

Kate noticed she'd left our any mention of Robert. Wise. Very wise considering how Vivian had been obsessed with him in Duncan's vision.

Beth crossed her arms. "I hate the rain. I'm not moving here." She took a deep breath. "But I'll visit regularly. Make sure these two don't get themselves killed."

Vivian smiled and quickly turned away as if she didn't want them to see. "What makes you think this offer would interest me? I have seen other Triumvirates rise and fall before you."

Vivian turned back to them. A spiral of small plants grew up around her in a horseshoe pattern. They didn't wither and die.

Kate was cautiously hopeful, but sensed the trigger wires laced between her words. She couldn't tell her about Duncan's vision. Her gut was very emphatic about the danger there. No one likes to be seen as lonely. Human or otherwise.

She thought of all the things she could say. How they could

keep her company. How they might learn from her. She could take a page from Robert's book and use beautiful and flowery words to charm Vivian.

But that wasn't Kate. And she knew about messed up families.

She put her hands on her hips and faced Vivian. "Your dad has done us a solid on more than one occasion, and I'm getting the feeling he thinks we're his pet Triumvirate. I don't like that. No one owns us. Not Caleb, not the Universe. So if you really want to piss your dad off, having us visit you regularly will do the trick."

Vivian seemed to ponder her words deeply. "As enticing as your offer is, I believe there might be something else I would like more."

There was a scuffle behind them and shouts that sounded all to familiar before the trees branches pushed forward two small bundles of clothing into the clearing.

Not bundles of clothing.

Emily and Patty.

CHAPTER 16

KATE RUSHED TOWARDS HER GIRLS AND GATHERED THEM IN her arms. Her heart thundered loudly in her ears. Every part of her wanted to run through the forest, right now, before Vivian could react. Get her girls back to safety.

But she didn't want to scare Emily and Patty. Her younger daughter was already scrutinizing her reaction with narrowed eyes.

"How did you two get here?" Kate studied their dirty and defiant faces.

Emily pushed her shoulders back. "Patty knew you needed her, and I couldn't let her go alone. Besides, we're family. We do things together."

Pride warred with fear inside Kate. "You were both very brave to go through the forest at night. Weren't you afraid?" Voice almost normal. Good.

"We had Caleb's crows keeping us company most of the way," Patty said.

"How do you know Caleb?" Sam asked.

Emily smiled wide. "We talk to him all the time. He's funny."

Kate felt dazed. Caleb? With her girls? She'd been trying to give them as normal a life as she could, but she suddenly realized how ridiculous that was.

Patty pulled on her sleeve. "You told me when I had that feeling, when I knew I could help, I needed to do it." Her eyes flickered across Kate's face. "Did I mess up?"

"No, honey." Kate kissed her forehead. "Though I'm still not happy you went off on your own into the forest, you did the right thing."

Patty smiled and color bloomed in her cheeks.

As much as she wanted to, she couldn't rewind what had happened. Apparently, both her girls had inherited the charge-in-to-danger gene from Kate.

Both Sam and Beth moved back to stand beside them. "Sounds like it's time to go," Beth said. "Now that the kids crashed the party."

But Kate knew they'd never make it if they ran. Not only would the owls attack, based on how their claws were clenching and unclenching the branches they gathered on, but Vivian could send her killer roots and vines after them. Then they still had the tunnel to make it through, and in the state they were in, Kate wouldn't be able to summon the lights again.

They'd come for the stones, but now all she could think about was protecting her children. They needed to get out of here safely.

Duncan met her gaze. Though his face was filled with despair, he nodded. "I'm sorry, Vivian, but the children aren't part of any negotiation. I withdraw my request for the dampening stones. We will leave your forest."

Kate blinked back tears. He was giving up everything they'd come for without hesitation. All those people at risk from RAVEN. People he was sworn to protect.

"Even when I have the means to save your *entire* town?" Vivian's voice took on a sly quality. "For centuries to come?"

A loud scraping filled the clearing. The base of Vivian's tree moved, a section of the wood sliding back and revealing a cluster of dampening stones. There were at least five she could see, with more in the back.

"Oh Lord." Duncan's whisper was ragged.

Vivian's gaze flicked to Kate's daughters. "To sweeten the deal, I can also teach you how to bring the stones back to life. In return, the girls will stay here, with me—unharmed, I promise."

She moved her fingers just slightly and the blackened stone by Duncan's feet rose into the air. It floated into the center of her tree, then emerged a moment later, glowing like new. Clear and beautiful. She let it fall on the ground next to him again.

Duncan just stared at it. Frozen.

Sam walked over and placed a hand on his shoulder. "I promise, we'll figure out another way to save your town."

Duncan nodded. "Thank you, Sam. I'll need all the help I can get." He looked over at Kate. "Because no matter the enticement, I would never trade your children." His eyes glistened with his own tears. "Ever."

Sam lifted a hand toward Vivian. "Is there anything else you would take in trade for the stones? Anything?"

"Mom, who is that woman?" Emily pointed at Vivian. Her typical whisper that was more of a shout. "She looks mad."

Vivian turned her attention from Sam and fixed it on the girls. She smiled, and it was as if the sun came out and bathed her in happy golden light. "Come closer, children. I can't remember the last time a child entered my woods."

It reminded Kate too much of the Wicked Witch of the West. If Vivian started saying "my pretty", they were taking their chances on an all out run for freedom.

Her body tensed, adrenaline rushing through her limbs. Vivian would have to go through her to get to her girls. "Girls, stay here." She kept their hands in hers.

Vivian frowned, and a cold wind whipped through the clearing. "I will not harm them. I would never harm a child."

Sam nodded at Kate. "She's telling the truth."

Vivian looked surprised, but the frown remained.

They couldn't run and make it out alive. If there was a way they could leave peacefully, Kate had to try.

Kate walked toward Vivian with the girls. "These are my daughters, Emily and Patty." She dropped her grip on their hands, but was ready to grab them back at the first sign of anything fishy.

Patty waved at Vivian, not looking worried at all. Emily just crossed her arms and jutted out her chin as if daring Vivian to do something.

Vivian crouched, her dress billowing out, and flowers

burst into bloom around her and the girls in a riot of yellows, oranges and blues. The air became warm, like Spring had arrived early.

"Do I frighten you?" Vivian's voice was soothing and musical, like a lullaby.

"No," Patty said. "You're the one who's frightened."

Kate was on hair trigger, waiting to yank Patty back.

Vivian looked puzzled, not angry. "Very little frightens me, child."

Patty smiled gently. "We're all frightened of being alone." She held out her hand toward Vivian.

The last thing she wanted was Vivian touching her daughter. Kate pulled her back a step. "I think it's time to go, honey. Say goodbye to Vivian."

"No." Patty gazed up at Kate. "This is the way, Mommy. The way we get to go home without anyone being hurt."

Kate looked at Emily, who just nodded. Beth shook her head and motioned for them to run.

Sam gazed at Vivian. "Promise us you will not harm nor change Patty in any way through your touch or by any other means."

Vivian's face became serious. "I promise."

"It's up to you, Kate," Sam said. "She's telling the truth."

"Please trust me, Mommy." Patty's voice was pleading. "I know what I'm doing. You said it wasn't a bad thing to use my gift to help others."

Kate gazed into Patty's eyes. This would be a deciding moment. If she didn't trust Patty now, they might lose any trust in the future. And her gut told her to let Patty do her thing.

"Okay, baby. I trust you."

Patty's face lit up, and she turned to give Vivian her hand once again.

Caleb's daughter stared at her hand for a moment, a shiver of fear dancing across her face, and then she took it.

Patty's eyes frosted white.

Kate gasped, but Emily touched her arm. "It's okay, Mom. She's like you."

Patty stroked Vivian's hand. "I see you with your daddy. Right here. Where you were born."

Vivian's intake of breath was loud. A flock of owls took flight, hooting and circling.

"Show me." Vivian's face lost its sharpness.

"Mommy, I want you to see too." Patty lifted her free hand towards Kate. She took it.

And suddenly, the forest fell away around them and was rebuilt in Patty's vision. Kate didn't know how Patty was sharing her vision with her, but she paid attention to everything.

The trees were smaller, and everywhere, the sun touched the tips of the branches.

Caleb walked into the clearing, his steps strong and sure. He was much younger. His skin the bark of a sapling—still pliable and fluid. A little girl was in his arms. No. Not a little girl. Not exactly. It was a collection of sticks and leaves in the shape of a girl. She looked about the size of Patty.

Kate sensed a tiny spark of life within her.

Like a firefly buzzing in the void of night.

"He gave everything he had because he loved you." Patty's voice was soft.

Caleb got on his knees, laying the stick girl before him. He looked up at the sky and spread his arms wide. "I kept the balance. Kept my word. Kept Entwine safe. Please grant me this wish."

Clouds gathered above, churning. The clearing was doused in darkness.

"You understand what you ask?"

The deep voice came from everywhere and nowhere. It was the same as the one Kate had heard the night they'd brought Robert to life.

The Universe.

Caleb nodded. "I've tried to keep her alive on my own, but I've failed. I need your help."

"A sacrifice is necessary."

"I know." Tears like fat raindrops rolled down Caleb's cheeks, but were quickly absorbed back into the wood of his skin. "I will do anything for my child. To bring her back."

The clouds disappeared, and the sun shone again into the clearing. A shaft blazed bright around them.

"So be it," the Universe proclaimed.

Caleb collapsed to the ground, beside the stick girl. A beautiful green glow rose from his chest. It hovered in the air above the two of them.

His skin darkened, losing its luster. His limbs thinned to narrow sticks. Everything that had made him vital fled from his body.

Kate wanted to turn away, but she couldn't.

The green glow dove into the stick girl, and she jerked. Once, twice, and the third time, her mouth opened and she drew breath. Sticks became limbs, hair flowed from the dark leaves around her crown. The berries for eyes dissolved and became real. She blinked and stared at her new hands.

Sitting up, she gazed at Caleb. He struggled to rise. She lifted him up to his feet as if he weighed nothing. And he looked like he barely did. Just a bag of sticks moving somehow.

Patty let go of Kate's hand, and she was suddenly back in Vivian's clearing.

Kate's cheeks were wet, her eyes sore from crying. "Caleb almost died giving you life."

Tears fell from Vivian's eyes, and every place they fell, flowers blossomed. Her hair filled with blooms as well.

"I didn't know." The otherworldly tone she'd had was gone. She just sounded like a young woman. Lost.

Patty nodded, her eyes back to their usual brown. "I had a feeling about you. Mommy says it's my gift. I knew you needed to remember." Her lips trembled. "Just like I do. Our daddies loved us very much."

Vivian pulled her into a hug. Kate didn't feel the need to stop it and wondered about the change. But everything inside her told her the threat was gone. Dispersed by her seven-year-old daughter, wise beyond her years.

"Thank you," Vivian whispered into Patty's hair. "Will you come back and visit me?" She gazed at Emily over Patty's head. "Both of you?"

Emily pursed her lips. "Will you teach me how to talk to your owls?"

Vivian laughed. "Child, you have gifts you don't realize yet. I will teach you many things."

Patty pulled back and touched Vivian's cheek. "I'll come back, but only if I can bring your daddy too. He misses you so much."

More tears flowed down Vivian's cheeks and she nodded. "Hold your hand out." She gestured to Emily. "Both of you."

Kate stepped forward. "Wait a second. Why?"

"You are a good mother," Vivian said. "Not quick to trust one such as I. But I seek to give your girls a symbol that will grant them safe passage through the tunnel into my lands. It will not hurt them."

Sam nodded at Kate and mouthed "green light".

"I'll need one too, then." Kate held out her hand. "And I'm first."

"Your left hand instead," Vivian said.

"What's wrong with my right?"

"My father has plans for that one."

Great. Just great.

Vivian smiled and plucked a flower from the ground, then wrapped its stem in a strand of her hair. She placed the flower on Kate's palm.

It sank into her skin, but she felt nothing. No pain, no sensation. Left behind was an etching of the flower in her skin. It had a faint sparkle in the outline, but unless you were looking for it, you'd never see it.

"Are you still Kate?" Beth asked. "Or have you been body snatched?"

Emily giggled. Kate laughed too. "Nope. Still me."

She let the girls do the same thing she had. Emily studied it closely, while Patty kept flashing her palm back and forth to have the moonlight catch the etching.

Duncan cleared his throat. "What would you accept for this?" He held the revitalized dampening stone in his hand. "It will hold off RAVEN a bit longer."

Emily frowned at Vivian. "He needs more than that. A lot of people could die."

Vivian's face softened. "And you know about death, do you not, little one?"

"My dad." Emily's face was strong, but Kate saw the tremble in her lip. "He died. And so will the people of Mr. Duncan's town if we don't help them."

Vivian rubbed her hands together, looking just like her father. "I will grant him these stones if you agree to come visit me every week."

"Woah, woah, woah." Kate held up her hands. "I've heard about Caleb's deals. And Sam's Bargains. I'm not letting my kids get mixed up in this."

Vivian pursed her lips. "Let's call this a friendly agreement. If the girls don't visit, I'll simply take back my stones."

Sam gave Kate a thumbs-up.

"And you need to promise that you will never harm or change my daughters in any way ever. I won't allow them to visit you without this assurance."

"I promise to never harm or change your daughters in any way ever." Vivian gazed at Emily and Patty. "I will give you an additional assurance as well. I will protect your daughters to the best of my ability, to save them from harm."

Sam gave Kate two thumbs up.

"Okay," Kate began. "Let's say they'll visit—"

"Mom," Emily interrupted her. "I've got this."

Patty nodded emphatically. "Caleb has been teaching Em all about deals."

"Oh, he has, has he?" Kate was going to throttle that ghost when she saw him. Well, she couldn't actually touch him. But Robert could. Teaching her daughter about deals. Who did he think he was?

Emily put her hands on her hips, reminding Kate of herself. "We'll visit once a month."

"Twice a week." Vivian countered.

"Twice a month."

"Once a week."

"Three times a month."

Vivian clapped her hands together. "Done." She gestured toward her tree, and five stones floated out to Duncan.

He gathered the stones into one of the bags they'd used to bring in the baked goods. "Thank you Emily, Patty." He gave them a bow. "And thank you, Vivian. I know you care nothing for the outside world, but this will save many lives."

Vivian looked at Emily and Patty. "Perhaps I will now have a reason to care."

The girls hugged Vivian, peppering her with questions about

what owls ate, could the land feel sadness, and did trees laugh?

"What just happened?" Sam asked looking as puzzled as Duncan.

Kate shook her head slowly. "What was supposed to happen."

No one died. Duncan would save his town. And a rift had been mended in a family.

Actually, in two families.

There wouldn't be any more secrets between her and the girls. If she'd ever needed proof they were part of all this, she'd just gotten it.

"THEY WON'T STOP TALKING ABOUT VIVIAN," BETH SAID, grabbing another bowl of stew from Kate. She ate like she had a hollow leg and never put on a pound. Kate would hate her if she didn't love her so much.

Beth looked over to where the girls sat, arguing over crayons in the kitchen. Patty wanted Sunset Orange, and Emily was bargaining for her to take Mahogany instead. "They're trying to get her dress just right."

Kate nodded. "I know. As soon as they woke up this morning, all they could do was go on about what they were going to learn, when could they visit. She obviously made quite the impression."

"Everyone have enough stew?" Kate raised her voice to cut through the crayon discussion.

Sam nodded as did Robert. Michael held up his bowl. Beth

sighed and grabbed an extra helping for him. She made her way over to their table and sat down.

Kate still couldn't believe everything that had happened last night. Her daughters tromping through the woods, saving them. She still needed to have a word with Caleb about what he was teaching them, but deep down, she knew his intentions were good. He was just lonely for company.

She knew she had a village helping her raise the girls, but she hadn't expected that the ghosts would pitch in.

Emily caught her eye, waving her over. Kate took her plate and joined her daughters at their smaller table.

"What is it, baby?"

Both Patty and Emily suddenly looked serious. Kate wondered if Patty had seen something else? Something really bad?

"Don't touch it, Mom," Emily said, "Not yet."

"Touch what?"

Emily put something on the table, on top of her drawing of Vivian. It was an action figure. It looked like a G.I. Joe. It was missing an arm, and mud crusted its side.

Whispers brushed against her skin. Kate looked around. Beth was laughing at Michael. Sam and Robert were busy snuggling. This old house carried sounds. But whispers?

Then a scream sliced through her ears. A woman's voice. She sounded frightened. In pain.

Kate stood up, eyes darting this way and that, but it was obvious no one had screamed.

Beth flashed her a concerned look.

Kate tried her best everything-is-okay-move-along smile.

She sat back into her seat. "Did you hear that?" she asked the girls.

"Hear what?" Emily asked.

Patty picked up the Sunset Orange and filled in a portion of Vivian's dress. "Mommy's hearing this." She tapped the rounded tip of the crayon against the arm of the G.I. Joe.

"You hear it too?" Kate asked.

Patty nodded, not looking up from her drawing. "But it's not calling for me." She lifted her eyes to Kate's. "It's calling for you."

Kate's stomach dropped like she'd just jumped out of a plane without a parachute. Well, it could call all it wanted. She wasn't going to answer. Besides, with needing another vision about RAVEN, she couldn't afford to be pulled into a random past memory.

Emily looked at the G.I. Joe. "Am I going to start hearing things and seeing things too, like Patty?" There was a mix of worry and hope in her voice.

Kate picked up the Periwinkle crayon and pushed the action figure further away with the dull end. "I don't know, Em. But whatever you end up doing or not doing, you're still perfect to me."

"Even if I'm not like you two?" Emily asked.

"It'd be boring if you were," Kate replied. "We need some variety in this family. And I have it on good authority that soon you'll be talking to owls." She pointed a finger at Emily. "But none in the house okay? I'm not cleaning up owl poop."

Both girls laughed, and Emily looked satisfied with her answer. She filled in the bottom of Vivian's dress with black.

"So, where did you find it?" she asked the girls. "The garden?"

"No." Patty looked disappointed. "*He* gave it to Emily. She went into the forest without me, Mommy. Again."

"Tattle-tale," Emily fired back.

"Teacher's pet," Patty responded.

Kate grabbed both their hands, getting their attention. She had a feeling who the "he" might be. A chill ran down her back. She shivered. "This G.I. Joe was given to you by Caleb?"

Emily nodded. "We were playing fort. His crows bring me sticks to build it, and it's so cool." Her eyes were alight. "We even have a moat. Caleb helped me dig it."

Patty pursed her lips. "I told you to wait for me so I could play too."

"You were playing ghost hunters with Riley," Emily said. "They're in love, Mom. It's gross."

"Are not!"

"Are too!"

Sam walked over. "Is there a problem?"

Kate looked up at her and found everyone's eyes and attention on them. "So far, only the usual sibling rivalry."

And a creepy action figure that's going to come to life and attack them all. Okay, maybe she'd seen too many horror movies, but that scream was not a happy one. And if the action figure came from Caleb, that couldn't be good.

Emily handed the G.I. Joe to Sam. "Caleb asked me to give this to Mom."

"What is it?" Beth came over, with Michael and Robert following.

Sam handed her the doll. "Maybe a gift for mending things with his daughter?"

Michael shook his head. "Caleb must know he owes you all a lot, but this feels like something else." He closed his eyes. "The emotions emanating from this thing are bad news."

Kate ate her stew, not looking at Michael. The fact that he felt it too was not comforting.

Everyone handled the action figure, and flecks of dirt rained down on the kitchen floor. Kate put down her stew. "People, I just swept the floor." She got up and grabbed the broom.

Sam took it from her and swept up the dirt.

Robert looked contrite. "I apologize for the mess we have caused. But I have found something of interest." He turned the G.I. Joe over, carefully capturing a few dirt flakes with his free hand. "There is a name on the bottom of the foot. It says Ollie."

Sam stiffened. "Ollie might be a nickname for Oliver. Caleb mentioned something bad had happened in the woods last time Oliver Wilson was there."

Robert nodded. "Something that he did not share with us. Could not share." He put the action figure back on the table. "I believe this is Caleb's gift to you for bringing Vivian back into his life. His only way of telling you what happened that day. And it must be something we need to succeed in our quest."

Beth crossed her arms. "I agree with Robert. Caleb's taking a big risk that the Universe might find out." She glanced at the ceiling as if the Universe was watching right now.

Kate sat at the table again. "The Universe sees everything, of that I'm sure. So, this must be an acceptable way to get us the information we need. Indirectly."

"And you'll need to use your powers to see it," Sam said. "There's a balance maintained."

"I don't want to touch it." The scream she'd heard sounded like someone was being murdered.

Beth raised a dark eyebrow. "We're not going to have to go through this again, are we?"

"Easy for you to say," Kate replied. "You don't have to get sucked into someone else's horrible memory." She stared at the action figure. "There's some nasty, shi . . . stuff that happened with that thing."

Sam touched her shoulder gently. "So, what do you want us to do?" She held up her fingers and ticked them off. "Commiserate, beg, guilt trip, or let you finish your stew first?"

"Damn, Sammy. You're always so smooth with the digs." Beth gave Sam a slap on the back.

Now it was Kate's turn to frown, knowing she probably looked like one of her girls. And as much as she protested, she knew she had to see what the G.I. Joe wanted to show her. Caleb had taken a risk to get her this information.

"Fine." Kate pushed her stew away. "I know you know I know that I'm going to do it no matter how much I argue." She looked at her daughters. "It's time for bed anyway. Head on up and don't forget to brush your teeth."

The looks they gave her were unyielding. In unison, they

both shook their heads. "We're staying." Emily's words were firm.

"I might come back as something mean—just for a bit, but it might scare you."

Emily took her hand. "We're not leaving. Family sticks together. Remember?"

Patty placed her hand over theirs. "We love you, Mommy."

"I've been seriously underestimating you both, haven't I?"

"Yup," Emily said.

"Pretty much," Patty added with a smile.

Kate couldn't help but smile back. "You can stay, but if you get scared, or if anything gets scary—" She gave Sam a pointed look. Her friend nodded. "—you let Auntie Sam know, and she'll take you upstairs."

"I can leave if you want," Michael offered. "You've already got a full audience."

"I believe your skills will be in need," Robert said. "Beatrice has shared you might be able to sense if Kate brings back emotions which are not hers upon her awakening."

Beth fiddled with her set of wooden spoons. "So, we won't need to potentially hit her with something?" Emily frowned at her, and Beth looked uncomfortable. "Sorry kid, I was just kidding."

Kate took her bowl to the sink. "Why do I always have to do the scary stuff?" she muttered to herself.

Sam came up behind Kate and whispered "I had to fight off a serial killer."

Beth put an arm around both of them. "I had to deal with

the fear of losing my two best friends. And if anyone repeats that, I will know." She kept her voice low too.

Kate hugged them, feeling safe for one brief moment. "Worst pep talk ever." She pulled back and looked up at them. Just a few months ago, everything had been different. Now she had them to lean on. It was still going to take some getting used to. But she was happy to try.

"We love you, Red," Beth whispered and kissed her right temple.

Sam kissed her left. "TOP powers activate."

Kate laughed. Couldn't help it. Okay, enough stalling. She gave them a final squeeze, and then walked back over to the table.

Sitting down, she opened up her hands, palm up. "Okay. Bring it on."

Robert placed the G.I. Joe in her hand, and like someone had pulled out a vacuum, the kitchen was sucked away to be replaced by a night sky, glittering with stars.

She looked down at her feet, finding grass below.

And blood.

CHAPTER 17

THE WORDS ON LOGAN'S COMPUTER SCREEN GREW FUZZY. He rubbed his eyes and took another sip of cold coffee. It was only seven p.m., but he'd been there since four in the morning, unable to sleep.

Kate was determined to go up against RAVEN. People were in trouble, which meant Kate would run headlong into danger. So he was going to give her as much information ammunition as he could find.

He'd been researching the shadowy organization all day. Calling old contacts and other stations to see if they had heard of anything resembling RAVEN. He didn't use their name, knowing that would likely flag something in the system.

"There's a call out on Miller Road." Constable Burns poked his head into Logan's office. "A car fire. I've already notified Reece at the fire station. I'm getting ready to head out there."

"Casualties?"

Burns shook his head. "Not sure. That's why I want to be

there. Kelly and Evens are already at the domestic disturbance at the O'Reillys."

This was the busiest Thursday night they'd had in years. Something must be in the air.

Logan stood. It felt good to stretch his legs. "I'll stay until someone gets back."

"Are you sure? I can call Mitchell to come in and cover the night shift."

"No. He's still recovering from the flu. It'll be fine." Logan walked past him to the coffee maker. Sheila usually kept it humming, but she'd already gone home for the night. "If another call comes in, I'll cover it."

Burns nodded and hurried out the front door, ringing the chime that went off every time the door opened or closed.

Logan filled the coffee filter with the necessary scoops and then added an extra one. He needed all the help he could get to stay awake.

The door chimed behind him.

"Did you forget something, Burns?"

"Hello, DCC Dunning."

Logan didn't recognize the voice. The hairs on the back of his neck rose. Something he still trusted in. Sheila called it his Spidey-sense. He called it his survival mechanism. It had saved him and Graham many times when they'd been growing up.

He turned around slowly, the coffee canister still in his hands. "Can I help you?"

A man stood by Sheila's desk. Tall. Muscular, but lanky. Red hair. Mustache and close cropped beard. Casual clothes, but expensive. Late twenties, early thirties. Dark green short jacket without any noticeable bulges for a weapon.

"I came as fast as I could. Sheila left me a voicemail. She said she was your assistant." The stranger looked concerned. Genuine. Logan didn't detect any of the usual tells. "She said Kate was in danger."

"Kate Banberry?" The stranger nodded. Logan put the canister down on the counter. Movements still nice and slow. He didn't have his billyclub on his belt. "Sheila went home a couple of hours ago. It had to have been a prank."

Confusion clouded the stranger's eyes. "If the call wasn't genuine, this means it's a trap."

"Who would want to trap you?"

"RAVEN. You wouldn't have heard of them. They're a—"

"Black ops military group," Logan finished his sentence. "Kate filled me in."

"I'm Duncan Forbes." He held out his hand, and Logan shook it.

The pieces clicked into place in Logan's mind. Kate had mentioned a Duncan who she needed to save when they'd been at Dr. Withers' house.

Duncan scanned the station. "Do you have a back door?"

"This way."

They'd gotten a few feet when the sound of cars pulling up outside reached Logan's ears. More cars than what his team had.

Logan pointed. "That way, down the hall and make a left. I'll lock the doors. Buy you some time."

He raced to the front doors, locking them. He doused the lights too. They didn't need to make themselves easy targets.

He slipped his cell phone out of his jacket. No signal. He moved to Sheila's desk, keeping low. Landline was dead too. He grabbed the radio next. Static. He switched to a different channel. The same.

Duncan came rushing back. "They've already got operatives outside."

Logan eased around to the side of the front window, looking through the slats of the blinds. There were at least five heavily armed men. Soldiers by their stance, though they weren't in any official uniform. They hadn't started firing yet, which meant they preferred Duncan alive.

The radio on Sheila's desk let out a shrill squeal and then a voice came on. "Come out, Duncan. Let's do this the easy way. If we have to come in there, people could get hurt."

"Where are your constables?" Duncan whispered.

"Out on calls." Most likely manufactured calls to get the station deserted. Logan wasn't supposed to be here. They'd probably hoped to capture Duncan standing outside the police station. Neat and clean.

"Is there another way out?" Duncan asked.

Logan had already run through the possibilities. He ran them again in case he missed anything.

Front window. Out.

Back door already covered by RAVEN.

Crawlspace. Half-filled with dirt. No exit.

Roof. No access points to get there.

Side window in the lunch room. It would be covered as well.

There was one option left. A tunnel. But he hadn't been down it in years. Not since he'd been initiated into the Freemasons.

He looked down at the tattoo on his arm. Maybe it was time something good came from it.

He put his hand on Duncan's shoulder to make sure he had his full attention. "RAVEN will come in here eventually, and I don't have time to booby-trap the station to give us any advantage. If I were them, I'd forgo the guns—too much risk they might kill you—and opt for either flash bangs or tear gas, or a combination with tranquilizer darts to take you fast."

Duncan's face dropped from worry into resignation. "What are our options?" He earned a notch of respect from Logan for not acting like the typical civilian and understandably losing focus when faced with a threat.

"Say something to stall them," he said to Duncan. "I'll get supplies from the back. And stay away from the windows. If they're using heat vision goggles, they won't be able to see through the walls. We don't want a preemptive snatch and grab."

Duncan clicked the radio. "Who are you?"

The voice was calm, in control. Logan didn't recognize it.

"You know who we are, Duncan. We've heard of your skills. How you can see specific times, places."

Logan left the sounds of the conversation behind and rushed back to his desk and unlocked his drawer. Got the key to the armory.

He raced to the armory and grabbed several knives, tear gas

canisters, masks, flashbang grenades, and two kevlar vests. The vests were old, but better than nothing. He shoved all the loose items into a backpack.

Logan slipped on one of the vests and ran back to Duncan.

"There's an old tunnel in the armory. I'm going to see if it's blocked. Keep them talking."

Duncan nodded. "Not many people know that I can direct my visions," Duncan said into the radio. "How did you find out?"

"Your friend Ken Allen told us what you can do."

"Ken wouldn't have shared that. You're lying."

Logan rushed back to the armory again. He pushed aside the desk he'd placed in front of the tunnel's hidden opening. When they were initiated, they'd been told the tunnels had originally needed keys, then combination numbers as they were updated with technology. Now, they were equipped with scanners. You just needed the right image.

He lifted up the piece of flooring covering the scanner and the sealed tunnel entrance. The scanner square winked green at him. Waiting.

Duncan's voice reached his ears. He was yelling at RAVEN. Not a good sign.

Logan dropped to the floor and placed his forearm with the Freemason's symbol over the scanner. The light moved up and down his arm.

A sharp hiss sounded, and then a cracking, fading into a rumble. The tunnel opened. The musty smell of mildew mixed with earth rose up from the opening.

Cobwebs coated the entrance. Logan quickly pushed them aside. The metal ladder was still there. However, the tunnel could be filled with dirt part way through. Whether or not this would lead him and Duncan to the side of the Scottish Glamour store five blocks down, he didn't know. But they were just waiting to be taken if they remained here.

He ran back down the hall. "This way," he hissed at Duncan.

Duncan dropped the radio and ran towards Logan.

"Were you screaming at RAVEN?" Logan asked, leading Duncan into the armory.

Duncan nodded. "I demanded proof of something before I would come out. They know I'm stalling, but they want me alive. I figured it'd buy us a little time."

Logan lifted his chin towards the dark tunnel entrance and handed Duncan a flashlight. "There's no time to confirm if it's blocked or not. Or it could cave in, killing us both."

Duncan's expression sobered. "I'm willing to take the chance. If RAVEN captures me, I'm as good as dead." He flicked on his flashlight and disappeared down the ladder.

Logan followed him, and then used the scanner on the inside wall to close the tunnel.

He only hoped they weren't exchanging one trap for another.

THIS WAS DIFFERENT. THE OTHER TIMES KATE HAD touched an object, she'd immediately felt the jostling for control in her mind. The feeling of being "other" because she was in someone else's memory—the memory from the object.

Why wasn't she feeling the dreaded pull sucking her in? This felt easy. Almost comforting. Like it was her memory. Which was ridiculous.

She looked around. It was her forest. Not a surprise considering where the G.I. Joe had come from. The night was cold. She could see her breath. Maybe Novemberish?

Blood. She'd seen blood. She gazed down. There it was. Near her feet. It belonged to someone she knew. No, someone Oliver knew. A flash of blue against the tree trunks up ahead told her she was right. She'd found her.

Who was *her*?

A surge of hope flooded her system.

"Rhona, where are you!" an angry voice shouted from behind her. Her vision shifted, she was losing herself, she was becoming . . .

Oliver turned around. His father was still a distance away. Oliver would might have time to save his mother. If his father found her first, he'd finish what he'd tried to do earlier.

He'd kill her.

Quickly covering the blood by pushing some leaves over it with his foot, he glanced back at the direction of his father's voice. Then he ran toward the flash of blue he'd seen between the trees.

He was tall for his age, all leg. At eleven, he was already the size of boys two or three years ahead of him. Each stride ate up the ground. He didn't dare run, for his father might hear the rustling of the leaves.

"Mother," he hissed. "Where are you?"

She peeked around one of the beech trees, twice as wide as she was. Blood soaked into the right sleeve of her jacket. His father had missed with his shot, only grazing her arm. "Oliver. Thank goodness. Where is your sister? We need to leave. Now."

He reached her in a few more steps. "You'll never escape with both of us, Mother. He'll find us."

She shook her head. "No. I can't leave you with him. Not now. Not now that I've seen what he's truly capable of. I didn't believe it before." Her eyes dropped to the blood on her jacket, then she looked up, her gaze latching on him. "If anything happens to me, you have to protect Mackenzie."

"Of course I'll protect my sister. I always have."

She gripped his arm tightly, almost painfully. "You don't understand. Mackenzie is special."

His mother wasn't making sense. "You need to leave, right now. He'll kill you if you don't." He pushed a small bag into her hands. It held all the money he'd been able to pull together. And his mother's passport.

Her red hair looked like fire in the stark light from the moon above. At 5'1", his mother was just a few inches taller than he was. His father's genes were strong in him, whether he wanted them or not.

She opened the bag and looked inside. Tears welled in her eyes. "I won't leave you and Mackenzie."

Oliver didn't have time for tears, and neither did his mother. "Come. I'll take you to Mackenzie." He took her hand and led her further away, through the woods. Away from his father *and* his sister. He'd left Mackenzie by the one of the old beeches where she loved to play. Far away from this madness.

"Oliver!" His father's voice rumbled through the trees. He was close.

"Go." He pushed his mother toward the edge of the forest and freedom. "I'll distract him. Help you get away."

His mother swayed on her feet, holding her stomach. He wondered if she were ill. "I won't leave you."

On impulse, he shoved his favorite G.I. Joe into her coat pocket. "Take this." It was still missing its arm, but it was his lucky charm. His mother needed it more than he did.

Her fingers closed around the G.I. Joe tightly. A single teardrop slid down her cheek.

A flash of pink through the trees caught his eye. His sister had found them. She threw herself into their mother's arms, crying.

"Come, both of you. Quickly." His mother turned to leave, but the crack of a tree branch told Oliver their time was up.

"Running off to meet with him again, Rhona?" His father asked.

His mother turned around. "James, please let us go."

Mackenzie stopped crying, but she didn't loosen her hold.

"You've sinned against God." His father joined Oliver, his gun in his hand. "Don't think I don't know about your condition."

"What condition?" Oliver couldn't help asking. He'd wondered if she were ill. Was she dying?

His father's face darkened even further, as if he were suddenly the night sky above. "Should I tell him or would you like to?"

His mother shook her head and looked down.

She was dying. He knew it.

"Your mother is pregnant." His father seemed to enjoy every word, a smile playing at the edges of his lips. "By another man."

Relief flooded through him. He didn't care she was pregnant. All that mattered was saving her.

"Father, put the gun away. We've found her. Let's go home." Oliver took a step toward him. The gun shifted to point at him.

"Step back, son, and let me do what I must. No one makes a fool of me. No one."

Oliver's mind whirled. Should he try to wrestle the gun from his father? Would he get shot in the process? If he pushed him to the left, the shot would most likely just graze his arm or shoulder. Going low to hit his stomach wasn't wise—the gun still had a chance to go off, and both Mackenzie and his mother were in range to be hit.

Before he could make a decision, a flurry of black exploded from the trees. Crows. Oliver threw up his hands against the feathers, the beaks, the claws.

But nothing touched him except air buffeted by the strong beat of wings.

Through the blackness, he saw his mother turn and run, carrying his sister. She got to the edge of the next row of trees. Was there a man standing there? He looked like he had a staff. That was ridiculous. Oliver was seeing things.

My father can't shoot through this. She's going to make it.

The crack of the gun beside him was so loud, his ears rang.

Oliver dropped to the knees, the crows disbursing as if the shot had been a signal.

His mother was on the ground. Oliver got to his feet and ran at full speed. He would get there before his father. After that, he didn't know. Didn't care. He had to make sure she was still alive.

Mackenzie screamed and it was like nothing he'd ever heard. It cut into his head. He felt like he would be ripped apart. His skin pulled back from his face, legs twisting underneath him, pushing him to his knees again.

Clumps of earth rose from the ground. The trees shuddered, cracking, branches breaking off and flying through the air. He rolled to the side to prevent being impaled by a nasty looking piece of beech.

His father came up beside him, dodging and ducking as well until a rock the size of a small dog hit him square in the stomach, bending him over. Another rock smashed into his head. He collapsed onto the ground. Blood soaking into his hair.

With his father incapacitated, this was Oliver's chance to get his mother and sister to safety. If only they could get out of the chaos caused by this sudden freak storm.

He rose to his feet, pushing against the wind. But it was too strong. It slammed him back against a tree, pressure crushing his chest.

His little sister wouldn't stand a chance. She had to take shelter. If only he knew where she was. He tried calling her name, but couldn't get a breath out.

Then he finally saw her. She sat crying. Untouched by the

maelstrom around her and their mother.

What?

His mother stirred, lifting her hand toward Mackenzie.

The wind died, and the pressure evaporated against Oliver's chest. He sagged down, leaning back against the tree.

When he finally was able to lift his head, his mother was gone.

Mackenzie walked over to him, half stumbling. "Sorry, Ollie." Her face was stained with dirt caught on her tears. "I didn't mean to hurt you."

He thought about the trees, the earth, the storm which had suddenly swept through the forest. "You? You did all this?"

His sister nodded. "But that man took her away." She pointed to where Oliver had seen the shadowy figure. "I couldn't stop him."

His mother had escaped. And his sister had incredible powers.

He glanced over at his father. Though he was bloodied, Oliver saw the rise and fall of breath in his chest.

For a brief second, he wished the boulders had finished him off. He should do it himself. Now. It might be his only chance. Leaving him alive meant he would continue the work at the facility. Oliver had seen what was done there. The experiments. His father believed they were saving the world, but Oliver knew better.

His father didn't seek to save the world. He sought to control it.

Oliver's hands opened and closed before finally clenching

into fists. He wouldn't become his father. He wouldn't kill.

Even if that meant that now that his father knew what his sister could do, Mackenzie's future only had one outcome.

RAVEN.

Logan coughed. The air felt heavy in the tunnel. But so far the passageway itself wasn't blocked, so he'd take a little discomfort in his lungs if they made it to the exit by Scottish Glamour—and hopefully beyond RAVEN's search grid.

He looked back at Duncan. There was only room for single file.

"How do you know, Kate?" He'd wanted to ask that question right away, but RAVEN had interrupted any chance of an interrogation.

"I met her through my brother, Michael. You know Samantha Hamilton, Kate's friend? She and Michael used to date."

Cagey.

"Known her long?" Logan dipped his flashlight down to show a deep puddle in their path so Duncan could avoid it.

"Not long."

"Yet you were willing to risk your life coming down to the station because you thought she was in danger?" Logan stopped and turned to face Duncan.

Duncan looked anywhere but at Logan. "This isn't really the time to dig into my motivations. RAVEN could be in the tunnel at any moment."

Logan didn't move. "Not unless they're freemasons born and raised in Rosebridge. Only we have this particular tattoo." He held up his arm toward Duncan. "Kate told me RAVEN is interested in people with special abilities. What are yours?"

Obviously nothing they could utilize as a weapon, as concealment or for escape, otherwise Duncan would have used it by now.

Duncan finally met his gaze. "I see the future. I'm helping Kate with her visions."

Not what he wanted to hear. The same type of ability as Kate. That already gave them a bond.

"Are you two dating?" From Duncan's fidgety stance, there was definitely something going on.

"No." Duncan ran a hand through his hair. "Not really. Nothing serious yet. We're just taking it slow and seeing where things go." He crossed his arms. "Are you asking in an official capacity DCC or because you're in the race too?"

"There's no race to win. We're talking about the heart of a smart, incredible and amazingly frustrating woman." Logan shook his head. "Kate will decide who she wants. Not us."

He turned and headed down the tunnel again, his steps dragging. Kate had known Duncan a short time and had already begun something. And they had shared abilities. Duncan was someone she could commiserate with.

But they did barely knew each other. Even Duncan was unsure where they stood. What they had was fragile at best. Logan had stability on his side. And affection. He knew Kate cared for him at least as a friend. And didn't the best relationships start as a friendship first?

He picked up the pace, his heart a little lighter.

"Has she always run straight into trouble?" Duncan's voice was hesitant.

"Always."

Duncan pulled on his arm, stopping him. "Look. I didn't realize you two had something going on."

"Nothing romantic." Not yet anyway.

Duncan studied Logan. "How long have you known her?"

"Five years."

Duncan whistled. "And how long have you been in love with her?"

He wasn't about to tell a stranger it had been love at first sight. She'd come into the station and tripped on the mop the janitor had left out. He'd helped her up, and as soon as she'd smiled at him, he'd been a goner.

"We're good friends." Logan lifted his chin. "I count that as an incredible blessing."

Logan turned and continued down the tunnel.

"So you're not worried I might steal her affection?"

Logan turned sideways to squeeze through a more narrow section of the tunnel. It looked like part of it had given way and flooded the tunnel with dirt.

"After seeing my brother's crazy obsession with Kate, there's no way I would get in the way of anything she wanted. And if that means you two become serious, if she's happy, that's what's important."

Even if it meant his heart was broken. He just had to trust she'd eventually realize he was the one for her.

"You really are a good friend to her." Duncan sounded almost disappointed. "She's lucky to have you in her life."

"I'm the lucky one."

Duncan remained silent after that. Just the sound of their breathing and steps in the tunnel. They finally came to the end and another ladder leading up.

"You should stay here in the tunnel," Duncan said. "Give me a flash bang and some tear gas. I'll take my chances."

"You'll need a distraction to get away. We're close enough in height that in the dark and with the tear gas masks on, they won't be able to tell us apart." Logan pointed up. "The tunnel opens up in the alleyway. You go one way and I'll go the other. Split their forces."

Duncan's eyes filled with worry. "They'll kill you if they catch you."

"You won't make it on your own. I knew what I was signing on for when I became a constable."

Duncan clasped his shoulder. "You truly are the better man, Logan. And it pains me to say that."

"If we both make it out of this alive, you'll owe me a beer."

"Deal."

They stared at each other for a moment longer until it was suddenly awkward.

"So, what's the plan, DCC?"

"When the tunnel door opens, you run left to the end of the alley and then a hard right. You'll see the forest straight ahead.

Once there, you should hopefully be able to lose them," Logan said. "I bet you Kate's forest ghost would help."

Duncan looked surprised. "You know about that?"

"I know about a lot of things."

"If I get away, I'll owe you a steak as well."

"Done." They shook hands, and Logan had a bad feeling it might be the last time.

Logan loaded a tear gas canister into the gun. Flash bang primed to pop. Mask in place. He watched Duncan do the same.

Logan climbed the ladder and placed his forearm against the scanner. It hummed, rustling back and forth. The ceiling above began to pull back over the ladder.

He peeped over the edge quickly. The alley was empty.

Scrambling up and out of the tunnel, Logan ran to the right. He heard Duncan's footsteps disappearing behind him as he ran the other way.

Logan stopped at the end of the alley and listened. No sounds except the wind. He peered around the side. RAVEN operatives were heading his way. From their stance, they didn't know he was there. It was most likely a standard search perimeter once they'd realized they'd escaped the station.

He hoped again he was right about the guns. He would really like to live through this night.

Logan burst out of the alley and ran straight across to the next one. Shouts and cries rang out behind him.

He ducked into the back entrance of the bakery. The door was recessed and would give him momentary cover. The operatives walked in front of him, their steps measured, eyes searching. He jumped out from hiding and fired the tear gas canister into the chest of the nearest operative. The flash bang went next.

Logan closed his eyes and rolled to the left, knowing he'd hit the steps leading down into the library's basement. The stairs were hard. He'd have bruises tomorrow. But it would take him out of the brunt of the tear gas' air flow.

He hit the bottom, and his mask cracked on the side. His skin burned just slightly, but he could still breathe.

The sound of choking and curses reached his ears. Then a radio crackled to life.

"We've caught him. Return to base."

The coughing faded. The operatives leaving. Then there was silence.

Their efforts had failed. Duncan had been caught.

He knew Kate would want to rescue him. He was part of her vision. Duncan had been in his charge and Logan had failed. He'd go with Kate to rescue him.

He slid his phone out from his pocket and called Sheila at home. She picked up right away, and he filled her in on what had happened.

"Get everyone back to the . . ." He broke off, his lungs seizing up. The teargas had pooled around him in the cramped space. "Sheila," he croaked.

His vision blurred. He dropped the phone. The dark pavement rushed up to meet him.

CHAPTER 18

KATE OPENED HER EYES AND FOUND HER KITCHEN surrounding her once more.

Everyone was gathered in a horseshoe pattern around her. She scooted her chair back.

"I'm not a science experiment, people. Give me some room." No one moved.

Michael shook his head. "I only feel confusion. Nothing dark." He smiled. "And she's mad. I recognize that energy signature. It's definitely Kate."

She knew they were just being cautious, but it still pissed her off. "Show's over. Can I get a glass of water?" She handed the G.I. Joe to Robert.

Sam gave her a glass of water, and she took a long drink. How was she okay? No coming back feeling the need to save someone? No big internal battle to retain herself. Did that mean there wouldn't be an issue touching objects any longer? Or was something else going on?

Both her girls sat directly in front of her. Knees almost

touching.

"Did I scare you two?" Kate tried to keep her voice easy and light. She still wasn't sure what she looked like when she touched an object.

Emily shook her head. "Nope. It's just like when you take a look-see." She narrowed her eyes. "But I could feel you still here. You didn't go away like usual."

"I felt it too," Patty said.

"Did you help me in there, Patty?" Maybe that's what was different. She had someone with her, grounding her, keeping her partially in the kitchen.

"I didn't do anything, Mommy." Patty scrunched her face up like she did when she was thinking hard. "My gifts are different."

"I'm glad your gifts are different," Kate said. And that Patty wouldn't have to go through what Kate did when she saw into an object's past.

"But it helped, right?" Emily asked. "Mr. Caleb said it would. He's really smart."

Kate got to her feet, everyone still watching her. She walked to the back door, looking out at the garden. There was only a half moon tonight, but it still brightened the darkness. A shadow moved by the tree line. Was it Caleb checking to see if his plan worked? She looked around, but didn't spot any crows.

"I found out it's Oliver's dad who runs RAVEN. Oliver was eleven years old in the memory I saw." She turned around and leaned on the kitchen island. The cold of the marble reminding her of the memory.

"Here, Mom." Emily had her cardigan in her hands. Kate shrugged it on and hugged her daughter. Patty ran over and hugged her too.

Kate just held onto them, onto their love like a tangible thing. For the first time, they were going through this together as a family. And it felt right.

She sat back down at the table and told them everything she'd seen and felt. Kate downplayed the intent-to-kill aspect of her vision, not wanting to frighten the girls, but she knew the adults would read between the lines.

Robert had made coffee while she told her tale. He'd gotten proficient at the process under Beth's guidance. Those two made a funny pair.

"Caleb tried to help them." Sam took the cup of coffee Robert handed her. "That much is obvious."

Beth turned her chair around and straddled it, leaning her elbows on the back. "But why didn't he go all attack-crows on the dad like he did to Graham?"

"I thought about that too," Kate admitted. "I think it has to do with whatever rules govern the forest. You, me, and Sam are part of TOP, so when Graham was trying to kill us, it would have upset the balance if he succeeded."

"Yet he did seek to prevent the murder of Rhona, Oliver's mother," Robert added. "And perhaps he was the one who secreted her off to safety as well." He sat next to Sam at the table. "I fear there is much we do not understand about Caleb's motives."

Michael had a notebook out. Just like Beth did. "Alright,

so to recap, we don't know what happened to Oliver's mother. His sister, Mackenzie, is either locked away at RAVEN or being used by them."

Kate touched his notebook with her finger. "We can't rule out that she might be a willing member of RAVEN. Her dad might have messed with her mind even further after her mom left."

Beth whistled. "I hope she's not a willing participant. If she had that kind of firepower at five years old, who knows what she could do now? Maybe crack a city in half?" Patty gasped. "Ooh, sorry kid. I'm not used to having little ones listening."

Robert put his cup down. "With your permission, Kate, I can see the girls to bed. Emily is already attempting to catch flies with her great yawns."

Emily tried to look miffed, but it was ruined by another yawn.

Kate gave them each a kiss on the cheek. "I think Mr. Robert is absolutely correct."

"But I'm not tired," Patty protested. Emily nodded in agreement.

"Well, I'm pretty tired," Kate said. "And I'll need both your help tomorrow to go through what we know and how to stop RAVEN. I want you fresh and rested. Can you do that for me?"

That perked them up. They bounced up and down like she'd announced a trip to Disneyland. Robert didn't even have to take their hands. They ran up the stairs before him.

Sam took a sip of coffee. "Are you really going to let them help with the planning?"

Kate nodded. "To cut them out now would damage what

we're starting to build here as a family. But I'll talk to everyone ahead of time to keep the discussions to the tactical side. Nothing scary, nothing that sounds like we won't succeed, etc."

"That's smart," Michael said. "Our parents did the same when we started to learn about the Covenant. It helped us feel included, bonded. Keeping secrets breeds mistrust and causes children to try to discover things on their own." A shadow passed over his face. "Sometimes with disastrous results."

"Yeah, you're not a normal family with normal family issues," Beth agreed.

Michael rubbed his eyes. "I think it's time I headed—" The sound of the Star Trek transporter blasted from his pocket. He took out his phone and squinted at the screen.

Michael's face had lost all color. "Glenna just texted. Duncan's gone. No one knows where he is."

Kate grabbed her phone from the charger. Two missed calls from Duncan. No messages.

"I'm calling Logan," Kate said. "He knows about RAVEN, and he can help look for Duncan."

Logan's voicemail came on immediately. She called the station instead. He sometimes worked late.

The line clicked. It was Sheila's voice.

"Sheila, it's Kate. I'm trying to reach Logan, and he's not answering his—"

"He's in hospital." Sheila's voice was rough with tears.

"What happened?"

"The station was attacked."

All the blood drained from Kate's face. She felt dizzy. "What do you mean the station was attacked?"

Michael tensed beside her. Beth shot Sam a worried look.

"He was trying to save someone." Sheila's voice shook. "He was exposed to tear gas. A lot of tear gas."

Kate clicked off the phone, her mind in a daze. Duncan was missing. Logan was in the hospital.

RAVEN had already made their move.

They were too late.

KATE DIDN'T WANT TO GO THROUGH THE HOSPITAL DOORS. Those doors led to bad memories. She just stared at them.

But Logan was inside. And she'd almost lost him.

"You can do this," Sam said. She and Robert had come with her to the hospital. "I felt the same way at the police station, remember? You just have to breathe through it and remember the this is different. You're different."

But it felt the same. Her heart still raced, her hands were sweaty, and her legs made of lead. The doors were only a few feet away, but they might have been miles.

"Is Beatrice here?" Kate asked.

Both Robert and Sam said, "She is." At the same time.

"Tell her I'm glad she's here. It feels a little less scary when she's around."

Sam held out her hand. "Did you want to hear what she's saying?"

Kate grabbed her hand right away and heard Beatrice's voice.

"I was with you, lass, every time you visited Paul. You were never alone. You'll never be alone."

Tears rushed to Kate's eyes. "I wish I could hug you."

"Well, we all have rules to follow and roles to play, Kate. The shackles of the past hold no weight for you now."

She knew what Beatrice said should be true, but her heart still felt heavy.

And if she didn't start moving soon, they would think she was a nut job or something.

She dropped Sam's hand. "Okay. Let's go." Robert opened the door for her. Kate stepped inside, breathing in the tart smell of alcohol mixed with the powdery scent of rubber in the air.

Those smells swept her away, bringing her back to Paul's chemo treatments. The second round had failed. Seeing him in his hospital bed looking so frail . . .

"Excuse me, Kate, were you here to see Logan?" Constable Burns had appeared in front of her. He nodded towards Robert and Sam.

She blinked her eyes, feeling slightly dizzy. "Yes. Is Logan allowed to have visitors?"

"He is. And I know he'll be happy to see you. Follow me."

Robert and Sam stopped in the waiting room. "This is from Beatrice," he said and gave her a hug. "And Beatrice also says we are to stay in the waiting room. Something about you needing privacy to finally tell Logan how you feel."

Kate felt her lips twist. "Did anyone ever tell her she's pretty bossy?"

Sam laughed. "Every day." She hugged her too. "Good luck."

Constable Burns took her down a hallway, then another, and pointed to the door at the end. "I've got to get back to the Station, but tell him I'll call him later with an update."

She just nodded, unable to speak.

Hospital rooms were on either side of her. There was a baby crying. She heard someone talking on the phone. Everyone unaware of what was happening around them. Of who was dying.

The door opened to Logan's room, and she heard his voice.

"I told you I feel fine." He sounded impatient, frustrated, and very much alive.

The tightness from her chest down to her stomach released, and she grabbed the wall for support. She took a deep breath and then another. Her legs finally moved, and she made it to his room.

Logan sat on the side of his hospital bed and pushed away the nurse's hands. "Tear gas effects wear off in thirty to sixty minutes once you're out of the dispersal range."

The nurse gave him a stern look. "We've rinsed your eyes and given you oxygen, but that doesn't mean you have a clean bill of health. And you need to keep putting this ointment on that rash for the next twenty-four hours."

"If I promise to follow your instructions, can I go?"

"Logan Dunning, you just settle down now. I've seen you in diapers." She winked at Kate.

Logan's eyes widened, but he stayed silent.

The nurse huffed, but appeared satisfied. "I'll see if I can wrangle up Dr. Lowry to dismiss you. But if you leave before then, I'll tell this lass stories that you don't want me to be telling."

"Yes, Nurse Briard." Logan flashed Kate a look.

"Don't worry, Nurse Briard," Kate said. "I'll make sure he stays put until the doctor gives the all clear."

The nurse nodded "At least someone has some sense." She left the room.

Kate went over to Logan. "Did she really change your diapers?"

Logan nodded. "That's the problem with living in a small town."

Kate tried to smile, but she couldn't. "I was so scared."

Scared you were dead. Scared you were hurt. Scared I would never see you again.

"You're trembling." Logan squeezed her shoulder. "I'm okay, Kate. You're not going to lose me that easily."

She hadn't seen this in any of her visions. Him getting hurt. But it happened anyway.

You didn't have a vision because you didn't need to save him.

She ignored her suddenly logical inner voice. She'd never imagined she'd put Logan in danger. "I'm so sorry I involved you in all of this."

Logan patted the hospital bed and she sat next to him. "The station and a threat against you was a convenient means to lure Duncan out. That's all. I'm just angry he got caught."

Kate shook her head. "And I'm angry they used me as bait."

"They must have known you two were seeing each other."

Though his words sounded matter-of-fact, she heard the hurt underneath.

She grabbed his hand. "It's nothing serious. I really just needed to figure things out."

Logan perked up. "Like what?"

She hesitated. He could have died tonight. Was she really going to keep quiet?

"I had to figure out how I felt about you. About us."

He stayed silent, but his thumb rubbed the top of her hand. It soothed her.

"At first I thought you might not like me that way." She met his gaze and smiled at the understanding there. "Then I came up with a list of reasons why we might not work. You know, the girls would never forgive me if I screwed things up. They adore you."

Logan brought her hand to his lips.

A shiver ran through her. Not just through her body, but through her heart. He rested his cheek against her knuckles, looking at her from under unfairly thick lashes.

"I love you, Kate." His breath danced over her skin. "It feels so good to finally say it."

Another shiver, quaking the dark shell around her heart. A crack. Behind the shell was where the potential of real anguish lie. A painful beam of light snuck in, burning the darkness with the beginning of hope.

She recognized the feeling inside her. And it was wild, bright, and definitely not safe.

"Damn it." She breathed the words.

Logan let her hand go. "What?"

"I've fallen a little in love with you."

A smile lit his face, moving up to his eyes, filling them with warmth. "A little can grow."

"That's what I'm afraid of." She hopped off the bed and turned away, eyes unfocused on the wall in front of her.

Imaginary moments played through her mind. What it could be like if they got together.

Waking up and seeing Logan next to her. Him helping the girls with their homework, then tucking them in. Rocking on the chair swing together, gray dotting both their hair.

Tears rushed to her eyes. If she had something like that again, like what she'd had with Paul, she'd be opening herself back up for possible heartache. Could she really go through that once more?

She'd thought it had just been guilt over not seeing Paul's cancer in time that stopped her from opening up, but it was fear too. Fear of feeling that anguish all over again.

She felt the warmth of his body behind her before he touched her shoulders gently. "I promise you, even if things don't work out, I will never abandon the girls. I care about them too much."

The conviction in his words was unmistakable. And if Kate knew anything about Logan, he kept his word. But she couldn't turn around. Not yet.

"And what about me?"

"What about you?"

"If we break up, would you still be my friend?" She realized all those other reasons she'd come up with before were really hiding what she feared the most—losing Logan as a friend.

"True friendship never dies," Logan said.

"Did you read that on a fortune cookie?"

He turned her around slowly. "You seem determined to predict an awful future for yourself. Things don't always have to end badly."

She let out a ragged breath. "That's all my visions are. Something bad happening. People being hurt, dying sometimes."

"But this isn't a vision, this is your life. Isn't it time you discovered what it could still hold?"

Intellectually his words made absolute sense. Emotionally, retreat mode was still vying for attention.

She'd believed Sam and Beth would come back into her life, would be the friends she'd remembered. And even through the pain, and years, it had happened.

Kate had always taught the girls to follow their heart, to listen to that voice inside. And that voice was telling her to take a chance. It sounded an awful lot like Beatrice giving her a talking to.

She looked up at Logan. "I guess I can't make you promise to live forever?"

He laughed. "Just like I can't make you promise to stop chasing danger." He grabbed the tissue box from the table and held it toward her.

She pulled one out and blew her nose. "Danger is my middle name, you know."

"Patience is mine." He cupped her cheek, his thumb wiping away a tear.

For the first time, she didn't pull back. She let herself feel not only his fingers against her skin, but the promise of what might be. What could be.

"I'm scared." Just saying it made her feel better.

"Me too. But since when has that ever stopped either of us?"

She took his hand from her cheek and just held it. "Speaking of scary things, I'm going to rescue Duncan."

"I know. I'm going with you."

No hesitation. Almost as if he'd been waiting for her to say it.

What if something happened and he got hurt? Or killed?

"Are you sure? It'll be dangerous."

He smiled again, crinkling the edges of his eyes. "Well, then I guess it'll be a good thing that you'll be there to protect me."

Logan knew about her gifts, loved her, and wanted to help her save Duncan. Her excuses were on the ropes, exhausted. There was absolutely no reason not to give this a chance.

Her breath caught in her throat for a moment. "Am I really doing this? Oh my gosh, I'm doing this."

"Did you mean to say that out loud?"

"No." Hopefully he thought it was about rescuing Duncan and not about him. Though with his keen cop senses, she was sure he saw right through her.

Logan laughed and took her in his arms, just hugging her. "Don't ever change, Kate."

"Don't worry about that."

She'd almost lost him tonight, but maybe it had been exactly the needed kick in her butt to finally listen to her heart.

I got it, Universe, okay? Please protect him.

Kate hugged him back with everything she had. They all needed to survive RAVEN and save Duncan. Which means she needed another vision. Somehow. Someway.

Otherwise, what was starting here was doomed.

They were all doomed.

THE GAZEBO IN KATE'S GARDEN LOOKED BEAUTIFUL, wreathed in fall leaves and flowers. Her gardener and the girls had outdone themselves.

It was time to strategize. Everyone was there. Including the unexpected Fiona Allen.

She'd showed up this morning with Jean. Her father, Ken, had disappeared, and after what Logan shared about Ken and RAVEN, they all suspected the worst. Ken was either dead or being held prisoner.

Fi wanted to help with the rescue, and Kate had to admit, her skill of seeing through things would come in handy.

Several crows cawed from the nearby iron trellis, a reminder that Caleb had his crows patrolling. No one put it past RAVEN to attack at any time.

Kate closed her eyes for a moment and lifted her face to the sun. It had been chilly all week, but today the sun was out in full abandon. It reminded her of the first time she'd met Duncan at the Forbes manor.

Hang on Duncan. We're coming.

"Isn't it dangerous to be discussing our plans out in the

open?" Lennox asked. He wore a fleece-lined leather jacket, a hat, gloves, and a scarf.

"I'm safe on my lands," Kate said. "Call it a gut feeling this is where we need to be."

"And we know that Kate's gut feelings are often correct," Jean said. Lennox scowled at her.

"You look funny." Patty gazed at Lennox's outfit.

Emily handed him a hot chocolate. "He's just cold, Patty. Be nice."

Lennox flashed Emily a grin. "Thank you very much, Emily. Your sister should learn from your example."

Patty stuck her tongue out at Emily, who ignored her to sit by Lennox.

"You were just speaking your mind, lass," Logan said and patted the seat beside him, reminding Kate of the hospital last night. Heat warmed her inside. Warmed her heart.

They just both needed to get through the RAVEN mission alive. Then they'd figure out what they had between them.

Patty sat next to Logan, looking very proud of herself. Kate had to admit, Logan was a better prize than Lennox. She was glad to see that even though his nose was still running from the tear gas, the rash on his neck had faded.

Kate had tried to get Beth or Sam to run the meeting. They were natural leaders. Kate had no new information, no new visions to help tell them how to succeed.

She glanced at her friends, hoping they might have changed their minds. Sam gave her a reassuring nod, and Beth simply stuck two thumbs up in the air. Well, she'd been pushing for them to treat her like an equal. Be careful what you ask for.

Everyone turned to look at her. Kate thought about hiding behind the planter, but they'd still see her.

"Everyone, please take a seat," Kate said quietly.

Her eyes scanned the crowd. Beth and Michael sat with Glenna just behind Logan. Sam, Robert, Jean, and Fi sat under the gazebo, shaded from the sun above.

"Beth, please share the intel from Dr. Withers." Kate lifted a hand toward her friend. Her voice was steady. Fake it 'til you make it was in full effect.

Beth stood and pulled out an envelope. "The doctor put this in the drop site. She finally gave us the address to the facility." She held up a piece of plastic. "And a key card for the main door to the lab areas. It's only viable through tomorrow—they are rekeyed weekly."

Michael nodded in approval. He looked tired. The circles under his eyes were almost black. Kate knew he was worried about Duncan.

"It won't do us any good on the doors that require retinal and DNA scans," Michael said. "But once we get to the doctor, she'll be able to handle the rest."

"And you can find her with your gift, right?" Glenna said to Beth.

Beth nodded. "I'll find the picture of her family. She brought it to the facility. It has a lot of meaning for her." She looked at Michael, Lennox, and Glenna. "When we're at the facility, I'll need one of you to ask me to find it. To save your brother. The request has to come from someone who really needs me to find the object. Otherwise it won't work"

Logan held his hand up. Kate gave him a quick nod.

"Before the attack at the station, I'd been doing research on RAVEN to try to find any information we could use," Logan said. "Beth shared the address with me, and I checked in with my cousin who works for the only outfit in town that hauls away medical waste. They service the RAVEN facility."

Glenna stood. "Can they smuggle us in?"

Logan nodded. "It's usually a two man run, done daily. He'll arrange for the other driver to call in sick tomorrow, and one of us will pose as the replacement driver."

"The drivers actually enter the facility?" Lennox asked.

"They do. I made sure of that," Logan said. "But they're only allowed in the back area where the medical waste is kept. My cousin said there are always guards, but just two of them. And only a key card is needed for the doors—no retinal or DNA." He lifted his shoulders. "After that, we're on our own. My cousin will take the truck and park it on the nearest road for when we're ready to leave."

Lennox raised his hand. "I'll pose as a driver. They already know the DCC's face. He won't get within a mile of the place."

"They might know you too," Emily said. "Mr. Allen could have given them pictures of your family."

"She's right," Fi said. "No matter what he did that night you went to our house, my Da wouldn't have said anything about our town without being forced to do so." Just the orange tips of her hair showed under her knit cap. "We can assume RAVEN knows everything he does."

Jean put her arm around Fi, but she shrugged it off.

The Forbes matriarch raised her hand. "Does Dr. Withers know where my son is being kept?"

"Technically, she won't see Duncan until tomorrow, per Kate's vision," Beth replied. "But she knows what Kate described. It's where they have the incoming stay before they chat with them."

Kate appreciated the way Beth kept things vague in front of the girls. So far, so good. She could tell by the girls' postures and expressions they were happy to be included. Which would make having them stay out of it more easy to enforce.

Sam turned to Kate. "Robert and I are going to contact the Warden, Sloane, today and see if we can get any useful intel."

"Is there anything I should do, Kate, besides charging up with electricity?" Glenna asked.

"No. At least not that I know of." Kate gazed at everyone. "I haven't had another vision yet to give any more information on what we need to do."

She had only glimpsed part of the story. She needed more.

"You'll get one, Mommy," Patty said. "I believe in you."

Several crows took flight, their black wings flashing in the sunlight. There was definitely someone watching them from the tree line. She knew in her heart it was Caleb.

She had to have faith the Universe would provide what she needed, just like Duncan had said.

But that didn't mean she couldn't push the issue with a little heart to heart tonight with the Universe.

And she knew exactly where she needed to have it.

CHAPTER 19

THE SUN BLAZED INTO BETH'S ROOM AND ACROSS THE TWO packages on her bed, even though they were headed into late afternoon.

Outside she still heard the voices of Michael and his mother as well as Glenna and Lennox. They'd stayed behind after the meeting.

She'd definitely bring her gun to RAVEN, because it was comforting, but they needed to incapacitate the operatives more quietly. Which is where the items in the boxes would come into play.

Beth opened the box from Lacey first. She'd contacted her as soon as Kate had her second vision. Her assistant had done an excellent job of bubble wrapping and padding the weapons.

The twin batons were worn on the handles, but the steel still gleamed. She touched the metal, remembering the first time she'd used these in a training session. She'd ended up scoring her first hit and scoring a new boyfriend. Josh had been an incredible instructor in *many* areas.

With a smile still on her lips, she unwrapped the stun gun. At almost three pounds, it was heavy, but you could deliver the jolt from all sides, not just the tip. It had brought down a two hundred and fifty pound opponent with just one blow. The aim was really key. The closer you got to the heart or head, the faster they dropped.

The other package was from an old buddy in Los Angeles. The one who'd tried to recruit her to his special band of fighters. She'd done a few practice jobs with them as an audition, but in the end she wasn't a joiner. Plus, she liked Carlos too much as a person. He was the most upfront, moral guy she knew. And she adored his family.

Best to cut ties when she did.

That way they'd never be used against her as leverage. She'd had enough of that in her life already.

The box was heavy duty. The scissors wouldn't do it. She took out her Kershaw knife and sliced the seams.

An envelope sat on the top.

Dura

It meant hard and uncompromising in Spanish. Her nickname with Carlos and his crew.

She opened it with her thumb, tearing a jagged edge through the paper. There was a note inside.

I know you won't ask for help, so I'm offering it. If the shit goes sideways, call.

I owe you.

Beth blew out a breath, and then put the note to the side, trying to quell the spark of light inside at his words. She'd never had anyone to count on after she'd been thrown into Juvie. Now there was TOP, though she still kept expecting Sam to suddenly disappear back into her old life. Leaving Beth behind.

Just like she did before.

Kate was solid. She'd told Kate she was her link to humanity, and she meant it. Kate was the only one she loved unconditionally. She'd die for her.

Hopefully it wouldn't come to that at RAVEN, but Kate was the best of them. She needed to live. No matter what.

"Okay, Marshall," she said under her breath. "Get your mind back in the game."

She used her Kershaw to open the first smaller box inside.

"Yes!" She clapped her hands, not caring if she looked silly to any ghosts watching. This was like Christmas.

A Prism 200C Backpack. Lean this baby back against a wall, and it mapped out what was on the other side.

Even though they wouldn't need one with this particular mission, given Fi's ability, she'd been wanting one for ages.

Knowing their track record, they'd be up against another Big Bad soon and this little baby would come in handy.

The next package was large. She'd asked for the Bodyguard Electro Gauntlet and Carlos had managed to grab one on short notice. He always came through.

The long black mesh gauntlet had a shiny guard for the forearm and a full glove to protect the hand. It could deliver up to 500,000 volts. It was for the left arm. Michael would fit this nicely.

She found the Xstat rapid hemostasis system plungers next.

Only two. She'd asked for five, but she'd take what she could get. Rather than using a tourniquet, you injected the pillow-like sponges into the wound. Coated in a homeostatic agent which stopped blood flow within 15 seconds, they inflated and sealed off the wound.

She'd seen these in action when a tourniquet couldn't be made. The soldier had survived because of one of these. What they were doing was insane, going into a heavily guarded military facility, and she would do everything possible to ensure everyone survived.

There was one last package. Carlos had given her an extra. The package had a picture on the outside taped to the paper. She knew right away that it was drawn by his daughter, Olivia. She'd be a little older than Emily now.

The picture had Olivia and her sister Louise along with their parents, and Beth was in the center. Olivia had put a heart over Beth's head.

She untaped the picture carefully so she wouldn't have to cut into it to open the package. Difficult to do with these damn tears in her eyes, but she managed. Another reminder of why she wasn't in their lives any longer. She couldn't risk it.

Beth opened the box. There were a series of smaller boxes inside. There were six. She opened up one and found a small dragonfly drone. These would be amazing in surveillance. There were instructions inside of how to pair them with her phone so she could see what their cameras saw. They weren't as small as a dragonfly, but just a little bigger. She'd fly them up by the ceiling.

Beth couldn't wait to play with her toys. She picked up her phone and texted Michael.

Up for a little sparring?

His reply came back quickly. *Verbal or physical?*

She giggled and then clamped her hand over her mouth. She didn't giggle.

Physical.

Just tell me where.

She gave him the location on the south side of the B&B. They wouldn't be disturbed there.

She had to admit, she'd underestimated Michael. He didn't back down from anything. Even when it disappointed his family.

They had a lot in common.

Maybe that's why he understood her? Why she felt comfortable with him because he wasn't as perfect as she'd first thought?

None of it really mattered anyway. He was only in Scotland for a little longer, she'd only be here for a bit too, and then they'd both be back in the States on opposite coasts. Long distance usually didn't work long term.

"Calm it down, Beth. You haven't even kissed him," she whispered.

Maybe that was the problem? If she liked a guy, it was either instant physical attraction or mutual platonic respect. She had a mixture with Michael. She wasn't used to that confusion.

She grabbed a baton and flicked it out, extending it with a snap. She'd stick to weapons. They were easier to understand.

And you could put them away when you were done.

Emotions were way too messy.

S
AM HANDED ROBERT BACK HIS RING. SHE'D HELD IT AND
called Sloane. As promised, Darrin had appeared and
whisked them away to Entwine. No questions asked.

She hoped Sloane could tell them something helpful about
RAVEN. She knew Kate was pushing herself to have another
vision, but if that didn't happen, they needed all the help they
could get.

Darrin led them back through the corridors, and this time,
they remained the pulsing wall of vines Sam had seen last time.
Nice to know they weren't wasting energy shifting, trying to
mess with her.

The Runner stopped before the same door as last time and
bid them both farewell.

Robert lifted his hand to knock on the door, but it opened
before he could get close.

They walked inside. The window in the distance showed a
large moon over trees.

The room was dark except for the glow of the fire. It appeared deserted, but Darrin wouldn't have left them here if
Sloane wasn't going to arrive.

Robert took a step forward, but Sam stopped him with a
touch on his arm. She knew she'd come to no harm here. She was
necessary for the balance. Robert, however, was an unknown.

"Take a seat." Sloane's voice came from a chair by the fire. She sounded tired. The Warden leaned forward, and Sam saw her profile.

"Has everyone gone home for the night?" Sam asked, looking at the nighttime sky in the window.

Sloane indicated the two chairs across from her. "Some have. But more have gone to the Game Room to make bets."

Robert and Sam sat down. The Warden looked the same as last time, but a bit more somber. Her pipe sat next to her on a small table, but it was cold.

The symbols on the side of her neck leading up into her hair were simmering bronze this time. They looked as if they breathed, going bright, then dark, then bright again.

"I did not realize there would be wagers in Entwine," Robert said. "What could you have to bet on?"

Sloane shrugged. "Many things. Time passes differently here, as you know. And boredom can set in. A wager here or there keeps the morale up."

Sam heard something underneath her words. "They're betting on us, aren't they?"

The Warden nodded and Sam felt again like she'd passed a test. "Yes, their wagers center around the Triumvirate. Your TOP, as you call it, might be the most short-lived one yet. Charging into RAVEN without a clue of what you're up against has set the odds high. That you'll fail."

Sam leaned forward. "And what about you? Are you betting for or against us?"

"For, of course. If just one of you gets killed tomorrow, it will upset my—" Sloane paused. "My future hopes for TOP."

Her ghost lie detector was showing green laced with red. Sloane was hiding something. And the fact that she'd bet, even for them, brought anger. From the soles of her feet up through her body. She knew she should remain silent. They needed Sloane's help. But she couldn't keep quiet.

"I'm so tired of this double standard." Sam's words were low, deep, bordering on the voice she used to summon the Bargain. She'd given up her powers long ago for this very reason. Feeling like a puppet to the Universe's whim. Forced to help ghosts, yet unable to say good bye to her parents when they'd died.

"Double standard?" Sloane eyed her with concern.

Sam lifted her hand toward the Warden. "We do your bidding, they bet on us to die. We don't do your bidding, and we're upsetting the balance. We're people. Not toys."

Sloane shook her head. "You've made your Bargain with the Universe for Robert. There's no backing out of the arrangement now."

Her matter-of-fact words just flamed the fire inside Sam. She remembered reaching for her parents in the burning car. Crying by the side of the road for their ghosts to appear.

"I made my deal with the Universe," Sam said. "But that doesn't mean my friends and I should be part of the entertainment to brighten the existence of *creatures* who have long forgotten what it's like to love." Her voice cracked. "What it's like to lose. What it's like to *die*." Tears filled her eyes, which only made her more angry.

Sloane grabbed her hands. "I remember." Her words were

gruff, clogged with emotion. "I remember it all." Matching tears were in the Warden's eyes.

Suddenly Sam was back in her childhood room. The first Rule had just floated into her mind. She'd been scared, but someone stood beside her. They'd placed a hand on her shoulder. Comforting.

Sloane released her, and the memory faded. Sam stared at her hands. Just what kind of being was Sloane?

"I'm sorry," Sloane said. "I shouldn't have said anything. Shouldn't have . . . why are you here?"

The Warden had regained her composure quickly. Tears gone. Face neutral.

Robert studied both of them. He took out a handkerchief and offered it to Sam. "We seek your counsel."

Sam wiped her eyes, thankful for Robert's steady nature. One of them had to hold it together. She didn't regret her outburst, she'd been angry for a long time. She still was. But Sloane had revealed something she hadn't meant to. Had she been there when Sam was a child?

Sloane lifted a finger toward Robert. "As always, on point. Eyes on the prize. How can I help?"

Robert took Sam's hand, his fingers lacing through hers. Her heart slowed just looking at him. Love was why she'd given her fate away. And she'd do it again. No hesitation. Which meant she had to put up with the Wardens.

Sam took a deep breath before speaking. "Do you have any information that could help us against RAVEN?"

"I do."

Sam and Robert looked at each other. Neither had expected the easy admission.

"And is there a cost for this information?" Sam asked.

"There is."

Robert gave Sloane a small nod. "I see you adhere to Caleb's school of enigmatic answers."

The Warden laughed and looked at both of them like they were precious. "I've had many a late night chat with Caleb. You'll have to get him to tell you about the sixteenth century soldiers who thought they could burn his woods. That's a good one."

"You mentioned if one of the Triumvirate is killed tomorrow that it will upset something," Sam said, "I'm assuming the balance?"

Sloane leaned back in her chair and suddenly had a drink in her hand. It looked like whiskey.

"You don't have leverage here on that count, Sam," the Warden said. "There have been many Triumvirates. And there will be more. Some are incredibly powerful. Others are wiped out before they can be used." She held Sam's gaze. "However, I don't want you to die, personally or professionally, which is why I told my Runners I was available to you. Always."

"So does this mean you are not requiring a cost after all?" Robert asked. His gaze was shrewd, locked on Sloane's face.

"There must always be an exchange. Nothing is truly for free, no matter what anyone says." Sloane's fingers tapped against her glass. "Love isn't free, neither is hope. Both are built on sacrifice. This will be a Bargain in every sense of the word."

Which meant if Sam agreed and didn't do what Sloane wanted, she'd suffer the consequences. Sloane was telling the truth, and they weren't going to change her mind.

"I need a glass of that." Sam looked at Sloane's glass. A matching one suddenly appeared at Sam's elbow on the table. She took a swallow. The whiskey burned down her throat, but it was just what she needed. "What do you want for the information?"

Sloane's lips rose up at the edges, looking much like the cat who ate the canary. "There will be a time coming soon where I will ask you to do something. You will do it. No questions asked."

Sam leaned back into her chair, mimicking Sloane's stance. This was her bread and butter. Bargain-making required finesse. "Will this thing you ask me to do end up harming someone I love?" Sam drained her drink, wondering if the whiskey was real or if her mind merely believed it was.

"No."

Green.

"Will it hurt someone I don't know?"

"Too vague to answer. I don't see the future like Kate does." Sloane gave her a sour look.

Green again.

Sam felt like they were playing poker, each waiting for the other's tell.

Robert remained silent beside them, though Sam noticed he had a glass of port at his table as well. It appeared Sloane had provided for him too.

"You wouldn't be making this a condition of our Bargain if I would do this thing willingly, so it's something I'm not going to like."

Sloane raised an eyebrow. "Perhaps. But whatever I ask will be in your best interest. You have my word."

Sam looked at Robert, hoping he'd see her uncertainty.

"If you could share a bit of the information you have on RAVEN," Robert said. "Perhaps Samantha would feel more secure in taking your terms. With an unknown boon to be given, we would need to ascertain if your information is indeed worth the potential price."

"You were always a good negotiator, even as a kid," Sloane said. "Your father taught you well." She drained her drink and put it on the table, where it immediately refilled.

"Did you know my father?"

"I did." She leaned forward toward Robert. "He was a great man. And loved you very much."

Robert's eyes glistened with moisture, though he remained stoic.

Sloane patted his hand. "I tell you what. When this is all done, if you both survive, I'll have your mom and dad brought here for a visit, Robert. So, you can talk with them."

Robert was on his feet immediately. He gave Sloane an incredibly deep bow. One that he'd told Sam was reserved for royalty. "I am once again grateful for your actions. Would I be able to bring Samantha as well?"

Sloane stood and gave him a hug, which he awkwardly returned. "Of course. You two should have a bright future if you don't mess it up tomorrow."

Sam wasn't able to figure out what Sloane's angle was. Or if she simply just liked the two of them? No wonder she got along with Caleb. They were both impossible to read.

She released Robert and gave Sam a long look. "And don't think I forgot Robert's other request."

"Proving you have information worthy of our wager."

Sloane sat down again, but on the edge of her seat. Her voice was excited, charged. "This won't help you succeed tomorrow, not in itself. But, I know someone who can help you bring down the head of RAVEN. Perhaps striking a serious enough blow from which RAVEN couldn't recover from." Her eyes locked on Sam. "Think of the lives you could save with RAVEN out of the picture. What would that be worth?"

Robert glanced at Sam. She gave him a nod. Sloane was telling the truth.

Sam already knew she was going to take the Bargain. Sloane knew it too. If she had a chance to end RAVEN for good, she had to take it.

The embers, the Universe's fireflies, were hovering near the ceiling. Waiting. They sensed her intention even if she hadn't spoken the words yet.

Sam exhaled through her nose. "Tell us what you know."

CHAPTER 20

WHITE PUFFS OF HER BREATH DISAPPEARED BEHIND KATE as she walked into her forest. The sun had dropped below the tree-line, leaving a faint sliver of orange topped with the approaching indigo of night.

Logan took up the rear with the girls. He'd insisted on coming, especially since she wasn't bringing Sam or Beth.

Emily and Patty had taken the opportunity to play bad guys and cops the entire way over.

Kate heard, "I'm the DCC, back down," coming from Emily in an unexpectedly deep voice, and then Patty's whine. "Why do I always have to be the bad guy?"

"How about, I'll be the bad guy," Logan said. "And you two are constables. First to catch me gets to be DCC. And my special hot chocolate." He ran past Kate, the girls fast on his heels. Their squeals and laughter filled the forest.

"I love that sound," Caleb said, walking around the base of a nearby tree. "Which is why I allow Emily and Patty to play in the forest."

Kate didn't jump. Maybe she was getting used to scary shit popping up unexpectedly. But her heart did the jumping for her.

Allow? Kate knew the old ghost loved playing games with her girls. They had regaled her just this morning with their past adventures. Apparently Caleb had become a fixture in their routine right after Graham was caught.

Kate smiled at him. "Thank you for letting them play. They love coming here." She sobered. "But after we get back from RAVEN, you and I are going to have a long talk about what you've been teaching my girls."

Caleb's smile moved to a frown. He nodded. "Agreed. Why are you here tonight?"

Kate cleared her throat. Sam had warned her he liked to be a bit dramatic and beat around the bush. A bunch. "You know why we're here. And what I want."

"A vision."

Well, she hadn't expected him to admit it. Not right away.

Kate rubbed her sweaty palms on the bottom hem of her shirt. "I felt the need to come here. Why?"

Caleb looked off to his left. "I do not dilly dally. Maybe you'd see that if you'd allow me to answer?"

"Who are you talking to?"

The ghost looked exasperated. "Beatrice, of course. Now if she will just hush for a moment, we can continue." He pursed his lips and then smiled. "As I was going to say, you came *here* because this is where you are from."

"I was born in Scotland?" No matter how much she'd

searched, she'd never been able to find out information about her real parents. Not even Bronson with all his connections had been able to discover the truth.

"Not born here," Caleb said. "Conceived here. Right in this forest."

Kate crossed her arms. "Over the centuries or even millennia you've been here, there had to have been other children conceived in this forest. Something beyond conception ties me to these lands."

Caleb's eyes didn't leave hers. "True."

The girls ran back through, this time with Logan chasing them. They stopped when they saw Caleb, and then ran to him yelling, "Mr. Caleb!" They wrapped their arms around his long legs.

"Wait a second," Kate said. "How are they touching you?"

Caleb grinned, looking like his younger self from Patty's vision. "My forest. My rules."

Logan just stood there, looking like he'd woken from a sleep. "Is that the forest ghost you told me about?" He looked at Caleb.

"It is," Kate replied gently. "This is Caleb."

Logan took a step toward the ghost and then stopped. "You saved Kate, Sam, and Beth from my brother, Graham. I don't know how to thank you for what you did."

Caleb gave him a nod, and then scooted the girls off his legs. "No thanks are necessary. They had already saved themselves. I was just making sure I did my part."

"Mr. Caleb says these are our lands," Emily said. "That we

belong here." A gust of wind blew through the trees, rustling the leaves. "Did the trees just say 'yes'?"

Caleb nodded. "You're learning how to hear them, Emily."

"You've always felt it, Mommy." Patty ran over to Kate. "It's our land. Let me show you the memories."

"The memories?"

"In the dirt." Patty crouched and pulled Kate down with her. "But we have to get underneath the surface."

Her daughter began to dig, and Kate helped her. After what had happened with Vivian, she didn't doubt Patty's words. After a moment, they hit the warm rich earth together.

The forest stayed around Kate, but suddenly everyone was gone except for Patty. It was now daytime. The leaves were just changing. And the trees were newer, younger. Light flooded the forest.

"I'm crafting this agreement because I need your help," a voice said. Kate turned and found a younger Caleb. Not as young as when he'd made Vivian, but younger than he was now. "The Romans will chop down my forest to build roads, walls."

She saw him a short distance away by a tree stump. A man was with him. Red, vibrant hair. Probably in his late teens, early twenties, he wore homespun clothes, and he had a boy with him.

"How can I help?" the man asked. "I have no army."

Caleb smiled, and it had the same crafty gleam as it did now. "By joining together, the Romans will not touch these lands. You need do nothing but accept our agreement. And build your shelter there." He pointed off through the trees.

Kate looked at the sun, the angle through the trees. The direction. Caleb had pointed to where her B&B now stood hundreds of years later.

The man spoke again. "And in return, my family will be protected?"

"It will be done," Caleb said.

"I agree to your terms."

"When your son is of age, it will be up to him to swear it too. And his children after that and so on." Caleb crouched to look at the boy. "Don't fret, Ewan. When the time is right, I will come to you."

Ewan nodded, looking too solemn for his age.

Caleb held his hand to the man. He took it, then hissed in pain.

"I've put a piece of my spirit in you." Caleb let his hand go. "My forest will recognize you now as a protector. And you will also be an anchor of Entwine."

The boy looked at his father, confused.

"That is the ghostly realm, my son." The man placed his hands on his son's shoulders. "Your sister was there before moving on to rest with your mother. Without Entwine, the balance would be lost between the living and the dead. Being an anchor is an important task that you will eventually take on your shoulders."

Patty tugged on Kate's jacket, and the forest shifted again in her eyes, like someone did the tablecloth-versus-dishes trick. Even though the dishes were still there after the tablecloth was yanked away, they were a bit wonky.

But it was the old trees again. Same twilight from before.

Kate stood and dusted off the dirt from her hands onto her jeans. Logan and Emily looked like they would burst, so she quickly explained what she'd seen.

"I'm a protector of the forest, aren't I?" Kate looked at Caleb, already knowing the answer, but needing to ask.

"You are."

Kate touched Patty's shoulder. "Your gifts are amazing. To show me the past like that."

"The trees and the land want to share their memories. They want people to know them. Know what they've seen." Patty looked at Caleb who nodded encouragingly, like she was repeating a lesson. "It's because we have a little piece of Mr. Caleb inside us." She held up the hand with faint etching of a flower from Vivian in her palm. "And now it's even stronger than before."

Kate stared at her girls. Patty could sense the future and now could recount the memories of the land and trees. And she was only seven. Would Emily develop a gift too?

"Fine, woman," Caleb said, his voice rising. "I'll let them see you if you stop haranguing me." He snapped his fingers, and Beatrice appeared.

Kate only knew it was Beatrice because she'd seen her when she'd gone back into Ray's memories. Beatrice had saved her with a swift kick in the ass when she needed it.

Kate rushed to her, but her hands went right through the ghost.

Caleb coughed. "Sorry, lass. That piece is outside my control."

Beatrice wiped her eyes, and Kate saw tears. "I'd be hugging you if I could, dear Kate."

"Who is that, Mom?" Emily asked. She walked towards Beatrice.

Beatrice leaned over, hands on her knees. "I'm a distant relative, lass. And I've been watching over you since you were a wee one."

Emily tilted her chin up, eyeing Beatrice carefully. "You've seen everything?"

Beatrice winked at her. "And nary a word will cross these lips." She glanced at Kate. "Oh, stop that frowning. If it was anything dangerous, I've always managed to warn you."

Kate raised an eyebrow, but her gut told her Beatrice was telling the truth. She trusted the feeling.

"Are you here to help me with the vision I need to have about RAVEN?" Kate doubted Caleb did anything by chance.

Beatrice shook her head. "You don't need any help, Kate. You have the means within you to call forth the vision you seek."

The words sounded extremely formal. Sam was the expert at these things. She suddenly wished she'd brought her, but she was still off with Sloane.

Kate had always suspected Caleb worked with the Universe, the Wardens, some higher power. Everything was connected.

Some of the pieces clicked into place. "The Universe didn't give me all the information I needed because it wanted me to come here?"

Beatrice nodded and made a come-on, come-on gesture with her hand.

"Because I'm supposed to have my vision here?"

This time Caleb gave her a nod. None of this helped—she still couldn't direct her visions. But there must be something tied to her being a protector.

Extra powers while she stood on this land?

The ground underneath her buzzed with sudden energy as if it wanted to answer her question.

Emily and Patty looked excited. Logan looked worried.

"Being here will somehow help me have my vision of RAVEN? To see what I need to see?"

Beatrice nodded. "But first you'll need to re-seal the agreement struck between your ancestors and Caleb."

She didn't doubt Beatrice told the truth. Kate trusted her completely.

"Why?"

Caleb stepped forward. "The agreement needs to be re-sealed each year to keep the connection stable. That's why your visions became more and more unreliable. It's part of why you black out now. You are part of the land, and the connection is weakening."

Picturing her grounding cord as a tree trunk diving into the earth had helped Kate with her visions already. Now she had a whole forest to ground her.

The question immediately sprang into her mind, and Kate didn't hesitate to ask it. "Who was the last person to re-seal this?"

"Your father."

Beatrice looked as shocked as Kate felt. "My father? Who was, or is, my father?"

Caleb stepped forward and took her hand. It felt like holding firm sticks, warm, with fire running through them.

"I know not where he is, lass, but he is still living. I would have felt otherwise." His words were kind.

The forest began to spin in lazy circles. Her father was alive. Caleb knew who her father was. Her real father.

Small hands wrapped around her leg. Patty. Arms went around her waist. Emily. They helped keep her steady. "And my mother? Do you know where she is? Is she alive?"

Caleb shook his head. "I know not. She wasn't a protector of the land, so I can't feel her here." He put a hand over his heart. "But I do know she risked much to make sure you were born."

"How—"

"Save your questions for later," Caleb said, his mouth set in a grim line. "The agreement needs to be re-sealed now. Before you run out of time." His eyes glowed green.

Time. Everything always seemed to come down to time. Not enough for Paul. Too much apart from her friends. Of course, there would be a clock on this piece as well.

"What do I need to do?"

Caleb smiled, and little pieces of bark flaked from around his eyes. "You'll know. For each Protector, it's a different vow."

Kate looked down at her girls. Patty's brown eyes were large, capturing the reflection of the emerging stars above. Emily's were determined. She reminded Kate of Beatrice.

"Do it, Mommy," Patty said. "The trees say it's time."

Emily rested her cheek on Kate's hip. "I'm with Pats. It's time."

"An anchor of Entwine," Kate said. "A protector of the forest. I guess I'm pretty important after all." She shook her head, feeling a bit dizzy again.

Logan walked over to her and placed his fingers on her heart. "Remember what I told you. This is what's always made you important. You read what's here. You see the good, the potential."

Beatrice beamed. "I always said he was the man for you."

Both girls grabbed him into their hug with Kate until Kate felt cocooned in a Logan, Emily, and Patty blanket.

So much love. And they all believed in her.

The words rolled off her tongue, easily. "I promise to protect these lands for always, until my last dying breath. And to hold Entwine fast as an anchor. I will not let go."

Both Emily and Patty shouted. "Me too! Me too!"

Caleb laughed. "I appreciate your commitment, but you'll get your chance when you're of age." Her girls both opened their mouths, no doubt ready to protest, but Caleb's hand in the air stopped them. "And you will get to make your own special oaths that are yours alone."

Emily pursed her lips, but nodded. Patty didn't look pleased, but she kept quiet.

Kate looked at Caleb. "And in return for my agreement, you will protect me and my family. For always."

"We have an agreement." Caleb's words were solemn. A flash of lightening shot over head and then the deep rumble of thunder. He held out his hand to her, and she took it.

Something pushed into her right palm from his. It wasn't painful. Just warm. He kissed her knuckles, his lips papery thin like dry leaves. When he released her hand, she looked at it. A shimmering tree spread over the tendons in her hand, the leaves just under her knuckles. It flashed green, brown, gold, before settling into a gilded bronze.

"I'm ready." Kate moved the girls from her into Logan's arms. She knew he'd take care of them. It felt amazing to have someone to depend on. Her heart expanded, knocking off a few more black flakes of armor.

"Ready?" Logan asked.

"For the vision I came for."

She suddenly sensed something next to her, the hairs on her arms rising from the cold.

The Death Vision.

"Do it," Kate said.

As you wish

The voice floated in her ears, elusive, like snow caught in a flurry. The vision wrapped itself around her in a cloak of ice. Kate shivered, and then clenched her teeth to stop from biting her lip.

Logan took a step toward her, but Emily grabbed his arm, stopping him.

The soil beneath her feet vibrated, dancing against her shoes. Energy rose up through the ground, winding about her ankles, her thighs. Everywhere it touched, warmth returned.

The cold, the heat, in perfect balance.

She was part of something larger now. Bigger than TOP. More powerful.

"Show me RAVEN."

CHAPTER 21

KATE'S KITCHEN TABLE WAS NOW COMMAND CENTRAL. A layout of the RAVEN facility was spread out before them. Sketched by Kate. It wasn't complete, but it was more than they'd had before her latest vision.

She'd seen Duncan again, but thankfully the same as before. He'd been attached to an IV, on a cot in a cell. They'd get there before anything else happened. They had to.

Beth and Sam hadn't made a reappearance in her vision. Maybe that means they'd be okay? That what she'd seen before wouldn't come to pass?

She tried to slow her breathing. Everyone who was going to RAVEN tomorrow gathered around the table. Lennox, Glenna, Fi, Logan, Michael, Beth, Sam, and Robert. No need to let them see how rattled she was.

Stu and Aggie would be on hacker duty tomorrow. Stu was ex-military and still had an active presence on the dark web. Aggie knew her way around computers from her days as a private investigator.

Dr. Withers had given Beth the access code to their system—it would only get them to the cameras, but that's what they'd need if they wanted to try to get in and out without alerting the entire facility. Stu and Aggie planned to use prior footage to create a loop.

Kate tapped the right side of the map. "This way leads to the sealed room I saw. I don't know if Mackenzie is in there, but I was shown that room specifically in my vision. It has to be connected to your conversation with Sloane."

Sam nodded. "Sloane said Mackenzie has been a prisoner for the last five years. When she finally refused to continue capturing innocent people in the name of RAVEN, her father locked her away."

"She definitely could cause some serious damage." Beth looked excited, no doubt imagining RAVEN's demise in an explosion of rubble. "If what you saw when you were in Oliver's memory is true."

Robert clasped his hands behind his back. "I agree Mackenzie would indeed be a formidable ally in our current mission. However, I am concerned for all the lives within those walls. Their safety."

Lennox looked like he hadn't slept since Duncan was taken. "Anyone who works for RAVEN already knows the danger in their line of work. I say we use Mackenzie if we can."

"I disagree," Kate said. "This is not going to turn into a slaughter. Not if we can help it." She might not know how they were going to pull this off, but it wouldn't be by all-out murder.

Logan touched Kate's shoulder. "Did you see Mackenzie freed in your vision?"

"No. I didn't see her at all. Just the room." Kate rubbed her eyes. "But I felt drawn to it. I know it's important. If she's not there, someone else is who can help."

She didn't want to think too hard about Mackenzie and the potential consequences of freeing her. They had to rescue whomever was in that room. That much she was sure of.

Michael gazed at the map. "Did you see where Beth and I should go?"

"No, but I think that's because Beth's gift will get you there. The vision didn't need to show me."

Kate looked at Glenna and Logan. "You two will need to make your way to the gate on the north side and short it out. That's the diversion I saw in my second vision that caused the alarm. It'll pull a good number of guards out to the gates. They'll need to inspect and confirm what caused it, then get it back up and operational."

"One section of the gate's electricity damaged takes out the whole gate?" Glenna asked.

"Yes. It's something they've been meaning to fix." Kate replayed the vision in her head. "But the major has been focused on the research. They've never had an attack on the facility, so they've grown lax."

Or maybe Oliver had always hoped someone would attack and save his sister? If he was still that boy she'd shared memories with, he'd have done everything in his power to save Mackenzie.

Which meant he couldn't save her. Not directly.

Glenna ran her fingers through her cropped blonde hair, making it stand up in tufts. "I can handle the gate on my own. Logan should stay with Lennox and keep your escape route clear."

Logan beat Kate to a reply. "You need someone to watch your back while you take out the gate. When we're done, we'll go back and help Lennox."

Glenna grasped Logan's arm. "Thank you." She looked like she wanted to hug him. "I don't usually get back-up."

Lennox made a rude noise. "Because you never accept it. Are you gettin' soft on me Glenna-girl?" His eyes were as light as his words.

Glenna punched his arm. "You wish, you big oaf. We'll probably be saving your hide in the end."

"Not likely." Lennox grabbed her hand. "You be safe, you hear me?"

Glenna squeezed his hand. "I will. You too."

"Wow, you really are chopped liver in your family, aren't you?" Beth said to Michael, hitting his chest with the back of her hand.

Glenna looked contrite. "I didn't mean—"

Michael cut her words off. "It's fine. So, Kate, what are you planning to do at the facility?"

"You *should* stay home," Lennox looked at her. "You've got no offensive powers."

His words weren't unkind, just matter of fact.

Logan gave him a hard look. "I don't want Kate going any- where near that place, but if you think the power of might is the only way to win, you're sorely mistaken."

Beth nodded. "What he said. Plus, Kate never gives up. Ever. She's a pain-in-the-ass that way."

Lennox looked bored.

"She's got near-sight." Sam's voice was firm. "It saved us at the Allens."

Lennox pursed his lips. "And how many times have you used this near-sight?"

"Twice." Kate crossed her arms.

"And can you control it?"

Kate looked at Sam, Beth, and finally Logan. She so wanted to be the hero they thought she was.

"No."

"This is Kate's vision," Robert said. "Without her, we would not know of Duncan's fate, nor would we have the tools to succeed. She goes with us."

Lennox raised his hands in defeat. "If you have a death wish, I won't stand in your way. Just don't take any of us down with you."

She dug her hands into her sweater pockets. The left one still held the Tardis toy Emily had given her. The right pocket held the dirt she'd taken from the forest. It tingled against her fingers.

She hoped she'd seen enough to save them. To save them all.

KATE COUNTED THE RIVETS ON THE BACK OF THE VAN DOOR for the hundredth time. Okay, maybe the tenth, but it felt like a hundred. They were almost to the facility.

Logan took her hand, and she realized she'd been holding her breath.

"It'll be okay, Kate."

He was risking his life for her, for all of them. Not because he had to, but because he chose to. Because he was a good guy.

She really didn't deserve him. But maybe she eventually could?

Kate kissed him on the cheek. He blushed, which made him look even more delicious.

She wanted to *kiss* kiss him, because they might die. But their first kiss was not going to be in front of Beth and the peanut gallery.

Beth was already lifting her eyebrows up and down and making rude gestures with her hands. Fi was snort-laughing next to her.

Logan gave both of them the cold emotionless cop eyes. Fi instantly shut up. Beth just frowned.

Michael nudged Beth. "Is that for me?" He gazed at the wicked-looking gauntlet she held in her hands, like something out of a movie.

Beth nodded. "This will take out the operatives quietly with an electric jolt."

Michael narrowed his eyes. "By 'take them out', I'm assuming you mean knock them unconscious?"

Beth pointed at the gauntlet's controls. "I've already put it on the lowest setting." She helped him slip it on. "I know you don't want to hurt anyone. This will just get them out of the way without permanent harm."

"Thank you." Michael's words were soft.

Beth looked up at him. "Yeah, well, I don't need to nurse you through any guilt later over killing someone."

He smiled with a glint in his eye. "Of course. I should have known it was a selfish decision."

Beth ignored him and turned to Fi. "You weren't part of my original planning, so no gadgets for you."

"That's okay," Fi replied. She took out a heavy duty knife sheath from her purse and attached it to her thigh. The knife she slid from the sheath looked dangerous. Serrated on the bottom by the handle, then tapering up to a deadly point.

Beth sat up straight. "Is that a Navy Seal SOG Tactical Knife?"

"My Da bought it for me when I turned eighteen." Fi's face fell. She slid the knife back in its place.

"We're using all our resources to find him," Michael said.

"And thank you again for coming with us." Kate leaned toward her. "We can use all the help we can get."

Beth handed Kate a long black rod with a rubber handle. "Speaking of help, since I know you aren't going to stay safe, here's a stun gun."

"Thank you, I guess?" Kate took it from her carefully, hoping she didn't stun herself by accident.

The van pulled to a stop. Lennox and Clay, Logan's cousin, got out and disappeared into the facility. If everything went well, the guards would be subdued, and they'd be back here opening the van doors to let everyone in.

Beth tossed Logan a small box. "When you're out by the gate, open this up. I already keyed it to your phone."

"Keyed it to—wait, how did you get access to my phone?" Logan said.

Beth just winked. "You'll see the picture from the dragonfly drone. It'll give you some warning of incoming solders." She flicked a quick glance at Sam. "I didn't get you anything because you have your ghost soldier with you. Not to mention how many other ghosts are probably in the facility."

Sam opened up her bag. "And I have these if the fighting gets up close and personal." She took out her iron daggers. Blue bits of light sparked from her fingertips and danced along the iron.

"Is that new?" Kate pointed at the light and iron combo.

Sam nodded. "The ghostly essence I've collected from my recent Bargains seems attuned to the daggers."

The door opened, bringing with it a cold breeze. Over Lennox's shoulder, the skies looked gray, the clouds effectively swallowing the sun. Kate shivered.

"Everyone have their vests?" Lennox asked. He pulled off the blonde wig he'd worn as a disguise, though Kate thought looking like Rod Stewart was not being under the radar.

They all nodded. Kate wasn't sure it was safer with the vests on—if RAVEN was going to shoot them, it would most likely be more bullets than the vests could handle.

"Stu has the cameras on a loop," Lennox continued. "He

said it'll be good for about a half hour, maybe a smidge more. Aggie somehow got wired into their coms. She'll warn us if they've made us. So, let's make it quick, people, and when we get out of this alive, I'll buy each of you a drink."

"Even me, brother?" Michael asked.

Lennox hesitated. "Rescue Duncan, and I'll consider it."

Michael nodded. Not really an olive branch, but better than what Kate had seen in the past.

Beth turned to the Forbeses. "Okay. Who's going to ask me to find the picture? The one of Dr. Withers' family. To save Duncan."

Kate expected Michael or Glenna to jump in, but Lennox beat them to it.

"Beth, I need you to find the picture of the doc's family." Lennox grasped her arm. "She'll take you to my brother. To save him."

The emotion in Lennox's voice startled Kate. But it was exactly what Beth needed. Her eyes turned black almost immediately.

Beth stared off into space, and then cleared the air in front of her like it was a mirror. "Yes. I see it." Her voice was multi-layered, as if someone spoke with her.

Goosebumps rushed up Kate's arms. She hadn't heard her voice sound like that before. Not even on her show. Was that new? It was creepy.

Sam lifted a finger towards the space around Beth. "Something there," she mouthed. Kate couldn't see anything.

Fi squinted at Beth, but just shook her head.

Robert leaned over and whispered to them both. "I see something too. It is a shape, or shapes rather. Not like the ghosts of Entwine." He stared at Beth a moment longer. "There are cords attached to Beth from these shapes. They are connected."

Beth jerked forward and then froze.

Michael looked worried. "Should we—"

Sam shook her head. "She's left her body, following the path to the picture. Give her a sec."

"At least that's the same," Kate said. Though it was still awful to watch. Almost like Beth was in suspended animation. She still breathed, but the life was gone, extinguished.

"She's coming back," Sam whispered. "I can see how it happens now."

Robert's eyes were wide. "It is beautiful."

Beth's intake of breath was loud and ragged. "I've got the location. Let's move."

They scrambled out of the van.

Logan hugged Kate. "I'll be back before you know it."

"You better. Otherwise I'm coming to save you."

He pulled back and smiled. "I've no doubt."

Glenna tugged on his arm, and they ran off toward the section of the gate they were going to damage.

The rest of them headed inside. The room Lennox led them into looked like a typical storeroom. There were racks of supplies to the left and the right, as well as a small desk by a door straight ahead. A tablet sat on the desk, playing *The Hobbit* movie, if Kate wasn't mistaken.

Metal drums marked "WASTE" sat up against the wall.

"Where are the guards?" Michael asked.

Lennox glanced at one of the racks. "I knocked them unconscious. I'll stay here and protect our way out." He held up a card key to Sam. "This will get you through that door and into the facility. Beth already has the one from the doc."

Beth looked at Sam and Kate. "See you soon." She hesitated for a moment, like she wanted to say something else, but then turned and headed to the door. With a quick swipe of the card key, Michael, Fi and Beth entered the facility.

"Don't do anything stupid," Sam warned Kate.

"You know I will."

Sam sighed. "I know. But try to stay alive, okay?"

"Deal."

They hugged each other.

Then Sam and Robert disappeared through the door, turning right to take them to the room which might or might not hold Mackenzie.

Lennox looked at her. "I hope you're right about everything."

Kate glanced at the door which had swallowed up her two best friends. "I hope so too."

She held up the heavy stun gun. Something told her before the day was done, she'd use it.

CHAPTER 22

BETH LOOKED AT HER PHONE. SO FAR, THE DRONE AHEAD showed the coast was clear.

"How far?" Michael asked. He brought up the rear, with Fi in between them.

"End of the corridor, we make a right, then two lefts, then another right. Door on the left." She flicked open her batons to full length. The steel reflected the lights above.

"I'm glad you know where you're going." Fi said softly. "So, we find Dr. Withers, and she takes us to Duncan?"

"That's the plan," Michael replied. "She'll also have John Anderson with her. He's one of the patients Kate saw in her vision. We need to save him."

Beth stopped and turned around. "Enough chatter," she whispered. "We don't know who we might run into."

They both nodded. Fi mouthed, "Sorry."

The kid meant well, but this wasn't the time to lower their guard. They could be captured at any moment.

Beth turned back around and continued to move quietly

down the corridor. Her senses were on full alert, listening for the sound of a boot heel, a voice, a click of a gun safety, but so far nothing.

Both Fi and Michael were silent behind her. She was pleased they'd listened to her warning. And a little impressed.

She had brought her gun, but that would be a last resort. They had to remain as quiet as possible.

Right turn. Next corridor was still showing clear.

"Company coming. Second door on the right." Fi's words were low.

Beth moved to the side of the door. As Fi predicted, it opened a few seconds later.

Two guards.

Beth's right baton swept under one of the guard's feet, flipping him back. He hit the floor, but had his hand to his earpiece almost immediately.

She jabbed the end of the baton with her fist into his diaphragm. He wheezed, struggling for breath. Beth punched him once, then twice. He was out.

Bodies slammed into the wall in front of her—Fi and Michael tag-teaming the other guard. Michael hefted him over his shoulder and pointed at the door they'd come out of. "We need to get them out of sight. Fi, any more inside?"

Fi stared hard at the door as if she'd burn a hole in it. "Clear."

"Help me with the retinal scan," Michael said. He crouched, and Fi lifted the guard's head and held his eye open. The door clicked.

They got the guards inside and out of the corridor. It looked like a typical office space. Two desks, bookshelves, computers. Boring.

"You two make a pretty good team." Beth searched her opponent to see if he had anything useful on him. Another card key. She pocketed it. And a picture of his kid. She wondered if his daughter knew what daddy did for a living.

"I used to help Michael when he practiced in town." Fi went through one of the desks.

Beth scanned the bookshelf while Michael searched the remaining desk. A slim black book emblazoned in red lettering on the spine caught Beth's eye. The title:

RAVEN: Leverage Is the Key to Change.

She quickly slipped it into her jacket. Light reading for later if they made it out of this alive.

A throaty *whoop whoop* of noise reverberated through her body, making her teeth rattle.

It was the siren from Kate's vision.

D ARRIN APPEARED IN FRONT OF SAM AND ROBERT, ALMOST as soon as they'd crossed the threshold into the main facility. A rush of relief flooded Sam. A friendly face.

"Sloane sent me to help," Darrin said. "I can take you to Mackenzie."

He turned, and they followed him down the corridor.

"And the cost?" Sam asked.

The Runner looked back over his shoulder. "This is included

in the Bargain you already made. For the future promise."

"Sloane seems to share great confidences with you," Robert said. "Have you worked with her long?"

"Long enough," Darrin replied.

Robert had asked exactly what Sam had been thinking. Darrin wasn't just a Runner. He was important to Sloane. Just as Sam and Robert were. What was Sloane's end game?

Darrin held up his hand, and they waited before turning the corner. Sam heard footsteps in the distance. Maybe a patrol?

"We need to wait for them to move on."

"Is Mackenzie dangerous?" Sam whispered. Sloane had kept dodging that question when Sam had asked.

Darrin turned and looked at both of them. "She's here against her will. She will want to leave with you."

Avoiding the question as expertly as his boss.

"How does Sloane know Mackenzie?" Robert asked. "She is neither a ghost nor one such as I, caught between two worlds."

The Runner straightened his gray vest, a movement Sam was beginning to recognize as a nervous gesture.

"Sloane has watched this organization from its infancy," Darrin finally said. "As you know, the Wardens have interests in both Entwine and the world of the living."

Sam nodded. "And like Caleb, Wardens can appear to whomever they want. Touch whomever they want."

Darrin didn't reply, but he didn't refute her words either. "The way is clear. Come."

They followed Darrin through the facility, trusting in his

guidance. But Sam's mind kept turning over his words. Was Sloane somehow attached to RAVEN? Had Mackenzie made a Bargain with her for her freedom?

They finally came to a stop. In front of a door at the end of the corridor. It was the only door.

And unlike all the others, it wasn't the same dull gray.

It was red.

Runners of energy seeped around the edges of the door, snaking down the hallway.

"Do you see that?" Sam asked.

Both Darrin and Robert nodded.

What if Mackenzie had been locked up for a reason? A really good reason?

Suddenly Sam wanted to turn back.

Robert took her hand. "Sloane would not have told us of Mackenzie and provided Darrin as a guide if this was not a challenge we could handle."

He was right. Sloane might not be telling them everything, but she didn't want either of them to die.

Then the hallway filled with a deep *whoop whoop* of a siren.

Sam jerked at the sound. It was a needed reminder of just where they were. RAVEN kept people as prisoners, experimented on them, used them. No one deserved that.

Even someone whose powers were dangerous.

Sam stared at the red door in front of them. In the sea of gray, the color was so rich and deep that she couldn't turn away.

Unlike the other doors, there wasn't a retinal scan. No tube.

No fancy equipment. Just a keyhole right under the knob, like Kate's front door.

Why something so low tech?

"I will look inside," Robert said. He slipped off his ring, putting it in his pocket, and walked through the door.

No matter how many times she'd seen him wink in and out of Entwine, it still made her catch her breath. And fear one day he might not come back.

"And I'll scout the nearby area," Darrin said. He disappeared as well.

Sam slid her hand into her bag, touching the iron daggers. They were as cold as ever. Like shards of ice. They lit the inside of her bag with blue energy.

Darrin appeared in front of her suddenly. She jerked out of her reverie.

"Guards are coming this way."

She scanned the corridor, but there was no place to hide, and it dead-ended in the door.

Sam put her face close to the wood. "Robert," she hissed. "The guards are coming. Can Mackenzie help?"

The heavy tread of footsteps reached her ears. They were getting closer.

Darrin walked through the door, leaving her alone again.

Great. So much for Sloane's help. If Sam could take the guards out, they might still have a chance. She'd be going up against heavily armed soldiers. Not great odds.

But if she failed, everyone would be captured.

Sam slipped the daggers out of her bag and tucked them

into the waistband of her jeans, under her shirt. She'd have to let them get close in order to use them.

Sam heard voices now. Two voices.

"I don't know why we have to check on her. Nothing came up on the monitors."

A sigh, then a deeper voice replied. "You know how the Major is about Patient 244. We have to verify in person. Make sure she's all right."

"I think he's too soft on her because she's his sister."

The deeper voice grew stern. "You want to tell him that?"

The other voice didn't respond.

Sam got on her knees, hands up, trying to look helpless, so when they came around the corner and saw her, they wouldn't automatically shoot. Hopefully.

She willed the blue sparks to stop flickering from her fingertips. They disappeared.

Arms encircled her from behind, pulling her backwards. Her body slammed hard into the door. She would have cried out, but the breath was knocked out of her. She gasped for air.

And then the door disintegrated.

Or rather she did.

After a few minutes of being on hair-trigger alert, waiting for something to happen, Kate finally walked over to lean on one of the desks.

"Someone's bound to come in here. No matter how fast

we are." The clock on the wall insisted it had only been five minutes since everyone had left, but it felt like forever.

"True." Lennox looked at his phone. "Which is why you're not here alone."

"I have this." Kate hit the button on the stun gun, and it crackled ominously. She turned it off quickly.

Lennox looked unimpressed. "So what do you think you're supposed to do here?" His tone normal. No usual acid burning on top.

"I don't know." Kate put down the stun gun on top of a file folder. "I never see myself in my visions, so I have no idea."

Lennox crossed his arms. "Yet you somehow knew you had to be here, risking your life?"

She slid her hands into her pockets. She moved her fingers through the forest soil she'd brought with her. It buzzed against her skin. The Tardis in her left pocket felt warm. She took it out and held it to her nose. It smelled of Emily's skin. She breathed in deep, feeling a brief moment of calm, and then dropped it back into her pocket.

She turned to Lennox. "I always have to try to stop my visions directly." Kate shrugged. "That's the way it's always worked."

Lennox snorted. "Not sure what help you'll be stopping this."

Kate stood up straight. "We wouldn't have had a clue as to where Duncan had been taken if it wasn't for me. What if me being here is the thing that saves your brother?"

"Starting to believe in yourself just a wee bit, aren't you?" He gave her a sidelong glance.

Her anger extinguished in a single breath. Lennox had been pushing her for a reason.

She still wasn't sure how she was going to save John, Duncan, Dr. Withers, and any of the others the Universe wanted her to, but this was where she needed to be.

"Why are you trying to help? It's not your usual approach."

Lennox shrugged. "I'd rather have you mad than scared. Better chance of success on this mission."

Kate gave him what she hoped was a sour look, but he just grinned at her. She saw the family resemblance to Duncan around the eyes.

She hoped he was okay.

We're coming Duncan. We're here.

Lennox's phone buzzed. A second later, a siren went off, sending a heavy vibration through the facility. Kate felt it through the soles of her shoes.

Logan and Glenna had been successful.

Her eyes went to the door they'd come through. They should be back any moment. Unless they were captured or worse.

Please let them be okay.

The soil in her pocket shifted against her hand, almost as if it moved on its own. Heat rushed up her legs, into her arms. Her near-sight was coming. She recognized the feeling now.

The siren continued to shriek overhead.

Suddenly Kate was outside. The siren was more muffled in the cold misty air.

Glenna and Logan were running toward the door into the room where Lennox and Kate waited.

No one was following them. They'd managed to damage the fence and not get caught.

A movement to the right caught her peripheral vision. Two soldiers were smoking. The gray of their uniforms melding into the metal of the facility.

"I can't believe the alarm went off again," one of the soldiers said. "What do you think it is this time?"

The other smiled. "Twenty pounds says its a tree limb."

"I say it's a squirrel. I'll take your wager."

Glenna and Logan came out of the gloom, right in front of the soldiers.

The soldiers had guns out immediately. Fallen cigarette butts smoking on the wet ground.

Gunshots. Logan's knee hit with a bullet, sending him tumbling to the ground. Glenna shot in the chest, blood blossoming through the threads of her cream sweater, spinning her around and going down.

One of the soldiers tapped his earpiece. "We've got intruders. Lock down the facility."

The familiar rubber band feeling pulled Kate back.

Back into the room where Lennox still grinned. Then his phone buzzed. The siren blared.

Time had rewound.

Her heart pummeled her chest with powerful bruising beats. Logan shot. Glenna possibly dead.

Move. She needed to move.

She grabbed the stun gun and rushed to the door.

"Glenna and Logan are coming back," she yelled. "And

we've got to take out two guards, otherwise your sister is dead and the whole facility is on lockdown."

She didn't stop to see if he was behind her. She wasn't a fighter. Didn't even know the simple self-defense techniques Logan always wanted to teach her.

But she had surprise on her side.

Kate flung open the door and ran at the two soldiers, going for their legs. She took them down in a tangle of bodies before they even had a chance to shout.

One of the soldiers recovered quickly, pinning her to the ground with his body. His forearm jammed into her throat. She could barely breathe, but she still had the stun gun in her hand.

She jammed it into his side. He fell off of her, crying out, but she shoved her hand over his mouth, stifling the sound. He tried to get up, so she hit him again with another jolt.

The other soldier had his gun out, but dropped it almost immediately, his hand burned. The metal glowed red.

He pawed at his ear, pulling out the earpiece, now a crumpled piece of foul smelling plastic and metal wires.

Lennox was instantly by her side. Two swift punches to the face and the soldiers were unconscious.

Kate sat up. Sweat coated her face and chest. She knew now how Sam had felt with Graham in the forest. She got to her knees and struggled not to throw up.

Lennox's hand lifted her to her feet easily. Almost off her feet. "I puked after my first fight too." His eyes were kind. "Inflicting harm on another, even in self defense, takes some getting used to."

Kate dropped the stun gun and leaned over, placing her hands on her knees. "I don't plan on getting used to it."

"That's what I said too," Lennox muttered under his breath.

Glenna and Logan appeared out of the gloom at a full run. They pulled up short.

"What the hell happened here?" Glenna asked in a harsh whisper.

Lennox slid one of the guards onto his back and headed toward the door. "She just saved your life, Glenna." His eyes flicked to Logan. "Can you grab the other one? We need to get them out of sight."

Logan gazed at Kate, eyes concerned. She gave him a small smile. Not because she felt it, but because he needed to believe things were okay.

Kate followed them mutely inside, her mind still spinning on what had happened. Did this mean they were going to succeed? Or was this just a lucky close call?

CHAPTER 23

THE INVISIBLE CORD CONTINUED TO PULL BETH FORWARD, towards the picture and Dr. Withers.

There was another door in front of them, marked "LABS". Beth took out the card key that the doc had given her. The door blinked green and opened.

They were almost there. The corridor before them was empty.

Beth pointed at the door they needed. The doc should be waiting for them. She took a step toward it to knock.

And it opened.

There was nowhere to hide. Beth, Michael and Fi froze where they stood.

The guard walked the other way down the corridor. He disappeared around the corner. The siren fell silent.

Adrenaline danced in Beth's system. They'd narrowly escaped that one. She hoped luck remained on their side.

She walked up to the door and knocked. The door whipped open, revealing Dr. Withers. The other doctor, Beth remembered his name was Bob, had John Anderson on his feet, half dragging him to the door.

"I can't go any further. I'm sorry," Bob handed John to Michael.

Dr. Withers injected John with something, and he started to come around. "I understand. It's okay." She gave Bob a quick hug and tucked her family picture inside her lab coat.

Bob looked at Michael. He turned his head to the left. "Hit me, but watch the eye. We need the Major to believe I tried to stop you."

Beth punched him before Michael could move. Hard enough to break a good number of blood vessels and crack his lip open, but no permanent damage. It would bruise horribly and do the job they needed.

The doctor stumbled back against the wall and then slipped back inside the lab.

"Nice," Fi said, admiration in her tone.

"Okay, where to next, doc?" Beth asked. "We've got to keep moving."

Dr. Withers pointed down the hall. "That door at the end leads to the intake rooms. It's not far." She looked at Beth. "There should only be one guard on duty. Carlson."

"Lead the way," Beth said and began to hustle them down the hallway. By her estimates, they had maybe fifteen minutes left before the cameras came off the loop.

They quickly reached the door. Dr. Withers provided the key card and retinal scan.

There was another door inside. This one required spit.

Beth shook her head. "I'd hate to have the job cleaning all of those each night."

Michael frowned at her. Probably worried she wasn't staying on task. Little did he know of her methods. She'd once told a knock knock joke right before she'd delivered her own knock of C4 plastic explosive.

You could die at any moment on an op. Why not have a little humor mixed in with the blood?

Fi grabbed the doctor's arm before she spit into the tube.

"There are two guards inside," Fi said in a low voice. "One on either side of the door. Duncan's in one of the cells unconscious. And there's someone else in the cell next to him."

The doctor's face lit with questions, no doubt about Fi's abilities, but they didn't have time to waste. They hadn't been expecting two guards. They had to time this right.

"Distract them when you go in, doc," Beth said. "I'll take the guard on the left. Michael you hit the one on the right. Fi, you protect the doc. Got it?"

"I'll protect Rachel," John said. He had color back in his face, and his stance was steady. Whatever the doc had injected him with had helped.

Beth nodded. "Everyone, try not to get shot."

They all nodded.

Dr. Withers spat into the tube, and the door clicked open. She walked in, calm, easy. Like there weren't fugitives hiding in the hallway.

"Dr. Withers, what can we do for you?" One of the guards asked. His voice came from the right.

"I was worried about the alarm, Carlson." The doctor's voice was steady. She turned her head to the left. "Hanson, any word on when the Major will be back?"

Beth tilted her head to the left. Michael nodded.

Michael rushed to the right. Beth ran to the left. She ran past the doctor, her eyes barely registering the cells against the wall.

Her baton caught Hanson in the kneecap. He yelled, his gun falling from his grasp. It hit the floor with a loud clatter.

Beth moved behind him, hitting his thighs and the small of his back.

Hanson spun, grabbing one of her batons, pulling her toward him. They both fell to the floor.

A shot whizzed past Beth's ear. Too close.

They both froze. Attacker and attackee.

"I don't want to hurt you, but we're freeing these people," Dr. Withers' said. She held his gun with both hands. John stood next to her, hands outstretched. Beth saw a shimmering field of some kind surrounding them.

"But you know what the Major will do." The guard looked genuinely scared.

"I know. Which is why you fought us and lost." The doctor's voice softened. "The camera feed is on a loop. They'll only see the aftermath."

John looked at the guard. "You were kind to me before, when I was first taken. Help us now. You know what they're, what *you're* doing is wrong."

Hanson pulled his hand away from Beth's baton. Defeat and

worry flitted across his face. "Hit me," he said. "And make it look good. I can't help you, but I won't fight you." His voice shook. "I've got a new baby girl at home. I can't risk it."

Disgust for RAVEN squeezed Beth's stomach in a firm grip. "Yeah, I know the drill."

She did as Hanson asked. The same as what she'd done for Bob. And she gave him several bruised ribs too. The doctor had been a lightweight, but Hanson was a soldier. He needed a bit more damage to sell it.

She leaned in close and whispered. "I promise, I will find a way to take this place down."

He squeezed her arm, and then got up and walked over to the cells, holding his wrists to be zip tied. Michael and Fi already had an unconscious Carlson secured to one of the cell bars with a zip tie.

Dr. Withers unlocked the cell holding Duncan. She rushed in and pulled out the tubes leading to an IV bag, putting a bandage quickly in place. She injected him with what looked to be the same thing she'd given John.

Duncan's eyes opened. "Where—how—Logan—Kate?"

Michael pulled him into a hug. "You're safe, big brother."

"I wouldn't promise that yet," Beth replied. "We still need to make it back to Lennox."

One of the other cells had a prisoner, as Fi had mentioned. A girl barely in her teens. With her dark hair and olive skin, she reminded Beth too much of Carlos' daughter. Dr. Withers injected her as well. She came around just as quickly as Duncan had.

They needed to get out of here now.

Beth looked at John, Duncan, and the mystery teen, assessing their potential help in getting out of here in one piece.

Duncan had visions, no help.

"What can you two do?" She pointed at John and the girl.

"Telekinesis and energy fields," John said.

The girl tucked her hair behind her ears. "I make things slippery."

A mixed bag of abilities at best, but she'd take what she could get. Beth nodded. "Okay, Superfriends. We want to get out of here quickly and quietly. But we might have to fight our way out. Do what you have to."

They all nodded.

She checked her dragonfly drones on her phone. The coast was clear.

Beth opened the door and didn't stop to make sure anyone was following. She knew they were. And regardless of their skills, this was all on her.

She hoped their luck hadn't run out.

S AM FELT WEIGHTLESS. SHE SAW EACH STRAND, EACH filament of the door as if she were in a completely new world. Her body was gone. Only her spirit remained.

There was something she had been trying to do. What was it? Her mind struggled to focus, wanting to become one with the door and stay in this incredible new land.

Then she saw a flash of silver. No, iron.

Her daggers floated beside her. Completely intact.

Daggers. Iron. Ghosts.

She was the Necromancer.

Sam tumbled backwards into Robert's arms and onto the floor of the cell.

She inhaled a ragged lungful of breath. "What just happened?" she managed, her voice barely a croak.

A hand appeared in front of her face, attached to an arm, attached to a woman in pale blue pants and shirt. Long red hair, braided to the side, and cold blue eyes. "He just pulled you through Entwine. And your daggers too. No wonder he's winded."

Darrin helped Robert to his feet, easing him to sit on the bed.

Sam took the woman's hand and got to her feet. The grip was firm, almost painfully so.

"I'm Sam and—"

"I know who you are. Sloane told me to expect you." The woman filled a bag with several books from the bookshelf. "I'm Mackenzie. And before you ask, I can't blast open the door." She lifted her pant leg to show a pack strapped to her calf, with a tube taped to her skin. "Steady injections to keep my powers on low. I had the choice of this or a coma."

Sam glanced around the cell. A small desk was to her left, a bed on the right, and every inch of wall space was covered in drawings. Many were of the forest. *Kate's* forest. Sam recognized Caleb's tree. Here and there were portraits of a woman smiling. She looked like Mackenzie. It must be Rhona, her mother.

And there was one of Rhona, Mackenzie, and someone who could be Oliver, based on what Kate had told them about her vision. Sam stepped closer to look at it. Mackenzie had captured the love and heartache so beautifully on their faces. Hands almost touching, but not reaching. Storm clouds behind them almost in the shape of a man.

Mackenzie tore the picture from the wall, tucking it into her bag with the books.

"These are incredible," Sam said.

A hint of softness quieted the tightness in Mackenzie's face. She pulled several more pictures from the walls, tucking them away. "They're just dreams now. Memories."

Voices sounded from the other side of the door. The same voices Sam had heard before.

Robert had barely pulled her through the door, and Mackenzie couldn't use her abilities. They needed the guards to open the door.

"Will the guards come into your cell?" Darrin asked softly. He met Sam's gaze, and she knew he understood their dilemma.

Mackenzie shook her head. "They'll do a verbal check through the door. Even with my injections, they're still cautious."

"Patient 244, check in." The deep voice called from the other side of the door.

"Will they come in if you don't respond?" Sam asked.

Mackenzie shook her head.

"Then tell them you're hurt," Sam whispered.

Mackenzie looked at Sam like she'd lost her mind.

Sam grabbed her arm. "I heard them talking earlier. Oliver's worried about you."

Mackenzie's eyes held surprise. "Ollie? He hasn't been to see me in months."

The deep voice called out again. "Patient 244, check in."

The other guard sighed. "Let's just go."

But using the Major's name, Mackenzie's brother's name, worked as Sam hoped.

"I cut my leg, Sergeant Bristol," Mackenzie said, and then motioned Sam and Robert to the other side of the door. When it opened, they would be out of sight. Darrin disappeared.

Sam grabbed her daggers. The ghostly essence immediately encircled the iron. And for the first time, the daggers were warm.

"No killing," she whispered to Mackenzie. Even without her supernatural abilities, Sam had no doubt Oliver's sister was deadly. Mackenzie gave Sam a tight nod.

"Check her vitals." Bristol said from behind the door.

"Dose is on target," the other guard replied. "Abilities neutralized."

"Please hurry. I'm feeling . . . I feel dizzy." She knocked over her chair, making a loud clatter, and then sprawled on the floor, her right leg under the bed frame.

"We're coming in," Bristol said.

There was a shift of metal, and then a hiss.

Both guards stepped into the room. Sam saw them from

around the door, which they had left wide open. Perhaps for a hasty retreat?

Bristol surveyed the room. "Help me get her up, Drummond." Together they lifted Mackenzie to her feet. Mackenzie went limp, pulling Bristol off balance giving Sam the opening she needed.

Sam rushed forward. She aimed high toward his shoulder and lower toward his hip, knowing one would score.

She'd seen what the ghostly essence had done to Ken Allen. Who knows what it would do combined with the daggers. She didn't want to kill anyone.

Bristol deflected her left hand, but her right scored a hit to his hip. She felt the blade slide into his skin like it was liquid.

He didn't cry out, just twisted, pushing her down and then rolling on top of her.

Just like Graham.

She couldn't breathe.

Frozen.

Summon us.

Dual voices filled her mind, speaking in harmony.

The image of her daggers blossomed in her vision, blocking out Bristol's flushed face.

Something smashed into her cheek, rocking her head back. Bristol's fist.

Summon us.

The voices were urgent now. Insistent.

Her hands burned against the iron like when she'd fought Ray, but the guard was alive, not a ghost.

She didn't know who she was supposed to summon. But if she didn't do something right now, it was over.

I summon you.

The ghostly essence fled her body in a rush, pulled into the daggers. Rather than just licking at the iron like before, the blades burned blue, the symbols on their handles blazing.

Bristol reared back to strike her again.

Her hands flamed hot, blue light filling the cell.

The dagger on his hip slid deeper. Sam shoved the other one into his arm.

Bristol's mouth grimaced, his eyes rolling up into his head. Tremors shook his body, and then he dropped, heavy and unmoving on top of her, but still breathing.

Sam released the daggers and shoved his weight off of her. The blue glow died.

A flurry of motion to her left caught her attention. Mackenzie roundhouse kicked Drummond back into the wall. He slid to the ground and didn't move.

"I don't need my abilities to take you out." Mackenzie lifted her foot to kick him in the head.

"Stop," Sam said. She sat up with Robert's help, and then got to her feet. Only a little wobbly. "We need to get back to the delivery room before the cameras come off loop."

Mackenzie lowered her foot slowly, a mutinous look on her face.

Sam picked the daggers up and slid them back into her waistband. She might have to get some sheaths for them.

She glanced at her hands. They weren't burned like usual.

And she hadn't lost consciousness. This was definitely different.

But her hands didn't spark any longer. She'd used up the last of the ghostly essence inside her.

Darrin appeared in the open doorway. "We've got to move fast."

They scrambled out of Mackenzie's cell and into the corridor.

With Mackenzie's abilities out of service, Robert still recovering from pulling her through Entwine, and her own lack of ghostly mojo, Sam hoped they'd make it back without running into any more guards.

"WE'RE RUNNING OUT OF TIME," KATE SAID, LOOKING at her watch.

Logan took out his billy club. "What's the plan if they don't make it back?"

"We go in. Find them." Lennox eyed the door to the interior of the facility.

"Which most likely would be suicide." Kate couldn't help saying what she knew they were all thinking.

"I'm not leaving my brother," Lennox said.

Kate found herself wringing her hands. She shoved them back into her pockets. Her right hand slid into the dirt from her forest. If she closed her eyes she could almost see it glowing in the distance.

Home.

A touch on her arm startled her. She opened her eyes.

"We won't leave anyone behind, Kate," Logan said. "And we'll make it out alive."

"I think I hear someone outside," Glenna said from her post by the back door. "Tell me again, brother, why we can't lock this door?" Her hands glimmered with electricity. "Or short it out?"

"Because that would immediately raise suspicion," he replied. "We let them come in and take them down."

They'd made it through so far relatively intact, and Kate prayed it would continue. The Universe wouldn't lead them here just to let them die. Isn't that why she'd had the death vision in the first place about RAVEN? To save people?

A shadow loomed to her left. She stumbled back, adrenaline surging up through her chest. It was a man. But the shelves behind him were still visible. A ghost. Had to be.

"There's a ghost here." Her voice came out in a whisper. The only ghosts she'd seen before were by touching Sam. Caleb didn't count and neither did his abilities by showing him Beatrice. He was a force all his own.

"I'm Darrin," the ghost said. "Sloane sent me. The Necromancer is trapped." He looked down at his hands, face drawn tight. "She'll die."

Darrin. He was the Runner who helped with Ray.

Kate saw his mouth continue to move. She knew he was speaking, but she couldn't hear anything else he said after that. Sam was going to die?

This couldn't be happening.

"Kate, what's going on?" Logan asked.

"Sam's in trouble," she managed to croak out of her tight throat. She knew what it felt like to only hear part of a conversation. And if they needed to save Sam, they needed to know what was being said.

"How do we save her?" she asked Darrin.

"Not we," he said. "*You.* Your near-sight will show you the way."

"But I can't force it."

"You forced your vision in the forest."

"That was different."

Darrin glanced down at her pocket. "You carry your lands with you."

"A pocketful of dirt is different than an entire forest."

Glenna asked. "Force what?"

"It doesn't matter. It's impossible." But there was the tiniest thread of hope in her mind. Sloane wouldn't have sent Darrin if there wasn't something they could do.

"Not impossible. Not any longer," the ghost said. "You've forged the agreement with Caleb. The connection to the lands gives you great power."

She had been touching the dirt right before seeing the vision that saved Logan and Glenna.

No. It couldn't be that simple, could it?

She eyed Darrin. "Sam's in danger, but you didn't say anything about Beth."

Distress filled Darrin's face. "You need to save Sam."

He was definitely avoiding. And wasn't happy about it. She needed answers from someone who could give them.

Kate put her hands on her hips. "Sloane, I know you're here watching. Come out, come out, wherever you are."

Darrin began to disappear. A woman walked through his fading form. Not really a woman. She looked in her early teens. From her partially shaved hair, Celtic tattoos, and intense gaze, Kate knew who it was.

Sloane.

Goosebumps raced up Kate's arms.

"The Necromancer is your priority," Sloane said. "No one else matters."

The goosebumps died, replaced quickly with heat and anger. "Both my friends are in danger because of my vision. A vision from the Universe, I might add. The Head Honcho." Kate took a step forward, and then another, until she saw the pores on the Warden's face. "I'm not choosing one."

"There's no way you can save both." The hardness fell away from Sloane's face. "I'm sorry, Kate, but you're too weak and untrained. We'll be lucky if you can save Sam." She shook her head slowly. "You've been right to doubt yourself and your abilities. You're not as strong as the others. Not yet."

Kate couldn't dispute Sloane's words. But Beth and Sam would never give up on her if the roles were reversed. And she wasn't giving up on them.

She looked down at her thumb, the one with the scar from their Blood Sister Ritual.

Even if she could force the near-sight, she wouldn't be able to see them both.

And she had the strong feeling that the danger they were in

was happening at the exact same time. To each of them.

But the near-sight was a new ability. Maybe she *could* see them both?

"You're right. I might not be as strong as the others," she said to Sloane. "But I'm the most determined." She took some of the dirt out of her pocket and put it on the nearest desk top.

"What are you doing?" Logan asked. His eyes searched her face.

"I'm going to save Beth and Sam."

He nodded. "What can I do?"

"I need your knife."

He handed it over without protest.

Sloane watched her. "You only have a few minutes. You won't succeed."

The knife shook in her hand. "I lost Paul, I almost lost Logan, and I will not lose another person I love. They're my family. If you aren't going to help, leave."

Sloane didn't move. Probably wanted to watch her fail in person.

The Warden would be disappointed.

Kate cut her thumb with the knife's point, at the scar. The beautiful tree symbol on her hand, the one Caleb had given her, glistened in the light from the bulbs overhead.

She took a handful of dirt and placed it on top of the tree symbol on her hand. Her blood mixed with the dirt. She squeezed her cut thumb, dripping more and more blood into the almost black pile.

The dark granules shivered against her skin, and then

moved. Sinking into her flesh. Energy burned from her hand, up through her body. She felt when the last particle dissolved into her.

The room disappeared. She was far away. Felt the wind against her leaves, the earth warm and comforting to her roots below, the sounds of all the creatures living within.

She'd seen much. Suffered much. And still she stood.

Just out of sight, she sensed Caleb and Beatrice.

"Going up against a Warden no less." Caleb's voice held a hint of laughter in her mind. "Both Sam and Kate are rule breakers."

"I'm not surprised about Kate. She's my kin, after all." Beatrice's pride was unmistakable. "You'll help her though, won't you? Help her save Sam and Beth?"

Those names brought Kate back to herself. She wasn't the forest. Not really. Not exactly.

Their presence began to slide away. She wanted to draw them back.

Caleb's last words were soft. "I don't need to help her. You know as well as I do just what she is. What she can do. She's the Oracle."

Suddenly she stood in front of the trees in Caleb's forest. Their roots ran through the ground, underneath her feet, bringing her energy, their life blood. Their branches creaked her name just like they had in Vivian's lands.

Oracle.

And this time another name followed.

Protector.

She held out her hands. The tree symbol blazed bright gold. Tendrils of light flowed from her fingertips. Just like they had the night Sam had sent the power of the Universe through them all.

The forest was alive with energy. The roots, the branches, the creatures all held within this space.

A stream appeared before her.

She saw everything.

The past, the future, the present. They flowed before her eyes in the glistening water.

She flicked her fingers to the left, and the past spiraled by her, caught on a new current, and out of sight. Clenching her right fist collapsed the future into a small ball, glimmering and glowing in the air. It was still malleable. Unknown.

The present was left in front of her. Like an escalator, the end kept falling and disappearing as it became the past. The beginning grew and stretched, reaching toward the future.

Kate spread her hands wide, releasing the future from its ball of light to rejoin the stream.

Everything played out before her. The present bleeding into the future.

There.

Blood and death. Images shimmered in front of her eyes.

That's where she would find Sam and Beth. See what she needed to see to save them both.

And with her next exhale, she walked forward and stepped fully into the stream of time.

CHAPTER 24

KATE FOUND HERSELF IN A HALLWAY OF RAVEN. SHE SAW Beth, Fi, Michael, Dr. Withers, Duncan, John, and a young girl—a teenager she didn't recognize.

Beth glanced down at her phone, looking at the image from the drone's camera. "Go back the other way," she hissed. "We've got company."

They quickly obeyed.

Two doors opened in the hallway before they made it out the other side.

Four guards came out of the rooms. They stopped, clearly surprised to see Beth and her troupe in the hallway. But the surprise didn't last long.

Everyone had weapons out immediately.

The young girl crouched to the floor, hands against the concrete.

The closest soldier slipped, scrambling to keep his footing. His gun fired as he fell, sending bullets wildly through the hallway.

His bullets caught John, Duncan, one of his own men, and Michael.

John fell to the ground, blood pouring from his neck, soaking into his hospital scrubs. Just like Kate had seen in her first vision. Duncan had been hit in the shoulder, but he still struggled to pull John out of the way.

A tranquilizer dart took Duncan down. John slumped against the floor, a red river of blood flowing towards the solders.

The girl crawled toward Dr. Withers, her leg bleeding, but darts took both of them to the floor, unconscious.

Michael was on the ground. Blood pooling under his body. He wasn't moving. Fi cried, shaking him.

Beth screamed, guttural and raw. Then she ran toward the soldiers, firing her gun.

She made it a few steps before she stopped screaming. A few more before she stopped breathing.

THE RUBBER BAND FEELING BEGAN TO TUG ON KATE, BUT with a single thought it fell away. She controlled this.

Sam. Show me Sam.

The pressure shifted, and she found herself hurtling forwards. Gray walls, darkness, and the shadow of someone, someone watching her, sped past Kate's sight.

And then she was in another hallway.

She'd found them.

Sam, Robert, and a woman, who she knew must be

Mackenzie. She had those same eyes she'd seen in the vision from the G.I. Joe.

They were running.

"Damn their routine patrols. Darrin was right. I can hear them coming." Mackenzie stopped quickly and lifted her pant leg. She yanked something from her calf and threw it to the floor. It clattered until it hit the nearest door and stopped. Kate saw fluid inside the plastic box and a needle.

"There's no point leaving that in now. I won't let them put it back in. I won't go back in that cell," Mackenzie said. "I don't know how much I can do with my powers, but I'd rather die then be locked up again.

Robert shook his head. "No one needs die."

They rounded the corner, Robert in the lead and came face to face with three soldiers.

Weapons were immediately drawn.

"Please, we mean no harm."Robert held his hands up.

One of the soldiers tapped his ear piece. "Patient 244 is out of her cell. And unmedicated. Two hostiles aiding." The soldier's eyes never wavered from Mackenzie. "Understood."

He took out that same tranquilizer gun Kate had seen before. The soldiers behind him leveled their guns towards Sam and Robert.

Mackenzie yelled, and the doors buckled like they'd been sucked back into their respective rooms. The lights flickered. The floor cracked. And the ceiling exploded overhead, showering everyone in metal and rock.

Kate looked down, and rivers of blood seeped out from

under the debris. Sam's hands reached for her, clenching and unclenching until they stilled.

AGAIN, KATE FELT THAT TUGGING. MORE INSISTENT THIS time. It would yank her out of the stream and into the present. And she'd have no time to reach and save both her friends.

Even if she somehow managed to explain to Logan and the others exactly where in the facility both Beth and Sam were, the odds were against them.

The only way to make sure there was a fighting chance was to have Sam and Beth see what she'd seen.

For them to know what was coming.

But how?

First she had to rewind more. Get to them both before what she'd seen came to pass.

When she'd moved her fingers before, she'd manipulated the flow of the past, the future. How had she known to do it?

I just knew. Somehow I just knew.

Maybe it was like Sam's Rules? How Sam knew what to do without being told.

Was it an Oracle thing?

Her vision grew checkered. She fought for control. She'd be back in her body in seconds unless she did something fast.

Grounding.

She needed to ground like Duncan had taught her. And this

time, she'd also incorporate the energy and power of her forest.

She realized now that she'd almost done it before, when she'd imagined herself to be a tree the first time she'd tried to ground.

The tree root, her grounding cord, filled the space around her. Then it dove down, tunneling through the earth, connecting with the core.

Earth energy flowed up, warming Kate's feet.

Tendrils spread out from her grounding cord, sliding through the land, reaching her forest.

The connection slipped into place easily, like it had just been waiting for her. Vibrations rumbled up her legs, moving through her body, just like what she'd felt in the forest.

She wasn't going to freak out. She could do this.

In front of her, the time stream slowed. The present and the future outcome for Beth shimmered up from the depths of the stream. Overlapping it was Sam's potential path as well. They became a competing jumble of images, no longer clear.

Kate needed to split the streams apart. That would be the only way she could give them each the vision they needed.

Somehow she just knew this.

But how was she going to split the time stream?

She needed a focus.

Something that controlled time.

The Tardis.

She knew she didn't have the figure physically with her, but when she reached into her left pocket, it was there.

The buzzing inside her from her forest combined with the

power of the earth energy and moved up through her arms, her hands, and into the Tardis.

She closed her eyes. "Split the streams," she whispered into the Tardis. "Split Beth and Sam's streams."

She imagined the stream parting, forking. On the left would be Beth's present and future. On the right would be Sam's.

Kate opened her eyes. The streams had split. Just as she'd imagined.

On the left, Beth was just walking into the hallway.

On the right, Robert was leading the way out of Mackenzie's cell.

What she needed to do next was completely crazy. And she'd probably die. Hell, they probably all would.

She slipped the Tardis back into her pocket.

"Here goes nothing."

She thrust her hands through the split time streams and grabbed Sam and Beth. Not physically, but through their connection as TOP. The Blood Ritual had left pathways, and she used them now, just as they used them to share energy when they touched.

Kate pushed her near-sight memories into them both.

Their eyes frosted white.

It was too much. She couldn't hold on. The present grabbed her and yanked her back.

Back into her body.

To the sound of screaming and gunshots.

CHAPTER 25

KATE BLINKED OPEN HER EYES. SHE FELT A HUNDRED YEARS old. Everything ached. She willed her body to move. Nothing.

This had never happened after a vision before. But what she'd done was more than a vision. She'd managed to see two futures and place that knowledge inside the heads of her friends.

She'd gone against the usual order of things. The balance.

This must be the price.

Had it worked?

Had she managed to save Sam and Beth?

A scream broke through the air. It was one of anger.

Someone had hidden her away behind one of the racks, propped her up in a seated position against a wall, but she could see through the open shelving.

Logan, where was Logan?

Sparks of electricity flashed in front of her, followed by Glenna. The floor reverberated like something heavy had dropped. A soldier raced past Kate's view. He was going to catch Glenna unawares. Kate tried to cry out a warning, but no sound came from her throat.

Glenna spun around, gracefully, like this was all a dance. And then she shoved her hands up under the solider's chin. They sparked with electricity, so white and bright.

His eyes rolled up in his head, foam coming to his mouth, blood spilling past his lips. As if she'd cooked his brain.

Kate wanted to look away, but couldn't. She watched the life leave his eyes.

He dropped to the ground only to be replaced by another soldier, who looked barely eighteen and scared. Glenna hesitated just a second, and his knife caught her in the side. She grabbed him, tumbling backwards, and Kate couldn't see them any longer.

Needles of pain shoved into Kate's temples.

Another scream of anger. It sounded like the same scream from before.

What she'd just witnessed, the flashes of light, Glenna killing the soldier, being stabbed, all played out again in front of her.

Maybe the after effects of being in the time stream?

Which meant she might still be able to save someone with her near-sight, but not if she sat back.

Kate barely felt the floor under her numb hands, but she pushed herself up and to her knees. Sweat rolled down her nose.

She crawled to the rack in front of her and grabbed onto the bottom shelf. The smell of burning metal caught in Kate's lungs, then burning flesh.

Lennox walked in front of Kate, just on the other side of the shelving. His hands outstretched. Two soldiers dropped their smoldering guns, their hands burned and blistered.

Lennox moved in quickly, breaking the neck of one of them with a hard loud twist. The other flew at him, but Lennox knocked him away like he was a pebble against the incoming tide. The soldier hit the wall and Kate swore she heard his bones break from the impact.

Someone yelled from Kate's right. Lennox turned and bullets ripped through his chest. His shirt filled with blood. Their bullets had penetrated the vest.

He stumbled on his feet, and turning, his gaze met Kate's. For the first time she saw fear in his eyes.

He grasped the metal rack, rocking it back and forth, leaving bloody finger streaks behind, but he fell backwards, out of Kate's sight.

She could stop this. She had to stop this.

This time it was ice picks in her temples. The pain was getting worse.

The burning metal smell, then flesh. Time had rewound again.

She wouldn't be able to prevent the soldier from firing at Lennox, but she could remove Lennox from the board. Give a diversion.

A sharp crack sounded. Lennox had just broken the solider's neck.

Kate didn't have a weapon. All she had was her body weight.

She knew as soon as she did this, she'd be exposed. But she couldn't let him die in front of her.

She took a step back and another, then pushed forward with everything she had.

The rack tipped forward, taking Kate with it. Lennox slid back out of the way.

She lay on top of the rack, unable to move. Someone flipped her over. She blinked against the light in her face.

The soldier with the flashlight smiled, and her blood chilled. His name tag said Colin Matthews. "The Major is going to enjoy experimenting on you." Matthews got on one knee and leaned down until his mouth was by her ear. His whisper was filled with a dark promise. "We know who you are, Oracle."

"Kate!"

She heard Logan's panicked cry, but couldn't see him.

Please let the time rewind. Please.

But this time nothing happened.

Either the Universe had abandoned her, or she was out of juice. Even breathing was an effort.

"Cuff her." Matthews pointed to another soldier.

Metal cuffs slapped onto her wrists. The initial cold was quickly replaced by a pulsing heat. The metal glowed blue.

Matthews and another soldier lifted her to her feet. She couldn't move her legs. They lowered her into a chair.

Kate's gaze searched the room. She found Logan. His arms were behind his back, restrained. Three guards surrounded him. He was bloody from a cut on his arm, but other than that, appeared to be in one piece.

Another soldier brought Glenna into view. She was cuffed

in the same type of metal that Kate was. They'd put a bandage on her side.

An unconscious Lennox was dragged out from behind a desk, a tranquilizer dart in his neck. Kate let out a quick breath. At least he was alive.

But they were all screwed. She'd be experimented on along with Glenna and Lennox. Who knows what they would do with Logan?

And her girls. Oh God. Her girls. They'd lose another parent. Patty would spiral again. Emily might too.

Her eyes immediately filled with tears. Somehow she'd thought they'd make it out of this. That the Universe wouldn't let her down. But she'd been wrong.

And she hadn't even saved Sam and Beth.

Their faces filled their mind.

She'd failed.

A breeze wafted against her face, coming from the door to the facility.

You saved us for a reason, Red. So we could save everyone.

Beth's voice slid through her mind. Obviously a hopeful hallucination.

They'd already tried to bond as TOP. To help each other. But they'd never been successful. Never been able to talk to each other like this.

We're coming, Kate. Hold on.

This time it was Sam's voice. She sounded like she was running.

A tiny flicker of hope sparked inside Kate.

"Take them to the intake cells," Matthews commanded.

"And what about him?" One of the soldiers looked at Logan. "We didn't detect any energy signatures."

Kate didn't need her near-sight to know what was coming next. To know what they'd do to Logan.

"Kill him," Matthews replied. "He's useless to us."

"But the Major didn't order anyone killed." The soldier holding Lennox spoke up.

Matthews took out his gun. "The Major isn't here. Any more objections?"

None of the soldiers replied.

Beatrice appeared before her. "Caleb sent me. It's all the energy he could spare. I hope it's enough to save you somehow." She touched her fingers to Kate's temple.

The energy wasn't enough to move. Her body was still a dead weight.

Matthews lifted his gun. He was going to shoot Logan.

But there was one thing she could still do. She willed the energy into her vocal cords and screamed.

Everyone turned to her. Matthew's gun was no longer trained on Logan.

It was pointed at her.

The door to the facility blew off its hinges, hitting Matthews in the back.

His gun went off.

CHAPTER 26

"JOHN, THE GUNS." KATE RECOGNIZED MICHAEL'S VOICE, though it sounded hoarse, like he'd been screaming.

Logan dropped to the ground and yanked Glenna down with him. Gunshots immediately rang out. The bullets hung in the air, frozen. John, the patient from her vision, held his hands outstretched. His face contorted with the effort.

Michael stood beside him, looking like the stuff of nightmares. Blood coated his blonde hair, turning it red.

Robert suddenly appeared behind a soldier, out of thin air. He grabbed his shoulders and slammed the soldier's head into one of the desks until he stopped struggling.

The dark haired girl she'd seen earlier crouched, hand on the concrete. Kate knew what would happen, had seen it in her vision with Beth. Those soldiers could kill everyone if their bullets went wild. John might not be able to hold everything back.

The girl met Kate's eyes and nodded. As if she knew. She stretched her other hand towards Michael.

The soldier's feet slid to the side and Michael grabbed his

gun, knocking him down. Another suffered the same fate. Somehow Michael kept his footing.

Mackenzie crushed her fists together and two of the closest soldiers folded in on themselves. Kate didn't know how else to describe it. It was like they were pieces of paper that had been crumpled up.

Even their screams had been swallowed.

"No!" Sam shouted. "You don't have to kill. Don't be your father."

The menacing look on Mackenzie's face dissolved into disgust. She dropped her hands and turned away.

Michael and Robert had already taken out the remaining soldiers. After the deafening sounds of screams and bullets, it was suddenly almost silent.

Just the sound of breathing and groans.

"She's bleeding," Sam said, rushing to Kate.

Had Matthews actually shot her? She had on a vest. She should be fine.

Sam looked at Robert. "Can you take her to the hospital, through Entwine?"

Robert shook his head. "I fear I would not have enough power to do so. It could instantly kill her."

Logan joined Sam, rubbing his freed wrists. "Dr. Withers, Michael, get over here." He unbuttoned Kate's jacket, revealing the vest. His fingers trembled. "Does it hurt, Kate?"

Usually he was unshakable. She knew she should be afraid to see him this way. But like her body, her emotions had somehow slid firmly into neutral. Like she was an observer, a viewer watching a television show called RAVEN.

"No. I can't feel anything, actually."

Michael hadn't come over yet, so this wasn't his doing, using his abilities to help take away the pain, ease her emotions.

"We'll get you to hospital and you'll be fine." Logan took her hand, but she still couldn't feel anything. "I'm bringing you home to Patty and Emily. I promise."

A flash of memory. The hospital. His cheek against her hand. Love. Her eyes filled. She blinked, her vision blurry.

And then almost immediately, her etch-a-sketch of emotion was wiped clean. Blank. Empty.

"Where are Beth and Duncan?" Kate asked, her voice sounding distant and tiny. Much the way she felt. Unattached.

Logan was upset. She knew by the way his brows pinched, but she needed to know Beth and Duncan were okay. That much was still important. Still lingering in her mind.

Michael walked over, shuffled actually. He looked exhausted. "Duncan was injured. I healed him as best I could, and Beth luckily had something we could use to stop the blood loss, but he still couldn't walk on his own. Beth made us go ahead." He touched Kate's forehead. At least that's what it seemed like he was doing, though she felt no pressure from his finger. "Said we had to save the day or some crap like that."

Kate laughed, an echo of a remembered emotion. Tears spilled down Sam's cheeks. She must have been more worried about Beth and Duncan than Kate had thought. She scanned the room with her eyes, the hallway beyond. Where were they?

Dr. Withers joined them. "Have you looked beneath the

vest?" she asked Michael. He shook his head. The doctor unstrapped the vest and pulled it away from Kate's skin. Very gently. Very slowly.

Surprise lit the doctor's face. "The bullet. I still see it."

Michael shone the light from his cell phone on Kate's chest. "It's barely penetrated. The vest must have slowed it down."

Sam looked up at the ceiling. "Thank you. Thank you Universe."

"I don't have anything for the pain," Dr. Withers said, "But we'll get you to hospital as quickly as we can."

"I'm not in any pain."

Michael looked at Dr. Withers. "Shock maybe? The bullet didn't hit anything vital."

A flicker of movement past Sam's shoulders caught Kate's attention, pulling her away from the doctors. She'd finally found Beth and Duncan. Through the open door. Beth shook hands with someone, but Kate couldn't see who.

Then Beth turned and grabbed a wounded Duncan from the ground, lifting him to his feet. His head lolled back and forth, barely conscious.

She handed Duncan off to Robert. Her eyes met Kate's, and the haunted look on her face dissolved into one of fear.

Beth was at Kate's side in an instant. "You let her get shot?"

"I wasn't here when she got shot," Sam snapped.

"Dammit, Sammy. I knew we shouldn't have left her alone."

A blast of indignation swept through Kate's mind. "I happened to save both your asses, so shut it." And just as suddenly, it ebbed and disappeared.

Beth flashed her a smile. "I'm less worried now. Yes, you did save my team at least." She looked at Sam. "Did you see—"

"I did." Sam nodded. "We would have died without you, Kate. All of us. You really don't need our protection. You haven't for a long time now."

Beatrice appeared in front of Kate, just behind Beth and Michael, wringing her hands on her apron. "We thought we were helping. I would have never given you that essence if I knew you'd be hurt."

"It's okay," Kate said.

"It's not okay, Kate." Beth ran a hand through her hair. "You've been shot."

Kate didn't bother to correct Beth, to tell her she'd been talking to Beatrice. Sloane had come back and had someone else with her.

Someone who looked familiar. Wait, not just familiar. She knew who it was.

No, it couldn't be.

It was her dead husband.

Paul.

CHAPTER 27

KATE JUST STARED AT PAUL'S FACE. HE LOOKED LIKE HE HAD when they'd first met. Dark hair, little smirk on his lips that always made him look like he was up to something. And the kindest eyes she'd ever seen.

Not like she'd seen him last, wasted away from the final rounds of chemo.

"Hey Kit-Kat."

She laughed at his nickname for her, and this time it wasn't a shadow of reaction. It was real.

"How're you doing?" Kate asked. "Wait. Stupid question. Sorry."

Paul smiled and walked closer until he was right behind Dr. Withers. "That's one of the things I always loved about you. Your faulty filter. You just say what you're thinking."

"Who is she talking to, Sam?" Logan's voice distracted Kate for a moment. Her eyes shifted to him.

"Paul." Sam's words were shaky.

Beth raised an eyebrow. "Wait, dead Paul? She's seeing

ghosts now?" Sam nodded, and Beth stood. "We need to get her out of here now."

Michael looked at Dr. Withers, who nodded. "We agree. She must have internal damage preventing her from moving or feeling anything."

"They do need to get you out of here," Paul said. "You're dying."

"I'm dying?" Kate's words were a whisper. There was a flash of something. Fear maybe, but then it was gone. Back to the deadness inside of her.

Paul nodded. Beatrice hit him on the arm. "Not yet, she isn't."

Beth looked as fierce as Beatrice did. "You're not dying, Red. I won't let you."

Logan lifted Kate into his arms. "I've got you." He looked around them. "I'll do everything I can to save her, Paul. You have my word."

Mackenzie joined them. "Something isn't right. We should have been overrun by now. Which means the way to the van is a trap. Get us out in the open where they have the advantage."

Glenna looked at John. "We'll check to see if our way is clear." They disappeared out the back door.

Beth looked at her phone. "Your cousin texted us both for an update. He's ready to roll."

The backdoor opened with a loud creak. Glenna's voice rang out. "No guards, no soldiers. It's entirely deserted."

"Mackenzie is right. Something is off," Logan muttered.

Kate looked for Paul, Beatrice, and Sloane, but they were gone.

They bustled out of the facility towards the exit and the forest beyond.

The cold air misted her breath outside. With each fast stride, the fence and trees bobbed in the distance.

Her eyes began to drift shut.

She heard Logan yell, "She's passing out."

Then she was suddenly someplace else.

CHAPTER 28

KATE FOUND HERSELF IN A STUDY WITH A COZY FIRE AND big easy chairs. A full length window sat behind a desk. Outside it was bright sunshine.

Not the night she'd just left. This was Entwine. Sloane's study. Just like Sam had described.

"I feel you behind me, Sloane."

Kate turned around to see not only the Warden, but Beatrice, Robert, and Paul.

"You're taking this surprisingly well." Sloane lifted a glass of what looked like port, in a salute. "But then you did hijack the time stream for your own purposes, Oracle."

"I've always been a Plan B-to-Z sorta gal, rolling with the punches," Kate replied. "Am I dead?"

The thought should have filled her with dread, shouldn't it? But it didn't. She still felt nothing.

Beatrice clucked her tongue. "It's as bad as we thought."

"Worse." Sloane frowned. "You're not dead yet, Kate. But both your body and your spirit are dangerously depleted."

"Spirit?" In the realm of Entwine, that word might mean a lot of things.

Robert stepped forward. "Your heart, your emotions. The things you feel that allow you to connect with others, like love. Or to warn you of danger, like fear, worry." His face was a mixture of the latter two.

She'd known there had to have been a price. "So that's why I'm not really feeling anything. It was the cost when I saved Beth and Sam, wasn't it?"

Sloane nodded. "No one has ever done what you did, however, in time you would have recovered."

Beatrice began to pace. "But as usual, you couldn't just lie still and let everyone else fight, could you? No, you had to run right into the middle of things."

"I didn't run. I could barely move."

Beatrice stopped and fixed her with a hard stare that quickly dissolved into admiration. "Even then, you didn't give up on saving lives. And I had to help you. Though I didn't know you'd end up shot."

Kate glanced at Paul. She kept expecting he'd go poof.

"Why are you here? Does this mean there's no hope, that I'm definitely going to die?"

Paul shook his head. "Just the opposite. There is hope."

Kate looked down, remembering again the last time she saw Paul. Not the robust man in front of her now. He'd been eaten away from the chemo. Just a shell.

"I'm sorry I didn't see your cancer in time to stop it." Her words were a whisper. A lick of guilt flamed inside her. "I never told you I could see the future, but when it mattered most, I was powerless."

"It's not your fault, Kate."

She looked up. "It is. It is my fault." The guilt grew, making her voice tremble. "I didn't *see*. I didn't see what was happening in time to stop it." She grabbed his shirt with both her hands. The fabric crumpled in her grip. She shook him, willing him to yell at her, do something. "I let you die."

The sob choked up her throat and spilled out.

She'd robbed her daughters of their father.

She'd failed.

Paul covered her hands with his own. "You didn't kill me, Kate. Cancer did that all on its own." His words were soft. "What you did do was make me feel loved and cherished up until the end." His voice broke then. Tears trailed down his cheeks. "And I could go willingly, I could stop fighting the pain and death marching through my body because I knew you'd take care of our girls." He let go of her hands and wiped her cheeks.

Her eyes burned along with her chest. "But I could have saved you if only I'd had a vision."

"You can't see your own future," Sloane said. "Like Sam can't see the ghosts of those she loves. It's the way it works."

Paul kissed her forehead. "If you need my forgiveness, you have it, Kate, but you know who you really need to forgive."

The usual regret churned together with the guilt inside her, but with less ferocity, less acid. Was it true? Had there been nothing she could have done?

Paul took her hand. "And you need to take a chance on love again. You promised me, remember?"

Kate squeezed his hand. "I am. It's just . . ."

"Just that you're still afraid you might lose Logan?"

She wasn't surprised he knew about Logan. Ghosts could be anywhere.

She pressed her free hand to her chest. "He's in here, Paul. In my heart. Somehow it happened." Tears filled her eyes, making all the ghosts blurry. "I don't think I could bear it if I lost him."

"Like you lost me?"

She nodded.

"So, do you wish we'd never met?"

"What are you talking about?"

Paul smiled, though it was tinged with sadness. "I died. I left you. Would it have been better not to have that heartache?"

"No, of course not. How can you even say that? We had years together. Two beautiful daughters."

Paul took her other hand. "Are you saying it was worth the risk?"

Kate looked at his left hand, his wedding band gleaming, almost shining. "It was worth the risk." Her words were barely a breath.

Sloane eyed her closely. "It's working. Now, Paul. The rest. Remind her."

Memories exploded in her mind. How they'd first met, and the awful coffee he'd made her drink. Emily's birth and the marathon labor. How Patty had come early, and they'd almost lost her. The blanket forts underneath tables. The magical smells of his cooking filling the kitchen. Paul playing with Barbies. Everyone making snow angels outside. The warmth of him next to her in bed.

The laughter. The sorrow. The love.

And then the images shifted to a place she didn't recognize. It was a beautiful house surrounded by the flowers and plants Paul loved. Paul walked out the front door with an older man and woman beside him.

She recognized them. His parents who he'd lost the year before he'd met Kate. It's one of the things they'd bonded over.

A soft meow made Kate look down. An orange tabby rubbed against her legs.

"Mr. Cuddles?" She petted his soft fur, recognizing that loud motor engine purr anywhere. They'd lost him to a car accident a few years before Paul died.

She heard Paul's voice in her head.

Would I rather still be with you and the girls? Yes. But it was my time. And I'm still surrounded by people who love me.

Death wasn't the end. It was merely the beginning of something new.

You promised me you'd be open to love again, Kate.

Keep your promise.

The shell around her heart, the one that Logan had already begun to crack, blew apart. Pieces of it fell away, disappearing into the darkness below. The bright light inside burned away the shadows of guilt and regret and anger.

The feelings were too much. Kate broke the connection to Paul, She dropped to her knees, back in the study again.

"I'm dying." The words brought crushing pain this time. Neutrality and numbness had been obliterated. "The girls, Paul. If I die, what happens to our girls?"

Pain filled Paul's face, but he remained silent.

Memories filled her mind. Seeing Patty face off against Vivian, so strong and kind. Emily's unwavering belief in family, in both Patty and Kate. Their arms around her. Their love.

How they wouldn't leave her when she had her visions, no matter how scary it was.

Her fingers gripped the rug, digging into the tufts. Hot tears rolled down her cheeks. Mucus dripped from her nose. Her mouth opened and closed, but no sounds came out. The anguish was too deep to rise. She would never see them again.

And Logan. She knew how she felt now. She needed to tell him, *had* to tell him.

Something amazing was just starting between them, and it would never have a chance now.

A chance.

Wait.

Sloane wouldn't have brought her here unless there was some way to stop this.

The thought galvanized her. She took in a ragged breath, then another. She lifted the bottom of her shirt and blew her nose on the hem. Getting to her feet, she stared at the Warden. "What do I need to do to live?"

"Do what you do best. Trust *this*." Sloane placed one hand over Kate's heart. And with the other hand, she snapped her fingers, and the study disappeared.

KATE OPENED HER EYES. SHE WAS BACK IN HER BODY AND back in a jostling van.

Sam's face loomed in front of hers. "She's awake. We're on our way to the hospital, Kate. You're going to be okay."

Usually Sam was an excellent liar, but Kate saw through her words easily.

Michael pulled Sam away. Though he whispered, she heard him. "She's fading. It's like her body isn't fighting at all. I don't think we're going to make it in time."

He was right. She was dying. Already it took all her effort to keep her eyes open. There was a waiting pool of stillness inside, beckoning her.

She knew the peace it gave. No feeling. No pain.

Logan was suddenly at her side. He grasped her hand, and she felt the callouses on his fingers.

She could feel something.

His eyes were red from crying, cheeks still wet with tears. "Don't give up, Kate. Please."

"I don't like our odds."

He smiled, just as she had hoped he would. "And when has that stopped us before?"

"I'm sorry I dragged you into this."

"I'm not." He pushed her hair back from her forehead. The heat of his fingers sent pinpricks of light through her. "You finally let me into your world. And you know you're not getting rid of me, so don't even think about it."

"I think you might just be as stubborn as I am." She laughed. More light traveled down her cheeks, her neck.

"I love you," Logan whispered and kissed her cheek.

"Lips," Kate said.

"Excuse me?"

"No cheek action. Not now. Kiss me. Really kiss me." She didn't know what was going to happen, but she wanted to kiss him at least once, with intent, not just by accident.

Something shifted in Logan's face. The worry disappeared, replaced by determination. "This will not be our last kiss." His words were firm.

"Aye, aye, Captain."

His eyes twinkled, some of the seriousness softening. Then he kissed her.

She felt his lips. Their softness. Also the love, the fear, but the hope inside him. A jolt surged through her heart, powered by the light he'd already awoken. She felt it beat. And felt it hurt. She cried out, couldn't help it.

Logan backed away, stricken. "Did I hurt you?"

"No"

Her body struggled to wake up, wanted to, but it needed something stronger. A stronger burst of energy. And she knew exactly how to get it. It had been in front of her the whole time."

"I need Sam and Beth. Now."

He didn't hesitate, pushing Sam towards her. She heard Beth's protests about being man-handled, but then she was by Kate's side as well.

"This better not be a death-bed confession," Beth said. She looked like she'd been crying too. "Because you're not giving up, Kate."

Things must be really bad for Beth to use her real name and not a nickname.

A shiver went through Kate, but she welcomed it. Proof she was still alive and could change things.

Kate met each of their gazes. "I can't move, so you're going to have to take my hands. And each other's."

Beth shook her head. "No way. We're barely holding you together as it is. We're not shocking you with the energy circuit thing we do."

Kate's vision began to checker. Winking in and out. She was running out of time.

"Grab my hands. Now."

Her outburst sucked away what little strength she'd had, but it'd be worth it if they would just agree.

A little color seeped back into Sam's face. "Bossy as usual. That's a good sign."

Beth didn't move. "We could cause more bleeding. We're almost to the hospital. We should wait."

"I love you, Samantha Eveline Hamilton and Tiffany Elizabeth Marshall." Kate's voice was a breathy whisper. She struggled to hold on to recite the oath to remind them. "When you need me, I will be your heart, your courage and . . . your strength." Her words slowed. "We . . . are sisters in blood."

I figured it out too late. I'm not going to make it.

Her fingers dangled into that waiting pool of peace.

She heard Sam's voice. "We can always agree on our love for Kate."

Beth's voice was soft. "Always."

And then everything flared so bright she couldn't see.

A charge of energy stronger than she'd ever felt ran through Kate. It flooded her body with heat. Everywhere it touched, life returned.

She felt her toes, her calves. Agony flared through her chest. She struggled for breath against the deep bite of her bullet wound, but she welcomed the charge of energy even as it brought more pain.

"What the hell is happening?"

She heard Lennox's voice, and it made her open her eyes. The glare of light hadn't been just inside her. The entire van was aglow, like someone had ringed it over and over again with white Christmas lights.

Kate looked at Sam—her eyes sparking lightning. Behind her stood Beatrice, Paul and Sloane, their hands alight with energy flowing into Sam.

A misty glow surrounded Beth, sending tendrils of energy down her arms and into the circuit. Beth's eyes glowed black, but this time with a ring of white.

Sloane had said to trust her heart.

She squeezed their hands, suddenly able to move, holding on to her best friends. The ones who'd come into her life at the time she'd needed them the most.

Then and now.

Tears ran down Kate's face. She'd risked everything to save

her friends, and without them, she would have died.

"You're hurting me, Pip. Ease up." Beth's grip grew stronger.

Sam squeezed harder too. "Yeah, Squeak. When did you get so strong?"

"I've told you both, I don't answer to Pip nor to Squeak." She pulled them both to her and into a hug. "I love you, my sisters."

CHAPTER 29

KATE LOOKED AT EVERYONE CROWDED INTO THE KITCHEN finishing up dinner. Baked chicken, mashed potatoes, and veggies. She wanted some comfort food for everyone.

She was planning to grab Duncan when the opportunity was right and finally clear the air between them. Her eyes went to where he sat with Beth and Michael. There was a softening between the brothers that warmed Kate.

Robert and Sam sat with them, but managed to look very intimate even though all they did was hold hands while gazing into each others' eyes. His ring from Sloane was back firmly in place.

She hadn't asked Beth yet about who she'd been shaking hands with. It had to be someone who worked for RAVEN. It was no accident they'd escaped so easily. And that RAVEN hadn't come after them for retribution. Something was going on.

But that was a conversation for a different time. A time when their lives weren't in imminent danger.

"She's incredible," Emily exclaimed, pointing at her picture of Vivian. Jean sat in between Kate's daughters and their detailed artwork of both Vivian and Caleb. Michael's mom was ooohing and aaahhing appropriately.

Patty held up her hand to Jean. "She gave us this."

Jean grabbed her hand, holding the flower etching up to the light.

Michael's father had made it as well. He looked like an older version of Lennox. Forbidding, even with his slight limp. "May I see that?" he asked Patty. She scooted over. "That looks like something I've seen in our archives."

No longer hiding her abilities away and being able to freely talk about what she could do had brought such a change in Patty. In both her girls.

Kate had changed too. The guilt was gone over Paul. Sloane had truly given her a gift. A gift of closure. She definitely owed the Warden one. A debt no doubt Sloane would call in eventually.

A sharp bark of laughter brought her attention to the table where Lennox sat with Bronson. They'd been exchanging war stories all night. No violent details around her girls. She'd already admonished them before the girls had arrived, after hearing of a harrowing adventure in Bulgaria. Thick as thieves, those two.

Glenna and Mackenzie devoured cake by the back door with Logan. Mackenzie had been standoffish at first, but had immediately bonded with Glenna. She'd already moved into the Forbes' manor.

Duncan approached with an empty plate. He had been out of the hospital for a week and was still moving a bit slow. "I'm stuffed." He smiled, crinkling the healing cut on his cheek.

She smiled back. "Glad you liked it. Could we talk for a moment in the study?"

He raised an eyebrow, but nodded, following her out of the kitchen.

They sat down by the fireplace.

"Logan's a good man," Duncan said.

Not the beginning Kate had rehearsed in her head a dozen times. "He is."

Duncan rubbed his beard with his knuckles. "Did I have a chance at all with you?" His tone was soft. Not accusatory or angry, just wondering.

Kate thought about his question, and then finally shook her head. "I don't think you did. My heart was already taken. I just didn't know it." She reached over and took his hand. "I'm sorry I hurt you."

"You didn't, not really. I knew it was something casual." He looked away, off into space. "What I didn't expect was the hope you gave me. That I might find someone who was interested in me for me, not for what I could do. And you know what happens when you hope?"

"I do. You open yourself up just a little." She squeezed his hand. "You're an incredible man, Duncan. Don't close yourself off again."

His eyes filled with tears. He pulled his hand away slowly.

"I'll try." Duncan got to his feet. "At least I lost out to the man who put his life on the line for me. Though now he's really going to rub it in my face."

Kate blinked back tears of her own and laughed. "He will."

Duncan gave her a side hug, away from his injuries, and kissed her temple.

"There you are," Glenna said from the doorway. "We need to get you home. You've already overdone it. I can tell."

Duncan gave her the stink-eye. "Who's older?"

"Who's wiser?" Glenna shot back.

Duncan raised his hands. "I give up."

Kate watched them leave before she headed back into the kitchen. She should have known he'd hijack her carefully laid apology with that insight of his.

Logan met her in the hallway. "How'd it go?"

"Better than I thought."

The tromping of small feet pounded behind Logan.

"You haven't shown him yet, did you, Mom?" Emily asked, joining them, Patty close on her heels.

"Of course I haven't," Kate replied. There was no way she'd ruin this moment for the girls.

Logan looked at Emily and Patty. "Show me what?"

They took his hands and tugged him toward the front door. Kate grabbed their jackets, making them put them on before they went outside.

Patty opened the shed door. Emily flicked on the overhead light. The parking sign she'd shown Logan was finally complete. The flowers were done. And there were even a few black figures that looked like they were meant to be crows. Caleb's influence.

And the girls had added four hearts beside his name.

Emily pointed to them now. "That's you, me, Patty, and Mom."

Logan wiped his eyes and laughed softly. "It's beautiful."

Patty smiled up at him. "We wanted you to know how much we love you."

He let out a ragged sob and crouched, hugging the girls to him. "I love both of you. So much."

Kate wrapped her arms around herself, trying to hold back the tears and failing.

"Why is everyone crying?" Emily asked. She pulled away and looked from Logan to Kate. "What's wrong?"

Kate laughed. "Nothing's wrong. They're happy tears."

Emily didn't look convinced.

"I bet you there might be a little cake left if you hurry," Kate said. "And I left extra frosting in the fridge."

Both girls brightened. "Bye, Mr. Logan," they shouted together and ran out the door.

Kate walked over and closed the door, locking it. Duncan hadn't been the only one she'd wanted to talk to, and she didn't need her girls interrupting. "One minute they're wise beyond their years."

"And the next, they're just kids."

Logan came up behind her and slid an arm around her waist.

She leaned back against his chest. "Last time we were here I was pretty clumsy."

"You were. And then you kissed me."

Kate turned around in his arms. "I did. Though it wasn't really a *kiss* kiss."

Logan's brows pinched together. "A *kiss* kiss?"

"You know what I mean. And the kiss in the van when I was dying doesn't count. I couldn't even move."

A mischievous look crept into his eyes. "You might need to show me what you mean."

She crooked her finger at him. He lowered his head until they were nose to nose.

"I love you, Logan."

It felt amazing to finally say it—and frightening too. But no tightness in her chest any longer. The shell around her heart had been decimated.

He smiled and kissed her nose. "I thought you were scared. That we might not work out."

"I still am. But nothing is certain. I've seen it. I've seen time." She touched his cheek. "Which is why I'm not wasting any more of it on fear."

She moved closer. Their lips met. Soft at first. Then more urgent. Her insides melted. Head to toe, molten lava. She abandoned herself to the kiss, fingers sliding into his hair.

Logan lifted her up, and she wrapped her legs around him. He walked them back to the low workbench and shrugged out of his jacket, laying it down on the surface.

"You're quite the multi-tasker, sir."

He gave her grin and eased her gently down onto the bench. Holding her gaze, he slid his hands under her shirt.

Her breasts started to hum the "Let's Get Naked" song. This

time she was humming right along with them. She pulled her top off over her head, careful not to fling it too far. They would eventually have to return to the house.

Logan followed suit, and Kate just leaned back and enjoyed the view. Toned chest with just a sprinkling of light brown hair. Strong shoulders, with that little cut she loved so much.

"You're so beautiful," Kate said. The Detective Chief Constable blushed. "Come here." He moved closer until she could see the flecks of amber in his eyes. She cupped his cheeks. He remained completely still, but she felt his heartbeat thrumming in his jaw.

"What do you want?" he asked. Ever the gentleman, waiting for her lead.

"The whole enchilada."

He laughed. It felt so easy, so natural being with him. Why had she fought it for so long?

"I'll get working on your order right away." Logan reached underneath her back. Her bra was a goner.

Hands braced on either side of her, he moved his bare chest up and down over her breasts. The friction was delicious. Her nipples tightened even more. Every move of skin on skin raised her hips to meet him, rocking against the enticing pressure between her legs.

She wanted his jeans gone now. And her pants. But then his lips found her breasts. Wetness and heat and suction. Oh my. Kissing his way down, he took the edge of her pants by his teeth, pulling them.

She wiggled out of them quickly. "Your turn."

Logan got off the bench and unzipped his jeans. He dropped them to the floor. And his boxer briefs next.

Kate stared. Ten points to Gryffindor. "How do you manage to hide *that* in your pants?"

"Well, usually you're not around making it difficult." Logan's fingers hooked the edges of her panties, pulling them down. "I'm going to need some help with this." He reached back into his jeans and grabbed a packet from his pocket.

Kate ripped it open carefully. There was no way she was going to mess this up. Her body would never forgive her. She rolled the rubber down his length slowly, squeezing and stroking him. Logan rocked back and forth in her grip.

She lay back down and pulled him to her. The pressure of him entering her almost made her orgasm immediately. She wanted this to last.

Didn't men use lists so they didn't lose their stamina? Maybe she should think about cookie ingredients to hold it together.

Sugar, flour, baking soda . . .

He kissed her, harder with each stroke, his chest hot against hers. One of his hands went to work down below, his thumb rubbing and circling.

. . . honey, salt, butter . . .

His lips moved to her neck, alternately nipping and kissing.

"*. . . chocolate chips,*" she moaned.

Logan laughed.

She held onto his shoulders, her body bucking underneath him, out of control. Faster and faster. The sight of him moving on top of her, inside her, sent her exploding, screaming his name. He tensed, his moans joining with hers. The sounds were beautiful to her ears. She kissed his cheeks, his eyes, his chin. Sweat clung to both of them.

He rolled to the side, lying next to her.

"It's a good thing the women of this town don't know how incredible you are in the sack." Kate tried to catch her breath.

"Oh really?" Logan arched an eyebrow. "Because they'd be beating my door down?" He flexed his arm, bicep at attention.

She giggled. "No. Because they'd have to go through me. And I have a mean right hook, you know."

"I know. My shoulder has suffered that plight."

She pinched his shoulder. "You can take it."

"I'll take you." He kissed her temple.

"Hazards and all?

"Hazards and all."

She rolled on top of him, intending another long kiss, but ended up knocking them both off the narrow workbench.

Logan's body cradled hers again, breaking her fall.

"We might need to Kate-proof the B&B." Logan said, laughing.

Kate tried to give him a stern look. He pulled her down for another kiss. She'd come to Scotland uncertain. Not knowing who she was beyond a mother and a wife. Not knowing where she came from.

But she'd found herself.

And she'd found love again.

ACKNOWLEDGEMENTS

What a time this has been!

I have to thank the Shearer Posse of friends, family, and loyal readers over these past months since the release of *Entwine*. Your support has been incredible!

From my book launches in New York and in Seattle, to private book parties, to all those who helped spread the word across social media—I could not have done it without everyone who showed up and believed in me.

I know many writers struggle for acceptance by their friends and family. I'm extremely grateful to be surrounded by such love and light.

My critique group has always been in my corner. Anne, Jess, & Troy—you helped get *Raven* to where it was meant to be. And a special thank you to my beta readers who gave me the feedback I needed to really bring Kate's story to life.

When I think back on the special moments since publishing *Entwine*, it feels surreal. Can this really be my life? Did I really make my dreams come true?

It is! I did!

To my sister, Kim, you are such a pillar of strength who I can always count on. You are more than my sister—you're my friend. From the NY Book Launch through writing *Raven*, you have been my biggest cheerleader. My life wouldn't be the same without you in it, seeester.

I worried when my niece and nephew grew older, that I wouldn't be as important in their lives now filled with new adventures and journeys. But they never wavered in their love for me. And sharing the NY book launch of *Entwine* with them was something I will never forget. Mary Kate and Charlie—I love you both so much!

My brother, John, and his girlfriend, Buffy, made my Seattle book launch extra special. They flew up from San Francisco to take part in my big celebration. I had managed to have all my family with me—from both my book launches—to see my dreams come true. It doesn't get much better than that. Thank you so much for being there for my special day. Hugs to you both—I miss you!

I remember someone once asking me why I lived in Seattle when I had no family here. They couldn't be more wrong.

To my Seattle family—through the years you have walked this road with me, never doubting I wouldn't have a book published. You were the ones who listened to my excitement when I took my first writing class, the ones who were ecstatic when I got my first agent, and the ones who cared for me through all my cancer battles. We might not be bound by blood, but we are bound by something even stronger—love.

I've lost track of the number of years I've known my best friend, Karen Weir, but it's long enough to know we were brought together for a reason. Thank you for all your guidance, your love, and your friendship. When my cancer came back just recently, you were there for me to lean on until I could stand on my own again. Looking forward to many more years of adventures with you, best friend.

Again, I must thank Jessica Petersen, who is not only my friend and editor, but also the cover artist for the Entwine trilogy. It's incredible that someone can be so creative and talented in multiple areas, but Jess is truly gifted. Through the ups and downs of editing and polishing *Raven*, I'm honored to have you as my partner. I know our future endeavors will both help us grow even more.

Through my writing coaching and course offerings, I'm thrilled to be able to help other writers on their path. Whether they're book writers or simply people who are trying to make a difference in the world and need guidance with their words, I know I'll be able to help them achieve their dreams. And in turn, the light I help grow, will help everyone they touch. Giving hope in the darkness.

Never again will I put any dream aside, even the ones I'm not sure yet how I will accomplish. As Kate says in *Raven*, "I've seen time and I'm not wasting any more of it on fear."

ABOUT THE AUTHOR

A NEW YORK TRANSPLANT, TRACEY SHEARER NOW CALLS the Pacific Northwest her home—a land teeming with ghosts, writers, and coffee shops.

The loss of both her parents and her own battles with cancer fuel her love of stories that explore how important our connections to each other are. And through her work as a mentor and coach, Tracey enjoys helping other writers realize their dreams.

Under the close supervision of her two rescue kitties, Cleo and Feta, Tracey is working on the next book in this trilogy. You can find her on Twitter and IG at @TraceyLShearer and at traceyshearer.com. You can also join her Motivated Magic Writing Group on Facebook for writing tips, trainings, motivation, and inspiration.